# Village Wives

SCEPTRE

*Also by Patricia Fawcett*

Set to Music
A Family Weekend
The Absent Child

# Village Wives

PATRICIA FAWCETT

SCEPTRE

First published in 1998 by Hodder and Stoughton
A division of Hodder Headline PLC
A Sceptre book



10 9 8 7 6 5 4 3 2 1



British Library Cataloguing in Publication Data

Fawcett, Patricia
Village wives
I. Title
823.9'14 [F]

ISBN 0 340 71852 8

Typeset by Palimpsest Book Production Limited,
Polmont, Stirlingshire
Printed and bound in Great Britain by
Mackays of Chatham PLC, Chatham, Kent

Hodder and Stoughton
A division of Hodder Headline PLC
338 Euston Road
London NW1 3BH

For my sister Maureen

A special thank you to Eunice and Maisie
for helping me with the research

# Part One

# 1

Tess O'Grady tried to get through to Andrew again as she drove past the gates of West House. Driving, using the mobile as she was, she still found time for the quickest of glances through the elaborate gatescreen towards the splendid peach-coloured Georgian building on the hill.

Dream on, Tess.

'It's me . . .' she said as her husband came on the line. 'I'm on my way home. I don't know what all the fuss was about, dragging me out at this time of the morning as if it was an emergency. It was just a mix-up with the fresh flower delivery, would you believe? The woman is quite capable of sorting it out herself. I'm just coming up to One-Mile Bridge and I'm not stopping for anybody, so I'll be with you in no time. I'll have to be on my way again in twenty minutes so have the coffee ready, darling.'

She did not wait for his answer, concentrating on making sure she pushed through and got right of way at the one-vehicle bridge. There was nobody in sight so she centred her car accordingly, slowing just enough to avoid catching the sturdy stone parapet. Whoever had built this bridge at this point at this angle wanted his head examining, but then she supposed when it was built there had not been any vehicles to worry about and it did feature on local scenic cards, one of Teesdale's ancient attractions.

Good God!

Who the hell was that?

Tess slammed on her brakes, wondering where on earth the pedestrian had sprung from, walking in the very middle of the bridge. Shocked, Tess took a few seconds to recover herself, clicked on a switch for the electric window and leaned out, prepared to let rip.

Then she saw *who* it was, the dotty old dear from the big house who seemed to spend her entire life traipsing back and forth to the village. No doubt she was one of those villagers who had been up in arms about the new housing development.

Well, tough! Bishopsmeade needed a shot in the arm, new blood. Already Tess was regretting moving here to the new development that the rest of the village so despised. She might have known village life would not be for her. Andrew liked it but then he was like that. Easily rooted.

The old dear, Mrs Makepeace – she must be a hundred if she was a day – was small and silver-haired and, although Tess had never spoken to her, she gathered she had a reputation for being a little eccentric. Her manner of dress certainly was and Tess did not approve. The day she lost her dress sense, she had given Andrew permission to shoot her.

Come on . . . get a move on . . . oh, come *on*, for Christ's sake . . .

'Good morning! Thank you,' the old lady mouthed, smiling, as she completed her journey across the bridge as if there was all the time in the world.

Tess managed a polite smile in return, pausing to make sure Mrs Makepeace was clear of the back bumper – just – before accelerating off and over the bridge with the panache of a Formula One starter.

Once over One-Mile Bridge, Constance Makepeace continued on her way. The interruption had been most unwelcome for she had been enjoying a moment of quiet reflection looking down onto the cool grey water. The bridge spanned the fat stream, one of many streams that joined up with the river that flowed deeply and silently through Bishopsmeade.

On second thoughts, quiet reflection was apt to provoke unhappy memories and so it was just as well the large car arrived when it did to interrupt her reverie. It was being driven by a woman, one of those new people from that so-called exclusive development of houses built on what was once the beautiful Church Pasture. Her late husband Hugh had taken the dogs for walks there and he would be so upset if he could see it today.

At the turn in the road, West House came into view but Constance avoided eye contact this morning. Ever since she had thought the thought last night, she had successfully avoided looking at the house. She kept her eyes averted even as she slipped past the high stone pillars and through the gatescreen. Four sets of topiary bushes edged the lawns, the drive leading straight up to the solid, square softly-hued building.

The mist and morning chill had evaporated and now a sparkle of September sunshine splashed against the house as she went indoors.

It had always been such a contented house, but Constance fancied this morning it had an air of disapproval about it.

It knew, of course.

But her mind was made up.

She would sell West House come the spring.

Whilst Tess O'Grady was waiting at the bridge, at number three Churchwood Close Yvonne Lonsdale was feverishly getting ready for the off.

'Mummy! We're going to be late!'

Portia, her oldest at eight, stood at Yvonne's bedroom door, an anxious look on her face, already dressed for school in grey and maroon. The other children, Samantha and Harry, could be heard arguing in the background.

'Nearly ready, sweetheart.' Yvonne put the finishing touches to her make-up, fluffed up her shoulder-length blonde hair before going downstairs. She refused to be rushed in the morning. She would die first rather than arrive at school in a mess.

Portia, bless her, had settled the argument and organised the little ones into a group in the hall complete with all the paraphernalia they needed each day. Yvonne checked the time, realising that, even though the village school was only at the far end of Front Street, they would have to go by car again or they would be really late and Portia would panic. Portia liked to be little Miss Perfect.

'Right, let's go,' she said, picking up the car keys and ushering them out into the cool of the autumn morning. They climbed into the car and she supervised the belting-up as there was the sound of crunching gravel next door and Tess arrived back in her flash top-of-the-range four-wheel drive.

'Late again, Yvonne?' Tess called maddeningly. She was never late, of course. She was also always beautifully groomed, dark and sleek as a thoroughbred horse, although she had it easy with no children competing for attention.

Unable to deny it, for they were by now later than usual and Portia was nearly wetting her little flowered knickers with impatience, Yvonne did the only possible thing and beamed back at Tess, glad she had taken the time to apply her make-up properly. She needed her war paint. Scented and powdered, she felt fit to cope with anyone and anything. Who did Tess O'Grady think she was anyway? Just because she was the proud possessor of Andrew, the sexiest man in Churchwood Close, was no excuse for swanning around like she did.

Yvonne fought against a little smile. Whether or not Andrew O'Grady was sexy was entirely irrelevant for he was totally out of bounds to an old married woman like herself. Robin and Andrew had not hit it off, poles apart as they were professionally. According to Robin, Andrew must be lacking in something to be satisfied with a career in accountancy.

'How is Andrew, Tess?' she asked, managing to keep her tone neutral, sensing also that the other woman was in a rush. 'Working from home now, isn't he?'

'Yes, and it's all going wonderfully,' Tess said, immaculate in a gorgeous red suit that went brilliantly with her bluntly cut jet-black hair. Long glossily-tighted legs peeped from beneath the shortish skirt. 'How is Robin? Heard from the high seas lately?'

Yvonne ignored the edge of sarcasm.

'Robin's very well,' she said. 'It's not exactly the high seas. It's an oil rig off Aberdeen.'

'Of course. You must miss him. I don't know how I would cope if Andrew was away so much.' She peered into the car, directed a smile at the children. 'Off to school?' she said. 'How lovely! I won't keep you then.'

'Oh, sorry, Tess . . . I'd almost forgotten . . .' Yvonne fastened her seatbelt, ignoring an anguished cry from the rear that the bell would be going any minute now. 'It's your big day today, isn't it? Your new shop opening?'

'It is indeed and I've had to sort out a panic at one of the other shops already. Not the best start.' She glanced at her watch. 'You won't believe the trouble I've had organising this event, Yvonne. It's the last time I'll ask an actress to open a shop. They have such an inflated view of their own importance. After all, who is this woman but a bit player in some soap? Her PA has a checklist a mile long. Still, it's terrific publicity.'

'And that's what it's all about. Say goodbye to Mrs O'Grady, children,' Yvonne murmured, negotiating the tricky reversing process over the heads of the bobbing children, and managing, despite Portia's gloomy predictions, to get them to school in time.

She kissed them in their proper order, reminding them to make sure they ate their apple after lunch. Harry was a touch tearful this morning. He had taken to coming into her bed during the night for a cuddle and, although it was disturbing her sleep pattern, she felt unwilling to deny the little boy some comfort. Poor sweet. He, more than his sisters, missed Robin.

'Off you go, sweetie,' she said, giving him an extra hug, propelling him gently forwards. Robin thought he was too soft by half but Yvonne saw nothing wrong in the little boy wanting reassurance. Time enough to grow up.

The girls dashed in, Harry turning to wave, bottom lip trembling.

Yvonne smiled encouragingly at him, clattered back to the car and drove home.

Tess, sparklingly attractive in one of her super-charged states, finally got away for the second time and Andrew, watching the car disappear down the road, decided he would have ten minutes exactly with the paper and a final cup of coffee before getting started on some work.

He liked this working from home lark. A bit of flexibility. It beat the hell out of charging out like a man possessed at seven thirty every morning in order to get to the office in time, and up here there was always the possibility that the village could be cut off by snowdrifts in winter. It didn't worry Tess. Her vehicle was built to get through *anything*.

Andrew had his coffee in the kitchen, his mind half on work and half on what he was doing for dinner tonight. He was trying out a new recipe, spicy lamb with baked potatoes and broccoli followed by apple sponge and cream. Hard to think that a year ago he was not sure how to boil an egg. When you applied yourself to something with a bit of enthusiasm, there was nothing to it.

The silence here in Churchwood Close had unnerved him at first. After nine o'clock, it was dead. The other day some character had turned up mid-morning, injecting some excitement into his rigidly imposed shopping, cleaning, cooking, working schedule. This character had been selling dusters and the like and, feeling sorry for him, Andrew bought some oven gloves knowing full well he was being conned.

Checking on the guy's movements afterwards, aware that the other houses were empty and that they were supposed to be operating a neighbourhood watch scheme, he'd seen him going up Yvonne's path next door and, rather to his amusement, he noticed she bought something too. The guy was grinning as he came down her path but then she was the sort to cheer any man's day. Friendly. On the day they moved in, she had been round with tea and biscuits and offers of help barely before the removal van had disappeared. For some reason, Tess, uncharacteristically crumpled after the day's events, had taken umbrage. Andrew couldn't understand it, although it later occurred to him that she might actually be jealous. Wonderful, of course, but misplaced. Good God, Yvonne wasn't his style! Altogether too fluffy for his taste.

Yawning, dismissing such thoughts, he glanced at the clock and went upstairs to his study. Two hours of concentrated work was worth a day of skiving about and flicking paperclips into wastepaper baskets, although he had to keep focused because frankly the view from the window across to the church and Staine Hill was a distraction. He loved Bishopsmeade, although he had no illusions that before too long Tess would be on at him to think about moving again. Itchy feet, Tess.

She was also ambitious, not just for herself but for him too.

The accountancy firm he had worked for since qualifying had done some staff pruning some time back and, egged on by Tess, he had taken up the redundancy terms offered and started up on his own. It was hard going though and, to his chagrin, he was stuck with box file jobs. He wondered how long he could keep up the pretence that it was working out. Tess believed him, but then she was not brought up to believe in failure. Her business plans grew worryingly more grandiose every day but Andrew had given up urging caution because she took absolutely no notice.

The view from the window finally claimed his attention after a couple of hours and he logged off his computer and stretched weary arms above his head. He would take a brisk walk this afternoon, get a breath of fresh air, maybe take the little path that stumbled towards the church and then swept round in the direction of West House and the hill. It was a hard slog, uphill all the way – Tess had done it once and once only – but he thought it well worth the effort. He was determined to keep himself in trim and he got sod-all exercise sitting at his desk all day.

If he craned his head the minutest fraction, he could see Yvonne hanging out washing. She was pegging out something pale blue and floaty, *wearing* something green and floaty.

Feeling a bit guilty to be watching her, unobserved as he was, he couldn't help a smile. Yvonne was some feminine lady, a sort of Dolly Parton meets English rose. Married to a deep-sea diver, of all things. Poor old Robin, having to make do with dreaming about her as he decompressed.

He went to make coffee, reflecting gloomily on some pretty obvious facts.

Tess's business – O'Grady's Floral Design, a range of florists with a distinctive touch – was blooming.

And *his* – personal friendly advice on tax returns, self assessment, PAYE, capital gains and inheritance tax – was struggling to keep its head above water.

When she found out, she would skin him alive.

# 2

Joe Sutherland was at his usual table, corner by the window, being fussed over. Seeing her, he waved across the room. Tess smiled as she followed the waiter, very aware of all eyes on her as she slipped slimly and easily between tables, kissing her father on both cheeks before sitting down with a big sigh.

The restaurant was a touch pretentious, as if embarrassed by its over-abundance of pinkness, but it was Joe's favourite, handy for him, just a couple of streets away from his office although he did of course use the car to get here. She had noticed it parked immediately outside, begging for a parking ticket.

'You smell nice, darling,' her father said. 'New perfume?'

She nodded, pleased. She had just changed from her usual Chanel, a touch bored with it. Her Gold Card this month would be absolutely horrendous, for this suit was also on it *and* various other transactions she would have to be reminded about. Andrew expected her to keep receipts, for God's sake.

'You *look* great too. New suit?'

'Yes.'

She could always trust him to notice her appearance. He paid attention to appearances, did her father. Her mother had been such an elegant lady, adept at spending money, and Tess liked to think she was keeping up the tradition. She owed it to her mother whom Joe had absolutely adored.

Andrew irritated her rather. He could not forget he was an accountant. He was tight. Quibbling about the price of the sitting room curtains when they were the focal point of the room. What the hell did he expect her to do? Buy material in the market and run them up herself? The designer whom she had commissioned had worked wonders on them, all that pleating and folding and hand stitching, and it had worked out at less than eight hundred which she thought was an absolute bargain. She'd told Andrew four and he'd been aghast at that. He was always wanting to know how much things cost, as if that mattered with curtains or clothes. You got exactly what you paid for with clothes.

Joe poured her a glass of iced water from the jug on the table before attracting the attention of the waiter. They took a moment to order and then he sat back, still managing to look very strange to Tess without a cigarette stuck between his fingers. Stephanie had apparently persuaded him to give up and this time it seemed to be working. It was amazing what a man would do for love.

His hands, below the stiff white cuffs of his shirt, were cared for, his nails neat and clean, his fingers adorned with several showy rings. Close to fifty now, he was a formidable presence, shortish with a bit of a paunch, true, but still managing with his superbly tailored clothes to cut a fine figure. Darkish hair, thinning and greying now, deep brown eyes, Tess's eyes, but a more rounded face. Tess had inherited her glossy almost-black hair, her fine features, her slender body, from her mother.

'How did it go this morning? The grand opening?' he asked. 'Sorry I couldn't manage to be there. Bloody meeting went on forever. This takeover's causing all sorts of problems. Ivan's put a new bloke in finance. Keen sort. Trying to make things add up, for Christ's sake.' The quick glance was sly. 'I thought Andrew would have been there for you this morning with it being such a special day.'

'He's busy.' Tess dismissed it with a smile. Joe had never entirely approved her choice of husband. To him, accountants were the pits of the professional world. 'It went wonderfully, Joe. It brought the arcade to a standstill. You should have seen the crowds. She was quite charming and rather regal. She wore pale blue with a big hat and she looked about sixty. Years older than she does on screen. It was rather a shock, in fact. I hope I didn't look too surprised.'

'That's actresses for you.' He waved at someone who had just come in before returning his attention to her. 'The coverage will drum up some business anyway, and that's what it's all about. Take my advice, Tess, and you won't go far wrong. After all,

I've been in the business of selling for more years than I care to remember. It's all about marketing, sweetheart. One brash TV celebrity is worth three brass bands. If I can't set you on the right track, nobody can. Fast track to the top for my girl, eh?'

He leaned across the table, put his hand gently on hers a moment.

Tess smiled and relaxed for the first time today. Following the panic phone call at seven, it had been a bit of a strain this morning and she hadn't slept very well, going over it again and again in her mind, coming up with all kinds of disastrous scenarios, the most important being that the blasted woman failed to show. Stress was good though. Essential. After all, what harm had it done her father? He thrived on it and she was the same. Life was so flat without it. She was lucky. One of the people who could take it. Andrew couldn't. Andrew was clueless when he was uptight.

Happily, she glanced round the restaurant. She was always so at ease with her father, at least when she had him to herself. It wasn't so easy when Stephanie was there, clinging to his arm, looking adoringly into his eyes. She tweaked the little pot of stiff flowers on the table. Artificial and my God, they looked it! Imagine a place as classy as this using second-rate artificial blooms from some tatty stall on the market, a job lot by the look of it.

'Have a word with the manager later,' Joe said with a grin, reading her mind. 'Oh and by the way, I might have a contract for you to supply some flowers for a wedding. We're talking big here, Tess, not some bloody two bit affair. They'll need flowers for the reception too. It'll be in Gosforth.'

'Fine. Sounds wonderful. Let me have the details later,' she said, her mind still on the morning promotion.

The new outlet was the most up-market of her shops yet, in an exclusive marble and mirrored arcade. There was a classy boutique, a shirtmaker, a perfumers and an Italian delicatessen and she was pricing accordingly. She was aiming at top clients there, no bargain pre-packaged blooms for under a fiver, but it would be worth keeping an eye on possible commissions. She had handed out her business cards like confetti this morning and something was sure to come from that. The boutique two doors away, for instance, had already enquired about a regular fresh floral arrangement for its window.

'How's Stephanie?' she asked at last, shamed into so doing although she couldn't in fact care less. She was sorry, she supposed she ought to be sorry, but she could not bring herself to like her . . . her *stepmother*, for God's sake, but she had learnt over the years how to deal with it. As long as she kept out of the woman's way except on occasions when meeting her could not be avoided, everything was fine. She had done her best, God help her, to be gracious about her father's second marriage and she knew, deep down, it was childish to feel as she did but she could not help feeling he had been disloyal to her mother.

What the hell! Stephanie probably couldn't stand her either but they managed to keep that secret from Joe. It was rather sweet that he thought they liked each other.

'Stephanie's very well indeed.' His face lit up when he talked about her, a fact that Tess found more irritating than appealing. 'She said to ask you when you two are going to get together? Shopping, perhaps?'

'I'll give her a ring sometime,' Tess said quickly, passing him a bread roll as a diversion. She never liked to look him in the eye when they talked about his wife in case the animosity showed. 'I'd love to see her but I am terribly busy. Is she selling any of those lovely paintings?'

'A few,' Joe said. 'The gallery looks pretty good though and we get our fair share of tourists up there. Keeps her amused anyway. Gives her something to do.' His smile flitted briefly. 'Between you and me, sweetheart, it costs me a fortune, the upkeep. Still . . . she's hardly Picasso standard, is she?'

Tess smiled sympathetically.

Stephanie was a former academic and looked it, something to do with Roman history, something dull as ditchwater anyway. At forty she had met Joe and within weeks she had given it all up, married him and now dabbled in watercolours although, to Tess's delight, not very well. She had actually had the almighty nerve to give Tess one of her paintings for her birthday present. A little personal gift, she had said in that cloyingly nice way of hers, so much better than a shop bought gift, don't you think?

She had also asked Tess if she might try to sell some of her work in the shops. So far, Tess had avoided giving a direct answer to that. In her opinion, Stephanie Sutherland was very effectively creaming off the money that ought by rights to be hers. Her own mother would turn in her grave if she knew. It still completely foxed Tess why her father should choose to marry someone with brains rather than beauty, for by no stretch of the imagination could Stephanie be called beautiful and her father was singularly uninterested in the arts. What did they have in common?

'This soup is quite dreadful,' she said, putting down her spoon. 'It tastes like washing up water.'

'Does it, by God? We'll soon see about that.'

Joe flushed, threw down his napkin and signalled the waiter, complaining loudly on Tess's behalf. Tess idly watched the fellow squirm. She had no patience with inefficiency or incompetence and, as the manager was hastily summoned, she and her father exchanged a slight mischievous smile. Joe loved it. Making a fuss. Nobody made a fool of him. Of course, he didn't often have the chance because if Stephanie were here she would have shushed him down, put up with insipid soup, just for the sake of harmony.

Andrew was the same and sometimes it irritated.

Andrew . . . her thoughts began to drift as the great soup debate went on all around for apparently nobody else had complained, content apparently to drink heavily seasoned washing up water.

'I don't give a bugger that nobody else has complained – *I'm* complaining.'

She let her father go on.

Three years on and Andrew was still letting it get to him. The baby business had upset Andrew more than it had her. Frankly, she had later realised that it had been a relief it happened the way it did because it had been a dreadful mistake getting pregnant in the first place. God alone knows how it happened. The point was that she was finished with babies forever although she hadn't got round to telling him. She hoped Andrew would see the sense of it because she did love him, of course she did, and she liked being with him. She wanted to stay married to him, just the two of them, and she was sure that, once he had accepted that she could not, under any circumstances, risk another pregnancy, everything would be wonderful.

After all, sex, now that she'd got over the worry of another pregnancy turning up out of the blue, was back to being just fine. As well as being a considerate lover, Andrew was a good listener too. She could grumble all she liked and it just bounced off. She thought they balanced each other beautifully. She saw herself as very much the dominant partner. Andrew was not entirely without fire – God, no – but he was quite happy to go along with what she wanted and even if he made a half-hearted protest, she could always get round him. She loved him for that.

'Right . . . that's that sorted out,' Joe said as the offending soup was removed and another starter was laid before her by a slightly huffy waiter. 'You'll like that.' He grinned as she picked up her fork. 'He can whistle for a tip, that bugger, for being so graceless. Should get this meal for free. I practically keep this place going and they can't afford to rattle me.'

'That'll help the expense sheet,' Tess said with a smile.

She knew all about his fiddles. He'd been at it for years at every company he'd been with. He would manage to charge today's lunch to the company, pay with the company credit card, although all he was doing was dining with his daughter. Tess delighted in these lunches. It meant they kept in touch and it saved the bother of time-wasting weekends over at her father's although they were due to visit soon. A magnificent home in Upper Teesdale, that went without saying, but Stephanie had managed to ruin it.

The woman was so insipid. She was in her middle forties now, already terminally grey and apparently content to be so. She bought all her clothes, as far as Tess could see, from Marks & Spencer or even BHS, was totally incapable of doing her own thing with them, jazzing them up a little, and so remained intensely boring. She was a keen homemaker, for God's sake, too. After years of living alone in academic isolation, she delighted for some inexplicable reason in having a man to look after. Fussed around Joe, practically brought him his slippers when he arrived home. Her father thought it charming. He was, it seemed, quite besotted. The traditional saying certainly applied. No fool like an old fool.

'Thanks for lunch, Joe,' she said, realising they had dallied long enough over it and she had things to do. 'I must dash. I need to drop in at the other shops this afternoon. See you soon.'

'Need any more money, sweetheart?' He spoke quietly, the question casual as he came round to her, helped her to her feet. 'You only have to say.'

'Stephanie wouldn't like it if she knew you were giving me money,' Tess said with a smile. She could handle her father just as she could handle her husband. She suspected her father had married Stephanie because he had been immensely flattered by the attention she showed him for, if nothing else, Tess conceded reluctantly that Stephanie had a winning smile.

'Stephanie doesn't know everything I do,' Joe said, to her delight. 'It's my money. I work bloody hard for it.'

He dug deep for his car keys, leading her to the car that he'd left parked on double yellow lines outside the restaurant. Company car, of course. Dark blue enormous Volvo with every extra imaginable, but then he was a director, as he constantly reminded everyone. Miraculously, yet again he had escaped the attention of the traffic warden.

'Can I give you a lift anywhere?'

'No thanks.' Tess glanced at her watch. Two hours was pushing it a bit for lunch. The girls would wonder where she'd got to. Not that she cared much what they thought but she had to show some diligence. 'I must get back. I'll tell Andrew you were asking after him,' she murmured, as he stepped into the car. 'And do give my love to Stephanie. I'll phone her soon. We'll have a girls' day out.'

She needed to talk to Stephanie in private anyway because, with her father's birthday coming up, Tess had an idea for a really super surprise party. Unfortunately, she would have to include Stephanie in the preparations if the surprise element was to be genuine.

She took a short cut via Eldon Square and walked quickly back to the arcade, loving the glossy Italianate feel of the pillars and the polished floor. The balloons and the fripperies were still out on show following this morning's grand opening. The 'star' – and Tess used the term loosely – had had another engagement so had not been able to stay. Tess frowned as she approached. The balloons could come down right away. Elegance and balloons did not go hand in hand.

She opened the door. There were no customers and the manageress and the two part-time assistants were chatting, standing up straight and attempting to look busy as she came through. The little fountain tinkled and splashed prettily and the scent of flowers was all around. Expensive, singly priced blooms.

'One of you . . . take the balloons down,' she called, as she went into the flower workroom at the rear. Taking off her jacket, she smoothed down her already smooth hair, redid her shiny red lipstick, and started issuing a stream of further instructions all at the same time.

# 3

'I know you and the Colonel were not local to the north east, Mrs Makepeace, but I am,' Ella Bainbridge said chattily as she poured the three o'clock tea. 'Born and bred over in Bishop Auckland. Did I ever tell you about when I was a little girl?'

Frequently.

Constance shook her head though, not wishing to spoil her delight at the re-telling, quite prepared to listen yet again to the gritty tale of Ella's youth, like something out of a Catherine Cookson novel. What a blessing she'd met up with her Bernard who'd rescued her from a living hell and married her, whisking her off thereafter to a remote farm in Northumberland. They'd lived in a tied cottage on the estate and Bernard Bainbridge, a farmer's hand by trade, was the sort of man quaintly referred to as the salt of the earth. Returning to their roots, they'd accepted the position as housekeeper/gardener handyman at West House gladly.

Of course, although Constance was happy enough to listen or pretend to listen to Ella, she rarely imparted any information about her own family, only little carefully selected snippets to keep the peace and please Ella. In fact, although most of the older inhabitants of Bishopsmeade knew something of the tragedies that had befallen her family, she preferred to keep the details shadowy, particularly pertaining to little Billy. The less known about that, the better. Hugh had concocted a tale and they'd stuck to it. Miraculously nobody had discovered the truth to this day.

'The youngest of eight I was and I very nearly killed my mother when I was born . . .' Ella went on cheerfully and Constance looked at her, her warning ignored.

Please God, not the drama of her birth!

Too late. There was no stopping Ella now. 'They must have bent my arm getting me out. Breech. Stuck fast I was. It was a shock for my mam. She said the last two before me just popped out like shelling peas. She never had any more after me. It put her right off, it did. Look at it, Mrs Makepeace, my arm . . . it's never really been the same since.'

'Good gracious.'

Constance looked at the offending arm which looked remarkably well to her. Remembering her own first pregnancy, she shuddered at Ella's choice of conversation matter, switched off her attention thereafter and let her ramble on. Ella liked to talk. Ella liked to get things out of her system by talking. Constance disapproved of such action. There was something to be said for suffering in silence.

It was her belief that some things were best not discussed.

Her first husband, Archie, and Hugh had been rather alike in many ways. Certainly in appearance and also in the way they preferred not to talk about things. It was the upper class way of dealing with both joy and sorrow. Hugh and she, for instance, had never discussed how they felt about losing their sons. He blamed her for Thomas's accident, blamed her also, ridiculously, for Billy. He had never actually said as much, but words were not needed to convey his thoughts. After Billy, through guilt probably, he bought her a silver locket to try to make amends. How foolish!

Going back to West House without a baby had been the hardest thing but she had never let Hugh know how she felt about it, for what was the point of that? Occasionally the memories came back at the oddest moments, like this morning, for example, as she leaned over One-Mile Bridge but she had learnt to live with that. Memories, good or bad, could never be completely erased.

She and Ella were in the kitchen at West House.

Ella Bainbridge, whose sixtieth birthday was coming up soon, had been with her now for fifteen years, fifteen interminably chatty years. She could, however, work and talk at the same time and she was a remarkably good cook and cleaner, got into corners, dicky arm or not.

The kitchen was huge, high ceilinged, but funnily cosy with the old range and they sat in the middle of the room, their feet on one of the proddy mats on the flagged floor, their cups on the scrubbed table. Constance was, despite Mrs Bainbridge's clear disapproval, enjoying, a little ahead of time, her third cigarette of the day. A genuine station clock, enormous, rescued some years ago, was anchored on the wall, ticking very deeply and solidly. It was never the right time but no matter.

Smith, an ancient ginger cat who had turned up on the doorstep some five years ago and taken up permanent residence, was asleep as usual, curled on the cushion of his favourite chair by the window. The big sash window, sparkling clean and uncurtained, looked out onto the east side garden, a wide expanse of sloping lawn, the leaves of the few trees just beginning to turn. Autumnal sunshine flooded in suddenly without warning and the two ladies sighed their pleasure.

Mrs Bainbridge, with no children of her own, mothered her. Before she left later this afternoon, Constance's evening meal would be prepared, all ready for her to reheat, cold items in the refrigerator, her bed made up, nightdress laid upon it and they, she and Bernard, were only a stone's throw away down in the village should they be needed at any time during the night. They used to reside at West House, staying in a small suite of rooms on the second floor, but recently they had acquired their own small property in the village, rather apologetically, and drove up to the house everyday in their little old car.

'That cat of yours over there . . .' Ella sniffed and glanced darkly towards the sleeping cat whom she never called by name. 'He's been in the blue bedroom again, on the chair by the window. Leaves orange hairs all over it. I have to pick them off by hand one at a time. Takes forever, it does. Trouble is, I can never catch him at it. Sly devil he is.'

'Yes,' Constance said with pride. 'He is indeed.'

'Eight of us, ten if you count mam and dad, in this little terraced street,' Ella went on, seeing she was going to get nowhere grumbling about the cat. 'Mind you, she did her best, my mam. She kept it spotless. And us. We had this tin bath she had to fill and then empty. We had a rota who got in first. And we only had one outside lavatory. Freezing it was in winter when you had to go. They don't know they're born these days. Did you know those new houses on Churchwood Close have *three* bathrooms? What on earth can you do with three bathrooms?'

'Indeed, Ella? I must say, for new houses, they do seem very large and well appointed.' Constance smiled, hoping to distract her, but it was not to be. She was in full reminiscent flood.

'She was from a long line of chapel folk. Stood no nonsense, although she was a good mother. She acted on instinct, she did. She would have nothing to do with some of the things the nurse said she ought to be doing. How many bairns have you had then, she asked her. She was before her time, Mrs Makepeace. The tales I could tell . . .'

Quite.

Ella Bainbridge had a bulky face with a broad flat nose, a large chin and small deep-set eyes. One of those ladies whom one felt sorry for, for she was really most unattractive to look at. Her heart was in the right place though, Constance knew with certainty, feeling a funny fondness towards her. Both of them, childless. It made for a sort of bond.

'And they have the cheek to talk about the good old days,' Ella went on, undaunted. 'Tough days for some of us. Although you had it nice, didn't you, Mrs Makepeace? Sounds lovely, that house you were born in. Cornwall, did you say? It's bonny down there, a bit warmer. I went to Brighton once. It's Bernard, you see, I can't get him to go anywhere. A right stay-at-home he is.'

'Brighton is nowhere near Cornwall,' Constance said. 'And in any case, it wasn't Cornwall. It was Devon.'

'Same thing,' Ella said dismissively, reaching for another ginger biscuit and lifting the cosy off the pot. 'Fancy another cup?'

'Thank you and it is not the same thing at all, Ella,' Constance told her. 'It's like Yorkshire and Lancashire. Quite different.'

She hadn't thought about her childhood home in a long time. It was quite a splendid house in its way, Smallcoombe Manor, although it did not compare to West House. The youngest sister of three, Constance was born in 1915 to Major William Parkinson and his wife Rosamund, and proved to be the child with the sunniest disposition, not difficult for she had belonged to a morose family. Three daughters had meant they were educated at home for father had not considered their education an important issue, not when they would marry sooner or later. Their governess had done her best and Constance had an enviable command of the Bible as the vicar knew to his cost, could manage an adequate conversation in French, could recite word for word numerous poems and passages from Shakespeare and had never forgotten her lessons on manners and deportment, but in the ways of the world her education had been sadly inadequate. Her father, on retiring from the army, had farmed and been a very considerate landlord to his tenant farmers, and her mother had passed her time being poetically delicate, trying in vain to provide her husband with a son and heir.

They had spent their childhood being quiet.

Constance sighed, seeing for a few seconds not the comfortable kitchen at West House but the almost medieval kitchen and pantry at the house near Totnes, forbidden territory in theory and therefore an especially exciting place to visit to catch a glimpse of the maids at work. Sometimes cook would pour them each a glass of ginger-beer if their governess was not looking, winking at them as she did so. Once Constance heard her calling them 'the poor little mites'. Wondered why.

A privileged life, of course, although at the time it had not felt especially so, for as a child how can one judge such things? All Constance knew was that they were one of the first families in the area to own a motor car, a Morris Oxford Tourer of which her father had been so proud, although she was happier riding on the trams when they visited Plymouth. They spent holidays by the sea in Weston-super-Mare, where Father unwound a little and helped them in their search for seaside crustacea. Even then they had to keep quite quiet so that they would not disturb Mother. All their life was geared to not disturbing Mother. Their visits up to West House to see Grandfather had been infrequent but memorable for all that. Everything had seemed so much bigger then and Grandfather Parkinson had been a most energetic and likeable man, much less strict than Father.

Constance drew a deep breath and brought herself reluctantly back to the present, flicking the cigarette towards the ashtray with a sigh. Her mother had spent all her life in a pale recline, sighing. Even Ella's mother, coping with the perils of having eight children and filling up the tin bath, sounded a lot more fun.

'Well, I can't sit here all day and you look ready for your rest,' Ella said briskly, removing the cups and carrying them towards the sink. 'Bernard wants a word sometime, Mrs Makepeace, about the pruning and the winter sort-out. Whenever it's convenient to you, he says.'

'I'm moving to my cottage down in the village in spring,' Constance said quietly, watching the woman's back as she busied about with soapy water. 'As you know, the present tenants will be leaving at Christmas. It's a decision I've reached after careful consideration. I would hope, of course, Ella, that the new people here will take you and Bernard on. I shall give you excellent references.'

'Oh, that won't be necessary, thank you.'

Ella's sturdy feet in brown lace-ups peeped from the hem of her heathery tweed pleated skirt. She wore a cardigan over her blouse in winter but today, September still, she was wearing just the cotton long-sleeved blouse buttoned to the neck and a silver brooch shaped like a swan. She had rather a pretty collection of brooches. Turning, she wiped her hands and smiled.

'I can't say I'm surprised. We've been expecting it, Mrs Makepeace. It's getting too much for you. You'll be much better off in that lovely little cottage of yours down by the river. Handy for the shops too and your teashop. It's not right, a lady of your age, trailing down to the village everyday.'

'That's not the reason at all,' Constance said, feeling the need to point that out. If it was up to Ella, she would do nothing at all, certainly never walk anywhere. Ella was a little over-protective and, although it was kindly meant, it was suffocating.

Ella looked unconvinced, rattling on in her unstoppable fashion, 'Bernard and me have talked about it. As soon as you go, we said, so will we, so there'll be no need for references. I'll help you out at the cottage, of course, if you want me to. It's not that I need the money, Mrs Makepeace, more something to do. I wouldn't want to work here though, not with you gone. It wouldn't be the same at all. And I expect the new people will want to make their own arrangements, don't you?'

'I expect so,' Constance said, relieved there would be no fuss. She had not of course expected any, for Mrs Bainbridge was remarkably resilient. 'I am telling you this, Ella, in strictest confidence. I do not wish it to be broadcast round the village. It will not be going on the market as such, you see.'

'You mean you're not putting it up for sale?'

'Not with an estate agent. They are much too concerned with money and as you know that does not concern me. They would insist on asking an inflated price and so I am dealing personally with the arrangements. My only concern is that West House has sympathetic owners and the price is therefore irrelevant. When I have found the right people, I will inform you. Until then this is between you and me only. Is that understood?'

'Of course.' Ella's eyes widened. 'My lips are sealed.'

'Good.' Constance gave her a final look. If rumours started, she would know who had started them. 'You're right, Ella. It is the right decision for me, although Smith will be awkward. He likes it here.'

They looked at the cat who, sensing their gaze, opened his eyes and stared at them before stretching and leaping off the chair, sauntering off to the cat flap and letting himself out in a huff of orange fur.

'You can't let yourself be ruled by him,' Ella said sternly. 'It's your life, Mrs Makepeace, and you must do what you think fit. Now don't you worry. Me and Bernard will help all we can with the move and I'll come and see you as often as I can at the cottage, even if you decide you can manage without me. I still haven't shown you all my photos. Three big shoeboxes full, Mrs Makepeace. Most of them from the farm.'

'How delightful! I shall look forward to that.'

On that rather threatening note, Constance retired for her afternoon nap.

'What did I tell you, Bernard man?' Ella said as he drove sedately out of the drive of West House the short distance to their little cottage on Fletcher's Yard. 'Leaving the house, eh? I knew it.

I knew there was something up with her. I could tell she was working up to telling me. I was beginning to wonder if she'd ever get round to it. I thought they'd be carrying her out in a box.'

'I'll miss the old place,' Bernard said with a sigh. 'I hope the new gardener knows what he's doing. It'll soon go to pot. Gardens do. Ideally, I'd like to work with him, part-time maybe, for a full season, show him what's what.'

'You're too conscientious, Bernard. You have enough to do worrying about our own little garden,' Ella told him. 'I've told her we'll stay until she goes. Only fair, isn't it? Poor old soul, I feel sorry for her, all on her own. She never lets on what she's thinking. Bit of a dark horse, she is. They always did keep themselves to themselves, people like her. Think they're better than anybody else just because they've got money. She once told me about this house she was born in. Grand sounding place in Cornwall. Or is it Devon? She's not a bad old stick though. She could be a lot worse.'

'That's right, she could. She's always treated us fair and square. And you should stop taking advantage.'

'Taking advantage? What are you talking about, man?' Ella asked.

'Stop being so nosy about her private life,' Bernard said, drawing up outside their cottage. 'She doesn't want to tell you. She's made that clear.'

'Secrets.' Ella clicked her tongue in exasperation. 'I can't bear secrets. I tell her *everything*, Bernard. Ever so interested she is in my family but she never says a dicky bird about her own. Not a lot, anyway. All I do know I get from other people.'

'It's none of your business, Ella pet. I bet she could tell a tale though. You can tell she was a bonny looking woman in her day.'

'Maybe. She's been married twice. I know that much.' She gave him a look.

'Fifteen years trying and you still haven't got to the bottom of it,' Bernard said with a wry smile. 'You must be losing your touch, flower. The rate she's going, she's going to take her secrets with her. To the grave.'

'Not if I can help it,' Ella said firmly. 'She needs to get it out of her system. Tell somebody. A person other than that cat of hers. She talks to him you know. I bet *he* knows.'

# 4

'You've missed the children. They're at school,' Yvonne said, carrying the phone to the sofa and flopping down. 'You know it's useless ringing at this time.'

'I wanted to speak to *you*,' Robin said. 'Sod the kids.'

She smiled a bit, knew he didn't really mean that to sound as it did. He loved them. She was sure he did.

'They miss you,' she said, trying not to sound too accusing. 'It's so confusing for them, all this toing and froing you do. We have to do something about it.'

'Like what?'

Yvonne heard his voice rise. Heavens, he had a short fuse!

'Like . . . you coming back home for good, of course,' she said. 'You can get a job round here. You working on the rigs has given us a good start but money's not everything. You know exactly what I mean. We've been through all this, Robin.'

'You've a bloody cheek, Yvonne. All you ever wanted was money and a big fancy house, new car, expensive clothes . . .'

'That's not true,' she said, wondering if it had been, once. If that was so, then what was the matter with her? She did have a lovely home, nice furniture, the children wanted for nothing, and yet it still wasn't right.

'It's not that I'm complaining . . .'

'Not much you aren't,' he said shortly. 'Look, Yvonne, I didn't ring so that you could start nagging me. You know as well as I do that I like the job. OK, it's not what I really want, you know that, but there's not many actual expeditions going on so it's the next best thing. I've got used to the hours and I've got some good mates. And we said we'd stick it for as long as we could. We knew it wouldn't be easy but what's the alternative? I wouldn't be happy with a factory job and it wouldn't pay nearly as much.'

'I know. But *I* miss you too,' she said. 'Can't you see that? It's not natural being separated like we are. If you were in the army or something that would be different. But you're not. We're doing this to each other from choice. I know it's a long way for you to come home just for a couple of days, Robin, but I wish you could come home every weekend. It wouldn't be so bad then.'

'You should have moved up here, you and the children,' he said. 'So don't go blaming me the whole time. I gave you the chance.'

'It wasn't practical. And you know I didn't like it up there. Sorry, but why should I move somewhere I don't want to be?'

'To save your marriage,' he said, very quietly.

'Oh, come on, it's not as bad as that,' she said, although the serious note had sent a sudden sharp tingle down her spine.

'Isn't it? I rang to say . . .' his voice lowered, temper cooled. 'I rang to say I'm sorry about last weekend. Things didn't work out too well, did they? You and me?'

'No.' She shook her head, filling up with sudden tears. Their wedding photograph, sitting on a bookshelf, seemed to stare accusingly at her, reminding her of the good times. Such smiling faces, so young and with such hopes! She'd looked absolutely wonderful in a froth of frills, felt it too.

'You're not still thinking you might be pregnant again, are you?' he asked.

'No. I wasn't pregnant. A bit late, that's all,' she said.

'Thank God. I don't want you using that as a weapon.'

'A weapon? For what?'

'For making me feel guilty, Yvonne. You're bloody good at that.'

She let it pass. It was hurtful that he could even think that but he had said it now and, if she was honest, it had occurred to her that if she was pregnant she might be able to persuade him to come home for good.

'We never talked, Robin,' she said after a short awkward pause. 'It's hopeless when you only have a few days off. It takes a few days for us to get to know each other again. I'm sorry but I felt a bit . . . well . . . awkward. Ridiculous, isn't it?'

'Oh . . .' To her annoyance he laughed. 'Are you talking about bed? Christ, what do you expect? We can't be expected to turn it on just like that. We've been married ten years. We have three kids.'

'I just thought . . .' she bit her lip. She couldn't tell him. She couldn't tell him how disappointing it had been. She had bought a new nightdress, made a special effort, and it had been a shambles. Furtive and unrewarding.

'Sex isn't everything, Yvonne,' he said and the way he said it made her feel ashamed.

'The children get so upset when you have to go back to work. They don't understand. Time doesn't mean much to them,' she said, moving onto a safer subject.

'Don't drag them into it. They're not the only ones with one parent at home. They're very proud of me. It's not everybody's dad who goes diving . . . I just work away, that's all. It's not as if we're divorced, Yvonne.'

But they might as well be.

She said nothing, wondering why their phone calls were so depressing these days. She was left feeling frustrated and irritated with him, every single time. Later this evening she would think of all the things she should have said to him.

'They look forward to you coming home,' she went on, contradicting what she'd just told him about time meaning nothing to them. 'They count the days. Portia has this big calendar and she crosses the days off.'

'I know. She showed it to me.'

'And then . . . you come home and there's the presents and everything, and we have to cram being a proper family again into a few days, then it's time for you to go back. Harry cried practically non-stop on the Monday after you went.'

'For Christ's sake! You spoil that child,' Robin said. 'Stop treating him like a baby.'

'He is a baby,' she said softly. 'He's only four, darling.'

'He's a little boy, at school now, and you've got to stop smothering him, Yvonne. Why do you have to mother *everybody*?'

'Maybe I could manage to fix something up and get a weekend up there with you,' she said. 'Get someone to look after the children.'

'Who?'

'I don't know, but you needn't worry. I wouldn't ask just anybody. I could ask one of the mums at school maybe.'

'Christ, Yvonne. Would you look after three extra kids for a weekend? OK, don't answer that, I know *you* would. But for most people it's too much to ask. They're a handful.'

'No, they're not,' she said indignantly. 'They're very well behaved.'

'Well, if you can organise it, it would be wonderful,' he said, managing, insultingly, to sound less than enthusiastic. 'We can book into a hotel, somewhere just the two of us. Having said that, it's not going to be easy to arrange. We've got a bit of a panic on at the moment.'

She wanted a weekend alone with him. A whole lazy weekend in some luxury hotel where they could relax, forget about the children for a couple of days, be together as they had been at the beginning, take time with each other, talk things through. She wanted to see if they could get back to where they had once been. There was still a chance that she could persuade him to give up the job and come home to them. She dismissed the brief thought that he was having an affair. She couldn't believe it of him because he'd never been that interested in sex, not even in the early days when they'd been together all the time.

All he was interested in was his diving and the sea. How could she compete with that? But she was after all his *wife* and she had the children on her side. A big commitment. Had he really got it in him to cast them off? It would cost him for a start in financial terms, and he was careful with money.

'But it will be all right if I can arrange it, won't it?' she said, even as the hope died in her heart. She knew she could not leave the three of them with someone else. She would just worry too much.

'I'll ring you again. Probably not tomorrow. In fact I may be stuck until Saturday. Give you a ring then, sometime in the afternoon, and don't whatever you do try to get me. It only causes mayhem.'

'But Robin . . .' She didn't have time to explain that on Saturday afternoon Samantha was out at a birthday party and she would be terribly upset if Daddy rang and she missed him.

It was too late.

He had already added a swift goodbye, an afterthought of a 'love you', and put down the phone.

# 5

The teashop on Front Street was run by a lady called Florence Green whom Constance had known for years, and it was exactly Constance's cup of tea, so to speak, with lacy cloths, fine floral china and a tiny centrepiece of fresh flowers at each of the tables. Freshly baked scones, a convivial atmosphere and no pressure to rush.

It was at the church end of Front Street, a straggly street that gently followed the lines of the village green, and further up there was the general store and post office, the butcher's, the baker's, the greengrocer's, a little restaurant, a couple of antique shops, the chemists, the village hall and the public house. The George, it was called, and she had never set foot in it. Not that she disapproved of drink, for she enjoyed her evening glass of very dry martini, but Hugh had considered public houses were not for them. Hugh had been a tiny bit of a snob.

This morning the teashop was full of cyclists. Young men in those strange skin-tight garments cyclists wear these days, carrying brightly coloured helmets with them. Constance did not quite see the necessity for such peculiar garments when surely a pair of bicycle clips and a cap would suffice.

'Mind if we squeeze in, madam?' one of them asked her.

'Not at all,' she said politely, quite unable to refuse them, even though the last thing she wanted was to share her table, for they brought with them a greasy smell of liniment. On the other hand, they looked very friendly, smiling at her as they perched, some too large for the chairs, beside and opposite her.

Poor Miss Green, toing and froing with trays and order pads, looked a little harassed and it was lucky she had the young girl to help this morning. Constance had been sitting alone in the cafe, awaiting her coffee and toasted tea-cake, when these people had suddenly and most unexpectedly burst in to take morning refreshment. In Constance's opinion, they would have been better served taking their tea at what used to be called a transport cafeteria, the teashop being for a more genteel client.

'We're just passing through,' one of the cyclists at her table said, stating the obvious. 'Round the dales trip.'

'How delightful!' Constance daintily prepared to eat her tea-cake. 'My late husband and I used to bicycle for pleasure when we were young. Regrettably, I had to sell mine off some years ago. A little stiff in the joints now,' she added, deciding she had better make the best of things, thinking what a bright trio the young men were.

She was bright herself, in what she believed they termed casual gear, wearing a buttercup yellow tracksuit today, fleecy-lined with black piping. She had only discovered such blissfully comfortable garments of late and, although Mrs Bainbridge disapproved, Constance had bought several. On a practical note, it meant cumbersome corsets could be dispensed with but Mrs Bainbridge considered such leisure garments totally inappropriate for an octogenarian and that quite delighted Constance.

They were having a few days of late summery weather just now which quite perked everybody up. Sleepy bees had done a dance in her back porch when she came out this morning and the meadows by West House were adrift with willowy pink and golden autumn flowers. The sky was high and blue. She had left Smith in a very perky state.

'Nice cafe,' one of them said when they had ordered. 'Come here often?'

What a civilised enquiry, Constance thought, smiling as she explained that she came every weekday morning and that she lived in the big house on the hill. They would be cycling past shortly and, if they looked to the left when they were over the bridge, they would surely see it amongst the trees.

Before long, they were all chatting away like old friends. The bicycles were propped up outside, many of them, and inside there was not a spare table to be had. Conversations ranged the length and breadth of the cafe, much laughter, and Constance felt quite a part of it all. It was rather invigorating and it certainly made a change from discussing the weather and the garden with Miss Green. She and Miss Green had just about exhausted talk about the garden. Miss Green was dreadfully dull, reminding her of her sister Eleanor. Eleanor had very little conversation either.

It occurred to her, as she listened to the young men telling her about some of the places they had visited, that she might have had a grandson by now, a grown-up one like these young people, if her children had lived. It was so sad that she had lost not only them but also grandchildren. A complete generation wiped out. Good gracious! She might have been a *great*-grandmother by now.

'Would you like another coffee?' the young man opposite asked.

Constance looked at him, smiled slightly, feeling her focus swim a little as it did when she thought about her lost children. The young man was very good looking in an artistic sort of way, less muscled than his companions. He reminded her just a touch of dearest Archie. Archie had had a gentle face, not too tall with an elegant slim body rather like Fred Astaire. Archie had also had flair, had quite set her pulse on fire with just one look from those grey-green eyes of his.

With Archie, it was love at first sight.

'And these are my sisters, Eleanor and Constance,' Grace said as she introduced Archibald George Lennox to them. Grace's look was pure triumph for Archie had not only an excellent pedigree of which their father thoroughly approved but he was also handsome and effortlessly courteous. He was also Grace's very first young man, for Grace, plain and a little plump, just eighteen months older than Constance, had no easy manner with gentlemen, her shyness managing to be excruciating rather than winsome.

Archie shook hands with Eleanor and then turned to her.

'How do you do? I'm delighted to meet you, Constance,' he said, stretching out his hand.

They had known instantly as they touched, her foolish heart had indeed skipped a beat, and poor Grace, totally unaware, had continued to twitter and laugh at his side as Constance smiled into his eyes and he into hers.

She was twenty-five when they married, a sweet little thing with a heart-shaped face, dark lustrous hair and sparkling expressive eyes that he adored. She felt she could admit to herself now that she had been beautiful once. But, sadly, it could not be denied that she stole him from Grace and, if there had only been a way to make it more bearable for her sister, Constance would have taken it but of course there was no way.

She and Archie fell madly in love and nothing, not even a distraught sister who understandably felt betrayed, could alter that. How could they deny it? Grace refused to believe it of them, turned nasty in a trice, and did not, understandably, attend their wedding. Archie believed firmly in fate and refused to let it worry him. After a brief tangle with her conscience, neither did Constance. As Archie said, to hell with Grace. It would have made no difference for, even if she had turned him down, he would not have returned to Grace.

They were married a mere four months after they met. There was an urgency about life, love, as war loomed. After being in the air cadet corps first at his public school and then at university, he was of course destined to go into the Air Force as a pilot, joining the Spitfire wing of 603 based in Hornchurch. He displayed a terrible enthusiasm for the idea of fighting in the skies and Constance tried in vain to dispel her own fears. Although it was probably unwise to consider bringing a baby into such a troubled world, she wanted Archie's child desperately, just in case . . .

'I'm sorry . . .' Constance stirred herself, realising the young man opposite was awaiting a reply to his offer of another cup of Miss Green's delicious coffee. 'It's very kind, but no thank you. It's time for me to walk back,' she explained. 'I have a small amount of shopping to do and then I have to walk back. I enjoy the exercise.'

'We could give you a lift on the handlebars,' one of them said with a laugh.

For a second she was rather shocked at his audacity then she laughed too. One had to display a sense of humour. Miss Green was sadly lacking in humour.

There was much scraping of chairs as the cyclists, all at the same time, exited. To her dismay, the young men at her table paid her bill too but it was too late to protest as they shot off towards the church in a two by two wheeled formation. Constance gazed after them, rather touched.

'Noisy lot. Filling up with carbohydrates,' Miss Green said with a smile, clearing the tables around, 'If only we had their energy, Mrs Makepeace, although you do very well for your age.'

'Thank you,' Constance said drily, before glancing at her small gold watch whose figures she had some difficulty in seeing. However, she would get a new watch with a bigger display before she would resort to spectacles. Spectacles were so ageing. 'I'll say good morning then, Miss Green, and I shall see you tomorrow as usual.'

She picked up her showerproof that she always carried in case of suddenly inclement weather and stood up, smiling at the only person left in the teashop. A young man, but not one of the cyclists. She had seen him before in here and Miss Green had told her that he was from the new houses. It was splendid of him to come in here, more than once too. And she had also seen him shopping in the village, carrying heavy looking bags home with him. A most agreeable looking man and she approved of the way he patronised the local shops. Supermarkets were such a dreadful innovation and she prided herself that she had never set foot in one. Nor would she.

'Good morning,' she said with a smile as she passed. 'Lovely day today.'

'Good morning,' Andrew replied, rising slightly from his seat, returning her smile.

Andrew, ridiculously concerned as he was about the village economy, was pleased to find the teashop so full and had in fact enjoyed an easy conversation with the cyclists himself. Nice bunch, and it poked at his conscience that, as a motorist, he could be a bit damned short with them, cutting in, that sort of thing. Tess was even worse. Tess had no patience with cyclists or pedestrians. Tess was dynamite behind the wheel.

He followed the old lady out a few minutes later. Funny old dear. Extremely well modulated tones that would appeal to Tess. Rather aristocratic looking with silver-white hair twisted at the back and pinned up and you expected her to be dressed in silks and furs, certainly not a hooded yellow tracksuit. He knew she was Mrs Makepeace from the big house for she had, somewhat reverently, been pointed out to him once in the post office. The Colonel's lady, apparently.

He was still reeling from a helluva row he and Tess had had last night. They'd started off happily discussing this surprise party she was planning for Joe's fiftieth birthday and suddenly they were off at a tangent and talking about babies. One of those things that exploded without warning from time to time. Entirely his fault for he ought to know by now that it was unwise, to say the least, to make any mention of the baby they had lost. They had made it up at bedtime, thank God, enjoying a somewhat subdued lovemaking. He'd made a private vow not to confront her with it again, the baby thing, not until she was ready. She was almost ready, he felt sure, but not quite.

Was he getting broody? He thought that only happened to women but, to his surprise, he'd found himself looking at Yvonne's three this morning as the Lonsdales set off for school, all smiles, walking for once, the little boy holding onto his mother's hand, the girls skipping in front. Chirpy lot. As far as he could tell, Yvonne seemed incredibly patient with them. He never heard her shouting at them, never ever saw her smacking them, and he often saw her carrying the little boy, although he was getting to the stage where he was almost past being carried.

He'd found himself thinking that they would have had a little three year old, he and Tess, if she'd gone ahead with the pregnancy. He knew, although it pained him dreadfully to think about it, that he would have loved the child no matter what, loved it even more if that were possible. Tess was reluctant to talk about it, had shut her mind to it he supposed, her way of dealing with it. Tess expected perfection in all things and that included a baby.

He dismissed it. No point. What was done was done.

He checked his watch and hurried along to the butcher's.

Shopping in Bishopsmeade, he was coming to realise, was not quite the same as going to Safeways. The whole thing was pursued at a much more leisurely pace. People chatted. The village butcher seemed to be bucking the general trend and doing a roaring trade. The shop was always full. The butcher knew everybody and did not rush. The first few times Andrew had found himself practically trembling with annoyance at the snail's pace, as they discussed all manner of trivial things but now he entered into the spirit of it. It hadn't taken long for the butcher, Ted Simpson, to get to know him too. He had the gentle probing question off to a fine art. The Gestapo would come a poor second. It meant, though, that he treated his customers exceptionally well. Amazingly, he remembered what you'd bought the last time, asked how tender the steaks had been, that sort of thing.

If Andrew had realised before he went in that Yvonne Lonsdale was just ahead of him in the queue, he might not have bothered. He'd decided a while ago that it might be better if he kept his distance. In his heart he knew he could take more than a passing interest in her if he allowed it. She flustered him a bit with those knowing blue eyes of hers. Today she was wearing trousers, the wide-legged satiny ones she favoured, white with a pink and white loose top. All a bit summery, Tess would say, considering it was getting on for October, although he thought she looked very pretty and was like a breath of fresh air amongst the generally anoraked queue.

'Hello Andrew.' She gave him one of her wide smiles. 'I haven't seen you for ages.'

'Busy, you know. I work from home now.'

'Yes. Tess said. Everything going well?'

'Fine.'

'I forgot the mince,' she said with a rueful smile. 'The children like mince. Shepherds pies and things. I expect you and Tess have something a bit more glamorous?'

'I use it for curries,' he said, worrying suddenly that this was bloody cosy and oddly feminine, standing in a queue at the butcher's talking about meals like this. 'It's easier for me to cook,' he said by way of explanation, wondering why he felt the need to explain. 'Tess doesn't feel like it when she gets in.'

'I'm sure she doesn't, not after a hard day,' Yvonne said with yet another glimpse of that gorgeous knock-out smile of hers. He could smell her distinctive flowery perfume from here and see the soft powder on her cheeks, the blush beneath, even admired the softly blue look of her eye make-up. He wondered what she looked like with a completely naked face. 'I haven't seen Tess for a while. She's always dashing about and looks so busy I don't like to disturb her. How did the shop opening go?'

'Terrific,' he said as they moved forward a pace. 'It was in the local papers up there. Nice picture. Tess looked great.'

'Who's next for the chop, ladies and gentleman? We mustn't forget Mr O'Grady, of course, standing there waiting his turn,' Ted Simpson called, wielding a fearsome looking knife and grinning and having the embarrassing effect of everyone in the queue turning to look at Andrew.

'I've been meaning to ask,' Yvonne said, once the queue settled. 'Does she do demonstrations?'

'What?' Startled, he looked at her. 'What sort of demonstrations?'

'Flower arrangements,' Yvonne said patiently. 'We're always looking for people to chat to us at school. We're trying to raise funds for equipment and we have special evenings. We charge a small entrance fee and we have a raffle. I've got myself roped onto the organising committee and I wonder if Tess would mind talking to us. Just a couple of hours.'

'I'll ask her,' he said, doubting it very much. Tess would be hard pushed to do any favours for Yvonne. 'She is busy though,' he added, preparing her for the worst. 'But I will ask. Any particular time?'

'Wednesdays,' she said. 'Any Wednesday will do. Seven to nine. We'd be so grateful if she could. It would make a change from slides of somebody's holiday and I know that it will go down well. Everybody will be so interested in the flowers. It's a gift, isn't it? Being able to arrange. I'm pretty useless, personally. I just bung everything in the vase and hope for the best.'

'I like your arrangements,' he said quickly. 'Tess's are a bit too artistic sometimes. They have to be explained,' he added with a grin.

She smiled uncertainly and for a second he regretted doing that, criticising Tess and thereby embarrassing Yvonne.

'I've been splitting some plants in the garden,' she said after a moment. 'I've been doing a late tidy up. Blitzing the side flower bed. The children helped, or rather hindered. Anyway . . . she's welcome to the cuttings.'

'Thanks a lot,' Andrew said, doing his best to sound keen, knowing that suggestion would go down like a lump of lead. *Their* borders were colour coordinated. Tess took it so seriously, jotting things down in a notebook, and there would be no space in her scheme of things for any of Yvonne's shambolic concoctions.

Luckily before they could be drawn further into their horticultural discussion, Yvonne reached the head of the queue. She beamed at the butcher whose face had turned a shade brighter. 'Hello, Mr Simpson. How are you this morning?'

'In fine fettle,' he said, looking at her with undisguised admiration. 'Those chump chops all right for you last time?'

'Lovely, thanks. I casseroled them.'

'Can't beat chump chops. Casseroled,' Mr Simpson said, addressing his remarks to the entire captive queue.

Tess, who shopped at the speed of light, would have stormed out by now, told him in no uncertain way where he could stuff his chump chops. Andrew glanced at his watch but it went unnoticed as Ted Simpson was not quite ready yet to get on with it. A few more seconds' pleasantry was called for.

'Got back all right then, did he? Mr Lonsdale?' He turned graciously to explain to the rapidly growing queue. 'Mr Lonsdale, Mrs Lonsdale's husband, works under the sea,' he said. 'In Aberdeen. Best mince, is it, for those lovely children? And I have some spicy tomato sausages, my own make, if you're interested. I know they like sausages and these are not like supermarket ones.'

Andrew waited patiently, taking the opportunity to check the display. He was doing pork chops with cider tonight, followed by a tangy orange pudding. He was a bit concerned at the combination of flavours but it was worth a go. He glanced at his watch again. Enough of this buggering about. He needed to get back and do some work before lunch. If Yvonne offered him a lift home, he'd take it.

He had no option, hemmed in as he was in the ever-so-slightly mutinous sounding queue, but to stare at the back of Yvonne's head as she attended to the business in hand. Even with the familiar clattering high heels she was still several inches shorter than he, a bit shorter than Tess. She was wearing her hair up today but fine golden strands escaped from the topknot and curled round her shapely neck.

He found himself desperately wanting to touch them.

# 6

Andrew was being a bore as usual about money. He was forever going on about it. If it had been up to him, they'd still be living in their very first place, a first floor apartment in that big house in Gateshead. What sort of address had that been!

Number One, Churchwood Close, Bishopsmeade, frankly, wasn't much better, not as an 'address'. Tess was going off this house quite rapidly. It was having people like Yvonne Lonsdale next door that did it. She had hoped they might be a little more exclusive. They might try putting it on the market, see what happened, see if they could drum up any interest and then they could look for something else. Unfortunately, here in Bishopsmeade, the good properties were few and far between and the only one she would really give her right arm for was the house up on the hill. Now *that* was some property.

Her mind returned to Andrew. Frankly he was being a pain. If it wasn't money, it was babies. He was becoming obsessed with babies and she had no wish to dwell on that subject so it was just as well she was being kept busy at the shops with trade pleasantly brisk. Three of the shops were operating smoothly but one was struggling, thanks to the incompetence of the manager. The woman had no affinity with flowers. As far as she was concerned it was just another kind of shop and that wouldn't do at all. Tess realised with irritation that she had made a mistake in taking her on, fooled into thinking that simply because the woman had a nice accent and dressed well she was up to the job.

She would have to have a word. Good God, she had given the woman enough chances, more than enough, and there was no alternative but to fire her. There had been customer complaints, more than one, and she couldn't risk her reputation going down the drain. As her father said, there was no room for sentiment in business, and after all, it wasn't as if it was the first time she had done it, given an incompetent the push. In fact, she hardly dared admit it even to herself, but the very act of doing such an unspeakably awful thing like sacking somebody rather thrilled her. It was just as well Andrew didn't have to do it. He would die a thousand deaths, would Andrew.

She took a final satisfied glance at the magnificent arrangement in the hall. She adored autumnal flowers and her shops were busily stocked with the chrysanthemums for church harvest arrangements as well as gladioli, dahlias and Michaelmas daisies. Autumn flowers had a certain boldness to them that she admired.

She had used a mass of golden tones and some leaves from the garden, taking time about trimming it, noting that the foliage was at that funny transitional stage. Come the first frosts all that would change and you could tell from the feel of the air that the first frosts were not very far away.

They were meeting Joe and Stephanie for Sunday lunch and, just as they were about to leave, Tess had started, for some inexplicable reason, to fuss with the flowers in the sitting room.

'Have you been touching these?' she accused, fixing Andrew with a look.

'Some were dead,' he said. 'I threw them out.'

'Dead?' she said, flushing her fury, 'Never in a million years. For God's sake, Andrew, I'm the expert. Leave the flowers to me in future.'

'Sure.' He snatched up the car keys, tight in a sudden sharp anger. 'You're welcome to them.'

He set off towards his car, leaving her to follow, not caring too much whether she did or not. She could make a mountain out of a molehill or, to be more precise, a bloody monumental fuss about some faded blooms. They had been very definitely dead. Crisp and dusty, crumbling under his touch.

'I hope you're not going to be sulky, darling,' she said, climbing into the passenger seat, 'because I'm not in the mood.'

'You never are.'

'What's that supposed to mean?'

'Forget it.' Andrew sighed, drove through the village, slowed down for the nasty bend near One-Mile Bridge, and accelerated up the hill.

'Just look at that house up there,' Tess said quietly, her bad mood over as quickly as it had begun. 'West House. Isn't it beautiful? I'm told the church holds various functions there throughout the year. The next time they have one, we must make sure to go. I want to see what it looks like inside.'

'I saw the old lady who lives there the other day,' he said. 'Mrs Makepeace. She said good morning.'

'Really? I've not actually met her yet but then I'm never around. It makes socialising so difficult and we really ought to try to be part of the community, Andrew.'

'I do,' he pointed out amiably enough. 'I buy what I can in the village. I support the local teashop.'

'That is very commendable, darling,' Tess said, leaning over to pat his knee. 'But I'm talking about a different kind of socialising. Meeting people with influence. Take this Mrs Makepeace, for instance. I should try to cultivate her friendship. I wonder if she goes to church?'

'You could go and stand outside one Sunday, take an inventory of people going in,' he said with a grin. 'Or you could just go to church. Why don't you? They're supposed to make people welcome, aren't they?'

'It's such a hassle. I don't want to get involved if I can help it because I'll no doubt be expected to supply free flowers and advice to the flower committee. But perhaps I ought. It does no harm to advertise your presence. The difficulty is, I've left it rather late. I should have done it straightaway. The first Sunday we were here. It's going to look odd now. As if I'm a born again Christian or something. You can't just suddenly turn up at church, for God's sake.'

He laughed, loving it.

'Darling, you are wonderful. You are such a snob. Trying to worm your way in with Mrs Makepeace just because she has pots of money. Your mother would be proud of you.'

'To get anywhere in this life, Andrew, you have to be a little devious. It's *who* you know every time. Ask Joe. He has a list of contacts a mile long. People he can call on at a moment's notice. *You* don't try hard enough.'

'I don't like that sort of thing.'

'Huh!'

He pulled back from starting a row. What was the point of talking about getting there on merit because you happened to be good at the job? He waited until they were free of a thirty-mile-an-hour limit in the next village before he tried a different tack in the conversation.

'By the way, Yvonne asked me if you'd do a demonstration for school. It went right out of my head.'

'Flowers, you mean?' Tess clicked her tongue. 'Honestly, people seem to forget I'm a professional. They expect me to do these sort of things for nothing . . . I don't suppose there's a fee involved, is there?'

'I don't know. I didn't ask. I shouldn't think so.'

'Pretend you've forgotten to ask me if she mentions it again. I really don't want to be involved, darling.'

'It's for school funds,' he reminded her gently, easing the car through the autumn lanes. Some trees were beginning to shed their leaves already but most were still clinging on, golden and crisping now. The morning Sunday sky had a high bright look to it, wispy clouds, lots of blue, but a pale sun.

'School funds? Is that supposed to make me feel guilty?' Tess asked with a short laugh. 'If I had children . . . if *we* had children,' she corrected herself, 'then that would be different, but as it is . . . well, I can't drum up a lot of enthusiasm for school funds. It's up to the parents. They had the little dears, after all.'

'You can be bitchy sometimes,' Andrew said, glancing sharply at her. 'It wouldn't do you any harm to give them a talk on flower arranging. You can do that sort of thing standing on your head.'

'On the contrary, it takes some considerable time to organise a demonstration. Time I can ill afford just now. You seem to think the shops run themselves.'

'I thought they did. I thought you had very good managers in them.'

'I do. Of course I do, but I need to oversee. It's my reputation.

And it's not just the shops. There's the weddings and funerals and dried flowers and postal flora . . . you have no idea what my job entails. There's the ordering and the selecting and the visits to the dried warehouse and wondering just how much I ought to diversify and . . .

'All right,' he said wearily, 'you've made your point. You're bloody busy. Even so, you could spare a couple of hours one evening surely?'

'You never listen to what I'm saying,' she said crisply. 'I've just explained. Why don't you offer your services? You can bore them rigid talking about financial matters,' she said with a quick smile, already unbuckling her seat-belt as they arrived at Romaldkirk.

The Rose and Crown was a popular venue and he parked some distance away to Tess's annoyance. Like her father, she always expected to park right outside the door no matter where they were going. Like royalty. Joe's car was already there but of Joe and Stephanie there was no sign.

'They'll be propping up the bar,' Andrew said, still irritated as they made their way towards the entrance. They ate out with Joe and Stephanie about once a month although Tess tried to get out of it if she could. Mixed feelings then. He liked this place. Excellent food. But somehow he did not relish a couple of hours in the company of his father-in-law and Stephanie. Stephanie, he had to admit, was hardly the life and soul of the party, although, unlike Tess, he had always felt that her affection for Joe was genuine. You only had to look at the way she looked at him to know she had not married the man for his money. She was just fairly quiet, that was all, and a bit shy, a little mouse quite dwarfed by Joe. It was impossible to think of her commanding attention in a lecture hall although she was bloody good at her subject, off like an express train if she got a sniff of it.

God . . . Tess was always accusing him of being too quiet in company and he would be the first to admit he was pretty hopeless at small talk, but Stephanie was something else.

'Now . . . before we go in . . . you're not to breathe a word about Joe's birthday party,' Tess said, pulling on his arm in the pub's porch. 'And I know it's ages off yet but Christmas might be mentioned and we haven't fixed things yet so if they say anything, you're to say that you insist they come to us this year. It'll sound better coming from you.'

'Oh I see. I thought you said we were going to them,' Andrew said, perplexed.

'Are you being deliberately obtuse? We *are* going to them,' Tess said, keeping her voice low. 'But we have to put up some sort of protest. I ask you, Andrew, when have I the time to prepare Christmas for guests? I shall be completely snowed under at work the week before. Stephanie has nothing else to do. If she's not buried in one of those boring research books, she's fussing with her paintings or sitting in that stupid gallery. And *she* has help in the house.'

A sore point. Tess thought they were made of money, that they could employ any number of staff. No matter that he did most of the domestic stuff anyway.

'Let Stephanie do it for once,' Tess went on firmly. 'She's into Christmas.'

'She always does it,' Andrew pointed out, even more puzzled. 'She puts on a great show. Look, Tess, what the hell *are* we doing at Christmas?'

'We are going to them, to Caryn Lodge,' she said, pulling a cheeky face at him. 'But we must offer them hospitality first. Get it? It's a little game we always play. As I've already told you once today, you are hopeless at being devious, darling. You have such an honest face, that's the trouble. I always know exactly what you're thinking.'

He followed her inside, smiling a little.

There was a minor panic in the bar. Joe was high-handedly directing operations and Stephanie, accompanied by a couple of members of staff, was on her knees minutely searching the carpet.

'Honestly! Her contact lenses again . . .' Tess muttered, face flushed. 'Well, if they think I'm joining in on *my* knees they can think again. These are very expensive tights and they are not for scrabbling about on the floor. You help them look, Andrew. I'll have a tomato juice if I'm driving back.'

She sailed past, announcing to her father and a myopic-looking Stephanie that they would catch up with them in a minute.

# 7

'What do you want me to do with all those clothes in the wardrobe, Mrs Makepeace?' Ella asked, struggling downstairs with an assortment of cleaning tools. 'All your good stuff? Your frocks and your blouses? Only it seems a shame seeing as you never wear them these days.'

The look she gave Constance said it all, for Constance was comfortably clad in a pale blue tracksuit this morning.

'I want you to leave them precisely where they are,' Constance said, rather regretting the sharpness of her tone as she saw the other woman's face flush. 'In any case, I do wear them sometimes. Contrary to what you seem to think, I do not spend my entire life in casuals. Sorry, Ella, but when I am dead, you have my permission to dispose of my clothes as you think fit. By all means, take some for yourself. But until that time, they will remain where they are.'

'Right you are then, Mrs Makepeace,' Ella said, in a bit of a huff, but doing her best not to show it. 'I'll put the kettle on then. That cat of yours is prowling about in the cellar. I can hear him. I hope he's not got himself stuck anywhere. There's a lot of rubbish down there.'

Constance smiled. It was most unlike Ella to show concern for Smith. She herself had no worries, for the cat was perfectly able to take care of himself in that respect. He was, she thought proudly, streetwise.

The 'rubbish' Ella referred to was hardly that. It was sealed-up boxes of belongings, of memories, that she could bring herself neither to look at nor dispose of. When she was gone, they could do what they wanted with that too although she liked the ancient

Egyptian idea of taking your precious belongings with you into the tomb. Safe there with you until some uncaring archeologists discovered them and took them away from you. She felt so sorry for Tutankhamen.

'You all right, Mrs Makepeace? You looked funny for a moment,' Ella said, looking at her with some concern. 'Did you go dizzy?'

'Not at all. I was thinking.'

She shivered, reaching for her cigarettes and comfort, and Ella, fussing with the teapot, spotted the movement, cast another glance her way, obviously not convinced that all was well.

'You haven't caught that virus that's going round, have you? Is that what's up? Virus? If they don't know what it is, they call it a virus, if you ask me. It was influenza that carried my dad off. Did I tell you?'

She waited for the slight shake of Constance's head before ploughing on happily.

'It came on so sudden. There he was, right as rain on the Sunday morning. We went to chapel as usual. All eight of us . . . we never missed. Mam believed we'd be struck dumb if we missed. Very superstitious, she was.'

Constance smiled as she took the cup Ella offered her. She had heard it all before, a hundred times, but no matter. Ella's memory was not quite so accurate as her own and the details charmingly changed a little each time it was recounted.

'Well, next morning, when he should have been off to work as usual at the farm, I feel only fair to middling, Hannah, he says. So my mam feels his head, says he has a temperature, lights a fire in the bedroom and pops him off to bed and just gets on with things. Baking for tea, you know. She spent nearly all her life in that kitchen of hers. Washing. Ironing. Cooking. Well, about seven o'clock or thereabouts there's a banging on the ceiling and she says to me, go and see what your dad wants now, hinny, and up I go. Burning hot by then he was, drenched in sweat, wild-eyed, wandering in his mind and it was all over bar the shouting. He lingered a few more days but it had got deep into his veins and they couldn't flush it out. They didn't have the same facilities in those days. Drips and things.'

Constance switched off as Ella started rattling on about the doctor who had visited her late father at the last. She knew it off by heart and had no desire to hear it again. She had other more important things on her mind. She was trying to find out who the young man in the teashop was. She gathered from Miss Green, although she had no means of verifying the statement, that he was a professional man, an accountant, fairly recently moved to Bishopsmeade, the new houses on the former Church Pasture, she rather thought.

Not trusting Miss Green, who was apt to get things fearfully wrong, Constance decided that the next time she saw him in the cafe – and Miss Green assured her that he came in from time to time about eleven in the morning usually – she would engage him in conversation. She was a little uncomfortable about so doing for she was not given to initiating conversations with strange men but this was different and, at her age, could in no way be misconstrued.

She would then, if he passed muster, invite him and his wife for tea so that she could see how they reacted to being in the house itself and, if Smith could be persuaded to join them, so much the better. Smith was such a good judge of character. Aware that Mrs Bainbridge disliked him, he avoided her.

'Dead,' Ella finished triumphantly. 'Passed over, they said. They sent for an old midwife who lived in the row to lay him out. She did the both. Bringing in and going out. My mam went to pieces. If it hadn't been for us bairns, she'd have . . . well, you don't need me to tell you, Mrs Makepeace. Funny, isn't it, how grief takes some people. She was never the same woman after that.'

'I know.' Constance sipped her tea.

She was never quite the same herself after Archie was killed. His plane was shot down on August 12th 1940 around teatime in the skies above southern England and a tiny bit of herself was blown up with him. She had felt a great shiver pass over her body on what must have been the very moment that he fireballed into the ground. Archie was – and this was something she never admitted to anyone, least of all Hugh – Archie was the great love of her life. She had tried to prepare herself for his death, knowing just how dangerous the missions were, but it was still so hard to bear. She was so young at a mere twenty-five to be a widow, too young, and, although she knew in her heart she would meet someone else someday, it was also hard to bear that thought for he, whoever he might be, would always be second best.

Her sister Grace wrote to her after Archie's death, quite obviously coerced by their parents into doing so. It was supposed to be a letter of condolence but there was much bitterness between the lines. In fifty or so years, there had been a miserly collection of letters from Grace, duty letters, letters she could count on the fingers of one hand. Letters that managed to spit words like venom over the miles.

There had been a final letter after Hugh's death.

She should have torn those spiteful letters up, tossed them onto the fire where they belonged but she had not. They remained amongst her other letters, a painful reminder to this day of how shabbily Grace considered she had been treated. She had married eventually, most certainly on the rebound, an older man named Alistair Curtis, but beyond that Constance knew nothing of her. They had met, briefly and bitterly, at their mother's funeral, scarcely exchanging a word, although Grace had mentioned that her husband was at home looking after their son. Constance had never heard anything further about the child who would, of course, now be a middle-aged man.

After their father's death a year after Mother died, Constance received a modest inheritance from the estate but the house itself, Smallcoombe Manor, was bequeathed to Eleanor. Now that she was dead too with no issue, Constance had no idea what had become of it. She would most certainly not enter into an undignified scramble for any monies that might have come from the sale of it. She had left Grace to deal with that and Grace had not seen fit to concern her with it. So be it. She did not even know if Grace was still alive or indeed if there had been any further children of her marriage. Constance had never set eyes on her for years and she suspected she would never set eyes on her again.

So much grief.

It – grief – had taken Hugh very badly too.

Looking back, she might have hoped that he would have been particularly strong, for her sake, but that did not happen. Instead, she had to be strong for both their sakes. She blamed the war and Hugh's experiences that he would not discuss either, not even with her. He kept so much locked away in his heart. He bundled up his miseries and thus they festered. The strict upbringing he had suffered contributed to that, the bottling it all up, but you could hardly say her own had not been strict too. She had not mixed with other children at all. The children in town were considered 'rough' and there were few girls of her class to befriend. If only she had been allowed to go to school. All her life, she had desired a true friend. Mrs Bainbridge, regrettably, because of her position in the household, could not be called a friend. Miss Green was the nearest equivalent even though her conversation was singularly uninteresting.

Smith, fresh from his exploration of the cellar, slipped into the room, miaowing a greeting before retiring to his chair by the window where he proceeded to upend himself in cat fashion and wash vigorously. Ella sniffed, wearing a supremely unflattering coral lacy cardigan today for the first time as October edged in.

'He'll be back here, that cat of yours,' she said. 'You mark my words, Mrs Makepeace. He'll be out of that cottage, up by the fat stream, over the bridge and be back here before you wonder where's he got to. I've heard tell they can cover miles. Territory-minded they are, a bit like Bernard. He doesn't like going off too far. Have you ever thought of asking the new people, whoever they might be . . .' she gave Constance an enquiring look but Constance said nothing. 'If they would be prepared to take that cat on as well. He'd like that.'

'I think not,' Constance murmured. 'We'll put his chair in the kitchen at the cottage. He'll soon settle.'

As she would.

She was convinced she would too but, as the weeks passed, it was a little nearer to the time she planned to move, and she must get on with the taxing job of finding the next owners of West House. Mr Wallace, who worked as an estate agent and valuer, came to church on a very occasional basis and last Sunday he had made a point of coming over and shaking her hand – enquiring after her health indeed! – as if he were the vicar himself. It was as if he knew. Gracious me . . . wouldn't he love to have a picture of West House in his window, pride of place, and wouldn't he love also to get his hands on a commission!

How could rumours start when nobody knew?

Except Mrs Bainbridge.

'You haven't mentioned my intentions to anyone, have you?' Constance asked later, as Mrs Bainbridge tidied the kitchen.

'Intentions? What might they be?'

'To move from West House,' Constance said patiently. Sometimes Mrs Bainbridge could be surprisingly obtuse.

'Indeed I have not. Not a soul.' She looked round indignantly, before sloshing the wet cloth on the floor and collapsing rather attractively onto her knees. There was a perfectly good squeezy mop but she neglected to use it saying she'd rather do it by hand then you knew what was what. 'Unless you count Bernard, but he won't say a word. Gossip doesn't interest him. We don't have any secrets, Mrs Makepeace. Husband and wives don't, do they?'

There was only one reply to that.

'You're not to say a word to anyone, Bernard man, about her moving from the house,' Ella told him when she took him and the lads a cup of tea. They had it in the big wooden shed in the kitchen garden. A nice cosy shed that they could shelter in if it was really bad. The lads, seeing that she wanted a word with Bernard, had, with a remarkable display of delicacy, retreated some distance away.

'I don't gossip,' he said, looking at her, meaning of course that she did.

'Nor do I,' she said. 'But she's got herself upset about it. She thinks somebody's been saying something and as we're the only people to know . . . how long can she keep it a secret anyway? People get to know things, especially in this village. You can't blow your nose without somebody noticing. And that butcher has you saying things you didn't mean to say. Crafty so and so he is.' She looked round to see where the lads were before continuing, in a lower voice, 'I've been down the cellar. Looking in boxes.'

'Now, Ella . . . that doesn't sound right.'

'I wouldn't take anything,' she said, flaring at his reprimand.

'I wouldn't dream of it. No, I was just seeing what there was. Letters and things. Photographs she doesn't want seen. Otherwise why would they be down in the cellar getting damp?'

'It's not damp in that cellar. I've seen to it myself,' Bernard said. 'Dry as dust.'

'Gathering dust then. Letters and cards. All sorts. She's never thrown anything away in her life by the look of it. Knitting patterns. Old magazines. Worth a fortune, I bet. I didn't have time to look properly in case she caught me at it, although she never does go down the cellar unless she wants to look at her wine bottles. I was going to say I was looking for that cat of hers if she did catch me.'

Bernard laughed, finished off his hot tea.

'When will you get it in your head? If she wanted you to know, flower, she'd tell you,' he said.

'She'd feel better if she told someone. A trouble shared is a trouble halved,' Ella persisted, taking the cup from him, giving him a look. 'You shouldn't drink it boiling hot like that. It'll burn your insides. Leak through your veins.'

She hadn't told Bernard about the babyclothes down there. Wrapped in tissue and then newspaper and then in a box. Little bonnets and mittens and silky things. Never worn.

# 8

It was quite by chance, although later Tess was to say it was fate, that she happened to overhear one of her staff mention West House.

'West House, *Bishopsmeade*?' Tess asked, pausing and looking up from the workbench where she was preparing a bridesmaid's posy. It was easy these days to get caught up completely with administration, management, staff rotas etc, and she liked to get back to bench work sometimes, finding nothing quite so satisfying as producing a work of floral art. It was one of the few times that she relaxed. She snipped at the pink display ribbon as one of the girls checked the address to confirm it.

'I'll take that,' Tess said. 'It's on my way home. Birthday bouquet, is it?'

'It's for a Mrs Makepeace, Mrs O'Grady. Doesn't actually say birthday,' the girl said, reading the card. 'It was a postal flora request from . . . let's see . . . somewhere in Devon.'

'May I check the flowers?' Tess asked, tying off the ribbon and examining the posy first, making sure it was absolutely perfect. Pale pastels as requested by the bride and it was indeed perfect.

She rose to her feet, leaving one of the girls to tidy up, knowing full well that her presence for most of the afternoon had an unnerving effect. They were a little wary of her and rightly so. She had no wish for them to be frightened of her – God knows she wasn't some sort of ogre – but a touch of respect was worth cultivating and that was why she insisted on Mrs O'Grady rather than Tess. It kept them in their place and on their toes. Their manageress had, to Tess's irritation, pre-empted her dismissal by announcing her resignation yesterday to take up a new post in a hardware store which would be eminently more suitable for her, pots and pans being less fragile than flowers. It meant another job advertisement and interview and next time she would make damned sure she got the right person.

Taking a final check that all was well, leaving the most capable assistant in temporary charge, Tess left them to it.

She placed the predominantly yellow bouquet on the seat beside her in the car and set off for home a little early, wondering if she should surprise Andrew first. Better not. He was entertaining a client this afternoon, somebody who was trying to avoid payment for services rendered. Andrew should learn to assert himself. Sadly, she conceded that her father was right. There was no place in the business community nowadays for nice uncomplicated people like Andrew. Being easygoing meant you were simply trampled underfoot.

She decided she would go straight to West House to deliver the bouquet. If she was lucky an invitation to step inside a moment might be forthcoming for she had also heard from sources other than Andrew that the lady of the house, Mrs Makepeace, was quite charming when you got to know her.

The house certainly was.

Tess sighed with pleasure as she stepped out of the car and had her first really close look at it. The colour of the stone was deeper than appeared from a distance, an apricot peach shade. Banks of monbretia near the house coupled with a profusion of tiny petalled white flowers glowed in the late afternoon sunshine. A hardy variety of roses, all pink, were visible in a side bed. A gardener was raking leaves off the lawn to one side and, seeing the car, he came towards her.

'She's not in, pet. Mrs Makepeace, that is,' he said, wiping grimy hands on his trousers. 'Do you want to have a word with my wife? She'll be able to tell you when she's coming back.'

'Thank you.' Tess clutched the flowers, reluctant to part with them as they were her excuse for admittance. Now that she was here, she was determined to see inside, just a tiny glimpse. Imagine living here!

'I'll see if I can find my wife in a minute,' he went on,

unhurriedly piling up the leaves. 'Just get these on the heap first, if you don't mind.'

'No rush.' Tess smiled, watched as he tipped the crisping leaves into a garden truck. 'Beautiful house,' she murmured, not holding out much hope of a useful conversation for he did not look the chatty type. 'It will fetch a fortune on the market, a house like this.'

He nodded.

'She's not bothered about that,' he said. 'Money doesn't bother Mrs Makepeace. She has plenty, you see. If I know her, she'll leave it to the cat's home. Thinks the world of that scruffy cat of hers. Smith, she calls him. Daft name for a cat, isn't it?'

Tess smiled with him at the eccentricity of old ladies.

What a waste of a fortune!

'Her husband left her a lot of money and she has no children,' he went on, in chatty vein. 'Lost a child, I think. You used to do in the old days. Me and my wife, we were never blessed that way.'

Tess nodded sympathetically, drawing his attention back to the house.

'How long has she lived here?'

'Can't say. Over forty years, I suppose. It's always been in her family. She tells me she used to come up from Devon when she was a little girl, play in these very gardens. They're both from down south though, her and her husband. He was a military man, a colonel, you know, and they moved up here sometime in the fifties, I think. He's long dead. Had an accident.' He nodded conspiratorially as if Tess ought to know the whys and wherefores. 'We never knew the Colonel although we've seen pictures. We've only been helping out these fifteen years past. She's reduced the staff over the years but we manage. She shuts up some of the rooms now. Grand place, isn't it?'

'It is,' Tess agreed and they stood a moment in silence, admiring it. Handsome, Tess thought, revising her initial impression, rather than beautiful. Symmetrical with its windows either side of the white painted door. Andrew would approve of this. He liked clean lines. Balance. Higgledy-piggledy unevenly timbered cottages did not appeal to him.

The gardener leaned his rake against the truck, sighed. 'All she wants, she told my wife, is to make sure it goes to somebody who loves it when she's gone. Nobody left in the family to leave it to, you see. Shame that, isn't it? Crackers about the house, she is. I know it's a fine one but, to my mind, it's *just* a house. No sense in getting attached to bricks and mortar, as they say. Needs a lot of repairs, it does, things I can't handle. Still . . . if I know Mrs Makepeace she'll be practically giving it away. They'll get it cheap anyway.'

'Who will?'

'The folks who move in when she's gone. She's decided to move down to the village to a cottage she has down there. In spring, she says. Not getting any younger, you see, in her eighties now. She doesn't hold with estate agents so she's going to find somebody herself, somebody she approves of. Queer carry on, isn't it? Mind you, pet, it's supposed to be a secret so I shouldn't be telling you by rights but you won't tell anybody will you. Keep it quiet, eh?'

'Absolutely. I won't breathe a word,' Tess said, smiling at him, forgiving him the 'pet', unable to believe her luck, still trying to take it in. This was just too good to be true. Was it true or was this man having a laugh at her expense, spinning her an almighty yarn? Looking at him again, she decided she had never seen anyone, apart from Andrew, of course, with such an open honest face. It *was* true then. She had stumbled on a secret.

'There she is now,' he said, smiling broadly. 'My wife. She'll sort you out.'

'Can I help you?'

Tess whirled round and smiled at the plump little lady who had asked. Showing her the flowers, she explained that she wished to see Mrs Makepeace.

'I can take them for you,' the woman said, admiring the flowers and declaring them bonny. 'She'll be back in a minute or two. She's gone down to the church hall. Some meeting or other. They're forever having meetings.'

'I would prefer to hand them over myself,' Tess explained patiently. 'Shop policy . . .' she added with a firm smile. She was determined that the woman was not getting her hands on them.

'Come and wait then. If you'd like to follow me,' she said,

striding briskly off through the hall heading for a door to the right. Tess, unable to linger, had an impression of height and length, dark carpeted stairs visible beyond an impressive arch. Rugs on the old polished floor. Gilt framed paintings hanging against a background of maroon wallpaper. A glossy leafed Christmas cactus in a blue and white pot, bare of flowers, sat importantly on a beautiful antique jardiniere and a couple of exquisite vases were perfectly positioned side by side on a spindle-legged tall table. Tess let out a deeply contented breath at the natural elegance. Mrs Makepeace was a lady after her own heart.

'You can wait in the sitting room,' the housekeeper said, opening a door. 'She won't be long. She's usually back by now but she will insist on walking, you know, when Bernard would be happy to run her down and she's a bit slower these days. Between you and me, if she stopped smoking she'd be better.' She stopped, probably aware of her indiscretion and Tess gave her a reassuring smile. Not a word, it said, will pass my lips.

The door closed behind her and Tess was left there, clutching the bouquet.

Looking round the room, she breathed out slowly. It was even better than her father's house. Bigger and better. She chose to remain standing, not having been invited to take a seat, the view claiming her attention rather than the heavy dark furniture and the bookshelves stuffed with ancient volumes. The view across the garden was wonderful and, in an instant, in her mind, she imagined she was living here and looking daily onto that view. It needed attention of course and a complete revamping of the interior and she would have to get new furniture because it would not tolerate a too-modern look. She would aim for a careful blend of old and new and – glancing at the faded velvet curtains – she would go for something fabulous for the curtains, cream-based, she thought, to gentle the whole scheme a little. Ginger and cinnamon for the sofas. Cream walls.

If she played this right . . .

The door opened.

'My housekeeper said you were in here,' the old lady who entered said with a smile. 'I'm Constance Makepeace. I do apologise for keeping you waiting but I've been down to the village. Oh . . . how enchanting! Are those for me?'

Feeling absurdly like giving a small curtsey, Tess handed the flowers over with a smile, waiting as the card was read.

'Oh . . . such a surprise!' Constance said, in delight. 'They are from a very old friend of mine from Devon – more of an acquaintance actually. We exchange Christmas cards and last year, when there was no card from her, I assumed . . . well, at our age . . . I thought she had departed. But she tells me now that she has moved from her old home and is in a nursing home. She remembered how fond I am of yellow chrysanthemums and sends them to apologise for the absence of a Christmas card last year. Oh dear, I must write to her at once.'

'How sweet of her to send you flowers,' Tess said, determined to stay put as long as possible. 'Would you like me to put them in a vase? I would be happy to arrange them for you.'

'Would you, dear? That would be so helpful. Mrs Bainbridge is no good at all with flowers. Too robust. And afterwards, if you have time that is, you must stay for a cup of tea.' She looked enquiringly at Tess. 'Good. I'll see if my housekeeper can find a vase for you.'

The ensuing fuss meant Tess achieved what she had set out to achieve. Filling the vase with water, she saw the sprawling kitchen, ripe for a fantastic conversion, a glimpse of what was now a slightly battered verandah but was crying out to be a light and airy garden room, had a good look round a very large bathroom upstairs although she dare not risk peeping into what must be bedrooms. To her delight, even the landing was big enough for proper furniture. The whole place was so *huge*. It could be home and office for her, offices for both of them in fact and so fantastic for entertaining. She could see the letterheading on the new stationery she would have to acquire: O'Grady's Floral Design – Head Office, West House, Bishopsmeade. Yes . . . it had a super ring to it.

Coming back into the drawing room after washing her hands, she was filled with a quite delicious excitement. It was fate. Fate that she delivered the flowers. Fate also that she should meet up with an indiscreet gardener. Bless the man!

'Milk? Sugar?' Constance charmingly attended to the matter

in hand. She was looking more like an old lady should today, wearing a double string of pearls and a twinset in a soft lilac colour with a dark skirt. 'I am awash with tea. The ladies of the church guild are such tea drinkers, you see. We were discussing fundraising events. We are, I regret to say, a little devoid of ideas. It boils down to the usual fêtes and jumbles, and of course the November bonfire. You must come to that if you can. It's a quite splendid evening. Now, you don't mind if I smoke, do you?' She was already reaching for a cigarette case. 'Would you like one? No, of course not . . . nobody does these days. Paranoid, I think that's the word. I'm over eighty and it's bound to get me in the end.'

'Really? Over eighty? And you're still walking down to the village every day? Wonderful.'

Constance gave her a shrewd look and for a moment Tess thought she might have made a mistake, been patronising. She wasn't very good with old people. Or children come to that. Desperately, she searched for something sensible to say but Constance, the polite hostess, beat her to it.

'Do you live locally?'

'I live in the village,' Tess said, accepting a custard cream with a smile although she never ate biscuits normally. 'In Churchwood Close.'

'Ah . . . the new houses,' Constance said with a wry smile. 'It's not your fault, I know, but I have to admit that I was totally against the whole development. The pasture there was so peaceful.'

'I understand perfectly. Unfortunately, I never knew the old pasture. I prefer old houses like this,' Tess said. 'This house is so beautiful. But, when you're just starting out, it's a matter of what you can afford . . . Oh, I'm sorry, I'm Tess O'Grady, Mrs Makepeace,' she added, stretching over and holding out her hand. 'I'm so pleased to meet you.'

'How do you do.'

Polite courtesies thus exchanged, they resumed their positions.

'You work in a florist's, then? What a lovely occupation that must be.'

'It's my shop,' Tess said. 'I trained as a horticulturist and now

I have four shops over in the Newcastle area. I also do private commissions, floral arrangements for offices and shops that sort of thing.'

'Indeed. You don't sound local, dear.'

'I'm not. My parents were originally from the north west but my father has worked in the Newcastle area for a long time now. He lives over towards Middleton with his second wife. My mother died a few years ago.'

'I see. Where were you educated?'

A little amused at the speed of the questions, feeling she was under serious scrutiny, Tess told her, blessing the fact that the private school she had attended over in the Lakes was well known. Rightly or wrongly – and Andrew would be appalled that it should matter – she knew that it damned well did. Constance Makepeace's pleasure showed. She explained that she had so wished to go to school herself but had been educated at home, which was nowhere near so grand as it sounded.

'And are you quite settled here, Mrs O'Grady? Here in Bishopsmeade?'

Tess's mind was at fever pitch ever since the gardener had spilled the complete can of beans. This was an important question. She knew what was expected of her for Constance obviously adored the village as much as the house and she was not going to fall at the first hurdle. Constance would never know that she was already becoming a touch bored with Bishopsmeade, was wishing they'd gone for something up on the Northumberland coast. She could not believe it of herself that she had chosen a brand new house. They had no character whatsoever and the drive from here up to Newcastle was so dreary.

But she would happily tolerate it if she could set off each day from here.

'I love Bishopsmeade,' she said. 'I fell in love with it when I first saw it. I said to Andrew – my husband – that we must get a house here. At the time we lived over in Jesmond but we'd been looking for some time for a place in the country. We settled for a new house because it was convenient, but we would love to move to something else someday . . . still in the village, of course. We're not intending to move. We're here forever.'

It struck home. She saw the quiet satisfaction in Constance's face.

'I felt exactly the same when we first moved here. Bishopsmeade has a way of drawing you into it, doesn't it?'

'It does indeed.'

'You mention Jesmond. That's interesting because my late husband's constituency was around Jesmond. He became an MP in the early fifties, shortly before we moved here. Sussex was much too far, you see, so we sold that property, although we did keep an apartment in London. In the event things worked out remarkably well because, when my uncle died in the early fifties, he had no children and so Hugh and I were happy to take this house on. Keep it in the family. The fifties.' She shook her head sadly. 'So very long ago. Before you were born, dear.'

Tess nodded.

'More tea?'

'No, thank you.' Tess decided she must not overdo it. The seed had been sown. 'It's been lovely to meet you,' she said as Constance escorted her out. 'I do hope you enjoy your flowers.'

'I shall and thank you for bringing them.'

Unable to stop a spring in her step, Tess walked to where she had parked the car.

She hardly dared glance back at the house, at its perfection, but she did, waving to Constance who remained smiling at the door.

She went over again in her mind what the gardener had said. Giving it away cheap. How cheap? As it stood, it was way way out of their price range but if the old dear was dotty enough not to mind about money then they might as well be the ones to benefit.

West House was as good as hers, she thought, as she drove across One-Mile Bridge.

Nobody else was having it, that was for sure.

Andrew would take some convincing, of course, complain that it was far too big and grand for them, but she was used to getting her way with him. The fact that he was utterly smitten with her helped. It was all a matter of choosing the right moment and a little gentle persuasion, and she was very good at that.

# 9

'It's only a few hours, Yvonne, on a rota basis, so it wouldn't be *every* week. I'm sure you can manage that.'

Yvonne smiled, trying in vain to hold out. Thin end of the wedge, she thought.

'It's not as simple as that. I mustn't take too much on. I have the children, Joan,' she said. 'What would I do in the holidays? And they're always getting surprise days off. Tomorrow, for example. It's a nuisance. It means it's impossible to make long term plans. I don't like to take things on that I can't follow through.'

'With this, there's no problem. You can always take them with you,' Joan smiled too, in some triumph. 'Failing that, we can always rearrange the rota if absolutely necessary. Come on, Yvonne, I'm so short of capable drivers and I know I can rely on *you* not to let us down.'

'That's what everyone says,' Yvonne said, not too dispirited.

She found it hard to say no when people asked something of her. And yet . . . she had to do *something* and, if it couldn't be her real work, then it might as well be voluntary do-gooding, damn it. She hated people to know about the voluntary work because of its very nature but the truth was, even though her speciality had always been with children, she did particularly like being with the elderly. You put up a guard most of your life, to protect yourself, and it was only when you were old, really old, that you could let it down. Be yourself. Take it or leave it. Old people for the most part were wonderful. Straight and utterly honest.

The trouble was that a couple of hours here and there added

up to a considerable time. Take this afternoon, for example. One afternoon a week helping out on a simple friendly-chat basis at Greenview Rest Home, one afternoon only so, in theory, it wasn't much, but it was a commitment nevertheless and she took commitments seriously.

With a sigh, she took the sheet from Joan and read it, knowing as she did so that it was already too late to back out. Joan gripped her volunteers like a vice and Yvonne was already resigned to becoming part of Joan's housebound library delivery. Joan was an institution, one of those amiable busybodies who were sneered at a bit but sorely missed when they were no longer around. Joan had received an OBE for community services last year and she still hadn't quite come down to earth. She accepted it, she told the local press, on behalf of her wonderful volunteers without whom she could do nothing.

It seemed to accompany her everywhere, sitting proudly on the desk now, whilst Joan hunted for her spectacles amongst a heap of papers. She was supremely disorganised.

'What does it entail?' Yvonne asked.

'Oh, thank you so much. I knew you would say yes. You, Yvonne, are one of my rocks. I have so few ladies of your age helping . . . girls, I should say,' Joan said happily, pouncing on her spectacles at last. 'Everybody your age goes out to work. Now, you pick the books up from the library where they are chosen for us and bagged and then all you have to do is distribute them to the clients. Eight in all as it stands just now. Hand them their books and if you can spare the time they'd love a little chat, perhaps offer you a cup of tea.'

'And then I just return the books they've finished with to the library?' she asked, admitting to herself that it didn't sound too taxing.

'Precisely. Simple. You'll love it. We have a lovely lot of people we deliver to. Three gentlemen and five ladies. Mrs Makepeace out at West House is new on the list.'

'But she's not housebound,' Yvonne protested. 'I see her about a lot. She walks into the village from the house. Every day as far as I know. She *is* the one who wears tracksuits and pearls, isn't she?'

'She is. A little eccentric, poor dear. She smokes, I'm afraid and, according to the lady at the general store, she gets through more than enough bottles of Martini. No, she is not housebound exactly but we do make exceptions,' Joan said seriously. 'She cannot carry the books all the way from the library van and so she asked if we could help. I use my discretion and we must be careful that we don't discriminate on the wrong grounds. I know she could easily afford to take a taxi, but that's really not the point . . .'

Yvonne nodded, not entirely convinced. However she would not argue. Constance Makepeace was a fixture here in the village, and spoken of as 'the Colonel's lady' in hushed tones by some of the residents of this nursing home. A lady with a mysterious past, it would seem.

'I can count on you, then?' Joan asked with an enquiring smile.

'Oh, all right,' Yvonne said, not entirely gracious but resigned to it. One more thing to add to the list of things she ought never to get herself involved with. When would she learn?

'Having collared me for something else, what do you want me to do now?' she smiled at Joan, picking up their coffee mugs. 'I have another hour before I collect the children from school.'

'Could you be an angel and take Agnes to the chemists? Give her a spot of fresh air. She wants some Oil of Ulay and some tissues. She particularly asked if you were in today. She likes you, Yvonne. I'm sorry, I know she's a bit of a grumbler but you can handle her better than anyone else.'

Thinking it wonderful that Agnes at ninety five was still caring for her complexion, Yvonne went to find her. She *was* in a grumbly mood as Yvonne helped pop her into the wheelchair, tucked a blanket round her thin heavily-hosed legs and pushed the cumbersome chair out of the rest home into the chill of the autumn afternoon.

'Freedom, even if it is perishing,' Agnes said grimly as Yvonne closed the door behind them. 'It's like being in prison in there.'

'No, it is not,' Yvonne said with a laugh, having heard it all before. 'Shame on you. You love it, Agnes.'

'You know nothing about it. You're only a slip of a girl,' Agnes said, lurching back as Yvonne bounced the wheelchair off the kerb.

'Sorry. I'm not used to driving this,' she said with a laugh, 'And I'm hardly a slip of a girl, Agnes. I'm thirty-four.'

'I was on my second husband when I was thirty-four,' Agnes said, capable still of surprises. 'You didn't know that, did you? Buried three of them, I did.'

'No, I didn't know that. You kept that quiet . . .' Yvonne struggled with the wheelchair over the grass of the green, taking a shortcut and regretting it as her heels began to sink into the damp turf. 'We should have gone round by the path,' she said. 'Sorry, Agnes, is it a bit bumpy?'

'It is. My insides are bouncing about like nobody's business. Still, you're a fine lass. Good job you've got a nice big bust on you. I always maintain you need a good bust to push a wheelchair. Some of these young nurses these days have no weight on them at all.'

Yvonne smiled down ruefully at the back of the old lady's head. Old people were wonderful all right!

'You'll catch your death in that,' Agnes remarked, peering round at Yvonne. 'Have you nothing warmer?'

'I don't feel the cold,' Yvonne told her. 'Don't worry. I have a lovely warm coat I slip over this in winter.'

'I hope you wear a vest, girl.'

Yvonne assured her she did or poor Agnes would have palpitations at the very idea of Yvonne vestless during the worst of a Bishopsmeade winter. She'd have a fit if she saw her collection of skimpy undies. She knew for a fact that Agnes wore knickers or bloomers that would take three pegs on the line, plus a pink brassiere, a corset with big clumpy suspenders, a vest and an underskirt.

'Are *you* warm enough, Agnes?' she enquired, as they set off down the path beside the green towards the little row of shops. 'Is it just the Oil of Ulay you want? I'd get you a nice fella too if I could but they're in short supply these days. Tell you what, if you see one you fancy while we're out, give me a nudge. Husband number four, what do you think?'

Agnes, ninety-five or not, laughed girlishly and Yvonne, relieved she was not offended, smiled with her.

It wasn't a bad idea, that.

The disgraceful thought came to her in a flash. With Robin a dead loss these days as he was, a nice fella for her too would indeed not come amiss. Somebody like Andrew O'Grady, for example . . .

# 10

Andrew watched Tess depart for work. The For Sale board was now pegged in a prominent position in the garden. When she got the house jitters, she didn't believe in hanging about. Her idea of putting this house up for sale, so soon, depressed but did not surprise him entirely. He suspected he had surprised Tess by agreeing to it so readily but he didn't feel prepared to put up with a prolonged sulk and he also was not so optimistic as she. He knew damned well that they would be unlikely to get a buyer for at least a year, probably longer, and a lot could happen in a year.

He was prepared to chance it. After all, he had made up his mind to go for a job if things didn't buck up a bit by Christmas. He had a good week to look back on and yesterday he received two cheques, long overdue and very welcome. A life-saver in fact. He had one or two jobs pending, including looking over the accounts of a market gardener who seemed intent on making his professional life as difficult as possible. He had turned up with his accounts, soil stained, all bundled together in a succession of grimy envelopes. Undated, most of them. Indecipherable, some of them.

Spurred on to do some work, he was constantly interrupted by the telephone. It seemed it never stopped ringing. It must be National Junk-Phonecall day. A conservatory saleswoman, some half-witted survey about what radio stations he tuned into, somebody trying to sell him a different phone system, a charity wanting him to do a house-to-house collection. In line with the junk theme, the morning post had all ended up in the bin.

Andrew returned to his desk after the latest telephone call

and tried to summon up a fresh bout of enthusiasm for the job in hand.

The doorbell rang.

Bugger! If that was Jehovah's Witnesses . . .

'Yes?'

He whipped the door open. Yvonne and the kids stood there, a forlorn little group huddling under a pintsized umbrella. The sky was leaden, leaves were beginning to fall at a steady rate, the temperature had plummeted, the rain felt cold and suddenly, autumn was here.

'Andrew, I'm so sorry to disturb you.'

She stood at the door in silken splendour. She was wearing a pastelly flowery ensemble, taking no account of the weather. Strappy high heels. Ankle length dress and a lightweight long scarf round her neck. Her daughters, pink-jacketed, looked up at him. Three pairs of beautiful china-blue eyes. The boy was a duplicate Robin.

'It's an emergency,' she went on. 'Otherwise I wouldn't bother you. A friend of mine – Lyn, she's called, from the cottage beside the post office – well, she's gone into labour and I've promised to drive her to hospital. Trust me, I'm always getting myself involved with things. You couldn't possibly . . .' She gestured towards the children. 'I wouldn't ask but I can hardly take them with me, can I? I'm Lyn's birthing partner, you see, as she's on her own. Her chap walked out on her. Can you believe that? She was eight months pregnant at the time.'

'Really,' he said sharply, not remotely interested in Lyn's predicament. 'Shouldn't they be at school?' he said, irritated to hell. What a bloody morning it had been!

'Holiday,' she said. 'One of those extra days they're forever slotting in. They've not been long back. Nuisance, isn't it? It would be today.' She adjusted the umbrella as the rain changed direction and blew straight at them. 'They'll be very good. They've got some colouring books with them and a jigsaw. That keeps them quiet for hours. I'd rather you didn't sit them in front of the television, if you don't mind. Robin and I strictly ration their viewing.'

'Mummy . . . ?'

'What is it, Portia?'

'Can we watch Tom and Jerry if you're not back? Can we?'

'If Mr O'Grady doesn't mind and aren't you forgetting the magic word?'

'Please . . .'

Andrew waited patiently. The bloody rain was bucketing down now and they were having a discussion on niceties.

'How long will you be?' he asked, aware he sounded a touch aggressive.

She shrugged. 'I have no idea. It depends how long it takes. You can't rush these things. I'll have to stay with her the whole time. I've promised and she's relying on me.'

What the hell could he say but yes?

He watched her disappear, heels delicately dodging puddles, and turned to look at the somewhat bedraggled trio left behind. Little Harry's lower lip was trembling and he clung onto his big sister's hand. Andrew felt a moment's helplessness. He knew sod all about children.

'Right then . . .' he began with exaggerated cheer as he felt three pairs of eyes on him. 'What shall we do, gang?'

'Take our coats off and dry our socks because we all stepped in that very big puddle by the gate. We've got wet feet,' Portia said in precise tones. 'And then may we have a drink, Mr O'Grady? Please.' She handed him a luminous orange lunch-box. 'Harry's sandwiches are in there. Samantha and I are not fussy. We eat anything.' She exchanged a knowing glance with her sister. 'Harry's a fusspot, Mummy says. He only eats treacle and peanut butter sandwiches. Mummy made them because she thought you might not have any in because grown-ups don't eat peanut butter.'

He realised he was holding three pairs of damp socks as they stood barefoot, Portia having arranged their sandals neatly in a row beside the wall.

'Is your heating on?' she enquired in an accusing voice.

'Well . . . yes.'

'You can put them on the radiator to dry, then,' she told him helpfully. 'That's what Mummy does. We don't mind not having shoes on because it's good for your feet, Mummy says.'

Andrew found them a towel so that Portia could organise the drying of the little feet and toes and then sat them at the kitchen table with their colouring books and a vast array of paints and crayons, draping the socks as directed on the radiator. Portia informed him they would eat sandwiches at half past three and may they have their drinks now, please?

Drinks?

He could have murdered a whisky and soda but instead he made double orange barley waters all round although Portia was worried that he didn't have a plastic beaker for Harry. She handed the glass to her brother with a single icy look that told him what would happen if . . .

'Give me a shout then if you want anything else,' Andrew said as they settled down with their drinks. He wondered if he ought to leave them but surely his baby-sitting duties did not necessitate him being glued to them for the remainder of the day. 'I'm working upstairs in my office. And don't touch anything.'

He left Portia in charge. That child would go far. She had that wonderful female bossy streak *plus* looks.

In the hall, his eye was caught by this week's floral arrangement. It was a bit more like it, he thought, for there was a lot of it tastefully positioned in a fat glass vase, reflected in the mirror. Leaves and berries from the garden and some blue multi-petalled flowers with fine feathery greenery. One of her shapes and textures things. He knew it all. He was the one who listened to her practice presentations.

She had suddenly announced the other evening, out of the blue, that she had volunteered to do one of these presentations, something to do with church, a talk on autumn flower arranging and, although he was pleased she had agreed to do it, he was a bit miffed because she'd refused to do the one at school and he'd already had to apologise to Yvonne on her behalf. Made him look a bit of a fool, that.

The Mickey Mouse lunch-box sat beside the vase and a tiny pink plastic handbag belonging to one of the girls. On the radiator, the socks, two pairs with lacy edges, steamed dry and the sandals were arranged in size order. Andrew smiled a little. The hall suddenly looked lived in.

Now . . . he peeped once more in the kitchen but all was well, the children busy and silent.

He had just entered the system on his computer when the doorbell rang. Not wanting to leave things for a moment, he carried on feverishly pressing keys and the bell rang once more. Phone calls. Doorbells. There seemed a conspiracy today to get him to do sod-all.

'I'll get it, Mr O'Grady,' Portia shouted up the stairs and, by the time he got there, a couple of strangers stood in the hall smiling down at Portia and Samantha and a paint-splattered Harry.

'Hello. I know it says view by appointment only on the board,' the woman said with a determined smile. 'But we were just passing, weren't we, Nick, and we have half an hour to spare and we were wondering if it would be terribly inconvenient . . .' She widened her smile, looking down at the children.

'They're not mine,' Andrew said hastily, realising that for once the house was in a bit of a mess. He had intended to leave the housework until later as they were having a simple meal tonight that did not involve hours of preparation. Half an hour's whizz round with the hoover would do the trick before Tess got in.

'Mummy's gone into hospital to help a lady have her baby. Mr O'Grady is going to make our tea today,' Portia explained as she led them into the kitchen. 'Harry only eats treacle and peanut butter sandwiches so Mummy made his because grown-ups don't like peanut butter.'

The woman smiled again.

'What charming children,' she said as she looked round the kitchen where the table was now covered with a selection of painting books and paint and murky painty water and soft drinks. Andrew felt bad about the state of the place. God, they had picked the wrong time to call. It was never as bad as this, not usually. 'Plenty of space, lots of cupboards,' the woman said diplomatically. 'Are you leaving the appliances?'

'Negotiable,' he said quickly.

He hadn't a clue. They hadn't discussed it. He hadn't expected anybody to come round for about a year. He didn't want a quick sale. They had nowhere else to go yet and he knew Tess would have her sights on something bigger and better. And, if they ended up discussing the state of their bank balances it would all come out. He needed more time. He needed to put these people off.

He pulled up the blinds so that they could see the garden. Rain lashed against the pane and the trees in the wood were barely visible. Behind him, he heard the woman give a small sigh of pleasure.

'We get a lot of leaves in autumn,' he said, 'Look at them just starting to fall. They drift in, have to be swept up, stick in the gutters, block the drains.'

'We like trees. Surely it's worth a little inconvenience to be able to look at them like this? You have a lovely garden.'

'Mrs O'Grady is a flower lady,' Portia pointed out as Andrew escorted the couple into the living room. Yesterday's papers hung about in that distressed way of yesterday's news. The patio, or terrace as Tess called it, managed to look uninviting, windswept and wet.

'Sorry about the room,' Andrew muttered, inexplicably feeling the need to pick up a newspaper, fold it.

'Not at all. Our fault. You weren't expecting us. It's very sporting of you to show us round at all.' The man spoke for the first time, bared his teeth in a grin.

Andrew quickly showed them the rest of the house asking the children to wait downstairs. To his relief, both the upstairs bathrooms were clean and tidy.

'We like living next door,' Portia said, meeting up with them again once they were back down. The other children were silenced by the strangers, staring up at them. 'We have our own bedrooms with our names on the door . . . mine says Portia's Room . . . and our own bathroom. We've got sea-shells and fishes and our own pink bubble bath. Mummy and Daddy's bathroom is in their bedroom. It's called on something.'

'Ensuite, darling,' the woman said with a smile. 'How lovely.'

Portia was unstoppable by now.

'You can take a short cut through the woods to school and the shops and there's lots of places to walk if you have a big dog. Daddy works in Scotland.'

'Diving with fishes,' Harry piped up suddenly.

'Right then. That's the lot,' Andrew said with a smile. 'Anything you want to ask?'

There was a blessed silence.

Samantha, shy, cuddled close to her sister on one side and

Harry, dark eyes huge, held onto her skirt at the other. Barefoot, with a few artistic streaks of paint on their cheeks, there was something poignant about the trio. Three very modern cherubs.

'We have a little girl just like you,' the woman said, gentling her voice and bending down. 'She's called Emma. If we moved here, you could play with her.'

Portia and Samantha beamed.

Andrew had no alternative but to look suitably impressed too.

'What are they doing here, for God's sake?' Tess asked, closing the door on the children who were sitting watching a cartoon on television. She turned on Andrew who had a guilty look on his face. 'And, more to the point, where is Yvonne?'

'She's taken some woman into hospital to have a baby. I don't know when she'll be back.'

'Oh, great!' Tess threw her jacket onto a chair. 'She's got a colossal cheek. How dare she palm them off on us?'

'On me,' Andrew said with a slight smile. 'I've been looking after them all day *and* I showed some people round the house. They just turned up on spec.'

'On spec? Honestly?' Tess eyed her husband with exasperation. 'When it says view by appointment that is what it means. Can't these people read? You should have told them it was not convenient.'

'If I'd turned them away, you would have complained. I thought you wanted a quick sale.'

'Yes, I do, of course I do . . . come on then, don't keep me in suspense, darling, what did they say? Did they seem at all interested?' A wave of excitement caught at her. It would be fantastic if they could sell at the very first attempt. A fluke but very welcome. 'Who were they? Do they have a house to sell? Will there be a chain?'

'Hang on,' Andrew said. 'You'll be pleased to know that Portia Lonsdale is a born negotiator obviously destined to go into estate agenting. She had them eating out of her hand. Never once mentioned a negative point.'

'And . . . ?' Tess could hardly control her impatience, irritated that he seemed so laid back about the whole business. She knew he was lukewarm about it but then he always was. She'd had to pull him out of the house in Jesmond by the scruff of his neck.

'Yes . . . they seemed fairly interested,' he admitted at last to her delight. 'But I wouldn't get too excited if I were you. We know from experience, don't we, that it doesn't mean a lot. It's the ones who seem positively disappointed who want to buy. We haven't got anything else lined up, have we, so it's hardly desperate.'

That was true.

In a sense.

'It's finished, Mr O'Grady. Portia's watching the news now,' Samantha Lonsdale appeared in the doorway, barefoot and sticky-faced. 'She wants to know if we may have another drink? Please,' she added, smiling up at Tess a little uncertainly.

'When will Mummy be coming back?'

This last question was from the small boy who looked suspiciously like he was going to burst into tears.

Tess smiled brightly at them, leaving Andrew to sort them out, patting Harry's head in passing, carrying her coffee into the garden room to get away from the television and Portia.

Even though she was proud of the garden room which she had florally furnished with great panache, she suddenly saw it and the whole house for what it really was. There was no comparison with West House. This house was overpriced and pretentious and no matter how hard it tried it could never be anything other than an estate house. Small and exclusive, six only, but still an *estate*, for God's sake.

Andrew knew nothing yet about West House. Time enough for that for, knowing Andrew, he was bound to pour cold water on the idea. He would come up with all sorts of reasons against it but she could get round him. She had, however, been unable to stop herself doing a bit of forward planning. No harm in that.

Sitting amongst a profusion of greenery on one of the cane chairs, she allowed herself a moment's daydreaming.

The dining room at West House, presumably on the opposite side of the hall, would also overlook the front lawns. As a complete contrast to the cream and cinammon for the drawing room, she fancied a more exciting scheme. She would need a big circular antique table, an important side piece, and a set of high-backed dining chairs. She had seen some materials in a shop in Eldon Square and had collected some swatches from them.

She had no idea how many other rooms there were but she would pay the same attention to detail in each room. She would save money by designing the interior herself but she would want it all decorating quickly. She was not going to live in a state of disrepair for long.

She wondered just what figure Constance Makepeace would have in mind. Something similar near Thirsk was on the market she noticed at a guide price of £350,000. That was out of the question even with help from her father, but if they could bring it down a considerable way then all was possible. Dare she hope for half price? Would Constance really let them have it for half its value if she thought they would really cherish it?

The unmistakeable sound of clattery steps outside made her put her cup down with relief. Thank God for that. The cavalry.

She smiled as she opened the door.

'Yvonne . . . is everything all right?'

'It's a boy. It all went very quickly at the last. It was Lyn from next door to the post office. You know her, don't you? I don't suppose Andrew told you who it was. Men can never remember details.'

'Come in . . .' Tess stood back as the children rushed through the hall with squeals of delight, grabbing hold of Yvonne as if they hadn't seen her for a week.

'I hope you've been good, you three,' she said, disentangling herself as Andrew appeared. 'Have they, Andrew?'

'As good as gold,' he said. 'Haven't they, Tess?'

'So I'm told,' Tess said, her smile fixed by now. 'I've only just got in.'

'A little boy. Six pounds five ounces,' Yvonne said happily, addressing her remarks to anyone who cared enough to listen. 'Alexander James. Lyn is thrilled but exhausted. You know how it is . . . ?'

Tess gave Andrew a warning glance. She was not being drawn into a discussion on birth. She had no intention of acquainting Yvonne with the facts. None of her business.

Yvonne thrust a box of chocolates forward.

'Thank you, Andrew,' she said, a faint blush on her cheeks. 'It was a terrible imposition. The three of them can be quite a handful. I hope you didn't mind me bringing them round, Tess.'

'Not at all,' Tess said quickly. 'It was the least we could do on this occasion.'

'Any time,' Andrew said to her irritation, saying a cheerful goodbye to the kids before disappearing into the kitchen.

Tess stood awkwardly at the door as Yvonne dallied on the path.

She never ceased to be utterly amazed at the finery in her neighbour's wardrobe. A cream silk skirt and top, a cream and navy scarf, hair looking fantastic and make-up obviously freshly applied. A jangle of bracelets caught at her wrist. She jingled and clattered so much.

'It was a wonderful experience,' Yvonne said, blessedly on the point of departure but managing an encore. 'It brought it all back. I wouldn't mind another baby . . .' she added in a low voice watching as her children set off down the path. 'Another boy to round things off.'

'You seem to have quite enough coping with three,' Tess said, not prepared to stand on the doorstep indulging the woman's maternal whims.

'Yes, I do. Of course I do. Just wishful thinking,' Yvonne said, 'Oh by the way, could you send some flowers to the hospital from me? I'll leave the choice to you. I know you'll do something absolutely gorgeous. Pink's her favourite colour.' She produced a twenty pound note and pushed it at Tess. 'Will that be enough?'

'Thank you. I'll deal with it first thing,' Tess promised, watching Yvonne swishing down the path, high heels dodging the puddles left by the day's rain, turning for a final wave before departing.

She needed to watch her.

Yvonne was a time-bomb.

Ticking.

And she did not want Andrew to be the man to defuse her.

# 11

Constance was enjoying an illicit cigarette, an extra one to the five she normally allowed herself. Purely a matter of self discipline which she felt so many people lacked today. She had received a sad letter this morning and it was her way of coping. She had always found cigarettes a comfort in times of sadness.

The day had been inclement but she had put on her mackintosh and wellington boots and taken a turn in the garden. She had walked the perimeter of the estate and even wandered onto the lower slope of the hill for a while, panting with the exertion, returning to the house feeling quite refreshed, cheeks tingling, although Mrs Bainbridge had tutted and fussed as if she'd been on a trip to the Antarctic, asking if she might add a splash of rum to the coffee she had ready and waiting. Constance had consented to the rum although in her opinion a bit of rain and a chilly breeze never hurt anyone.

Mr and Mrs Bainbridge had departed at length amidst their usual hullabaloo and the house was now silent. The curtains were drawn, there was a fire in the sitting room hearth and Constance had drawn her chair up to it. Smith was curled on her knee, apparently asleep, and she stroked his back absently.

She had written to her acquaintance in Devon to thank her so very much for the flowers only to find her letter returned with a short kindly note.

'Her swan-song . . .' she told Smith. 'For some reason she must have thought of me at the last and decided, goodness knows why, to send me flowers. How very odd. Perhaps she didn't have any real friends either, Smith. We scarcely knew each other because she was more my sister Eleanor's friend.

Older than me. Goodness . . . she must have been in her nineties.'

It was a shock to think that, if Eleanor were alive, she would be ninety-one.

She looked across at the cluster of sepia photographs on the little table, her attention caught by one. Christmas 1920, she knew for certain. Wearing a dainty little petal-skirt frock in pink shantung, she recalled, with a broad silk sash to tone, she was sitting in between her sisters, clutching her new doll. There had been a doll's perambulator too that she had quite adored. For a moment, as she gazed at the photograph, a moment caught forever, she felt that familiar sadness for what was past. Eleanor, who had remained a spinster, was demure to the end, devout and almost as desperately dull as Miss Green from the teashop.

Eleanor was long gone but Grace, so far as she knew, was still alive. At least she had not heard to the contrary. She must be an embittered old lady. Sometimes guilt nudged at her, for hadn't she made her sister's life a misery? Hadn't she been responsible for that? Who knows how things might have worked out. Perhaps if Archie had married Grace, he would not have been killed. Ridiculous as it was, Grace most certainly believed that.

*You're so pretty and perfect, Constance Parkinson, but underneath your skin you're wicked. Wicked to do that to me, your own sister. I would never have done it to you. Never. I would die first.* Constance could hear Grace saying the words in that quiet wishy-washy voice of hers. Grace had no personality either.

After Archie died, Constance remained in the house they had shared in London because she was reluctant to return to Devon as a newly widowed lady even though her parents wished it for they worried for her safety. Her mother had uncharacteristically fussed but Constance had been adamant. She would be perfectly all right in London even though her mother was right and it did turn out to be the most distressing year of the war with Plymouth, too, dear Plymouth, suffering heavily, although her family had remained safely cocooned at Smallcoombe Manor.

Constance never felt brave nor stupid remaining in the capital at that time because she knew, with the same certainty that she knew Archie would never survive the war, that *she* would. She had a small staff in the London house who looked after her as well as they could. Bombs fell close enough but not that close. There were hardships but there were ways of getting round them.

The main reason she did not return to Devon was that she did not wish to face Grace who blamed her most unfairly for Archie's death. Grace had taken the news very badly and had fallen to pieces and – the ultimate sin – let herself go completely. Constance, pulling on all her reserves of dignity and decorum, never did and felt precious little sympathy for her sister, having quite enough to do with mourning the loss of her husband.

It was only when the war ended that she finally visited Devon for a long summer holiday, intending to spend it in contemplation of the future. She and Grace were both in their thirties now and Grace looked it. As well as having singularly dull mousey hair that never shone, she was also of an ill disposition, still managing to be appallingly shy and trying to hide it unsuccessfully by adopting a brusque manner. So it was all the more amazing how she attracted the attention of yet another man.

He was just a little older than Grace, a man whom Grace met at a house party at an acquaintance's over in Cornwall. A man who made it clear from the beginning that he did not wish to discuss the war. He had participated fully in the war but it was now a closed chapter, he said, which, although it intrigued them greatly, they had to accept. His manner, friendly enough, changed quite dramatically and not for the better whenever the war was mentioned. Their father told them not to mention it too often as he suspected the man had had a 'bad' war. So did Archie, Constance told him tartly.

Flattered by his courteous manner and elegant good looks, Grace blossomed and began to take a renewed interest in her appearance and Constance helped dress her hair and advise her on what to wear, for Grace had little natural dress sense. Times of course were difficult, particularly at the drapers, and it was so tiresome that there was short supply of various essential items but style was style and it could still be accomplished although it required a little more effort.

Constance began to hope that perhaps someday Grace might forgive her. Even though there was now a new man, the resentment was still there, under the surface, bubbling. Archie's photograph still sat on the little desk in Grace's room. She and Grace never talked of him. Nobody in the family ever talked of him.

'My sister Grace had no style, Smith,' she said, as the cat elaborately rearranged himself on her lap, fractionally digging his claws in. Constance gently admonished him before continuing. 'And I'm afraid she never made the best of herself.'

Smith purred. He fully concurred.

'So you could say she only had herself to blame. There was I, in my thirties, granted, and with a past in that I was a married lady, a widow, but I was still so lively, so determined not to lose my sparkle entirely. The only way for me to recover was to start to live again.'

There were picnics, dinner parties, all that summer as Grace waited for the proposal. In private moments when mother and daughters were alone, wedding plans were discussed for Grace was to be married in the nearby village. Eleanor, although rather too old and definitely too plain, insisted on being bridesmaid and Constance was asked, with ill humour, to be matron of honour. For a brief time, Grace's animosity was almost erased, her plain features took on a glow that was almost attractive. She quite simpered whenever her man was around and wore her hair in the style of Lauren Bacall whom she admired. She did not *look* like Lauren Bacall, however.

Constance sipped her Martini thoughtfully. She had chosen to dress for dinner tonight for no special reason other than that she desired to wear her ivory evening gown once more and she wished to eat in the splendour of the dining room. Eating alone was quite boring but she had stretched the meal out, the simple meal Mrs Bainbridge had prepared, pretending there was a companion opposite. It worried her a little. Talking to herself. Talking to Smith was perfectly permissible but talking to *herself*!

As she had discussed with herself at length over dinner, she was not getting very far in her efforts to find a suitable family to take over West House. It was proving difficult because it had to be done with discretion. One could not advertise for suitable applicants in the local paper.

The family she chose must not know they were the chosen ones until she announced it. She would mark the occasion with a dinner party over which she would impart the good news. A final dinner party with her as hostess at West House.

The young woman who had delivered the flowers from her acquaintance in Devon was certainly worth getting to know a little better. Tess O'Grady had been to a very good girls' establishment, spoke very nicely, and that had to count for something. She was giving the ladies of the church guild a talk soon on flower arranging, a charming notion, and she had insisted on waiving the little token fee they paid their speakers. How very nice of her but then she had seemed a pleasant young woman. Modern, of course, with her hair and clothes but Constance approved of that. She liked women to be strong. She was strong herself in so far as her upbringing would allow. No woman of today would allow their husband to dictate to them as Hugh had done. They would have argued, quite rightly, for what they believed to be the proper thing to do. If only she had been able to do so.

She finished off her drink in a single gulp, ground her cigarette into an ashtray and reached once more for her case. She lit up again, shocked to find her hands shaking as she did so, very nearly dropping the lit cigarette onto the cat in her agitation. Luckily Smith was bombproof and merely shifted a fraction before resuming his position.

It was quite amazing how powerful the emotions were after all these years.

How vivid the memories.

How very strong the guilt.

The proposal that the Devon household waited patiently for, eventually came, that summer long ago. It came during a heavenly summer ball at Smallcoombe Manor on a balmy evening following a glorious day. The war was over at last, there had been the joy and excitement of VE Day, and once again, in the midst of the celebrations, Constance's euphoria was tempered by sadness as she was reminded of dearest Archie who had not returned.

She put that aside, however, determined to enjoy the ball. Grace was beside herself with anticipation for the ball had been arranged by their parents with the full expectation that a betrothal announcement would follow. The formal drawing room was cleared of furniture to make a small dancing area and all the best people were invited. All the pent-up emotion of the war years could at last be thrown off and it promised to be a superb evening.

Constance, during the course of it, was invited to take a stroll outside.

Their steps echoed on the flagged stepped path that led to the lower garden and the views over the softly rounded hills of the Devonshire countryside. The war, the bombing, were already becoming distant.

She sighed, very conscious of the nearness of her companion.

'I know you've had a most difficult time, Constance . . .'

She nodded, not daring to speak, for this evening there were memories of Archie too, Archie here with her in this very garden, Archie proposing marriage at almost this very spot.

'And I understand and am happy to accept that it may take some time for you to grow to love me as I love you . . .'

She caught her breath, glanced up at him. His profile reminded her a little of Archie and, from within the house, they could hear the recording of Ella Fitzgerald singing 'Everytime We Say Goodbye'.

Romance as well as the scent of roses was in the air.

'My darling Constance, I know this is a little rushed but will you do me the honour of becoming my wife?'

'But what about Grace . . . ?' she looked at him in astonishment.

'What about her?'

'I thought . . . we all thought . . . that you and Grace were serious about each other,' she murmured, as, within, a slow delight kindled. She had done it again. Really, it was too bad of her.

'Did you?' His smile was amused. 'Well I never.'

What on earth would Grace say this time?

She oughtn't to do it a second time. That was just so very cruel.

She could say no to him and let Grace have her man this time.

However, she looked up into Hugh Makepeace's eyes and her smile said it all.

# 12

'You've missed them *again*. Do you ever look at the time when you ring, Robin?' Yvonne said, taking off her coat with one hand before sitting down by the phone in the hall. 'I've just taken them to school. The phone was ringing as I came up the path.' She took a deep breath to calm herself down. 'What do you want?'

'And it's lovely to speak to you too, darling,' he said with a short laugh. 'Does there have to be a reason?'

'At ten to nine in the morning I should think so,' she said with a sigh. 'Sorry . . . you've caught me on the hop. I'm in a rush. I have to tidy up, put the washing in and then I've got some voluntary work to do.'

'Christ! Why do you bother? The point of you not going out to work surely is that you are there for the children?'

'I am there . . . here . . . for them,' she said. 'I fit in the other things when they're at school. Don't start, Robin. You know damned well I miss my job but if it's a question of choice then there is none for me . . .' she tailed off, not anxious to start him off.

Too late.

'Go on, say it,' he said angrily. 'I messed up your career. Having the kids messed it up rather.'

She kicked off her shoes. New ones and they were pinching her. She gripped the receiver tightly in her sudden anger.

'I am saying nothing of the kind, damn you,' she said. 'One of us needs to be here and it might as well be me. I'm happy with that and I know I will go back to work later when it's not so difficult. And I resent you saying that about the children, Robin. I love them and I wouldn't be without them for anything.

Although . . .' she hesitated, wondered if she ought to say it. 'I do resent the fact that you seem to opt out of all your responsibilities to them.'

'How the hell do you work that out? I'm earning the money, aren't I?'

'I could earn it too,' she said. 'At one time, don't you remember, I was earning more than you. You were *between expeditions* at the time.'

'My work fluctuates, you know that.'

'And mine was secure,' she said, annoyed to be reminded of it.

'How the hell have we got onto this?' he said. 'I rang, in fact, to tell you . . .'

'Sorry.' She sighed heavily. 'Sorry, darling. It's been a bad morning so far. Harry wasn't well last night and he came into my bed at two for a cuddle. He went off again but I was wide awake for hours. I didn't get to sleep until about four. I feel like death.'

'Cry off your voluntary work,' he said, emphasising the words nastily.

'I can't do that. They'll be expecting me,' she said. Tired, she felt weepy and this difficult conversation when she was feeling like this was too much. 'What was it you wanted to tell me?'

'I've had a spot of news. What would you say if I took up a diving job on an overseas expedition?'

'Have you resigned?' She held out a slender hope that she might persuade him to come home. An expedition was out of the question, of course. She saw little enough of him as it was.

'No. But you remember the French guy I used to dive with?'

'Yes.'

'He's come into money so at last he can afford to fund this venture he's been trying to get off the ground for years. He couldn't get commercial sponsorship, which is unbelievable considering what an important dive it's going to be. It's a deep water hollow with underground caves and they need experienced men. It's dangerous but don't worry. We know what we're up against. He's trying to get together a really terrific group of divers. It's the sort of stuff I dream about, Yvonne. It's new territory, never been explored before. The dive of the century.'

She caught sight of her face in the mirror, the sudden annoyance understandable. Would he ever grow up?

'The dive of the century?' she repeated, and he did not notice or chose to ignore her sarcasm.

'You bet. It'll catch everyone's imagination. It'll be a real challenge. It'll beat the hell out of oil rigs anyway. God knows what we'll find. They're filming it for a television documentary and we can sell the story to popular as well as geographic magazines. It's not *just* the money, of course . . .'

'For how long?'

She couldn't help the exasperation in her voice as she recognised the barely suppressed excitement in *his*. Fine for him. Swanning off to somewhere exotic and leaving her to cope with day to day life. Oh, when would he come down to earth? When would he stop acting as if he was starring in 'Raiders of the Lost Ark'? Adventure stopped when you had a mortgage, a wife, children, stopped for most men, that is.

'Six months initially, with the prospect of an extension to do other things. Jean-Louis has all sorts of stuff planned,' he said. 'But they'll pay my fare back home every six weeks or so. Long weekend.'

'Long weekend every six weeks or so,' she echoed. 'Well, thank you very much, Robin. That's great. That is really great.'

'I'll still see you. What's the problem?'

'The children,' she said flatly, realising he hadn't even asked after them. 'It's not fair on them. They want a proper daddy. One who's here most of the time. I'm fed up with making excuses for you. I don't think you've even set foot in their school, have you? The staff don't know you, that's for sure. I think some of them believe you're a figment of my imagination. Did we get married so that we could spend most of the time apart? It's unnatural.'

'I might have known you'd be unreasonable. I am going to take the job,' he said after a moment's silence. 'I've already given Jean-Louis the thumbs up. This was just a courtesy call to let you know. We go in the New Year so I'll be home for Christmas. If you want me, that is. If you don't it's no big deal. I'll be up to my eyes in sorting out my stuff.'

'Let me think about that,' she said, trying to take it all in. 'I wish you wouldn't do this. Take me by surprise. You've ruined my day, Robin.'

'I have to go. I'll let you know the details later. Oh, by the way . . . I can let you have an increase in your allowance. I have some bonuses due.'

'Thank you,' she said dully.

'Bye then. Love you,' he said.

'I'll tell the children you called,' she said hurriedly but it was too late.

The line was dead.

The courtesy call over.

Tess held the dogwood in her hand and surveyed the arrangement. She chose her colours carefully, liked to complement the surroundings, but in the end all it boiled down to was a good eye.

Andrew, poor love, had no eye. He gave no thought to composition or texture or height. But then, lots of people were in the same boat when it came to artistry, floral or otherwise. Look at Yvonne . . . her house was an absolute mismatch of patterns. She seemed unable to make her mind up as to what theme she wished to pursue. You had to have a theme.

Take West House, for example. Discreet elegance was the only possible way you could play it and Constance Makepeace managed that very well although obviously it was all a touch old-fashioned. Tess had already decided what pieces of furniture were going with them but mostly they would have to start afresh. She wondered if her father might be agreeable to another small loan . . . Of course, she would not mention it to Andrew for he got huffy when that was suggested. She already owed a considerable amount but Joe was easygoing about repayment and it was understood she would pay up, with interest naturally, as soon as she was a little more established. The shops were on an up-curve, but only slightly. Times were tough, and flowers were unfortunately considered a luxury item.

The dogwood still clutched in her hand, she frowned at the arrangement. Yes . . . she was rather pleased with it. She liked the lighter touch of the wild clematis, the love-in-a-mist seedheads and the contrasting red leaves. Here was the place to experiment and she needed to think up a suitable arrangement for the demonstration she would shortly be doing.

'You finished . . . ?' Andrew hovered, jingling car keys. 'Looks very nice,' he muttered as she dallied still.

Taking no account of his opinion, Tess nodded, dispensing with the dogwood. It was fine. She dared not think about the gracious reception hall at West House. Everything would be on a grander scale there, arrangements would be so important.

After an initial flurry, there had been no further interest in their house. She had entertained some hopes for a while of the couple who had turned up on spec for they had returned. Tess had made them coffee and provided orange juice for the fractious child who accompanied them and for a few days she had waited anxiously to hear good news from the estate agent. But now, the middle of October already, she decided she must cross them off the list. Stupid, but she felt a quite irrational dislike of them as a result.

'Why you have to decide to fiddle with flowers when we're just off is beyond me,' Andrew said unhelpfully as they went out to his car. 'You know what Stephanie's like about people being on time.'

Tess sighed. They couldn't put it off any longer, she supposed, going to Caryn Lodge for lunch. Stephanie had rung Andrew during the week and, taken off guard, he couldn't think of an excuse, so here they were.

'I've been thinking about this party for your father . . .' Andrew said once they were underway.

'And . . .' Tess glanced at him with irritation. She sensed a big 'but'.

'Are you quite sure about it? Will he thank you for a party?'

'Don't be ridiculous. Of course he will. He'll love it. In fact, he would be terribly disappointed if we did nothing. If I left it up to Stephanie, we would be doing absolutely zilch. She's such a nuisance, Andrew, quibbling about the cost when I'm footing the bill, for God's sake. It's my treat.'

'Want any help with the organisation?'

'No. It's all in hand.'

Her mind on the party, she let him concentrate on his driving. The hotel was booked, the entertainment arranged, but she still had to firm up on the invitations . . . so much to do and so little time to do it. Trust Andrew to harbour second thoughts on the wisdom of it. She knew her father better than anyone, including dear Stephanie. This party would be the highlight of his year.

Once they were on the road over the moors it was quiet, but you had to watch out for the occasional straying sheep and rabbits who seemed to have taken leave of their senses today, darting in death-wish fashion in front of the car.

When they moved into West House, they would be able to hold such events there. Just think of it. She would at last be able to entertain properly. How could she ask more than four people to dinner at Churchwood Close without them practically sitting on each other's laps? They had rather lost touch recently with their friends. Some of them she was happy enough to lose but one or two of them were very influential and she really ought to keep track of them. You never knew when you might need to call in a favour from an old friend.

She sighed, bored with the journey. So-called scenic views did nothing for her at all. October had started wet and it looked set to continue, although this morning, having rained all night, it was drying out and the sky had a shaken fluffy look about it. They had driven through a funny mix of weather on the way, showery at first then sunny, and there . . . a rainbow of theatrical perfection pointing towards Middleton-in-Teesdale and their destination.

Her father's grey stone-built house was a few miles to the south of the market town, in a secluded spot. The long curving drive ended abruptly to the side of the house with a flower bed close in so that plants and flowerheads brushed against you as you passed. Andrew parked the car and they stepped out into the high cool air, higher than Bishopsmeade and feeling it. Tess shivered, pulling her jacket closer, setting off towards the entrance.

The extensive mainly-grassed grounds ended at the road at a clump of rhododendron and laurel, and over the road, the sparkling silver of the Tees meandered through fields, a patchwork of many shades of green, a few isolated farms, sheep, and almost opposite the village of Middleton, easily picked out nestled under the hilltops as it was. Stephanie, after a lifetime of city living, loved it here, knew the names of all the hills; Scarney, Harker,

Green Fell. The breeze that always seemed to waft round the house ruffled Tess's hair and she frowned, smoothing it down.

'Come on,' she said impatiently, turning to see where Andrew was. 'I'm cold. What are you doing?'

He was examining the front of the car, straightened up after a moment. 'Think I hit a rabbit back there,' he said. 'Hope I'm mistaken but I thought I felt a bit of a bump and there's some blood and fur on the bumper. Poor old thing, eh? Hope it's not lying hurt somewhere.'

'Oh darling! What a shame! Still . . . it's done now, it can't be helped,' she said crisply, jigging him along, sighing as she saw the stricken look on his face. 'Get the flowers for Stephanie, would you? They're in the back.'

Her father and Stephanie were just on their way out to meet them. Tess rushed forward to embrace them both, leaving Andrew to follow with the flowers. Stephanie, bespectacled today, was wearing her slippers and Tess was unable to hide her irritation. She knew they were family but even so. She would never dream of entertaining in slippers.

There was a delicious smell as they entered the hall. Tess wrinkled her nose appreciatively, taking hold of her stepmother's arm in a conspiratorial manner as they went through into the sitting room for pre-lunch drinks. Her father fussed with glasses and aperitifs, he and Andrew standing close, straight down to talking business as usual.

The ladies exchanged a smile.

'So good to see you, Steffi,' Tess whispered. 'You and me don't see enough of each other. When are we going to get together for some shopping? Give me a call and I'll see if I can find a slot in my diary.'

Stephanie nodded, checking to see Joe was not listening.

'I need a new dress,' she said quietly. 'For you know what.'

She smiled up at Tess in childish delight.

Stephanie adored secrets.

# 13

Constance was doing a little shopping in the village when she saw the young man from the teashop. He was on the opposite side of the road, accompanied by three small children. Miss Green had surely been mistaken in saying he had no children. She approved of the professional parental manner with which he was shepherding them along. Two golden-haired sweet little girls and a dark-haired son.

Since the last time she had seen him – sometime last month, she thought – their visits to the teashop had failed to coincide, so she had been unable to gently quiz him. Seeing that he was heading for the little play-park beyond the green, she abandoned the butcher whose breezy manner she did not quite approve of in any case and crossed the road in the family's wake.

This was rather fun.

Spying.

Hugh, who like Constance had spoken excellent French, had been in intelligence during the war and took the whole concept of the Official Secrets Act very seriously, so much so that anything he might have divulged to her later was purely accidental. He never meant her to know anything, not even that he had been involved in intelligence work, and it irritated. Secrets between man and wife indeed!

Once the war was over, everyone seemed to be telling their story but not Hugh. He talked of it sometimes in his sleep, speaking urgently, sometimes in French, with fear in his voice, so that she would climb out of her own bed, go across and shake him awake at once, worried for him. You can tell me, dearest, she would say, but he would shake his head. It wasn't something he wanted her to know about, he said, and whilst she accepted that he was only trying to protect her, she minded that he did not think she was up to knowing the truth.

The children were muffled up in anoraks and trousers and Constance, sitting on a chilly bench, watched from a discreet distance. Shrieks and laughter. He was very good with them. Joining in with them in a very natural manner, pushing the swing for the smaller girl, on hand but not intruding as the boy scrambled clumsily over a climbing frame. The more she saw of him and his family the more she liked the man. She wondered about his wife. If his wife was of a suitable standard then perhaps she had found her family. Perhaps she need look no further.

Of course it would be unwise to make any decision without consultation. After all, there was always the chance – absurd though it was – that the family of her choice might not wish to live at West House. She would – what was it? – sound them out.

She was very bad at this easy chat that people engaged in nowadays. She had been taught to hold back with strangers, to retain her reserve and to talk about the weather if in any doubt. She quite deplored this current trend to call everyone by their Christian names, even bank employees. She had therefore absolutely no idea how she would make friends with this man and his family. It was rather a dilemma. Perhaps Mrs O'Grady might know him as they both lived in the new houses. She would ask her. After all, *they* had been introduced and she did intend to invite her and her husband over for tea sometime. She had to have more than one iron in the fire, a spare in case her favoured family backed out.

That decided, Constance stood up, the cold seeping through her rear most unpleasantly. She walked passed the butcher's, ignoring his cheerful wave, deciding she could not face him and the jovial chat that to her mind verged on the insulting. It was his business to serve and not ask questions. If she found the meat not up to standard, she would most certainly inform him accordingly. She would ask Mrs Bainbridge to purchase the meat this week as she was always offering to do. She went instead to the little general store and off-licence where she purchased a small carton of single cream as a treat for Smith and a generous supply of cigarettes.

* * *

Andrew decided he wouldn't tell Tess that he'd had the children for a few hours this morning. Half term. He'd volunteered, in fact, when they were on their way out with Yvonne who had a hair appointment. They were complaining in that dragging-feet way of children, not wanting to go, and he'd said if they really didn't want to, they could stay with him instead.

And so they did.

They'd walked with him down to the shops, helped with the shopping, and because they'd been very good, he'd let them spend some time on the play-park on the way back. He'd not enjoyed himself so much in a long time. It was cold and fresh, one of those days when it felt good to be back indoors in the warm. Pink-cheeked and tingling. Ears cold. They'd had hot blackcurrant juice and biscuits when they got back and, as Yvonne was not due back for another hour – what the hell was she having done to her hair? – he'd asked if they would like to help him make some little cakes.

They'd mixed and measured and messed about generally and it was something of a miracle, given his own considerable inexperience with baking, that in the end the cakes were recognisable as cakes, let alone edible. Portia helped him clean up afterwards, extra fussily, sleeves pushed up, whilst the two little ones pored fascinated over his chessboard, playing some sort of highly imaginative version of their own.

'Harry said the "s" word this morning, Mr O'Grady,' Portia said, passing him the dirty cutlery. She spoke very quietly, looking carefully at him, gauging his reaction. 'Mummy didn't hear but if she did, she would be very cross. Mummy says only grown-ups can say those words. She says naughty words sometimes after Daddy rings. He makes her cross.'

'Does he? The "s" word?' Andrew said faintly, out of his depth with this, seeing that Portia was not going to let it pass. 'Dear me.'

Portia tugged at his arm, mouthed the word 'shit'.

'Well . . . you mustn't tell tales,' Andrew said, trying not to smile. 'Harry is very naughty but it might be best if we don't say anything.'

'Why?'

'You can take two cakes home with you, two each,' Andrew

said firmly, deciding that changing the subject was preferable to a long discussion on the psychology of parental overreaction. 'And, because you did the most work, Portia, you can choose your two first.'

Blessedly, she fell for the diversion and, minutes later, the little cakes, iced with cherries on top, were bagged up, ready for the off. By the time Yvonne arrived, newly coiffured, freshly scented and smiling dazzlingly, Harry's misdemeanour had been temporarily forgotten. Andrew made no mention of it.

He got down to some work when they went, the house strangely silent without them. After a few solid hours at the computer, a few necessary phone calls to clients, he went to make himself a coffee and, as he sat drinking it, eating one of the cakes Portia had left for him, he found for some inexplicable reason he was thinking about their baby, the baby that never was.

You thought you'd forgotten and then something, a little thing, was capable of bringing every sodding moment back.

Was Tess right? Had he really been as useless as she suggested when it came to the decision? The consultant and the counsellor they talked to had been at great pains to explain all the options but Andrew had known, as he held Tess's hand, that the decision was already made. She had made it.

The staff were supportive but Andrew had been unable to rid himself of the feeling that the decision to terminate was ultimately a selfish one. Tess was thinking not of the baby but of herself. Understandable, and he had told himself not to be critical of that. He had been so conscious of doing the right thing and indeed, on the very weekend when they found out the results of the amniocentesis test, they stupidly went shopping to try in vain to take their mind off it and they'd stumbled across a family with a little boy in tow, a boy with those familiar facial characteristics of the Down's Syndrome child.

'Oh, God . . .' he heard Tess say at his side. 'Get me out of here.'

Andrew had seen the look she gave the child. Worse, the parents of the child had seen it too, heard her agonised whisper surely, and, as he rapidly followed Tess out of the shop, he looked back and tried to offer an apology. All he could remember was their gentle manner, the way they talked to the child as he tried on his new red shoes, a happy looking child.

By the Monday, the decision was made. Tess was in hospital.

On the Tuesday, the baby, a boy, was born dead, almost four and a half months after he was conceived.

# 14

Stephanie always rang her at the most inconvenient moments.

'Oh thank heavens, I've caught you,' she said, as one of the assistants passed the phone to Tess. 'I tried the other shops and nobody seemed quite sure where you were this morning. And I tried your mobile but there was no answer.'

'Look, Stephanie, what is it? I'm rather busy,' Tess said, for this, the smallest of her shops was in a central narrow alley where she stocked her cheaper range, most of the flowers already bunched up and packaged in cellophane as in the supermarket manner. Bargain offers, two bunches for the price of one, that sort of thing. She used local growers a great deal for this outlet. In fact, she tried to make it as much like a market stall as possible, opening as it did straight onto the street. Even though she deplored the downmarket aspect, it had a very good rapid turnover.

'I'm so sorry to bother you when you're so busy, Tess, but I wanted a word about Joe's party,' Stephanie said in a low voice as if Joe was standing within earshot, although presumably at this time of day he would be at the office. 'I'm a little worried as time is getting on and I hadn't heard from you. I wondered if you have any more details that I should know about?'

'It's all arranged. What else is it you need to know?' Tess said impatiently. 'I've booked the function suite at the hotel and I've managed to get hold of a jazz quartet to provide the music. Preferable, don't you think, to having a DJ? They're going to do us what they call the deluxe buffet. There's nothing for you to worry about at all, other than to make sure you get him there on time. You can pretend . . . well, I'll leave that up to you,' she went on, assuming the woman could come up with something even though she was spectacularly unimaginative. 'As for numbers, I've had about thirty definites, some possibles and several can't-make-its. Are you quite sure we haven't missed anybody off his work list? It could cause terrible problems if we inadvertently leave someone off. You know what a back-stabbing organisation he works for.'

'Yes I do. I wish he'd do something less stressful, but that's Joe, isn't it? I think we have informed everybody,' Stephanie said, sounding worried. 'I managed to get hold of an internal telephone list. I'm so sorry but I had to let his secretary in on it so I do hope she'll be discreet.' Her sigh was huge.

'She'd better be,' Tess said sharply, wondering why on earth she'd left Stephanie to deal with *anything*. The secretary wouldn't be breathing a word on pain of death if she'd dealt with it herself.

'I'm not very good at this sort of thing, Tess,' Stephanie went on, stating the obvious. 'All this secrecy. I'm sure someone will tell him. How can we hope to keep a secret when over thirty – forty – people know about it? I keep getting telephone calls in the evening and Joe's starting to look at me oddly. I don't think he suspects it's a party though.'

Tess sighed. Couldn't the woman handle her own husband, for God's sake?

'People love secrets, Steffi, and they love surprises too,' she said. 'They can't wait to see the look on his face when the lights go up and we start to sing Happy Birthday. I shall brief everyone on what's expected.'

'Yes, but the thing is, Tess . . .' She hesitated and Tess frowned into the receiver, willing her to get on with it. The girls were all busy serving and a couple of customers looked like they were on the verge of giving up. People shopped through this alley at a frantic rate of knots. Twenty seconds if you were lucky was all you got from their attention span and that was why she did such a bright special offer display to grab them. Last St Valentine's Day, they'd actually run out of red roses here as a result of a very effective roses-and-romance display.

Stephanie was having trouble saying it, whatever it was.

'What?' Tess said sharply, not bothering now to hide her

impatience. 'Look, Stephanie . . . I must go. Why don't you ring me at home later?'

'I can't,' she said. 'How can I? I have to ring when he's not in. You see, the thing is I'm not sure Joe wants a surprise party. He says not to make a fuss.'

'Nonsense. He's just saying that,' Tess said, wondering if Andrew had been having a word. Andrew was depressingly unenthusiastic and it was contagious to someone as indecisive as Stephanie. 'You know Joe as well as I do. He'll be the life and soul. He'll be disappointed, take it from me, if you don't do something.'

'Are you sure? Tess . . . ?'

'Yes?' She gritted her teeth. Stephanie could be so *annoying*. God knows how the students had put up with her for two or three years.

'And another thing that's been bothering me. You are happy to come to us at Christmas, aren't you? I know you wanted us to come to you this year and it occurred to me later that I might have been a bit pushy . . .'

'We shall be delighted to come to you,' Tess said. 'We are looking forward to it. Nobody can do Christmas like you, Steffi. You are superb.'

'Oh really, do you think so . . . thank you. It's my very favourite time of year,' she said happily. 'In fact, Joe thinks me quite mad, but I've already started to plan. When I was single, I used to dream of doing a Christmas for a family. I love all the preparations and I'm going to make my own decorations . . . we're going to put lights on the tree outside. What do you think?'

'Wonderful. That sounds lovely. Don't do a thing about flowers, of course. I shall bring those.'

'Thank you. I thought I might cook a goose. Is that all right? Because, if you really don't like the idea, I can always stick to turkey to be on the safe side. What do you think?'

'Whatever,' Tess said, relaxing a little because the queue had eased. 'Whatever you do, it will be superb. You're such a good cook.' She pulled a face into the phone. Butter the woman up at all costs before she did the unthinkable and took up their invitation. Andrew was no help either. He'd managed to sound properly disappointed when their own invitation was turned down. 'We still talk about the delicious meal we had last Christmas,' she added desperately, worried she might be overdoing the praise just a snitch.

'I do but try,' Stephanie said with that infuriating breathy laugh. 'So that's all settled, then?

'What is?'

'The surprise party. All I have to do is get him to the hotel for eight o'clock. Buffet and a dance, isn't it? I don't know what to wear, Tess. We couldn't possibly fit in our shopping trip sometime this week, could we? He wouldn't think it at all odd because we've been talking about it for ages.'

'Why not?' Tess said recklessly, wanting to cut short the conversation so that she could grab a bite to eat. She was doing her flower arranging demonstration in St Cuthbert's church hall this evening and she wanted to get home early afternoon and put her feet up for a while. 'Saturday all right for you?'

'Oh lovely . . .' Stephanie's delight showed in her voice. 'Shall we go in my car?'

'No. Mine,' Tess said.

Stephanie, for reasons best known to herself, insisted on running a five or six year old little Citroen that in Tess's eyes had certainly seen better days. She was not turning up in Newcastle in *that*. Bad enough that she had to go shopping at all with Stephanie, who would turn up dressed in a chainstore item as usual. When you shopped in exclusive boutiques you had to look the part.

Still . . . a day's shopping would be fun and she needed a new dress herself for the party. All sorts of influential people would be there, for Joe knew everybody who was anybody in the local business world. It did no harm at all to cultivate contacts; you never knew when you might need them.

# 15

Yvonne stopped her car outside West House, reached over the seat for the bag of books. She had made good time this morning, enjoyed delivering the books and having a chat with everyone. Mrs Makepeace was her last call, so she had time for yet another cup of tea or coffee if she was offered one. All in all, it had been another of those hectic mornings, with Samantha in a panic this time because she'd forgotten that she had to take some leaves and things into school for a nature project and no, they would not do tomorrow, she needed them *now*.

For Yvonne, in the middle of organising their breakfast, it had meant a hasty scrambling about at the bottom of the garden in her dressing gown for a suitably varied selection. Although it was a fine bright day, there was a heavy dew and she had rushed back indoors, her bedroom mules sodden, her nightdress damply clinging to her ankles, to where Samantha was waiting right at the kitchen door hopping from foot to foot in a spasm of anxiety. It was worth getting wet feet though to see the way her little face lit up when she saw the bundle of leaves.

Smiling at the memory as she climbed out of the car carrying the bag of books for Mrs Makepeace, Yvonne looked round a moment, taking in the quiet beauty of it all, admiring the gardens, the way the lawns fell away, merging, it seemed, into the meadows beyond. She closed her eyes a moment and the silence and sweetness of the air wrapped round her.

It was the first time she had been here, this close, and she was suitably impressed. Feeling for some reason a bit nervous, absurdly wondering if she ought to be going to the tradesmen's entrance, she walked over to the front door and rang the bell.

After a moment, there was the sound of footsteps from what seemed a great distance.

'Oh, come in . . .' The woman who answered the door was not Mrs Makepeace.

She led Yvonne into a spacious entrance hall and left her there, going through to another room at the rear and announcing in a loud voice that the woman from Bishopsmeade Volunteers was here with the library books. Did Mrs Makepeace want to see her or not?

There was a definite stress on the 'or not' and Yvonne bristled a little at that. The woman had given her a look that Yvonne was not unfamiliar with. Blonde hair and a good bust, as Agnes might say, meant one thing only where some people were concerned. Tess O'Grady looked at her in exactly the same way. Women often did. It meant they thought she possessed one brain cell, over-exerted at that. Men looked at her with a quite different look.

'You're to go through, she says,' the woman said with the barest attempt at a smile. 'And do you want a cup of tea or coffee, she says to ask?' There was no doubt from the way she said it, she was willing Yvonne to refuse.

'Thank you. A cup of coffee would be lovely.'

'Right you are. Go on in.'

Yvonne stepped into the room, tapping on the door that was ajar.

'Thank you so much. How delightful!'

Constance Makepeace waved at her to come across the room, across a vast expanse of Chinese rug in shades of vivid turquoise and yellow. It was such a bright room, flooded with autumn sunshine. The walls were lined with bookshelves and there were two windows, one looking onto the side lawns and the other onto a terrace and a rose garden, a few late roses still hanging on providing a splash of colour. A fire, a real one that would fascinate the children, burned in the grate.

'Do sit down,' Constance Makepeace said with a smile. 'My housekeeper will bring the coffee in shortly. Now, who are you, dear?'

'Yvonne Lonsdale,' she said, sitting down in a yellow armchair.

'Do you want to see my identification?' She rummaged in her bag for it. 'You can't be too careful, Mrs Makepeace.'

'That will not be necessary.' She shook her head. 'You have the books, do you not? And this is the day for them. That is sufficient proof to me that you are who you say you are.'

'Would you like to see the books?'

'Presently.' She reached for a cigarette case, lit one. 'I assume you don't . . .'

'I used to,' Yvonne said with a rueful smile, 'And then when I was expecting my first baby I thought it best to give up and I never started again.'

'In my day, they didn't mind you smoking when you were in what they called an interesting condition. They thought, quite rightly, that it calmed the nerves,' Constance said. 'It's most kind of you to do this, Mrs Lonsdale. Thank you so much. I do so look forward to receiving my books.'

'It's a pleasure.' Yvonne relaxed a little although the room made her feel she was in an expensive antique shop. 'Do you read a lot, Mrs Makepeace?' she asked, trying to break the ice, feeling that this lady would be rather difficult to get to know, stilted and formal as she was. Easy does it, then. One toe in the deep end.

Constance nodded. 'Every evening. Five or six pages before I turn out the light. Such a pleasurable occupation. Do you read, Mrs Lonsdale?'

'I wish I had the time. With the children – I have three children – and my husband works away from home, so it's rather difficult. Most of the reading I do is bedtime stories although Portia, my eldest, can read for herself now.'

'Portia? What a pretty and unusual name!'

'Isn't it? My other little girl is Samantha and our little boy is Harry.'

'Charming names all. I may have seen you down in the village. You do live down in the village?'

'The new houses. Churchwood Close.'

'Ah . . . yes, I thought so. Last evening, we had a most delightful talk, a flower demonstration, at the church ladies' guild, given to us by somebody you will probably know. Mrs O'Grady.'

'Oh yes, Tess. She's my neighbour.'

'Charming woman. She presents herself beautifully. Discreetly.'

Yvonne nodded, not quite knowing what to say, feeling the slightest reprimand had just been issued. She supposed she was looking very 'bright' today in a primrose yellow dress with some dangly fun earrings and a jingle of gold bracelets.

The coffee blessedly arrived and Mrs Makepeace dismissed the housekeeper with a nod. She gave the impression she was used to servants in the easy manner she dispensed with her.

'There's a young man I believe lives in Churchwood Close whom you might also know,' Constance went on when their coffee was poured. 'I have seen him recently and I wonder if you might enlighten me as to who he is. A tall man, with three children. Two little girls and a small boy. Mrs O'Grady suggests I may be mistaken.'

'I don't understand. Are you sure he lives in Churchwood Close?'

'That's exactly what Mrs O'Grady said and so I must conclude I was given the wrong information.'

'There's only me with children,' Yvonne said thoughtfully. 'And Robin's away. Oh, I know what it will be . . . you might have seen Andrew with the children down in the village. Andrew O'Grady, Tess's husband. He baby-sits sometimes for me.'

'I see . . .' There was a pause as she handed Yvonne a plate of biscuits. 'So, what you are saying is that they are not his children?'

'No. They're mine,' Yvonne said with a smile, bemused at the understandable mistake. 'He is very good with them, though. They like him a lot.'

She struggled with the conversation after that. Mrs Makepeace, ever polite, was stiff and not very forthcoming. Yvonne took the opportunity during a lengthy pause to bring out the books and let her see them. Detective stories as requested.

'Most of our ladies like romances,' she said as Constance pronounced them satisfactory. 'A love story.'

'I have no time for romance. Love at first sight, all that nonsense! I like to exercise my mind and detective stories are such a puzzle,' Constance told her with the slightest of smiles. 'I like to try to unravel the plot as I go. Romance is far too trivial for me.'

They were interrupted by the arrival of a ginger cat, who had slipped in through the half open door. He gave a loud miaow to announce his arrival before coming over to them, tail up in the air, fluffing against Yvonne's legs a moment. She leaned down to stroke him and he regally allowed it before he was off, leaping or rather scrambling onto the arm of Constance's chair, scratching at the peach silk as he did so.

'His name is Smith. Or at least that is the name I have given him. I have no idea what his original name was or where he comes from. He has lost a little of his bounce,' Constance explained, touching his head softly. His presence subtly altered her. She became instantly a little more receptive. 'His age, you see, Mrs Lonsdale. He keeps it secret but we, the vet and I, have decided he might be about eighteen. He has few teeth and a ragged ear as you see. By no means perfect.'

'I think he's handsome,' Yvonne said stoutly.

'So do I.'

Constance glanced at the clock that sat on the mantelpiece as it chimed eleven in a high-pitched staccato manner.

Her time was up.

Quickly, Yvonne rose to leave, explaining that she would see her again in a fortnight's time.

'Mrs Bainbridge will see you out, Mrs Lonsdale.'

Constance Makepeace inclined her head graciously.

The audience was at an end.

'Blonde bombshell that's what they used to call women like her,' Ella said with a sniff. 'Jayne Mansfield or Marilyn Monroe. Yellow frock and high heels and lipstick. And did you see those earrings and the bracelets? At this time of the morning? I couldn't take my eyes off them. I bet she never gets down on *her* knees to scrub the kitchen floor.'

'You needn't either, Ella. It's quite unnecessary.'

'Be that as it may . . . she's not the sort you can imagine in a pinny, is she?'

'Indeed not. A little too flamboyant for me. However, she is doing charity work,' Constance pointed out. 'So we must give credit for that. She tells me she lives in the new houses.'

'I know. I've seen her and those children of hers. Bonny they are, I'll give her that.' Ella deftly removed ornaments, dusted beneath and around, replaced them. 'Are you putting the house up for sale then, Mrs Makepeace?' she asked suddenly, unexpectedly. 'I wouldn't ask, only Bernard's getting bothered. He says he might need to do some extra clearing out round the back.'

'It's all in hand,' Constance said, deliberately vague. 'He is just to continue at the normal pace. No need to worry at all. By the time I move to the cottage in spring, all will be resolved.'

'Right you are then.' Ella stuffed the duster in her pocket, looked round with satisfaction. 'That'll do then, I think. Spot of lunch, Mrs Makepeace? What do you fancy?'

'Thank you. I think I would like a softly boiled egg and some brown bread.'

'I'll get on with it now.'

Ella departed and closed the door quietly behind her.

Constance reluctantly decided against another cigarette and leaned her head on the back of the chair instead. Mrs Lonsdale's flowery scent was still around although it was quite pleasant. Smith, not liking an upset to his routine, had disappeared but would be along later.

She was rather tired, in fact. And also a little disappointed at the way events had turned out. Meeting up again with Mrs O'Grady last evening, she had once more been extremely taken with her. She had been quite charming, given them a most informative talk and she so obviously adored flowers. A love of flowers signified a sweet nature in Constance's opinion. Mrs O'Grady had offered to help them with the church arrangements should they so wish, although Constance knew that idea would not meet with a positive response. Church flower arranging was quite another matter.

That aside, Constance thoroughly approved of her. Mrs O'Grady was always so smartly dressed, last night in an expensive green suit and cream blouse. Just for a moment, Constance had felt quite nostalgic for the days when she too was called elegant but comfort must take pride of place now.

Afterwards, as some of the ladies prepared the refreshments, she had taken the opportunity of having a few words with her. After drawing a blank on the subject of the identity of the man with the children – now of course resolved – she had asked Mrs O'Grady and her husband to come to West House for afternoon tea, Wednesday week. Mrs O'Grady – Tess, wasn't she? – had seemed quite delighted at the idea, said her husband too would be so pleased as he had long admired the house from afar.

The fact that they had no children was not after all so important. They were young. They would have children in due course. Children perhaps born at West House. How lovely. Under no circumstances, of course, would she consider the young woman who had brought the books this morning even if she had seemed to be quite taken with dearest Smith and he with her. Very scented and made-up and buxom. Certainly not the sort of woman to live in a house like this. One simply could not take people out of the class they were born into. It never ever worked.

Perhaps she had already made up her mind. If Tess O'Grady's husband was as nice as he appeared to be, then there would be no more doubts.

She would ask Mrs Bainbridge if she would mind waiting at tea. So much more civilised if someone served. A dying art, of course, and Mrs Bainbridge, untrained as she was, did not alas do the job with any degree of competence. She blew hot and cold on how she treated Constance. Over-familiar on occasions and quite aloof on others.

Once upon a time, Constance reflected with a sigh, servants knew exactly how to behave. When she and Archie married, they had a small staff of four in the house in London, retainers borrowed in fact from the much more substantial country property of his parents. Four was the minimum almost. Archie's family were Gloucestershire stock, very much landed gentry, although Archie was the third son so would not inherit the estate. Archie did not mind that. After the war, he planned to go into the construction business for there would be a great demand for housing, he said. He very much wanted to make money from his own ventures, a little unhappy with living off the family name.

A dream never fulfilled.

The onset of war was a volcano erupting and Archie's death was something she chillingly anticipated. Archie's mother had been a great help, spending a good deal of time with her after Archie was killed. It was she who suggested the services of a doctor friend of hers to help with Constance's forthcoming confinement and Constance, knowing nothing about pregnancy, had accepted gratefully. She recalled how well she had felt during her pregnancy, suffering none of the sickness that she had expected. She owed it to Archie to keep herself well. Archie had been delighted at the prospect of becoming a father and the fact that she carried Archie's child within her body was some small consolation.

The ladies of the family, with the solitary exception of Grace, spent a lot of time making baby garments until the big chest of drawers in the nursery was full of tiny clothes, the Chilprufe vests, the napkin squares, the bootees and mittens, the sweet little cardigans. All in white, of course. She would often go into the nursery and just take things out of the drawers, touch them, hold them against her face, put them away again.

There were some problems with supplies, of course, but she had the money to by-pass most of the difficulties, and she remembered to this day her choice of a Beatrix Potter design for the nursery curtains, heavily lined with a closely woven coloured casement. Great care had to be taken in the black-out that there would be no gaps of light if baby had to be attended to during the night. She felt sure she would have a son whom she would name after Archie, of course. Archie's mother quite depended on it.

A nanny was engaged and her room beside the nursery made ready. About ten days before the baby was due, a nurse arrived to help prepare Constance for her coming ordeal. The nurse, a starched and stiff presence, was dark with bulbous eyes and she did not have a cheerful disposition, which made Constance increasingly nervous as the days passed. Within her body, the baby kicked and tumbled before settling into a quiet state just prior to the delivery.

Constance shifted uncomfortably in the chair, a whimper

involuntarily passing her lips. She did not wish to release the memory but it was too late. It was suddenly so vivid.

Ante-natal care in those difficult days even for women of her class was fairly basic, so the problem of baby's awkward lie went undiscovered. The doctor who, it turned out, had delivered Archie, was well past retirement and out of touch. His examinations of her had always been conducted in a swift and perfunctory fashion.

When she went into labour it was hours and hours before the nurse felt it necessary to call him out to assist at the birth and when he arrived he was – well – not up to the job and his breath smelled most unpleasantly of whisky. The pain . . . she whimpered again at the memory. She was dragged about the bed, told sharply by the nurse to be quiet and stop making a fuss for the servants could hear, and eventually, after frantic whisperings in a corner that absolutely terrified her, the doctor started bringing clattering instruments out of his bag and the nurse told her he was going to have to pull baby out for they were getting nowhere.

She felt the tears on her cheek. Wiped them away quickly lest Mrs Bainbridge should see them when she came in to tell her luncheon was ready.

'It was a girl, Mrs Lennox. Born dead,' the nurse said briskly afterwards, her eyes betraying no emotion. 'Too big for you. She's made a mess of you. No, it's no use taking on. It's just one of those things. Keep still and then I can attend to you. You can have a look at her if you want in a minute when the doctor's cleaned her up.'

Margaret Rose Lennox. Margaret, despite being unfashionable these days, was such a pretty name, every bit as pretty as Portia. She had chosen it in honour of the Princess Margaret Rose who was such a beautiful little girl too.

There was no consolation, for this time, with the death of the baby, Archie was well and truly gone. She mourned him afresh as well as the baby and she never saw Archie's mother again. When *her* mother arrived to see her, Constance was lying-in, looking she supposed as pale and interesting as all those tragic heroines in the romantic novels she read at the time, trying desperately to recover her spirits.

'Everyone sends their love, dearest,' her mother said. 'Your father, Eleanor . . .' the slight hesitation was noticed, '. . . and of course Grace.'

It helped a little to see her mother even though neither of them knew what to say. Mother had been torn by her feelings of loyalty to Grace and sympathy for Constance. She remembered her mother had said little about the baby, merely stroked her hair and smiled her sympathy, the pain showing in her eyes. Perhaps, after all, although she had never said it, her mother had loved her.

Effortlessly, Mother saw to the arrangements, even paid the incompetent doctor and the sadistic nurse, whom Constance never wanted to set eyes on again. When she finally did get on her feet again, everything had been removed from the nursery. Everything of Margaret's. The nanny had left. Her maid meant well, of course, but Constance knew where the baby things had been put and recovered them later when she was more able to cope with looking at them.

'Come on, Mrs Makepeace . . . it's all on the table,' Ella's voice broke into her thoughts. 'Been dozing off, have you?'

'Not at all. Thank you, Ella, I will be with you presently.'

Constance gave her a look, refusing to be rushed, rising in a few moments a little dizzily before going through to the kitchen where they would take luncheon.

# 16

There was nothing doing with the sale of their house. A few enquiries but nobody at all keen to pursue matters further. With little joy on his business front, Andrew was resigned now to getting a job come Christmas, although he had said nothing to Tess, reluctant still to admit defeat. Tess had other things on her mind. The party for Joe was assuming ridiculous proportions but before that they had received out of the blue an invitation from Mrs Makepeace to have tea at West House.

Tomorrow afternoon, and Tess was acting as if it was a summons from the Queen.

The second half of October had been very wet, the whole country suffering. Wet and windy and the flowers in the beds had finally given up, drenched, drooping and utterly depressed. The lawn was sodden, mackintoshes and umbrellas in constant use, and Yvonne had given up pegging out the washing.

The phone rang and he sighed as he went to answer it. He hoped it wasn't the estate agent with some good news. An obscene phone call would be preferable to that. He could not risk a sudden quick sale. It would leave them with a pounding headache anyway because they had not looked at anything else. It rather surprised him, that. Knowing Tess, he had expected to be dragged along to something they could not possibly afford every weekend. Next time, he knew, she wanted a one-off older detached house, in decent grounds, something like her father's house, something therefore that was in all honesty out of their reach. Would she spend all her life reaching for what was just out of reach? He knew she would accuse him of being a stick-in-the-mud but this constant scrambling up the ladder wore him out. He was happy enough frankly with what they already had.

'Andrew . . . it's me, Yvonne,' the voice said, slightly breathless. 'I'm so sorry to disturb you but can you possibly do me an enormous favour?'

He couldn't for the life of him understand why she was ringing. They were so close, they could have conducted this conversation with the aid of two plastic cups and a taut thread.

'What favour?' he asked suspiciously. 'I'm working.'

'I know and I'm so very sorry to interrupt. The thing is I'm in a pay phone at the supermarket in Darlington.'

'Oh . . . are you?'

'You're going to think me a complete fool but can you come and get me? You're never going to believe what I've done. I can't believe it myself. I've locked my handbag in the car and it's got the car keys in. I slammed the door and it was locked. I can't get in. I can't get home.'

Oh God!

'Oh, Andrew,' she went on, sounding comically frantic, 'I couldn't think who else to ring. It's been a horrendous afternoon. I have this trolley, absolutely overflowing, with wobbly wheels and everything. I've just wiggled it across the car park in the pouring rain, loaded everything into the car and now I don't know what to do and I've to pick the children up at half three. I'd left it all a bit late in any case. I was late setting off and . . . what are we going to do?'

She stopped, sounded like she was going to cry. Andrew sighed, not liking the sound of the 'what are *we* going to do?'.

'Aren't you with the AA? Something like that?' he asked crisply. 'You can ring them and they'll sort you out. They have spare keys, I think.'

'We didn't bother with that because we're covered with the new car thing. I could ring the garage where we got it, I suppose, but they're over in Sunderland. It will take absolutely ages. The thing is there is a way out. Can you bring my spare keys? Would it be too much trouble?'

'Where are they? How do I get in your house?'

'There's a front door key under the flowerpot with the pansies nearest the swing. I know, I shouldn't, but it's just as well I did, isn't it? Take that and when you get inside the house, my spare car keys are in the blue vase in the hall window. Got that? Look, Andrew . . . I've borrowed money for this call and I'm running out. Can you come? Please?'

'I'll be there as soon as I can,' he said.

'Oh . . . you're an absolute angel.'

Bugger.

He waterproofed himself, went in search of keys, found them, and drove snappily in more ways than one to the supermarket. The car park was fairly full and it took him a while to locate her, a vision in a long suedy pale green mackintosh standing beside the car, waving to attract his attention, sheltering under a big black umbrella.

He wound down his window, passed her the keys.

'I am so pleased to see you. Do you want any shopping while you're here?' she asked brightly. 'We can have a coffee.'

'No, I do not want any shopping. I thought you were in a hurry anyway,' he said with gritted teeth, ignoring an annoyed hoot from behind for he was disconcertingly half in half out of a space. He slipped the car into gear, managed a brief smile directed towards Yvonne, even though he could have strangled the woman. 'I'm going home. I've got work to do.'

'I shall follow you,' she said. 'And when we get back, I insist you come in for a coffee and a slice of my chocolate cake. Double layer with cream and nuts. The children love it. No – no arguments. It's the very least I can do. See you later, Andrew.'

And she was off back to her car.

Bloody dizzy woman! His annoyance spilled over on the journey back and he found himself wondering just why he was quite so irritated. After all, it was the sort of thing that could in theory happen to anyone although he couldn't see it happening to Tess. He parked his car once they were home and, when pressed again, said he could spare time for a quick coffee. Just a quick one.

'There . . .'

Once inside, she slipped off the mackintosh and adjusted the belt of the dress beneath. For some reason, he was less inclined these days to mention to Tess the moments he spent with Yvonne and the children. He felt just a bit out of his depth on this one.

He hoped he was wrong but he had the feeling that Yvonne had him in her sights, was circling prettily before homing in for the kill. It was hardly the thing for a man of the world to admit but, although he was bloody flattered, he hadn't a clue how to handle it. He loved Tess. He wasn't cut out for an affair.

'What absolutely foul weather!' She ran a towel through her hair, fluffing it dry. 'You all right? We've made good time actually. I wasn't quite so pushed as I thought. Do you mind if I just unload the shopping first?'

'I'll give you a hand.'

He was sorry he'd offered as bag after bulging bag was brought in and deposited on the kitchen work-top. She would put them away afterwards, she said, getting on with making the coffee.

He took a seat as directed on one of the high stools at the kitchen breakfast bar. She kept the place very clean, he noticed, his new-found domesticity surfacing. It was so obviously a family kitchen. On the walls were pinned a collection of drawings. Children's drawings. One that caught his eye was of a deep-sea diver, arms stiffly outstretched, smiling through his face-glass, surrounded by brightly coloured smiling fishes and sea-shells, the water crystal clear and blue.

'It's Daddy,' Yvonne explained unnecessarily catching the direction of his glance. 'Sweet, isn't it? Samantha's very good at drawing. There's a self portrait somewhere. Oh yes, there it is. Isn't it a shame?'

'What?'

'That they see so little of Robin.'

'Yes, it must be difficult for you with him being away so much. Thanks . . .' He accepted a mug of coffee, smiled at her, sorry he'd been a bit terse before. She couldn't help it, he supposed, if she was naturally scatty.

'It is difficult. In a lot of ways.' She pushed a generous portion of cake and a little pastry fork towards him. 'It's lonely and I'm not very good at looking after the house . . . plugs and things.'

Andrew sank the fork into the soft mixture as she watched with a satisfied smile. The sponge was wonderfully light and, just for a moment, he had a notion to ask her for the recipe. But he did not.

'I don't mind helping out with things like that,' he said. 'I know Robin would do the same for Tess if positions were reversed.'

'I'm sure he would, although I bet she wouldn't lock herself out of her car.' She glanced at the clock on the wall. 'Sorry . . . I'm going to have to fly. I must be there when they come out. Oh . . . you won't mention this to Tess, will you? I know she doesn't have much of an opinion of me but this will convince her I'm a complete idiot.'

'Not if you don't want me to, although it could happen to anyone,' he said, although he knew she was right. Tess just did not *do* things like that.

In the confined space of the hall they jiggled for position, accidentally touching.

'Sorry . . .'

Hastily Andrew took a step back. Her perfume was lovely. Her hair very pale. Her eyes very blue. And there was a hint of colour in her powdered cheeks.

'Andrew . . . before you go . . .' She held onto his arm and looked at him with those big beautiful eyes. 'I can't apologise enough about today. I am mortified to have caused you so much trouble. May I at least pay for your petrol?' She blushed even as she offered and he smiled, shook his head. 'Are you sure? Well . . . thanks again.'

And before he knew what was what, she reached up and kissed him.

Took him completely by surprise.

Kissed him so gently on the lips.

*Kissed* him.

He escaped to his house as she set off with a cheerful wave to get the children. The rain had not let up at all and he shook himself dry when he got in. Catching sight of himself in the hall mirror as he did so, he saw that he was grinning like a fool.

Tess spent so much time deciding which outfit to wear that it was a miracle they got up to West House for three thirty.

'Leave the talking to me,' she said as they waited at the door. 'Just back me up when necessary.'

Andrew grinned at her, bemused by the whole thing. A tea date!

Just as the door opened, he felt Tess's hand in his. Pleasantly surprised by the gesture, he gave it an encouraging squeeze. He had no idea why she was getting herself so worked up about this.

He thoroughly approved of the home-baked spread but the atmosphere in the quiet of the drawing room at West House was so refined that they picked rather at the food. To his surprise, for he hadn't realised she knew Constance Makepeace that well, Tess rushed over and kissed her, gushing about how lovely this was. She'd brought flowers, of course, but then she always did. Thank goodness they were not too elaborate, just a few sprigs of something blue.

'We've met already although we haven't been formally introduced,' Constance said as she shook hands with Andrew. 'At the teashop in the village. Do you remember?'

'Yes.' He smiled, taking a look round the room, liking what he saw. Tess was right. This was some house although quite out of their range. He couldn't understand what Tess was on about; some sort of devious plan was afoot, no doubt, and he decided that caution was advisable. He would indeed let her do the talking if that's what she wanted.

'I have such happy memories of visiting my grandfather at West House when I was a little girl. I never imagined that one day I would live here. When we first moved, my husband and I, we entertained frequently,' Constance told them with a gracious smile. She was dressed for the occasion in twinset and pearls, pearl studded earrings also today. 'We had to entertain although my husband was never keen on the social side. It was part of the job. My late husband was in politics, Mr O'Grady,' she explained politely. 'He retired at the 1955 election because of ill health, a nervous problem. However, he achieved his ambition. We might have returned to live down in the south of England but we chose not to. We felt quite settled here.' She gazed happily round the room. 'As I say, this is a splendid house for entertaining. Do you entertain very much?'

The question, although directed at him, was answered by Tess.

'We would love to,' she said, giving him an adoring look. 'Wouldn't we, darling? But the house is so small. With our business connections – both of us – we should entertain much more than we do. If only we had a house this size . . .' she sighed, looked up at the ceiling as if praying for it to happen. 'It's out of the question, unfortunately,' she added, taking a delicate nibble out of the cucumber sandwich.

'And you, Mr O'Grady . . . Tess tells me you are an accountant,' Constance said. 'I had an uncle who was an accountant. Of course, in those days it was quite different. One had to add up figures.' Her eyes twinkled and Andrew warmed to her. He liked a sense of humour. Tess didn't actually possess one.

'Computers and calculators now,' he said. 'They do it all for you, Mrs Makepeace.'

'Do call me Constance,' she said. 'And I shall call you Tess and Andrew. It's against my nature to be so informal but one must move with the times. Thank you, Mrs Bainbridge, that will be all,' she said, inclining her head as the lady finished fussing. 'You may clear away later.'

Andrew gave the housekeeper a quick smile as she swept by, amused at her expression and the raising of the eyebrows directed at him alone.

'It is very much a family home, West House,' Constance continued when the door had closed behind Mrs Bainbridge. 'I do so hope that one day there will be children living here again.'

'Oh, yes . . . what a wonderful place for children,' Tess said, eyes shining, looking once more at Andrew. 'Isn't it, darling?'

He nodded, pleased at her response. He hadn't seen her act so positively when children were mentioned for a long time. Could it be that at last she was coming round to the idea of trying once more?

'You hope to have a family then?' Constance enquired with a slight smile as she filled the teapot with hot water from the silver jug. 'If you'll excuse my impertinence in asking.'

'Of course.' Tess smiled, looked across to him. 'We always wanted a large family, in fact. But we decided it was best to wait until we are really finally settled in the house we want to stay in. The forever house if you like.'

'It's bad enough moving with just two of you,' Andrew said with a smile. 'Although babies don't always wait until the right time, do they? About three years ago . . .'

Tess shushed him with a look and luckily Constance seemed not to notice, messing about with milk and sugar as she was.

'I always imagined I would have a large family,' Constance said, once their cups were refilled. 'But sometimes things don't work out quite as planned.'

Her voice made it perfectly clear that there would be no discussion on that point and Andrew glanced anxiously at Tess, aware that sometimes she was less sensitive than he, willing her not to ask any questions.

She did not.

They talked about the village and Constance told them something of its history and of the history of the house itself, and afterwards she took them on a conducted tour that lasted some considerable time. Room after room. A library. A gentleman's study. Upper rooms that he supposed were the original servants' quarters. A hotchpotch of kitchen areas. Little corridors and funny little larders. A bathroom that was out of the ark and a separate lavatory that was the size of their shower room.

Tess would have lingered but Constance was brisk and they returned to the drawing room at last where she bade them sit down again. Andrew refrained from glancing at his watch. He had hoped they might take the chance to make an exit when they were in the hall but the moment passed.

A ginger cat joined them this time.

'It has been most pleasant,' Constance said, smiling down at the cat as it circled the rug. 'Thank you for joining me this afternoon. And I do hope that both of you will be able to come along to the bonfire party on November the fifth, of course. The event here was initiated by my husband Colonel Makepeace many years ago and the entire village is invited, with the ladies of the church guild providing the refreshments. Hot soup, baked potatoes and sausages – Mr Simpson's own, I believe.'

'That sounds wonderful,' Tess said. 'Thank you. We shall certainly be along. Won't we, darling?'

Relieved as Constance finally rose to her feet, Andrew smiled his agreement. It sounded fun, in fact. More fun than tea. The children would enjoy it. He must remember to mention it to Yvonne.

A final flurry and they were off, Tess in the passenger seat this time.

'It went very well,' she said. 'Don't you think?'

'OK. A bit best-behaviour stuff though, wasn't it? I thought you said there wouldn't be cucumber sandwiches?'

She laughed. 'And a silver teapot? The genuine article too. It was so elegant. I was terrified you were going to break one of those beautiful china cups.'

'I am house-trained you know.' He smiled, not offended. 'She was a bit short with that housekeeper, wasn't she?'

'It's how they behave, people like that,' Tess said. 'She's from a different era, Andrew. She's very classy, don't you think?'

'Why did she ask us? Or does she do it to everybody in the village? Are they all waiting with bated breath for their official invite. Is there a rota?'

'Don't be flippant. There was a serious purpose,' Tess said and he noticed her hesitation before she continued. 'You know I mentioned that West House might be ours? Well . . . I've been told by a certain source whom I shall not name that she intends to sell it. Next spring. She's moving into a little cottage she owns.'

'Is she now? She didn't say anything.'

'No. I know she didn't.' Tess laughed. 'And I know why she didn't. We're not supposed to know, you see. She's busy deciding who's to have it. She wants to sell it to us, Andrew. I just know she wants to sell it to us.'

'Does she?' At a loss, he shook his head. 'Are you sure? You do get some mad ideas sometimes. We couldn't afford it anyway.'

'Not at its true value, no, but she's not interested in money. We have to take it slowly. Give her time to come to a definite decision. But we have made a very good initial impression. Thank you, darling, for being so nice to her.'

'No more than she deserved,' he said. 'She's a nice old lady. A bit stiff and formal, but nice.'

'She has a very expressive face. Didn't you notice? I think she's hiding something. Something in the past. Did you get that impression?'

'Yes. Sorry, I nearly blurted things out about the baby. Can't think why.'

'It wasn't the right time to tell her about that,' she said. 'It might come in useful later.'

Useful?

'You sounded pretty cheerful back there,' he said as he pulled into their drive. 'That bit about us having a family. Does that mean you feel ready to talk about it again?'

'For God's sake, Andrew,' she said, slipping out of her seat-belt and turning to smile at him. 'You are an idiot sometimes. Didn't it dawn I was just saying that to sweeten her up? I didn't mean it for a minute. I'll say anything she wants to hear. She can't hold us to anything once the house is ours. And *no,* I am not ready to talk about that, so please don't even try.'

She was off.

Locking up, he followed more slowly.

He'd just been taken for a ride.

# 17

Constance was going to have a word with her solicitor at some point to draw up the necessary documents. She had almost decided that she would let the O'Gradys have West House for a sum to be arranged. Something easily within their grasp. She knew she could not give it away for that might cause all manner of legal complications and Mr Nicholls her solicitor would huff and puff at such action. He would complain in any case that she was being foolish.

She knew him well, however, and he knew that, once her mind was made up, that was it. He would know better than to drag out a sulk, legal or otherwise. She could telephone now, this very moment, but there was no rush, was there? She had set spring as her target for moving and spring it would be. She wanted as little interruption to her life as possible and she certainly did not want the new people, pleasant as they were, impinging on her whilst she was still in residence. Measuring up and such like.

The good news – and she knew they would be delighted, both of them – the good news could wait.

She had felt a touch unwell this morning, had staggered down to the kitchen to make her early cup of tea and returned promptly to bed. Mrs Bainbridge would be along shortly but, in the meantime, she would rest and perhaps forego her visit to the teashop. Smith had followed her upstairs and was now sitting – Ella would explode with indignation – on her bed.

The tea helped relieve her queasiness but she resisted the impulse to get up and remained where she was. For a moment, when she had entertained the O'Gradys to tea, she had felt quite ridiculously like confiding in them about dearest Margaret. She had not of course. She had never confided in anyone. After the birth, she had been relieved when she realised that her family preferred not to discuss it. She had certainly not talked to the servants although they had been extra nice to her.

'People are embarrassed by tragedy,' she told Smith, waiting for him to complete his ablutions, before patting a spot beside her. 'There . . . you are a very clean cat,' she said, stroking his silky back. For his age, he was remarkable. That made two of them. 'You see, Smith, after Margaret I had no desire to have another child. One could not substitute. What a ridiculous idea. Margaret was Margaret. And, in any case, I was so frightened of going through it again. I was a little afraid of men. Oh, I was flirtatious enough because I was beautiful and beautiful women are flirtatious, but sex – excuse me – was quite different. Hugh understood, at least I think he understood. He knew all about Archie and Margaret and how I stole Archie from Grace. So unfortunate that it should happen a second time, although Hugh seemed to find it amusing. He was aware of my feelings before we married. He said he loved me and we would work things out. I wonder though, sometimes, if Grace was right.'

Grace had accused her of taking Hugh simply because he was hers. All her life, she said, Constance had taken things that belonged to her. It began with dolls when they were small, graduated to items of clothing and then to her men. Grace maintained that Constance did not want Archie nor Hugh, not really, but because they were Grace's . . .

Grace was wrong about Archie. She had so wanted Archie.

Perhaps Grace was right about Hugh but it was her fault for being so timid about such things. She ought to have fought like a tigress for her man instead of letting him go so feebly.

She wondered if she ought to talk to the cat about such private things. Sexual matters were not something one ought to talk about. Although she and Hugh shared a bedroom, they did not share a bed for some time after they married. There was only one way as far as she was concerned, one sure way, to avoid another pregnancy and that was abstention from sexual intercourse. And so they abstained. For almost a year. She chose not to enquire what other arrangements Hugh might have made during that time but, whatever they were, he was discreet. There was the apartment in London and his club where he spent weekends on occasions and she did not accompany him. London had too many unhappy memories for her. All their married life, he had kept in touch with a close circle of his friends that she chose not to become intimate with. It meant weekends away on his own from time to time visiting his friends up in Scotland and over in the Lakes. She rarely accompanied him, quite content to stay at home. She supposed it was fair to say that their marriage, although not exactly one of convenience at the outset for she had entertained romantic dreams for a while, had eventually turned into that.

There was a knock on the door and, hastily in a comic panic, Constance shooed Smith off the bed lest Ella should see him.

'Are you all right, Mrs Makepeace?' Ella was full of concern. 'You should have rung and we would have come earlier if you were feeling poorly. Oh dear, you only look moderate and that's a fact. I don't like your colour.'

'I am all right now. I was a little queasy first thing,' Constance said with a smile. 'I shall get up in a few minutes but I will not be going down to the teashop. Perhaps you would be so kind as to inform Miss Green or she will worry.'

'Right you are. I'll do you some dry toast, Mrs Makepeace, and another big pot of tea. Down in the kitchen in half an hour. Shall I draw the curtains for you? It's not a bad day although there's a touch of frost on the hill.'

'Thank you.' Constance inclined her head and Mrs Bainbridge closed the door.

Arrangements were in hand for the bonfire evening. The vicar was nominally in charge of proceedings, organising the bonfire which was piling up in one of the side meadows. There would be fireworks and they would stand round the bonfire warming themselves. Constance looked forward to it for it was always such a splendid event and this year the O'Gradys had promised to come along so that would be extra special. Their very first bonfire supper at West House. She so hoped they would continue the tradition and now that Tess had been persuaded to attend church, there was no reason why they should not. Poor Tess. She had so wanted to come along to St Cuthbert's but been a little shy at the thought. Constance knew why. Some of the ladies of the church guild were most off-putting. Tess need have no fears. Constance would make sure she was made very welcome. She would see to it personally.

Toast and tea were waiting in the kitchen.

Mrs Bainbridge sat down with her.

She had bad news to impart. Mr Porter, the retired postman, had dropped dead last night. Just like that. Keeled right over. But then he'd had this flushed look for years. Unhealthy in Ella's medical opinion. Mrs Keller's cottage on Lilac Lane had been broken into and her jewellery stolen. And Mrs Laidler had been rushed off to hospital. Ella had been unable to ascertain yet what was the matter with her although in her opinion she'd been a bad colour for months. Yellowish tinge. Liver, isn't it? Or was it kidneys? Poor woman. Lost her husband last year to cancer. You can get caught with things if you're at a low ebb. Something to do with your immune system, she'd read.

'Are you feeling any better yourself, Mrs Makepeace? Your colour's a bit better now.'

'Yes, thank you.'

'Nice couple, weren't they? The young couple from Churchwood Close who came for tea?'

'Yes, Ella. Very nice. Quite charming.'

'Any particular reason, Mrs Makepeace? For them coming for tea?'

Constance sighed. 'In confidence, Ella – and I mean in confidence – I think I would like them to live here.'

'Oh . . . I thought that might be it. I think that's a good idea,' Ella said with a smile. 'Very classy, she is. Smart suits she wears. There'll be flowers all over. She has a knack with flowers. And he's a nice man. You only have to look at him to know. You can tell with some people, can't you? My Mr Bainbridge for example . . . I knew the minute I saw him. I just knew he'd look after me and I was no picture even when I was young. Love at first sight it was. Do you believe in that, Mrs Makepeace?'

'I'm glad you approve my choice,' Constance said, choosing to ignore the question. It was none of her business. 'Nothing must be said to them yet, though. I want to choose my moment carefully. After Christmas, I think. Yes, Ella . . . the more I think of it, the more I see them installed here. Tess wants a large family, you know. And she loves the house. I showed them round. They both loved it, in fact. I watched their reaction very closely. They will look after it for me. I am making the right decision, aren't I?'

She looked at Mrs Bainbridge, surprised to find herself asking the question of her housekeeper. It was unlike her to have doubts. Perhaps she needed reassurance.

True to form, Mrs Bainbridge provided it.

Ella looked round her own little living room with some pleasure. There wasn't a thing out of place. They had a red fitted carpet, a three piece suite, a nest of tables, and Bernard had made some shelves beside the fireplace where she could put her ornaments and some books, mainly his gardening books, for one of his pleasures on a winter's evening was sitting reading. She liked tapestry work herself although she had to watch she did not overdo it on account of her bad arm.

It had been nice enough living up at West House up on the top floor but she had started to worry about what would happen when Mrs Makepeace passed on. She'd always wanted a little place of her own. She wouldn't thank you to live in that big house nor could they afford it. The heating bills for a start would be a king's ransom. No, she and Bernard were better off in their own place. After all these years they finally had their own place.

It was cosy and clean and Bernard had his bit of garden. Everything they ever wanted.

It was the best decision Mrs Makepeace had made for a long time, moving out, although Ella wished she'd do the right thing and put the house with an estate agent, do everything proper. All this underhand business . . . but then she was such a one for secrets. The couple she had picked seemed nice enough. He'd given her a lovely smile when Mrs Makepeace had gone all hoity-toity like she sometimes did. Liked to remind you who she was, the Colonel's lady, from a nearly titled family down in Cornwall or wherever it was.

'According to Miss Green at the teashop . . .'

Bernard shook his head, sitting across the fire from her in his chair. He lit his pipe. Smiled at her in that way of his.

'Not gossip is it, Ella pet?'

'No it is not, man. I was just asking a few questions about Mrs Makepeace,' she said. 'Out of neighbourly concern. Some of it I knew already, of course, but I had to let her talk once she got started. She does very nice scones with homemade jam. Anyway, she told me that when they moved here, he – that husband of hers – was in Parliament. They had a child. A boy. Three or four he was, or so Miss Green thought. I guessed as much although it's like getting blood out of a stone getting Mrs Makepeace to tell you anything . . .' she leaned forward conspiratorially, lowered her voice. 'Listen to this . . . Miss Green says they went up to Scotland on holiday. It was Coronation Year, she thinks . . . Well, they came back without the little boy or at least they came back with his body. Mrs Makepeace was in a terrible state but she did not want people to know all the gory details so all she would say was that it was the result of an accident. Anyway, he drowned.'

'I know,' Bernard said quietly. 'She told me once.'

'Who did?'

'Mrs Makepeace.' He puffed on his pipe, unconcerned.

'Bernard Bainbridge! And you never told *me*!' she said, voice rising. 'We don't have secrets. Why didn't you tell me?'

'I didn't want to talk about it. It upset me,' he said. 'She was very matter of fact. One day she just said that . . .' He thought hard a minute. 'She said that if I didn't mind, Mr Bainbridge, she would prefer me not to talk about the fat stream because her little boy Thomas had drowned up in Scotland and it was inclined to remind her of it. Well . . . that was it. I haven't mentioned it to her since.'

'I have,' Ella said with a frown. 'Oh dear me. I mentioned it when I was talking about that cat. Fancy her not telling me and telling you. Funny woman she is. Drowned? I wonder what happened exactly. How did he drown? Did she tell you that?'

'I don't know. Does it matter how? It doesn't matter whether you drown in a bath or in the middle of Loch Lomond. You're still dead.'

'Poor soul. It doesn't bear thinking about, does it?'

'No.' Bernard leaned back in his chair. 'That's why I don't.'

# 18

Yvonne knew that Andrew was avoiding her. It was of course because she had kissed him after all that fuss with her keys at the supermarket. She didn't know why she had done it because she might have known he would react like that.

She was beginning to develop extraordinary feelings for him and she was frankly worried sick about them. If she didn't know it was impossible at her age, she'd say she had a crush on him. There'd once been a boy when she was fifteen whom she'd hankered after and she felt hot now at some of the awfully indiscreet things she had done to try to grab his attention. He had never of course given her a second glance, not once, for he had been nineteen himself and he had thought himself much too sophisticated. It happened to all young girls and was just part of growing up.

But now she *was* grown up and she had to stop thinking silly thoughts like this. She was a married woman and it didn't matter at all that it was falling apart around her, for Andrew was married too and therefore out of bounds. Whether or not *he* was happily married was completely beside the point. Maybe Tess was different at home, softer and nicer. Maybe.

She had big problems of her own.

Robin had cried off the next weekend he was due home. Something about his holiday quota, something to do with him having given notice, that she did not understand, something that sounded suspiciously like an excuse. What she did understand was that it was too late for them. She had, in their very last telephone call, given him an ultimatum. Them – her and the children – or the expedition. He had told her then how much he loved them all, how much he wished he could settle into an ordinary job, live with them all the time, how much he had agonised over what to do.

She waited for the 'but' and of course it eventually came. She did not understand, he said, what diving meant to him. Not the sort of commercial diving he'd been doing these last few years, God no, but what he called proper diving.

He could not turn this chance down. If he turned it down, there were half a dozen other divers just waiting. Jean-Louis had some fantastic dives planned, any number of them, and Jean-Louis had done him this tremendous favour asking him to come on board knowing full well he was married with a family. He normally played safe and went for single guys, guys who had no strings attached.

That had really done it. That he thought of them as an encumbrance, as his 'strings'. She had exploded, she remembered, although having a full scale row on the phone is not at all satisfactory. Calming down at last, spoiling everything by weeping, she recalled his own voice as he tried to make her 'see reason', as he put it. Surely she'd seen it coming? Each time he came home it was getting harder and harder for him to adjust, for them to adjust. It was not fair on the children either. They would be better apart. They each coped in their own way with being alone. The children were well adjusted and happy and they would accept and understand the principal of divorce if it was put to them in a matter-of-fact way.

'Don't tell me how to deal with them, Robin. I've been doing it on my own for long enough,' she said, weary of him now, only half listening to the pitiful excuses.

Long term, he just couldn't face it. Domestic life. It was better that he admitted it, that she recognised it now, that they went their separate ways, or did she want it to drift on for years as it could do?

'You should have thought of all that when we got married, before we had children,' she said, bitterness surfacing. 'You should have stayed single, Robin. Oh . . . just go and enjoy yourself but don't expect me to sit here and wait for you to tire of it. I want a divorce.'

'That's what I'm trying to say. You shall have one,' he told her, the relief in his voice the final nail in the coffin. He would make sure she was all right financially, he told her, she and the children. He would be able to pay off the house and he would continue to provide her with her allowance until such time as she felt she could manage without. He hoped she would find someone else eventually.

She couldn't stand him being *nice* to her.

She had cried herself to sleep that night, quietly so as not to disturb the children, and since then she was coping on automatic pilot. Taking the children to school, spending her days as she always spent her days, picking them up from school. The house had never looked so sparklingly clean. Routine was a comfort. All the time she was trying to remember the old days, the good times with Robin, but they were fading fast and all she could remember now was how she had lost him to the sea. Melodramatic but true. It might have been easier if she'd lost him to another woman.

She'd been up to West House a couple more times with the books for Mrs Makepeace. The last time the housekeeper had dealt with her, making her wait in the hall, saying that Mrs Makepeace was taking a rest and would be unable to see her. It didn't matter. Yvonne saw the expression in the woman's eyes, the same expression as before, and although it hurt a little, it didn't really matter. Nothing mattered much. She supposed she would have to think of some way of resuming her career if it was possible. She needed independence. She had no wish to rely on handouts from Robin forever.

She sighed and turned her attention back to the matter in hand. It was her afternoon at Greenview Rest Home and Joan had asked her to take Agnes a cup of tea and maybe have a bit of a natter with her. The staff were a bit worried because Agnes was depressed.

Oh really!

'They tell me you're down in the dumps, Agnes,' she said as soon as they were settled with cups of strong tea and a slice of jam Swiss roll. 'Do you want to tell me why?'

'No. That's my business, girl,' she said briskly. 'Anyway, what's up with you? Don't look your usual self.'

'And what is my usual self?' Yvonne asked, raising her eyebrows.

'Blonde and real bonny,' Agnes said with a sly glance her way. For ninety-five she had surprisingly sharp eyes beneath the out-of-style spectacles. 'And you're not afraid to wear proper frocks and nice high heels. Fat behinds squashed into those blue trousers it is nowadays and nothing else. You brighten up my day, Mrs Lonsdale, and that's a fact.'

'Do I?' Yvonne smiled a little, looked out of the window that overlooked Front Street and the green. 'Good view, haven't you? You can see everything that's going on from here.'

'I can,' she said with satisfaction. 'Makes being in prison worthwhile, having a view. No bars on the window.'

'Don't start on that, Agnes. I'll take you out for a walk now if you want, this very minute.'

'I don't want. You're dangerous with that wheelchair, girl. I don't trust you. You'll fire me off into the road one of these days.'

Yvonne smiled across at her. Despite the fact that she'd been coming to Greenview for about a year, she knew very little about Agnes at all. All she did know was that she liked her. She must have been feisty when she was young. Still was.

'I see those children of yours regularly,' Agnes went on after a moment. 'Going to school. Coming back. That older girl seems to like talking.'

'Portia's a chatterbox,' Yvonne said with a proud smile. 'We try to walk most days. If we're in a rush we have to use the car but I don't want them to get into the habit of doing that. They should walk.'

'You're a sensible lass, then. Who's that fella who sometimes picks them up? Worried me it did the first time I spotted him. Who the hell's that, I thought, with Mrs Lonsdale's children? I knew your husband was away. I nearly asked somebody to ring the police.'

'That was Andrew. My neighbour. He baby-sits sometimes. Sometimes he just picks them up for me if I have something else on. I've started going to an afternoon class on Tuesdays and Thursdays and he says he doesn't mind looking after them for a while until I get back.'

'Does he not have children of his own then?'

'No.'

'Married, is he?'

'Yes.'

'Recipe for disaster, that,' Agnes said, blowing on her tea before taking a sip. 'You mark my words.'

'Oh no, it's perfectly all right. I trust him with them.'

'I didn't mean *that,*' she said, showing her yellow teeth. 'I meant you. You're married, aren't you? And he is. Both of you to somebody else.'

'Yes.'

'Well then . . .'

'Well what? Honestly, Agnes, are you going daft?' she said, feeling herself go hot. 'I don't know what you're trying to imply . . .'

'Yes, you do,' she said at once. 'You're blushing, girl. A married woman at that . . . blushing.'

'It's you, you old bat,' she said cheerfully, deciding to go for attack. 'You have nothing better to do than invent all sorts of intrigue. Intrigue in Bishopsmeade . . . honestly!'

'I may be an old bat,' Agnes said delightedly, 'but I'm a clever old bat. You forget, Mrs Lonsdale, that I buried three husbands. I know all there is to know about gentlemen. They're all the same, every single one. They have trouble with their instincts, you know. We can twist them round our little fingers, we can. Out-manoeuvre, you see. It took me two goes before I struck lucky. The first two were mistakes. I'll tell you about them some day. But the last one – my Jimmy – he was my half. You know what I mean?'

'Philosopher now, are you, Agnes?' Yvonne smiled, glanced at her watch. She didn't want to cut the conversation short but she was getting a bit pushed for time.

'What's he like then?'

'Like? Well . . . he's a very nice man. Quiet. The children like him a lot. Samantha's always talking about him. It's Mr O'Grady this, Mr O'Grady that . . .'

Agnes sniffed. 'I didn't mean *him*. I meant your husband, Mrs Lonsdale. It's funny how he was the one to spring to mind. This Mr O'Grady.'

'I see. Sorry . . .' Embarrassed, Yvonne dared not look her in the eye. Wily old bird!

'You'd better get yourself off to collect those children of yours,' Agnes said, the yellow teeth flashing. 'And if you want to talk about it, here I am. Stuck here. Not going anywhere. Can't get anywhere under my own steam these days.'

'I'll take you out for a walk next week whether you want to go or not, you old meddler.'

Yvonne collected her belongings together, smiled to show she had not meant any offence.

'I'll remind you about that. You can push me up the hill if you want,' Agnes said, giving her a sharp look up and down. 'Get some of that fat off your behind. We'll talk some more about your love life. Nothing you say will shock me. I've seen it all.' The sigh was one of content. 'Thank you, Mrs Lonsdale. I haven't had such a good talk in a long time.'

Joan pounced on her before she left.

'Cheer her up?' she asked. 'Oh, good . . . I know I can rely on you.'

Andrew was beginning to enjoy the time they spent together, him and the children. He treasured the little moments. It miffed Tess, of course, so he didn't say too much about it, although just now she was totally preoccupied. This promised to be one helluva surprise party. He hoped Joe would appreciate all the effort Tess was putting into it.

After The Kiss, he had avoided Yvonne for a while, desperately embarrassed, but when they finally did meet she greeted him as if it had not happened. It was a touch disappointing. Had it meant nothing to her? Had it really just been a little impulsive thank-you? She ought not to have kissed him on the lips, though.

So he would forget it as she obviously had. He concentrated on the children instead. Portia Lonsdale was some little girl. Bright and intelligent, and he liked the way she wasn't palmed off with half an answer. Portia wanted to know what was what. If she kept that up, she'd end up as some no-nonsense female in a suit rather like Tess. No . . . not quite like Tess for Portia had a gentle streak in her that often showed in the way she treated the younger children. Maternally inclined, Portia.

She came out with all sorts of indiscretions, though, which

could be embarrassingly direct. For instance, Mummy had said a naughty word and banged the telephone down on the table the other day, knocking the vase over. Daddy had been cross on the phone, you see, Portia explained earnestly, and Andrew had had to stop her there before she said something more.

He smiled a little. Poor Yvonne, for it sounded as if she was letting it get to her, being stuck here on her own. However much he wished he could help in some way, he had no time to spend on her problems as he had enough of his own. Tess was driving him mad these days. She was all business. She was excluding him more and more from her life and he did not like it.

The tea party at West House had been a bit of an eye opener. Was she really so calculating? Did she intend to wheedle her way into Constance Makepeace's affections, that nice old thing, just so she would let them have her beloved house, for it was no exaggeration to say it was beloved to her? Andrew was uncomfortable about the whole damned thing. He would never have gone with Tess if he'd known the reason why they were there. As to her telling Constance, quite clearly, that they intended to have a family, a large one at that, when she had no bloody intention . . . that was unforgivable. That had really shaken him. For the first time ever, he'd looked at Tess with fresh eyes. He didn't want to ask her outright for he was almost afraid of the answer, but he was beginning to think now that he would never be a father – at least not with Tess.

When you took away the sexual attraction he felt for her, and it was still there, what was left? Not much, and the thought scared him because, although he still loved her, he was finding this hard to cope with. Her callousness. He saw now that he'd suspected it after the baby but had refused to believe it.

He sighed, felt a little hand slip into his and looked down at Samantha.

'Cold?' he asked. 'Come on, let's hurry back.'

It was foggy and very chill at three thirty in the afternoon and icy steam drifted across the surface of the fat stream as they crossed it on their way home. They had got into a routine these Tuesdays and Thursdays. Juice and sandwiches or cake when they got in, nothing elaborate, just something to keep them going until Yvonne got back and they had their tea proper. She certainly fed them well from the glowing descriptions they gave. As requested, he did not sit them in front of the television . . . well, only occasionally . . . and despite tuts from Tess, he had bought a few books and games to keep here so that they had something to occupy them.

'Right gang, coats off,' he said as soon as they were in the warm.

It was getting dark already on such a dismal day and he drew the curtains over, piling their anoraks on the stairs and leading them into the kitchen. Samantha presented him a little shyly with a picture she had drawn. Endearingly, it was of him. Wearing his green shirt and jeans. His hair had a touch of Afro about it and his ears stuck out alarmingly as did his arms but he imagined, as he dutifully admired it, that somewhere, somehow, she had caught the essence. Yvonne was right. Samantha was artistic.

It could pass for Robin at a pinch, he thought, as he placed it reverently on the table. He could hardly keep it. On the other hand, why the hell not? He was certainly not throwing it away, not when Samantha had taken such trouble with it. Her name – Sam – was printed in big uneven letters at the top.

Portia helped put the sandwiches on the plates. Carefully put the jam tarts on another, sticking her finger in a bright red one so that she could claim it for herself.

'My daddy's going to live on a ship,' she told him, looking guilty as he caught her licking her fingers. 'In the Mediterranean.' She said the word slowly and carefully and absolutely correctly, as if she was spelling it out.

Andrew said, 'Is he? I'll show you where that is later on the map.'

'I know where it is,' she said. 'Mummy showed me. He's going to dive in the water. Find a cave. Find the treasure. He won't be able to come home for a very very long time because he's going to live there for ever and ever. But he still loves us. Very very much.'

'Right.'

Calmly, Andrew carried the plates to the table. Poured out their juice. This did not sound good. This sounded to him as if Robin was giving up on them. However, he couldn't quiz Portia.

That wouldn't be right. He would have to pretend he did not know if Yvonne said anything at all.

As was their habit, he left Portia in charge of them for a half hour whilst he did some work in his office but tonight he could not concentrate. Poor Yvonne. How could Robin do that to her? It sounded very much as if he was going off on some expedition and just leaving her.

One thing he did know. If Yvonne was his, he most certainly would not leave her. Not for a minute.

He heard Yvonne's car and was waiting for her when she rang the bell.

'They haven't been any trouble, Andrew, have they?'

Her entry words. Almost a password.

'Not at all. They've had a sandwich and a jam tart,' he told her, watching her closely. She was much the same as usual, pretty in blue, but was there a slight puffiness round the eyes? Could she have been crying?

The children, under Portia's supervision, were getting their coats on and Samantha had retrieved the picture from the table to show her mummy.

'Oh, how nice!' Yvonne said with a smile. 'Look, Andrew . . . Daddy.'

'It's not Daddy,' Samantha said crossly. 'It's Andrew.'

'Mr O'Grady to you, please,' Yvonne said with a fixed smile, folding the picture carefully. For some reason, Andrew had the oddest feeling it would not find its way onto the kitchen wall.

Over the children's heads, he and Yvonne exchanged another smile. She was looking gorgeous in a fluffy blue sweater and a softly flowing darker skirt, her hair up tonight, clustered earrings glittering, her neck smooth and pink, face just a little raw from the early evening air.

'We'll see you Friday for the bonfire,' she said as they got ready to leave. 'We're looking forward to it.'

She was not looking at him now, busying rather with the children.

'Say *thank you, Mr O'Grady, for looking after us,*' she instructed as usual.

They piped up and he smiled, waving as they went down the

path. When he closed the door on them, it felt very quiet. A little lost.

Tess would be home soon and it would be party, party, party. Thank God it would all be over soon.

Yvonne had taken the picture with her, which was a pity. He thought of it, the child's basic drawing, and felt a stupid lump in his throat. Nobody had ever done that before. Liked him enough to draw a picture of him. Just as well it was gone, though, because it would have irritated Tess if she had seen it. In a strange way, it was as if she was jealous of his attachment to them.

He went to make the tea and, by the time Tess rushed in, it was all ready. Because he felt a bit guilty about his earlier thoughts, he made a very special effort. Pale blue cloth, candles, the best china. A creamy chocolate and walnut concoction for dessert that had taken ages and looked wonderful.

'I haven't time to eat,' she said. 'I have about a hundred final phone calls to make. You have no idea, Andrew, how much organising this is taking. And Stephanie is no help whatsoever.'

'I thought you told her to leave it to you,' he said, looking at the heap of curry. 'Sure you won't eat?'

She shook her head.

'Stick the rest of it in the freezer,' she said, as she headed purposefully for the phone.

# 19

Tess was growing impatient at the lack of interest in their house. Nobody this last month, and it was a loose end she could do to tie up. She would switch estate agents, for this one was proving worse than useless. Wouldn't it be wonderful if she could just casually drop the news to Constance sometime? *Oh, by the way, we've sold our house and we're on the look-out for something else in Bishopsmeade. A bit of a panic, really. The people who are moving in want to get things off the ground so goodness knows what we shall do until we find the right house.* Maybe it was something to do with her extreme old age but Tess felt that subtlety was lost on Constance.

On top of all the worry about this, she was concerned about Andrew and that bitch of a woman next door. She had him hanging on a string. Blondes, busty ones at that, could very nearly get away with murder. Just who the hell did she think she was, dumping the kids on him like she did?

Once it could be forgiven, just about, but not any more, not when it was happening on a regular basis now.

She'd had it out last night, not very satisfactorily, with Andrew. He'd been a bit huffy anyway because she hadn't wanted his damned curry. She didn't know why he bothered making such a fuss about meals. If he shopped in town, he could get a week's supply of frozen dinners from Marks & Spencer and just pop them in the microwave. They did superb curries but that wasn't good enough for him, was it; he had to spend hours chopping and dicing and acting like a martyr. Andrew was being a pain, in fact, ever since they'd been to West House for tea. The only good thing to come out of that, was that if

Andrew had been fully taken in, then surely Constance would have been too.

'Yvonne would have to pay somebody else,' she told him last night. 'A considerable amount at that. I don't know how much per hour.'

'Pay for what?'

She looked at him, mystified sometimes at his complete innocence.

'For baby-sitting,' she explained patiently. 'It's beyond a joke. You are working at home, for God's sake, earning a living, and it's time you told her that. It's not fair of her to keep dropping those three off at any old time and expecting you to drop everything and look after them for a couple of hours or whatever. That first time – all right, that was an emergency – but recently . . . honestly, Andrew, she has no business joining an afternoon class or whatever the hell it is she does – have you asked? – for all we know it could be something extremely sordid. She might be operating a brothel. She looks the sort.'

He pounced angrily on that and she wished she hadn't said it. She hadn't meant it. It was just a joke. OK, it wasn't very funny but it was coming to something when he couldn't take a joke now, not about Yvonne. He said again that it was only an hour and a bit and he didn't mind in the least.

'I mind,' she said, unwisely unable to let the matter drop. 'I mind a lot. I mind that she's getting away with it. If you won't tell her, Andrew, then I will. And you know me, I'm not afraid of speaking my mind. Just you tell her straight she has to make proper alternative arrangements for the children and you're very sorry etc, etc, but you're too busy to help on a permanent basis. How does that sound? Reasonable?'

'Leave it with me,' he had said.

Tess sighed now as she thought about the conversation. She didn't believe for a minute he would do anything about it so it would be left to her as usual to sort out, but it would have to wait its turn.

Tonight it was her father's surprise birthday party and she felt dizzy herself with anticipation as she dressed for the party. She was going along early leaving Andrew to follow. She was after all the organiser and she wanted to check personally that everything was in hand. Two of her girls had been there all afternoon attending to the flowers, the arrangements exactly to Tess's requirements; the hotel up in Gosforth had a wonderful reputation for providing perfect buffets, the jazz quartet was confirmed today, and the guest-list was complete.

She was wearing a new dress. The little black dress with those little special touches that made it worthy of its price tag. Stephanie would be wearing a new dress too. A scarlet affair that would drain all the colour from her but for once she had been adamant and Tess had been unable to persuade her otherwise. She was glad the shopping trip was over. It had not been a success for Stephanie tended to forget the purpose of the visit, drifting into old bookshops given half a chance, browsing through shelves of boring old books. She had even bought a few text books on the Roman Empire. Oh, well, each to his taste. The books had set her off and she had given Tess what amounted to a lecture on the journey home. It was only as Tess recognised names, could acquaint it with an old television series starring Derek Jacobi, that she could show any interest whatsoever. They had the video somewhere amongst their huge collection. Pretty good, she remembered. She must watch it again soon, refresh her memory.

On the journey to the hotel, she memorised the names of all the people who mattered, people in Joe's organisation who pulled all the strings. Tess greatly admired her father. She closed her eyes to the fiddles for, after all, didn't everybody do it given the chance? He'd hopped about from organisation to organisation for the last ten years, always one step ahead of them, moving on before the shit hit the fan, as he had once said to her.

She must make sure she circulated tonight, make sure people were aware who she was, make damned sure they took her name on board. She would have to ditch Andrew while she was doing this because he was singularly unhelpful, hopeless at playing up to people.

It had annoyed her considerably that he'd thought fit to mention the coming bonfire evening at West House to Yvonne. She was now of course bringing her family along and Andrew had even fixed it, damn him, that they were walking up together in a big happy gang. *Walking* up! It would take God knows how long to walk when it was minutes by car.

Perhaps it wouldn't be too bad after all as the children would want to get a grandstand view of the fireworks being lit. Yvonne would have to stay and supervise them and Tess and Andrew could slip away and help with the refreshments. Anything to ensure a prominent presence. They had to be seen. Constance had to see them.

First things first though, and she must concentrate now on Joe's party.

It was going to be just superb.

Arriving at the hotel before any of the guests, Tess checked the arrangements one last time. All that remained now was for that simpering stepmother of hers to get her father here on time, suspecting nothing, of course. Tess thought they had kept the secret. She had spoken to her father on the phone only yesterday and he had not given any inkling at all that he knew. In fact, he had seemed a touch preoccupied and when she questioned him as to why, he had said it was nothing for her to worry her pretty head about. Coming from anyone else, she would have clocked them one for that, but she allowed it from him. Having a man, be it father or husband, who worshipped the ground you walked on was an advantage the sensible woman ought to play up to for all it was worth.

She left the musicians, who certainly looked the part in their cream jackets and crimson bow ties, to tune up. There was a beautiful white piano, gleaming saxophones, clarinets and other instruments, and they were set up on a small stage off to one side. It was a gracious function room, long and narrow, gold and red, and the curtains were undrawn so that the guests could look out onto the softly lit garden. People could take a turn in the garden later in the evening if the champagne got the better of them.

Tess greeted people now, a few early stragglers, as they arrived, splitting them off easily in her mind into work and social people. There were some friends of his, long lost friends, whom Stephanie had asked along. People who would no doubt remember her mother. A touch insensitive of Stephanie, for those people were bound to compare the two wives and, like West

House and Churchwood Close, there *was* no comparison. Some of these people, Tess noticed with irritation, looked distinctly the worse for wear already and they hadn't even started. Tess was not remotely interested in them.

His colleagues from work she kept a close eye on, having made damned sure they knew who she was and what business she was in. A bit off, perhaps, to tout for any actual business here tonight but, if the opportunity presented, she didn't see why she should act coy. Might as well grab it if she could. The big bold arrangements had one of her pink-edged display cards in a prominent position so there was no doubt they had been done by O'Grady Floral Design. Just in case, she had a few business cards tucked into the little black clutch bag she was carrying.

Joe's boss of bosses was called Ivan Oakes, a tall slim snake-like man with black eyes and an arrogant manner. Early forties, Tess imagined, considerably younger than her father anyway. Joe had opposed the appointment a couple of years ago and was off-hand when he talked about him, dismissing him as some sort of computer upstart. There'd been rumours a while back about takeovers but Ivan had scotched them and her father had not mentioned it again.

'Mr Oakes . . . so glad you could come along,' Tess said, smiling as she reached him and a gangly-looking gingery woman she took to be his wife. 'We've had such fun these last few weeks trying to organise this without my father knowing. Thank you so much for keeping the secret. It can't have been easy.'

'I hope nobody ever organises a surprise birthday for me,' his wife said anxiously, glancing at him. 'I should die.'

'You don't know Joe, darling, like we do. He will love it,' Ivan said, holding onto Tess's hand a little longer than necessary, rather too firmly at that for her liking. 'We can always rely on him when it comes to the social life as his expense sheet proves. He reckons half his job is conducted over lunch. Or dinner.'

'Or breakfast?' Tess suggested with a laugh, managing to extricate her hand without it looking as if she was snubbing him.

'Still, as long as the orders keep on coming, we can't complain, can we?'

Tess caught the look he exchanged with his worried wife, felt a moment's anxiety herself, but couldn't think why. Joe had been with the company far longer than Ivan so there shouldn't be any serious problems that her father couldn't handle. Joe could hold his own in the dirty tricks department, headed it in fact.

'Do help yourself to nibbles,' she said. 'I'll be back to you later. Must circulate.'

Andrew had drifted in, standing just inside the door a moment, looking terrific in his dinner suit. For a split second, quite without warning, her heart tumbled as in the old days. Ridiculous. For all his faults, and he had a good many irritating ones, he was dishy as hell. Awkward as hell too, just now, about this baby thing. He had a problem, he told her with that serious look of his, about lying to Constance Makepeace. Tess had no patience with it. For God's sake, did he or did he not want West House? What harm was there in saying they intended to have a large family if that's what dear Constance wanted to hear? If it pleased her to think that, then where was the harm? They weren't swearing on oath, perjuring themselves. The trouble with Andrew was he was too damned intense for his own good sometimes and far too honest.

'Darling . . .' She kissed him, pulled him into the room. 'Look like you're joining us, won't you? And do please smile. Go and talk to the people over there . . .' She indicated the group assembled near the far window. 'They're all old friends of his. God knows who most of them are. I have to keep circulating amongst the people from his office. Be careful what you say if you talk to Ivan Oakes. We'll catch up with each other later. OK?'

The band started jazzily up.

Tess looked round, pleased. They were good. Thank God for that. People began to relax, everybody looking oddly excited at the prospect of what was to come. The cake was huge. The presents, masses of them, were assembled on a separate table. Tess had no intention of letting Andrew know just how much this was costing her. Too much, of course, but this was one of the best hotels in the area and, like the dress, the quality showed. This had to come out of her own pocket. She could hardly ask her father to pay for his own surprise.

When they lived at West House, they could hold functions such as this at home which would please Andrew as it would save money. Tess wondered about knocking the library and second sitting room into one to make one huge salon, as it were. It would be wonderful for parties, although it was not the sort of thing to mention to Constance who would not want one single brick removed. She treated the place as if it was some sort of shrine but then she was a bit odd. Look at the way she fawned over that scraggy cat. A mere moggy, hardly pedigree.

'A word, Tess . . .'

'Of course, Ivan.' She gazed up at him through lowered eyelashes, a measured sexy look. He was a very sensual man and her reaction to him was deliberate. It was worth a try. Why not use her considerable sexual appeal, within reason? She had no intention, after all, of sleeping with him. In fact, sexually, she found him repellent. 'How can I help?'

'Would you like me to give a speech? Nothing elaborate. Just a few simple words to celebrate the old so-and-so reaching his half century. How fortunate the company's been to have him with us these past few years, that sort of thing.'

'Would you? How lovely! I'm sure my father will be delighted.' She glanced at her watch, pulled a wry face. 'Ten minutes to go. Stephanie did say they should arrive on time, so I think that perhaps we should quieten everybody down. He thinks he's coming for dinner, just the two of them.'

'And you've arranged all this to surprise him? He's a lucky man.'

Tess glanced sharply at him. She hoped it would never be necessary for her to enlist his help with her business. Quickly now, with the help of a little drum roll, she got everybody's attention, asking them to be quiet so that in a few more minutes, when they were told the car had arrived outside, they could begin the count-down.

'You will play Happy Birthday to You properly, won't you?' she said to the leader of the quartet, offending him profoundly but not caring. She did not want a jazzed up version that nobody recognised. In any case, she was paying them enough, so who were they to complain? 'When I give the signal.'

'You look beautiful,' Andrew murmured at her side. 'How much did that little number cost?'

'A lot,' she said, flashing him a smile just as she got the signal that the car had arrived in the car park.

'Quiet, everyone.'

Silence and a few subdued murmurings from the assembled guests. Smirks and smiles. The musicians' hands were poised. Listening hard, Tess could hear her father's voice, then Stephanie's girlish giggle.

The door opened and they stepped inside.

Tess gave the signal.

Surprisingly in key, they all launched into Happy Birthday to You, followed by a big round of applause for the birthday boy.

For a minute, her father looked quite startled and then, to Tess's relief, his face broke into a big smile and he rushed forward to greet everyone.

# 20

'Joe seems to be enjoying himself,' Andrew said, eventually finding Stephanie near the buffet table. 'Here, let me hold that for you while you get something to eat.'

'Thank you,' she said. 'But I've had something already and to be honest, Andrew, I'm almost too nervous to eat. I've had butterflies all day, worrying about it. But . . . you're right . . .' she glanced over to where Joe was holding court amongst a circle of his colleagues. 'Tess was right, as usual. He does seem to be enjoying it.'

'You look very nice tonight,' he said, knowing how much she needed reassurance. 'That's a lovely dress.'

'Do you really think so? You're not just saying that? There was ten pounds off it. I don't think Tess likes it very much.'

She smiled, blushed. Grey-eyed, grey-haired. A mouse of a woman who, although frighteningly intelligent, kept that pretty much to herself most of the time. She had a lot of startled hair, anxious eyes, but a winning smile when she chose to use it. She alternated, for no obvious reason, between academic-looking spectacles and contact lenses, and in fact Andrew preferred the glasses. She wore them now and they suited her. 'Tess did wonderfully well with the arrangements, didn't she? Not a hitch,' Stephanie went on after a moment. 'I offered to help but she wouldn't hear of it.'

'That's Tess.'

They smiled, struggled a bit with the conversation. Andrew never knew what to say to Stephanie and she obviously had a similar problem. Rather to his relief, she was whisked off by someone, her presence required because the presents were about to be opened. Andrew stood off to one side, alone, not minding. He was not a social animal.

He watched Tess. Dark and vibrant and vital, looking absolutely fantastic in the black dress, plain at the front but dipping almost to the waist at the back with two narrow straps crisscrossing. Smooth pale back. She must have sensed his glance, for she turned suddenly and looked at him quite wickedly.

'Audrey Oakes . . .' A woman with unruly red hair stood in front of him, smiling with determination as you did at these sort of events. 'You are Tess's husband, aren't you? She pointed you out to me. She's a wonderful woman, your wife. So energetic. And the flowers are beautiful, aren't they? I do believe it's a talent to know just what to choose. I spend a fortune on flowers and they never ever look right. I thought perhaps she might do the flowers for us in reception at the offices. Not that it's anything at all to do with me, but whenever I visit Ivan I find the reception area so very dull. I shall have a word with him.'

'Thank you. I'm sure she will be delighted,' Andrew said, a little surprised she wasn't doing it already. Joe had slipped up there. Missed a chance. Unless he had thought that fiddling a floral contract at his office was a bit near the knuckle. 'It's great that everyone turned up tonight.'

'I suppose they thought they must,' she said. 'Sorry . . . that sounded dreadful. What I meant was that it is something of a special occasion as I understand he may be leaving us, sometime next year.'

'Is that so?' Andrew sipped his drink. 'The first I've heard.'

'Oh, goodness. I've been indiscreet.' She pulled a face. 'Forget I said that. In fact, you *must* forget I said it or Ivan will be so annoyed. He tells me things in confidence, you see, and I'm not always sure whether they are for public consumption or not. I'm always putting my foot in it.'

'Don't worry. I shan't say a word,' he told her, looking towards Joe who, with Stephanie's help, was now opening his presents amidst great shouts of laughter as he held aloft a pair of silver tanga briefs. Andrew tried to attract Tess's attention but she was nowhere to be seen so he helped himself to another drink.

He found himself watching Ivan Oakes. They had exchanged a brief word earlier and, in fact, Andrew had not taken to him much. Now he thought about it, Joe had seemed a bit peculiar lately so it was possible that he did know something but was keeping it quiet yet. He could hardly believe it of Ivan, though. You wouldn't come to somebody's birthday party if you knew that you were about to give that person the push. You wouldn't go to the trouble of giving a speech on their behalf?

Would you?

There was just something about the whole atmosphere of this party. Of course it was a happy occasion, but all his colleagues from work were exceptionally cheerful, almost too cheerful. Trying very very hard. As for Joe . . . well, he hadn't liked to say anything to Stephanie, dared not say a word to Tess, but he had caught Joe a few times in unguarded moments and he wouldn't like to bet more than a fiver that old Joe *was* enjoying this. It was unthinkable that Joe would be given the push unless he had finally been rumbled and nailed. Or could it be that he was leaving from choice, with another job lined up that he hadn't yet told them about?

Doubtful, because it wasn't like him to be secretive about things like that.

Watching the proceedings quietly, the feeling firmed up that something was wrong.

He felt quite sure Stephanie was unaware of it but he was less certain about Tess.

Tess moved in mysterious ways.

# 21

There was a coffee morning at West House for the ladies of the church guild to make final arrangements for the bonfire evening. They were great ones for organising. Their fancy cars were parked, more or less, all over the drive. Somebody had managed to run backwards into the flower bed near the house and made a real mess of the plants. Bernard would go spare. Ella had been up and down the hall, opening the door, letting them in, taking coats and hats, for what seemed ages.

Happier now in the kitchen, she made the coffee and piled the freshly made buttered scones onto plates. She didn't have much patience with them, these ladies with their loud posh voices, but there it was. You had to put up with it. They all had more money than tact. She'd been extra early so that she could make a couple of batches of scones first and then give the rooms they would be in a special do for they were the sort to miss nothing. Sure enough, two of them had piled into what they called the 'loo' directly they arrived. You'd think they could have gone before they came, for most of them lived in the village or nearabouts. What it was, of course, was that they were just having a nosy, seeing what that downstairs bathroom was like, seeing if Mrs Makepeace had changed that wallpaper yet. She hadn't, but then she wouldn't now, would she? Little did they know that this would be the last time they'd have the bonfire here at West House unless the new people wanted to carry on with it. By rights, Ella thought Mrs Makepeace ought to tell the ladies this morning. Such a one for secrets she was.

These ladies would be all over what Ella considered *her* kitchen tomorrow night for the bonfire. The day after she'd have it all to sort out. Every single pan would be in the wrong place. The store cupboard would be all a pickle. They rooted, they did. Peered in packets and suchlike.

'Out, man,' she ordered as one of the lads who worked for Bernard opened the back door and started to come in. 'I'll bring your tea out in a minute. I've only got one pair of hands. I've got a coffee morning on and that takes priority.'

She was not having her clean kitchen floor full of muddy footprints. That cat had already left a little trail of his pawprints leading from the cat flap all the way over and she'd been on her knees at seven with the damp cloth. He'd be on the chair in the blue bedroom now, keeping out of the way while the ladies were here. He didn't like too much fussing. He never got any from her. Baby tigers that's all they were, cats. Hunters. Sank their teeth into baby birds. She had no time for them. Mrs Makepeace treated him like a prince. Special milk for him that cost nearly fifty pence a carton and biscuits and the best cat food. Turned his nose up at the own-brand stuff now and wouldn't touch semi-skimmed for love or money.

'Mrs Bainbridge . . .' a voice gushed, belonging to one of the committee members, a tall lady with thin pursed lips and a maroon knitted suit. 'May I help at all? Carry the scones for you, perhaps?'

'Go on then,' Ella said, a little overawed, forgetting the woman's name, smiling instead. 'Is everybody here now, Mrs . . . er . . . ?'

'Bamber-Price. Yes . . .' there was a hesitation and the plates of scones was put down once more on the table. 'Tell me, Mrs Bainbridge . . .'

Ella looked at her. She noticed that the kitchen door was closed.

'Is Constance well? She seems a little out of sorts. It's all right, you can tell me.'

'She was queasy a while back but she's all right now,' Ella told her, in no mood, with the coffee all hot and ready, for a gossip. 'Got a lot on her mind, you see, what with one thing and another,' she added mischievously, not able to resist.

'Oh . . . I thought so. She's seemed a little secretive lately.'

'She always is.'

Ella checked the tea trolley, then set off, leaving the woman no option but to follow with the scones, bursting with curiosity.

Bernard would be proud of her discretion.

The fact was she had been down in the cellar again, digging in boxes, looking for clues. Clues to what, she didn't really know. All she knew was that there was something that Mrs Makepeace was not telling. Whose were the baby clothes? Not the little boy Thomas who had drowned, for these were brand new, the sort of things you collected together for your layette. Individually wrapped in tissue. She must have lost at least one baby. Oh, yes . . . hadn't she once heard tell of that? She'd need to make enquiries.

As for her husband, Colonel Makepeace as was . . . well, a problem with his nerves she'd heard, on account of his war experiences. He'd died in a shooting accident in the Lakes but what if she'd killed him? People like her, in her position, could get things hushed up. Now that would be terrible, wouldn't it? A lovely old dear like her. Although she did have a set to her mouth sometimes that made you think. She'd caught her once or twice lately daydreaming with a very funny look on her face. Suppose, all these years, she'd been working for a murderess. What a tale she could tell!

She pushed open the door to the drawing room with her knee.

'Oh . . . well done, Mrs Bainbridge!'

'The scones look wonderful, Mrs Bainbridge!'

'Just black for me, Mrs Bainbridge.'

The cat was in the room, as large as life on the window ledge, joining in. Ella was kept busy pouring coffee and tea, smiling all the while. Masses of different scents and a profusion of perms.

'Do you mind if we borrow your kitchen tomorrow?' someone asked, picking up a scone. She had red lipstick on her teeth, Ella noted with satisfaction. 'We shall be here during the afternoon because there's so very much to do. We have to heat the soup and do the sausages – and shall we do beefburgers for the children, do you think?' This latter question addressed to the ladies, not Ella.

The suggestions poured forth.

'Garlic bread and baked potatoes with various fillings.'

'I have some pumpkin pies left from Hallowe'en.'

'Don't forget the pease pudding.'

'And dips. We must do dips.'

'What about drinks? Mulled wine, perhaps? Or non-alcoholic punch?'

'Why *non*-alcoholic?' Constance enquired, the first time Ella had heard her speak.

'Some people will be driving,' someone said. 'And we don't want a repetition of last year do we?'

'Someone can keep an eye on him this time,' Constance said.

They laughed nervously and looked at Ella.

She knew full well they meant the vicar but she wasn't saying anything.

A small silence fell.

'You will be at the bonfire evening, Mrs Bainbridge?'

'Oh yes,' she said.

After all, somebody had to clean up after them.

They, none of them, for all their airs and graces, had a clue how to do that properly.

Constance was glad to see the back of them. And so was Smith. He had been surprised to see them all but stoically had remained, incredibly patient with them, with their pats and strokes and oohs and aahs, suffered being picked up by one cat-lover, but he was now as fed up as she.

Constance did not fuss him, leaving him to recover. She assisted Mrs Bainbridge in clearing the remainder of the clutter from the drawing room before slipping on her outside jacket. She fancied a walk up the hill. She hadn't taken a walk up the hill in ages.

'I'm going out, Ella,' she called. 'I am going to take a stroll up the hill. I may be late for lunch, so don't worry.'

'I'll have to hoover the drawing room again. Crumbs all over,' was Ella's parting shot. 'And we go to the trouble of providing them with serviettes as well . . .'

Constance ignored her. It was her job, after all. And she was rather offended, in fact, with the off-hand manner in which Ella had despatched the ladies on their way, appearing as she did unannounced with a pile of coats and hats and dumping the lot on the drawing room settee for them to sort through themselves. One did not do that. One or two of her guests had been quite taken aback. She would have a word later.

Bernard was busy too, muttering, on his knees by the bed near the house replanting things, but Constance did not pause to talk, merely passing the time of day with him. She took the path that snaked through the rear gardens and led eventually through a narrow gate onto the hill path itself. It was November chill now. Raw. She was glad she had slipped gloves on. The heaped-up bonfire was visible in the clearing in the top meadow and it would be quite splendid tomorrow when it was lit. It promised to be a dry evening, thank goodness, so that would be one less problem to face.

The bonfire evenings had started when Thomas was small. They held them at the vicarage in those days but it was so difficult to get the fire lit in that often waterlogged garden beside the river. A damp squib as often as not, so Hugh had come up with the idea of holding the event instead at West House where it was higher and considerably drier. Even the vicar, the very same vicar, whose social skills were lamentable, had heartily approved.

The path up to the top of the hill started beyond the house in a fairly leisurely fashion, and then much later it forked, one path for the young and energetic, the other longer but less steep for everyone else. There was a bench at this branching point, most welcome, where you could sit and make your decision as to which path to take. Constance, checking it was quite dry, sat down for a cigarette.

The house and gardens were visible from here as was the church and village. A group of trees, though bare now, effectively hid the vicarage and river from view. Constance lit up, breathing out slowly and surveying it all in a single sweeping glance. Very much the same as always except for the new houses of course which, she had to admit, did merge in reasonably well after all.

She had told nobody today about her decision to move but she had been extremely aware the whole time that this was the last bonfire evening at West House to be given with her gracious permission, as it were. Turning points. All through one's life, there were turning points. The last this, the last that. Significant moments ought to be so special but they were not always.

She had said goodbye to the house in London where Margaret was born without a backward glance. However, she had fonder memories of the house in Sussex where she and Hugh had lived after their marriage. She liked it there, liked the proximity to the sea which, if she was honest, was something she missed. When they left it for the last time to come up to County Durham, Thomas, who suffered greatly from travel sickness, had been ill, she recalled, just at the crucial moment when she had meant to peer from the car and catch a last, very last, glimpse of the house before they were gone forever. Attending to her little son's needs, she missed it and there had been no point in asking Hugh to go back. Why go back?

Sweet memories of that house, of course, for that's where she had taken Thomas home as a splendidly healthy two-week-old baby. After Margaret, she had insisted on a hospital delivery for Thomas with the very best care and all had gone well. Thomas was so like Hugh. Hugh had been quite delighted at the birth of his little son and had been so considerate to her too. He agreed quite willingly to her request for not only separate beds but separate bedrooms for a time.

Time enough for another child for, after the successful delivery of Thomas, she now felt able to contemplate having another child, a daughter perhaps, when Thomas was four or five. She wanted to enjoy her son in his early years in undiluted form. And enjoy him she did. He was an angel, as people so often say of children who die in infancy. Try as she might, she could only remember the good times with Thomas. He was bright and intelligent and had he grown would have made her so proud. Hugh had intended that, after a local preparatory school, he go to Westminster Boarding School and then Cambridge and then he hoped he might go into the diplomatic service. Thomas's life was mapped out and Constance knew he would not have let them down for, even as a little boy, he was endearingly anxious to please.

The holiday in Scotland was intended as a break primarily for Hugh who had been under severe strain. They stayed at a friend's home in the west of Scotland and, because the weather was so agreeable, they spent a lot of time outdoors. Wonderful picnics as of old. And then, on a day's private excursion to the small loch, Constance did the unthinkable and took her eyes off her son for a moment. She was busy laying the white cloth for the picnic. Carefully unwrapping the food her friend's cook had prepared for them, for her, her friend and their little son who, although a little older than Thomas, got on so well with him. Her friend was a chatterer and the conversation was cheerful and genial. The little boys were playing by the water and later, agonising in her mind, she thought she recalled the splash but could not be sure. They continued to make preparations for the picnic. How food takes on a different quality when eaten out of doors! There were sandwiches, tiny filled pies, cheese and the rosy red apples Thomas adored. Thomas was growing well and had a hearty appetite.

Little Ian returned alone carrying his fishing rod, red-faced, running, panting, pointing. Incoherent when he finally reached them.

By the time they reached the loch, of Thomas there was no sign. The branch on which he had dangled over the water was broken off. She remembered the sudden icy cold that wrapped around her. She remembered someone saying that the loch shelved away very deeply very quickly. She remembered somebody screaming his name. Not her. Her friend. She remembered the handyman who had been working nearby stripping off and diving in. Searching. Surfacing. Searching. Surfacing.

On the bench on the hill, she shivered, pulled her jacket closer, closed her eyes and felt the cold high breeze on her face, heard the sound of it as it whistled and whipped through the heather. There was no reason, of course, why she should not continue to take a walk up here when she was living in the cottage but she knew she would not. In fact, she might never set foot in West House again for it would be too painful.

The last glimpse of anything was always painful.

She dropped the cigarette, ground it with her foot, rose to her feet, looked up at the hill but decided not to push for the summit.

Instead, she made her way slowly down.

# 22

'We're ready,' Yvonne said, as he opened the door. 'Are we too early? Sorry, but the children are so excited.'

So was she by the look of it, cheeks pink, eyes bright, smile huge, her hair almost hidden by the floppy red hat she was wearing. Her coat was long and black and he could hardly believe the wellington boots.

'Come in a minute. We aren't quite ready yet,' Andrew said, although *he* was. It was Tess who was holding them up, buggering about with a mountain of clothes that lay discarded now on the bed. What on earth to wear for a bonfire party? Oh, the agony of indecision!

They gathered in a group in the hall as he closed the door and shut out the cold evening air. It had been a stormy sort of day, grey clouds skimming overhead, never properly light, but the evening had brought a welcome change and the wind had died down. It was perfect for a bonfire. Cold but dry.

'Hello everybody,' Tess said as she came downstairs, smiling.

She was back to wearing the very first thing she had tried on tonight, Andrew noticed. A cream padded ski jacket and long dark brown skirt, brown leather boots sticking out from under it. No hat, but a long cream and brown scarf draped loosely round her neck. 'Isn't this wonderful? We're all going to a bonfire party,' she said brightly, looking down at the children.

They stared at her, nodded but said nothing. They didn't know Tess. They were a little unsure of her.

'Right, gang,' Andrew said, clapping his hands. 'Let's go.'

A lot of people, most of the villagers in fact, were walking up to the big house this evening and it was a clear starry night, the occasional rocket soaring and splitting in the sky, the sound of the crackle of another bonfire nearby as they crossed One-Mile Bridge. Their breath puffed out as they walked, there was a sparkle of frost on the path and they took their time climbing the hill. Up ahead, the house was lit like a Christmas tree.

Before long, the two ladies were walking behind, chatting, with Andrew and the children in front.

At his side Portia skipped.

'Is it a palace?' Samantha asked as they made their way up the long drive.

'No, silly. It's the big house,' Portia told her, 'where Mummy takes the books for the lady. Isn't it, Mummy?'

'What's that, darling?'

'Something about books,' Andrew said, turning to smile at them. He was pleased to see that Tess seemed to be getting on with Yvonne for once. She had been a bit quiet, in fact, since Joe's birthday party and he knew something was wrong, something connected with it. He had tried to bring it up this evening as they got ready for the bonfire but she had shaken her head, told him they would talk later.

So, whatever it was, he had that to look forward to.

They reached the house at last where the ladies of the church guild were waiting to direct them round the side to the meadow where the bonfire was just about to be lit. There was a slight embarrassed furore about who would pay the admittance charge as this event was to raise funds for the church. In the end, despite Andrew's protests, Yvonne insisted she pay for herself and the children at least.

'For God's sake, it's only seventy-five pence. Does she have to make such a fuss?' Tess muttered at his side, tugging his arm as he would have set off to follow. 'No, let them go. I've told Yvonne we'll catch up with them later. You and I are helping with the refreshments.'

'Are we?'

'Yes,' she said. 'I told you. Oh, look . . . there's Constance.'

She was off, gushingly, towards the old lady and Andrew followed more slowly, realising as he caught Yvonne's little wave that he would have much rather gone with her and the children.

It was bloody tearing him apart these days. These feelings. He found himself looking out for her when she came back from school, watching from the window as she climbed out of the car and went up her path. Worse, sneaking a peep from his office window whenever she was working in the garden. The feelings of liking her that he had known for a long time were subtly changing. He knew it. He was denying it so far but he bloody knew it. He just didn't know what to do.

As for Tess . . . all her faults that he knew about, had put aside for years, were rising to the surface like bubbles and they could no longer be popped, forgotten about. He did not like some of the things she was up to these days.

Contrary to expectations, he was not required to help this evening. Bossily shooed off by the other ladies. Tess was in the thick of it, however, doing the beefburgers with a good deal of aplomb and gallons of tomato sauce, trying to look as if she did this sort of thing everyday. She had managed to insinuate herself onto the same refreshment stall as Constance and there they were chatting away merrily.

He sighed. Shook his head. Sure he'd love to have this house, who wouldn't, but fair and square, not in the underhand way that Tess was contriving. He looked up as fireworks exploded in the sky, gold and blue and white, the sparklets of light falling from them, the children squealing their delight. There was a not unpleasant smell of slightly damp grass, gunpowder and woodsmoke. Quickly, he strode over to the fence where they were keeping the crowd back and eventually found them.

'There was a guy, Mr O'Grady, on top of the bonfire,' Portia said. 'Wasn't there, Mummy?'

'I think it was supposed to be the vicar,' Yvonne murmured. 'At least it bore an uncanny resemblance. It was the hat that did it. Probably one of his old ones.'

They laughed. Whoever it was supposed to be, he was well and truly alight as the bonfire crackled and hissed sending out odd gushes of heat in what was turning out to be a bitterly cold night.

'Cold?' Andrew asked as, beside him, Yvonne shivered.

'Just a bit. I forgot my gloves and my hands are cold. Stupid, wasn't it?'

It was tempting to say 'hold my hand' but he did not. How could he when Tess was here? It was different with the children and Samantha and Harry soon had a hand each, their eyes wide, their little faces aglow as they watched the display.

'I don't remember displays like this when I was little,' Yvonne said, hands firmly in her pockets.

'Don't you? You poor old thing,' he said, giving her a quick smile.

'Less of that,' she said, smiling too. 'What I was going to say was that I didn't see an organised firework display properly until I was at the first school I worked at.'

'You worked in a school?'

She nodded. 'I taught. I gave it up before we moved here. It was too difficult you see with my own children. Childcare was becoming horrendous.'

'You're a schoolteacher?' he asked, quite astonished. 'Good Lord . . .'

'Don't sound so surprised,' she said, bemused by his surprise. 'Now you're going to say I don't look like a schoolteacher, aren't you?'

'Well . . . no. It's just that . . . OK, you don't look like a schoolteacher.'

'It was a special school,' she said quietly. 'I loved it.'

'Yes, I suppose the school you teach at is pretty special to you.'

'I don't mean that. A *special* school,' she said. 'Special-needs. For pupils with learning difficulties.'

'Oh . . . I see.'

He hid a smile. It irritated Tess that she had never found out what Yvonne used to do for a living. Working as a secretary and doing the boss the odd favour was one of the kindlier options she had come up with.

'Not the sort of thing to discuss at dinner parties,' Yvonne said quietly, as if she was reading his mind. 'It tends to get a little serious and some people . . .' she did not need to say Tess, it was implied . . .' some people are embarrassed by it.'

At his side, Samantha jumped up, slipped his grasp.

'Can we have something to eat?' she asked, looking up at Andrew as Yvonne bent down to refasten Harry's boots. 'Can we? Please.'

'You may have something to eat,' Yvonne said absently, straightening up and holding her son close a second.

It was so natural a gesture, so loving, that Andrew was oddly moved by it.

'Come on, let's see if we can find Tess,' he said cheerfully, breaking the mood, leading them off towards the house.

The children bounded ahead and he and Yvonne walked more slowly.

'They can call us Andrew and Tess,' he said. 'It's a bit silly, this Mr and Mrs O'Grady lark.'

'I prefer it, if you don't mind,' she said firmly. 'I don't want them to become too familiar and I think it encourages them to respect grown-ups. There's too much of this first name business nowadays.'

He glanced at her, surprised and a little amused at her earnestness.

'That's the sort of thing Mrs Makepeace might say, but all right. If it's that important to you . . .'

They reached the beefburger stall where Tess was looking hot and bothered. Andrew didn't like to tell her there was some tomato sauce on her cheek. Constance was beside her, nominally dispensing little paper plates and napkins, but Tess seemed to be doing all the work.

'Yes?' she enquired, through gritted teeth, he could tell, as he and Yvonne and the children appeared. 'What can I get you? We have onions and pickles and chopped tomatoes and cheese slices and two lots of sauce.'

'I'll get these, Yvonne. My treat,' Andrew said hastily before she started rummaging through her handbag for her purse. 'What do we want, gang? Have we decided?'

He caught Constance Makepeace looking at him quite closely as he collected together their ridiculously convoluted orders. He could never quite fathom Constance's looks.

He could Tess's, though.

Hers told him plainly that he was in for it when they got home.

The children were asleep, worn out with the excitement. Arriving back tired and way past their bedtime, it had been a quick hose-down under a warm shower, a shampoo to get the smoke out of their hair, pyjamas and bed for them. Yvonne was too upbeat herself to sleep for a while and she sat in the living room in the half light of a reading lamp, relaxed and happy.

They had had a lovely time tonight, one of those times she knew the children would remember with affection, and she knew why. If there was one reason to pin-point just why it had been such a success, it was Andrew. The children liked him so much and, in a way sadly, they talked about him more these days than they did about Robin.

Children were remarkably resilient, but then she knew that. They looked at situations with their unbiased eyes and saw things for precisely what they were. They didn't try to make excuses or see all sides or be rational. Things were so wonderfully black and white. They liked Andrew, they did not like Tess, and that was that.

No agonising from them about why they liked him. No worrying that it might be getting out of hand. No longings, of course, no adult longings like she had. For a while tonight, together, the five of them, it had all seemed so . . . so perfect. Robin might be their father but she had to face up to the fact that he had no time for them. He'd never been the fatherly type. When he was home, he never applauded their sometimes pathetic little efforts to attract his attention. Rarely praised them. She was sure he did love them in his way but his was a selfish way. It did not include them any more, in fact it never had.

'Mummy . . . ?'

She turned, saw Harry at the door in his Batman pyjamas clutching his old adored teddy bear.

'Come here,' she said softly, opening her arms to him. 'Aren't you sleepy?'

He shook his head, gave a big, big sigh. He looked so like Robin sometimes with the soulful eyes. When Harry was grown up and she was old herself, he would be a constant reminder. In that way, Robin would never leave her. Gently, she settled her little son against her soft bosom, stroked his sweet-smelling dark hair. Crooned one of his favourite baby tunes. Sometimes he fought against these precious little moments, struggling and saying he was a big boy now and didn't want cuddles, but just now he was content to stay put and quietly listen.

She must not cry herself for Harry was sensitive to her unhappy moods.

She felt tears well up though, at the way it had all fallen to pieces lately.

She wished there was someone to hold and cuddle her, to murmur that everything would be all right.

She wished Andrew was here.

As far as Tess was concerned, the evening had only been a partial success. Oh yes, she had managed to get time alone with Constance during which she had made further determined efforts to impress her. She had told her all about her father's home up the dale, comparing it with West House although making sure that the latter came out on top. Constance must have no doubts that Tess thought West House the best. Constance must be made to realise that nobody but she, Tess, must be considered as a possible candidate. She was destined to live at West House.

Constance would keep going on about families, though, and babies. The house was rather bored with one person, it needed a family she said. It ached to have a family living in it once again.

Tess, although beginning to think the woman was distinctly peculiar, had obligingly enthused, saying she couldn't wait to be pregnant, but they were waiting until they felt finally settled. Throwing caution to the wind, she embroidered the story still further, tossing in all sorts of impossibilities such as her giving up her career and devoting herself to motherhood. Fortunately, Constance seemed happy enough to accept all these fairytales at face value.

'You are lucky, dear, to be happily married,' she had said then. 'I do not know your husband very well, of course, but I must say I like him. He has a most pleasing demeanour. He is perhaps a little old-fashioned, if I may say so, which I find a charming trait. A courteous man, and there are so few about these days.'

And then, just after this cosy conversation, what did Andrew do but appear at their stall complete with Yvonne Lonsdale *and* her battalion of kids looking for all the world as if he was part and parcel of them. He might as well have had his arm round the woman, they looked so comfortable together, and when a couple were that comfortable together, it had to spell trouble. Constance had surely noticed, although of course she was far too polite to say a word. What the hell did Andrew think he was up to? Did it not occur to him that it might look a little odd?

A full scale row was best avoided, though, because she had a favour to ask of him first. One thing for sure, she was going to scupper this thing with Yvonne, if there *was* anything, before it got properly started. God . . . she'd caught the woman looking at him a couple of times and there was no mistaking the look. She would hardly win a prize in the subtlety stakes, Yvonne. The bitch was quite clearly out to get him. Well, she could forget that! Tess wasn't letting go of Andrew that easily. She wasn't sure just why it was so important to be married, particularly now that she had decided there would be no family, but it was useful. In so far as she needed a man, Andrew would do nicely.

'Run a bath for me, darling, would you?' she asked when they arrived home. 'My hair smells of smoke.'

He came close and sniffed it. 'So it does. Quite nice.'

She smiled. 'No, it is not. You might bring me a glass of wine up. I'll go straight to bed afterwards.'

'OK.' He went to get glasses, calling out that the children had enjoyed themselves, hadn't they? And Yvonne?

'Yes. And for once in her life, she was suitably attired,' she said, the memory of their returning home still piercingly annoying. Happy families. Andrew hoisting Harry on his shoulders, for God's sake, because he had stopped dead in his tracks and said he couldn't walk one more step. Thank heavens, it was past their bedtime and there was no question of them coming in for a post-bonfire discussion.

Next year, *they* might be hosting the bonfire evening. She would graciously consent as Constance did, but there would be one or two changes. No silly refreshment stalls. It was like something out of a fairground. No, they would have something a little more sophisticated, and it would be by invitation only so that they didn't have the entire village coming along.

She was reclining in the bath when Andrew brought her wine up, her body tantalizingly half concealed under the froth of scented bubbles. She needed him to be slightly off-guard and the time and place were carefully chosen.

'Thanks, darling.' She made herself more comfortable, smiled. 'No . . . stay. I want to talk.'

'It's distracting,' he said. 'But go on. Let me guess . . . is this about Joe?'

'Do you know something too?' she asked, catching something in his expression. 'Something you've not told me?'

'I'm not sure. It was just that Mrs Oakes said something about him leaving the company. She was upset after she'd said it, worried about being indiscreet. I didn't say anything at the time and I didn't want to say anything later in case Stephanie didn't know.'

'It sounds pretty serious,' Tess said, sipping her wine. 'I suppose you'll find out eventually, but he was pissed off about the party. He's been trying to keep a low profile at the office, you see, and being the centre of attention rather put paid to that.'

'Did you tell him it was all your idea?' Andrew asked. 'Or did you manage to put the blame on Stephanie?'

She glanced at him sharply. She had done precisely that, in fact, but she was not going into details.

'Joe tells me they are being taken over and there's going to be a big reorganisation,' she went on calmly. 'He's been asked to provide an expense account update for the new financial director. He's spitting feathers.'

'Oh, Jesus . . .'

'Exactly.' She allowed a slim smooth leg to appear above the water line. 'Problems. But surely it's possible to sort them out, particularly his expense sheets. I wonder, darling, if . . .'

He looked at her, smiled a little. 'Are you working up to asking a favour of me? Bit of a cheap trick, don't you think?' To her irritation, his quick look at her was bemused rather than lustful. 'Sorry, it won't work this time, darling.'

'Cheap trick?' she said, sitting up indignantly. 'What do you mean?'

'You know what I mean and the answer is no,' he said, picking up his glass of wine and heading out. 'I thought you knew me better than that, Tess. I do not fiddle accounts.'

'It's family,' she said, reaching over for her glass and nearly spilling her wine in her agitation. 'That's different, surely. That doesn't count as fiddling.'

'Did you seriously expect me to agree?' He felt a sudden sharp anger. She didn't even have the guts to ask him outright. She had to resort to this, trying to sway him by flaunting herself. 'How can you ask me to do something unprofessional? Something that could really land me in it?' he said, hand on the door. 'Some of us have a few more scruples than that.'

'For God's sake . . .' she stood up, stepped out and wrapped herself in a big warm towel. She had maybe underestimated his professional loyalty, his irritatingly po-faced attitude to his job. There was still time. She could still win him round. He still found her irresistible. She followed him, wrapped only in the towel, into the bedroom where he was tidying up the clothes she had left on the bed. 'Stop being so bloody boy-scoutish and stop acting like a housewife too,' she said. 'And listen to me . . .'

'No, Tess. You listen to *me*. He's on his own, that father of yours,' he said, and his eyes were cold. Remaining cold even as she allowed the towel to slip a tiny beguiling bit. Incredibly, he didn't even seem to notice. 'I wouldn't lift a finger to help him get out of the hole he's dug for himself. He's behaved like a cocky little kid getting away with it for years. The answer is no, Tess.'

'I know you don't get on, the two of you, but won't you do it for me, darling?' she asked, hitching the towel up and going over to him. Looking him right in the eyes. She knew she looked wonderful. Warm from the bath. A little pink faced. Hair damp. Poor Andrew. She could wrap him so easily round her little finger. Triumphant, she let her gaze travel slowly over his face, lingering on his lips.

As she had known he would, he pulled her towards him and kissed her then. Roughly. She murmured appreciatively, and wriggled a bit in his arms, breathing a sigh of relief.

And then she made her fatal mistake.

She repeated the question.

And got the same answer.

No.

# 23

Up at West House, Constance was a little worried. It was not proving to be quite so simple as she had thought. Tess was a beautiful girl, most pleasant and helpful, and Andrew was indeed a charming young man.

But . . . something was not right and she was a little concerned.

It was perhaps as well she was not impulsive or she might have told them about West House already and she knew she must be absolutely sure before she said a word.

Everyone had left. The ladies of the church guild had promised to return tomorrow morning to help Ella clean up the kitchen and a couple of the men were also coming along to help Bernard and the boys tidy up after the bonfire. It was still smouldering and would do so for most of the night. There was that wonderful smoky smell everywhere but the stars were on their own now, fireworks finally fizzled out.

She had been out last thing, when everyone had gone, to catch another glimpse of the bonfire before she retired. Poor Smith was distraught with the noise of the fireworks and had disappeared into the cellar earlier. Worried about him, she had to wait until Ella was gone before she went to look for him. It was cold tonight and she did not want him to spend all night in the cellar in a frightened state. He had taken to sleeping in her room, on the big comfortable armchair by the window, and as soon as she stirred in the morning, he leapt onto the bed and greeted her.

The cellar light was very bright. Dazzlingly so.

Carefully, she walked down the steep stone steps, holding onto the handrail. The cellar quarters were very large, two rooms in fact, the roughened walls painted white, the flagged uneven floors swept. She had a small wine cellar, neglected of late, and a large collection of shelves housed all manner of bottles and jars.

'Smith, where are you, darling?'

A tiny frightened miaow and a glimpse of a ginger head. And she smiled, edged past some boxes and called encouragingly to him to come out because everyone had gone now and the fireworks were over for another year. There was milk waiting for him in the kitchen and some of his biscuits.

Someone had been in one of the boxes.

Ella probably. Constance knew that Ella was consistently annoyed at her refusal to tell her innermost secrets. It was the box with the baby clothes, Constance noted, one that she would have been advised to part with at the time.

Without looking at them, she closed the box properly. In the box next to it, undisturbed, she noted, were her letters. She kept them all. Extremely long, intensely boring letters from Eleanor who had loved the art of letter writing. The letters from Grace. Not only bitter, she now realised, but gloating too. In Grace's eyes, she got what she deserved.

Archie's letters were all here too, the ones he had written to her before they married, the ones she had opened with trembling fingers at the house near Totnes, the ones she had hidden from Grace if Grace should be so – well . . . *graceless* as to read them. Archie had been a romantic and the letters were to be treasured, taken out occasionally and lovingly read. It was appalling to think that a man like Archie, so thoughtful and kind, should be shot out of the sky and despatched in a ball of fire.

As for Hugh . . . there were just a few when he had been away in London on business. Surprisingly terse, and she had no idea why she bothered to keep them. She blamed what happened in the war, whatever it was, for the dreaded moods of despair that could overtake him without warning. All right, Grace, she sometimes felt like saying, he might have been happier with you. He and I were never meant to be. You might have understood him better.

But it was her sister's fault. If the positions were reversed, she would have fought tooth and nail for Archie, despatched Grace without a moment's hesitation. As for Hugh . . . well, if Grace had even come up with a reasonable protest she might have backed down.

Poor Hugh.

Constance never read his final letter for it had been destroyed.

His friend Walter had been most discreet. He telephoned with the news and she had known at once from the gravity of his tone that it was very bad news. Hugh was to spend a long weekend with Walter over at his home near Keswick with a few other weekend guests. Hugh had asked if she wished to accompany him but she had refused. Hugh was very depressed but he had been so before and had she really thought, as she bade him farewell, that it would be the last time she would see him? Had she really thought as he stepped into the car and turned to wave that it was the last glimpse ever?

She rather thought she had.

Walter's news, therefore, was not unexpected. He was in total agreement with Constance that they must avoid scandal. The Makepeace name had to be protected. Walter was a surgeon, a man of influence. He told Constance that, in the quiet of his library the evening before, he and Hugh had enjoyed a glass of whisky and a cigarette. To Walter's distress, Hugh had spoken to him of suicide and indeed the circumstances of the death next day confirmed that, but, because he was a doctor and had moved the body to try to see if there was anything that could be done, it was easily explained away as an accident. Hugh had been rather clever about that for he had admitted he was concerned about protecting the family name. Hugh was nothing if not an honourable man.

'Are you all right, Constance?' Walter had asked, as the words sunk in. 'You may leave me to sort everything out. The inquest, believe me, will record a verdict of accidental death.'

'Was there a note?' Constance asked after thanking him for his help.

She noted the hesitation.

'I'm sorry. I feel badly about this and I do apologise, Constance. In the heat of the moment, it was unfortunately disposed of.

I found it in his room and I was most anxious that nobody else see it.'

'That's all right. I understand,' she said, although there had been a moment's anger that he should have had the audacity to do such a thing. Her letter after all. Hugh's letter to her.

The inquest did indeed record a verdict of accidental death. A trip when climbing a stile, a loaded shotgun, and that was it.

Poor weak man.

Hugh died in late November and that very year, with him finally gone, with nobody left to question her motives, she made a few discreet enquiries. When she felt able, years later, she started the Christmas visits.

# Part Two

# 24

'"White Christmas", it was called, starring Bing Crosby,' Agnes said with satisfaction. 'Mind that door, don't let it swing back on me.'

Yvonne shot the wheelchair through the gap in a sudden flurry, the door shutting with a slam behind them.

'You'll be the death of me, girl,' Agnes went on, adjusting her ruby-red felt hat. 'And to think they let you drive a car too.'

'I'm all right with the car. I just can't get the hang of this thing,' Yvonne said. 'Everything's stiff. Right, Agnes, where do you want to go?'

'The south of France.'

'No. Seriously?'

'I am serious,' she said. 'I fancy a bit of warmer weather. Perishing it is here. When I'm a hundred and that's not so far away, I'm going to see if I can't get a trip on Concorde. They like that sort of thing in the papers. First flight at a hundred. They'll want to take a picture of me swigging champagne. Daft old bat, they'll say.'

'Sure you don't fancy a parachute jump instead?'

'No, cheeky. Concorde will do fine.'

'It sounds a lovely idea. I'll see if I can arrange that for you. Joan's got people she can ask about that,' Yvonne said. 'So . . . what was it you were telling me about "White Christmas"?'

'It's my favourite song. My Jimmy, my last and best husband, was a great fan of Bing Crosby, and he had a lovely voice too. Used to croon to me, he did, the daft old thing – my Jimmy, I mean, not Bing. I was just saying what a lovely film it is and they put it on every Christmas. I'm looking forward to that this year,' Agnes said. 'Vera Ellen, I think she was called. Blonde like you but a lot thinner.'

Yvonne smiled. Agnes would do well to remember that she was in control here and they were on a downward slope.

Downward slope . . . her life felt like that too just now. What tiny glimmer of hope she might have had that she and Robin could still sort things out was gone. Snuffed out like a candle.

Robin was not coming home for Christmas as he felt, probably rightly, that it wouldn't solve anything and just might make things worse. She would have to tell the children sooner or later that she and Robin were getting a divorce but she was waiting for the right moment. At least they had been spared listening to rows nor would they have to suffer growing up in a tense, uncomfortable atmosphere. It wouldn't be a great deal different for them. She loved them so much. She had enough love in her for it not to matter if their daddy was gone. Not much, anyway. For all his faults, Robin was not a vindictive man, just lethargic. She would try to make sure it was amicable. Oh God, an amicable divorce!

'He had a lovely deep voice, Bing Crosby,' Agnes went on.

She was wearing a fur coat. A real fur coat. It surprised Yvonne and made her realise that she hadn't actually seen one for years. It was quite beautiful. A brown silky coat, the patching of the individual skins showing quite clearly. Mink, Agnes told her, a present from her last but one husband who'd had money even if he had precious little else to recommend him. She fancied being buried in it, in fact, although it might be a bit warm underground in a fur coat on second thoughts.

'You are the limit, Agnes,' Yvonne said with a fond smile as the old lady cackled at her own joke. All her wits about her indeed. She found herself hoping that, whatever might happen, Agnes would hang onto those wits she so treasured. She did not want to see her without them.

Agnes had made a special request for Yvonne to take her out so that she could buy some Christmas presents for the nursing home staff. First stop the newsagents. Letting Agnes ramble on a little, not really listening, Yvonne pulled the wheelchair to an abrupt halt, half on half off the pavement waiting for the traffic to clear.

Perhaps in a way it was better that Robin was not coming home for Christmas. She and the children would be just fine on their own. She might invite Agnes. And then she would explain to the children how they must be extra kind to her because she was a very old lady. Yes, they would like that and it would be good for them. And Agnes would be delighted.

'Now, Mrs Lonsdale, take me in, if you would, and then could you wait outside until they call you? I have something private to attend to.'

Yvonne, used to the old folks and their need for privacy, did as she was told.

It was December and the children were getting very excited. They were making paper chains at school and the play was next week just before they broke up for the holidays. Portia had a starring role in her class's nativity play and was terribly earnest about learning her lines properly. Samantha, less dramatically able, was in the angelic chorus and Harry refused to say what he was doing which was a bit worrying and meant she would have to snatch a private moment with his teacher.

Outside of school, people were developing that frantic look that Christmas brings but Yvonne was determined that this year she would enjoy it too. She would keep it simple. Too many presents confused the children and made them snappy. They would enjoy a traditional Christmas this year and she would do her best to keep the commercial content to a minimum.

Standing outside the shop, she hoped Agnes would not be too long because she was a bit sniffly today, caught the same cold probably that the children had had. Since the bonfire party, they had all been a touch under the weather although the O'Gradys seemed to have escaped the bug. Tess was looking wonderful as usual these days, wearing a fantastic looking big-collared winter white coat over her suits when she set out in the mornings. Yvonne saw Andrew but not so often, for he only looked after the children on one day now for a mere half hour after school. Tess had said something to her that had made it perfectly clear that they were becoming a nuisance.

The conversations between her and Andrew when she collected them had been brief recently to the point of terseness. She wondered if he was really as fed up with them as Tess was making out. She suspected not, but it didn't matter. It was just as well anyway, before things became too complicated. She had caught him looking at her sometimes, and then quickly looking away, and she knew it would not be too difficult to – well, to seduce him . . . if she wanted. She did not want that and she had better stop this silly tendency of hers to tease.

In the meantime, she had to do her very best to make sure that Christmas was happy for the children if not for her. Their first Christmas apart since they were married. The divorce was not going to be in any way complicated and should go through at the normal pace. She had not yet actually told the children, not even mentioned the word, but she thought they might know of it, have some inkling of what it meant. She wasn't the only parent at school to have marital problems.

Robin would be off soon to his base in Italy from where they would be setting sail, anchoring off the coast so that they could begin the dive. He would write, he promised, to the children. He had sent her a generous cheque to buy presents for them and she was to get something for herself too.

'She's ready, your lady,' the shopkeeper came out to tell her, and Yvonne collected the wheelchair and an excited Agnes who wanted Yvonne to help her wrap the presents for everybody when they got back.

'What will you be doing at Christmas, Agnes?' Yvonne asked her as they got to work with the sheets of bright Christmas paper and the matching bows. There were boxes of chocolates and biscuits and soaps and lavender wardrobe sachets. Agnes was taking it very seriously, crossing names off a list as they worked.

'Watching "White Christmas" if they'll leave me in peace,' she said. 'Then having a turkey dinner whether I like it or not and I don't, and then a sing-song round the piano and bingo though I'd rather play bridge. And then another film after the vicar's called to pay his respects, a disaster one if we're lucky. The trouble with that place, Mrs Lonsdale, is that too many of them have lost their marbles. It gets on my nerves watching them. Some of them are only youngsters in their early seventies.'

Yvonne made up her mind.

'We'd like you to come to us on Christmas Day,' she said

quietly, not looking at her. She snipped at a piece of red ribbon, tied it round the wrapped parcel. 'We won't have turkey. The children prefer chicken. Robin will be away on business so there's just me and the children this year.'

'Away on business? At Christmas?' Agnes clicked her tongue. 'Letting you down, isn't he?' Her glance was shrewd. 'You don't have to feel sorry for me, Mrs Lonsdale. It's kind of you to ask and don't think I'm not grateful but all in all, I'll be better off here. It's not as bad as I like to make out and after all children don't like old people around.'

'Mine do,' Yvonne said stoutly. 'They don't see their own grandparents. Robin's father never comes near and my parents live in Australia. The rest of my family is out there, you see, and they went to join them. So, we're on our own. Please come. I want you to come. I want to cook for somebody other than the children, another adult, or I'll be eating shepherd's pie and pink instant whip with hundreds and thousands on top for Christmas dinner. Their favourite meal.'

'I'll come on one condition. Can I watch "White Christmas"?'

Yvonne smiled.

'We'll all watch it,' she said.

# 25

'I just wanted a quick word, Andrew. Have you a moment? I've come to issue an invitation. The children would like you to come to their Christmas concert,' Yvonne said, smiling as she came into the hall. 'Tess too, if she can make it. The more the merrier. There won't be a full house exactly. Most mums and dads are working, you see, so it's mainly grandmothers and child minders. It's Thursday afternoon at two o'clock.'

'I'd like to, but . . .' Andrew struggled for a plausible excuse.

He was working extremely hard to try and stop a potentially explosive situation here. He and Tess were going through a rough patch as, obviously, were Yvonne and Robin but that didn't mean he and Yvonne should try changing partners. Why the hell should that work any better? Marriage wasn't just something you could toss away at the first difficult hurdle.

The excuse presented itself suddenly.

'A job interview,' he said, which was partly true. The fact was he had to phone to fix up a convenient date and it might as well be Thursday.

'A job? You're going back to work then? I mean going *out* to work,' she corrected herself with a laugh.

'I'm thinking about it,' he said, refraining from launching into the whys and wherefores.

'Oh . . . they will be disappointed, but I'll explain. I find they're generally pretty reasonable when I explain things properly. Well . . . some things.' She smiled, hesitated, and before he knew what was what he had invited her for a coffee.

'Haven't seen you for ages,' he said, as she followed him into the kitchen where he had indeed been just about to make himself one. 'Not to talk to, anyway. Oh . . . sit down, it won't be a moment.'

'Thanks.'

It was two thirty on a stormy December afternoon. One of those days when the light is on from getting up to going to bed. Dark. Dismal. Depressing. December. At least Yvonne brightened things up considerably, in a pink high-necked sweater and long velvety pink skirt. Lots of thin gold chains round her neck and the usual jangle of bracelets. Her engagement ring, a single diamond, sparkled and her finger nails matched the pink of the sweater. He liked the attention to detail. Tess paid heed to that too but somehow on Yvonne it was more obvious, or was he simply noticing it more?

Here she was, an oasis of warmth on one of the shortest greyest days of the year.

'Snow's forecast for Christmas,' Yvonne said. 'The children are very excited about that. Will it upset your travelling plans? Tess said you're driving up the dale to her father's.'

'It could be a bit tricky but we'll manage,' Andrew said, handing her a mug of coffee. 'What about you? What have you and Robin got planned? Just a family Christmas?'

There was a little silence. She reached for a spoon and stirred her coffee vigorously a moment.

'Robin will be away, I think,' she said, and he noticed how bright her eyes were, the little toss of the head, the defiant look. 'It's such a nuisance but it's something he can't get out of. Essential maintenance and somebody has to do it.'

'On the rig?'

She nodded and he waited, giving her the chance to say something about the Mediterranean. Or had little Portia got it completely wrong? Children did get the wrong end of the stick sometimes.

'Everything's OK, though?' He regretted the intimate nature of the question but he had to know.

'Oh, yes. Everything's fine.'

'Good.'

They smiled awkwardly and he pushed the box of biscuits towards her.

'Shortbread,' he said stupidly, still looking at her.

There was a sort of luminous quality about Yvonne that he had not noticed before. A most definite glow. The sort of glow that used to surround Tess. Or could it be that the glow was there simply because he had fallen in love with the woman. He did love her and it wasn't just physical even though he fancied her like crazy and wanted more than anything to get her into bed. No, it wasn't just that . . . he loved her and the kids for lots of other reasons.

'Is everything all right with you?' she asked after a moment. 'You seem a bit . . . well . . . unsettled. Is it because of your job?'

'I'm just a bit down,' he said. 'You know how it is. It's thinking about Christmas, I suppose. Last Christmas I had a feeling that maybe this Christmas we might have a baby around.'

'Oh . . . I see.' She smiled. 'Perhaps next Christmas, then?'

'If only,' he said and he saw the sympathy in her eyes, blurted it out before he could stop himself. 'We lost one, you know. Three years ago when we lived over in Jesmond.' He hesitated a moment, 'There was a medical problem, baby was going to be handicapped . . . it had Down's Syndrome . . . and we decided it was best to terminate.'

'Oh, no. Poor Tess,' she said softly. 'And poor you. I did wonder, actually. She has this look on her face when you talk about babies. Come to think of it, I might have been a bit insensitive. I'm glad you've told me because I'll be more careful in future. It must have been a terrible experience for her.'

'It was. You expect everything to be all right, don't you, and it *was* all right at the eleven week scan but then, at fifteen weeks, she had the double blood test.' He smiled a little. 'I don't know why I'm telling you. You know all this, of course.'

'Oh yes. It all takes time,' Yvonne said. 'Then you have to wait for the results.'

'We weren't too anxious. We assumed everything would be OK. But it showed a probability . . . just that . . . that the baby might have Down's. We were advised then to have the amniocentesis test and after that we were nail biting for two weeks. Tess just cried the whole time. She was inconsolable. We thought it happened to older women and Tess was only twenty-six at the time.'

'Oh, Andrew . . . how awful.' She shuddered her horror. 'I just sailed through all my pregnancies and it's so hard to imagine it.'

'Once we decided to go ahead with the termination, she was induced and had to go through labour and baby was born dead.' He felt himself fill up with emotion, drew a single deep breath to control it. 'I saw him. Tess wouldn't look. We had a service later, the hospital chaplain conducted it for him and for a couple of other babies and he was cremated. There's a little plot reserved for babies. Tess refused to go and I haven't been there since. Frankly, I don't think I could face it.' He sighed, in control, thank God, pleased that he had talked about it, pleased that he could do so now in comparative calm. 'Bloody awful experience all told. What would you have done, Yvonne? If you'd been faced with the same thing?'

'Oh . . . goodness, what a question,' she said, her hand stilled on the table very close to his but not touching. 'That's not a fair question, Andrew. I'm not sure, to be honest. I just don't know. I'm not sure I wouldn't have made the same decision as you and Tess did.'

'Would you?' He felt oddly disappointed, had felt sure she would have gone through with it. 'Why?'

'There are a lot of things to consider. If you have other children, you have to think about them. A handicapped child takes a lot from you. Remember, I did work with them. Some of the parents are wonderfully strong, others not so strong. If you asked them the same question, would they have gone through with it had they known, then I think you'd get a half and half reply. Some would do the same again, some wouldn't. There's no easy answer and there's no right answer either. Don't fret about it, Andrew. It was the right decision for you and Tess even though I think children with Down's Syndrome are beautiful.'

He tried a smile, not quite succeeding.

'Tess would not agree,' he said.

'I don't mean in a conventional sense,' she said earnestly. 'Let me try to explain, and this is why I don't bring it up at dinner parties because it all gets a bit fraught,' she added with a smile. 'Something happened to me years ago that had a deep effect on me, in fact I think it was that that made me decide to specialise.'

'Go on,' he said as she hesitated.

'Sure you want me to? OK. Once, when I was in college, I was with a group of people at a social evening and one of the couples there had brought along their Down's Syndrome child. He sat right beside me and stared at me. Solidly. At last his mother couldn't stand it any longer. Stop looking at Yvonne, she said, it's rude to stare. And then he leaned very close to me and he said, "I like you". And he smiled at me. And, do you know Andrew, it was one of the loveliest things anyone had ever said to me. I've had a few compliments over the years but that has to rate the most sincere. Do you see what I mean?'

'Yes, I do,' he said, looking at her and taking his time about it. These last few minutes had convinced him, if he needed convincing, that there was a helluva lot more to Yvonne than you would think.

'Well . . .' She blushed, did not look at him. 'The point I'm trying to make . . . what *is* the point I'm trying to make? I've lost my drift.'

'You're trying to convince me that we did the right thing,' Andrew said. 'The doctors said that too. And so why the hell do I still think we made a terrible mistake.'

'Guilt,' she said. 'That's quite common. You have to put it behind you. For Tess's sake. Next time it will be fine, I'm sure. Has she had counselling about it?'

'There won't be a next time,' he said, even as it finally dawned on him. 'She's made that clear.'

'Oh, well . . . she'll probably change her mind. Goodness, is that the time?' Yvonne clattered to her feet, smiled very brightly. 'I must go.'

Damn.

He hadn't meant to say any of that, he thought, as he watched her disappear up her drive. Confession time, was it? He felt better for having said it though. Sometimes, even though you were well aware privately of the truth of the matter, it needed to be said, spoken of, before it became fact.

And the fact was, although he still loved Tess in a way, he no longer liked her very much.

* * *

'It's always Christmas when things happen, you mark my words, Mrs Makepeace,' Ella said darkly.

She was halfway up the stepladder decorating the Christmas tree. Constance stood at the foot of the steps holding them. The whole room smelt deliciously of pine needles. Bernard had set the tree up beside the window in the sitting room. One week to go, and for Constance the decorating of the tree signified the start of Christmas proper.

'And it makes it worse, you see, if something awful happens at Christmas,' she went on, stretching a little ambitiously over to the top of the tree. 'Do you want the fairy on top? Or the star?'

'The fairy,' Constance said, worried that Ella might fall. 'Do be careful, Mrs Bainbridge. We should have waited for Bernard.'

'He's neither use nor ornament. He'd have been off these steps, the tree with him,' she said with a sniff. 'No head for heights, you see. Something to do with his blood pressure, I think. Goes dizzy, he does. He has to sit on the edge of the bed a full five minutes before he gets up. There!'

She wobbled her way down and they stood to admire the result.

'Thank you. It looks lovely,' Constance said, switching on the little candle lights. Outside, the heavy morning frost was clearing only slowly from the lawns and the sky was a pale speckled grey. Snow was threatened, or rather promised, for Christmas Day itself.

'Road accidents, drink driving and the like, people popping off with excitement, and it spoils Christmas for ever for the ones left behind. Reminds you. Take my oldest brother, for instance . . .'

'How about a cup of tea?' Constance interrupted firmly. The story of Ella's oldest brother's shocking exit from this world was a north-eastern tragedy to rival a Greek one and she had no wish to suffer it again.

Ella, a little put out, stuffed the unused decorations in the box.

'I'll pop this down in the cellar first and then I'll put the kettle on.'

'A word about the cellar, Mrs Bainbridge . . .'

'What about it?' she asked guiltily. 'I had to move some of the boxes around the other day when I was looking for that cat of yours. I thought he'd got himself stuck. It's not for me to go looking through boxes, Mrs Makepeace.'

'No, it isn't, Ella. And I would prefer it if you don't.'

'Right you are.' She looked like a little girl caught out doing something naughty. 'About Christmas, Mrs Makepeace . . . I'm sorry to keep going on about it but are you quite sure you don't want to come to us? Me and Bernard would love to have you. I'm doing a turkey and a ham and a lovely strawberry trifle with fresh cream. I feel terrible leaving you here.'

'There's no need,' Constance said with slight smile. 'On Boxing Day, Smith and I will be perfectly all right on our own. The cold meal you plan for me will be adequate, and after all it's just another day as far as I'm concerned. On Christmas Day, however, I would like you to come up to feed Smith. I shall be gone early and won't return until past his teatime.'

'To your usual Christmas place?'

Constance nodded. Ella was bursting to know where but she had no intention of telling her. She was looking forward to it so much. From choice, she had kept the visits over the years to Christmas only.

'A great niece, is it? Did I hear you say you went to visit a great niece?'

Constance did not answer.

'Did I hear you mention a cup of tea, Ella?' she asked instead, taking a seat as Ella went huffily out.

Smith was exploring the Christmas tree. He circled it slowly, sniffing it, ginger fur softly brushing against the fine glass ornaments, not dislodging a single one. Satisfied at last, he came over to Constance and leapt onto the arm of the chair and thence to her knee.

'Ella is beside herself with curiosity. If only she knew, Smith,' Constance whispered. 'She would be quite ecstatic at the scale of *my* tragedies. It would keep her going for simply years.'

# 26

Excitement tingled in Stephanie's veins. Christmas Eve. Caryn Lodge was a dream. Festooned from top to bottom. Outside, she had strewn coloured lights over one of the firs. She had made a laurel and red eucalyptus wreath for the front door with a sumptuous red satin bow to finish it off. Rather naughty, perhaps, because Tess did such special ones herself and would perhaps bring one along. She hoped Tess would not take it the wrong way. Tess was so difficult. For no reason sometimes that annoyed look would cross her face, the one Stephanie tried desperately hard to avoid. She was certainly not trying to out-do her stepdaughter.

Tess and Andrew were expected later and when they arrived they could relax and enjoy a glass of spicy punch and one of her melt-in-the-mouth mince pies. She had spent a frantic few days in the kitchen finishing off, enjoying every moment, and there was enough food to feed an army. As well as the usual cake and desserts, she had made candies and sugared confections. She had her Christmas menu written out and timed to perfection. The personal Christmas crackers, home-made of course, were filled with a few little extravagances, ready.

The sitting room was newly decorated in shades of dusky pink and she had – she hoped it wouldn't look too presumptuous – hung a couple of her paintings on the wall. She had had a good pre-Christmas session at the gallery, selling quite a number of her paintings to local people. She hoped they were buying them because they liked them and not just because they felt sorry for her. Joe said she put too low a price on them but she had no confidence in her work, her artistic work. Of course

Joe enthused, but then he loved her and would not hurt her by telling her otherwise. Conspicuously Tess did not enthuse which was probably a more accurate assessment. She still had not offered to take any in the shops and Stephanie did not wish to ask yet again on pain of receiving a blunt answer.

Having a stepdaughter who was an expert florist was a bit nerve-racking and she so wanted Tess to approve her efforts. On the mantelpiece, she had removed the ornaments and in their place was a careful arrangement of holly from the garden, blue pine, rosehips and golden glass pears.

There were two Christmas trees. Joe had grumbled a bit about all the fuss but he did not understand her love of Christmas, grumbled every year about the extraordinary effort she put into it.

One tree was in the hall and one in the drawing room. The one in the drawing room was decorated purely in white and silver with satin bows and pearls and on the table she had arranged some white gladioli, longiflorum lilies and spray carnations. The flowers that Tess would undoubtedly bring along would find a home elsewhere.

She went across to the window to check on the weather. Wonderful! The garden was plain, essentially a big lawn with an island bed but beyond, the gentle bump of the hills pushed upwards and from the back of the house, other hills stretched into the distance and there was no sign of any other habitation. After years of being hemmed in by other people in the various bedsits and flats she had frequented, this was bliss. Everyone had thought she was married to her work, and she had been until she met Joe. His fiery personality and wicked eyes had quite overwhelmed her and she handed in her intention to resign at the end of term leaving them in a dizzy shambles workwise but not caring greatly for she was in love.

And she still was.

She was worried about Joe a little. Something was wrong at work but he wasn't telling and that worried her even more. He was not the sort of man who discussed his work with her but then he did treat her so like a woman. The little woman at home who did not understand such things. It amused and delighted her to play along with it. Why not? She knew that Joe adored her and that was all she needed to know. But she really wanted to tell him that if the worst thing happened and he found himself out of a job, it wasn't the end of the world. She could always go back to work if necessary and also, if necessary, they could move to something a little more modest. She wouldn't mind. She would miss this house, of course, but as long as she and Joe were together and happy, who cared about where they lived?

Fat flakes of snow drifted down, steadying themselves as if descending by parachute, already beginning to have an effect on the landscape, a soft sifting on the hill peaks. Soon it would be so silent, that special hold-your-breath silence that snow brings. A nuisance though, just at this very moment when both Joe and Tess were somewhere on the road. Once they were all here, her family, then it could snow for all it was worth.

Happily she looked round, deciding that everything was quite perfect. She had the wine and the food. She had decided on turkey at the last because Joe had finally admitted he did not care for goose, and there were individual Christmas puddings with brandy butter. Once again, her mind turned to food.

The sound of the car and the crunch of gravel roused her. Oh, thank goodness, there was Joe. He had to work until the very last minute at the office and she had worried that he would be very late. Quickly, she fluffed her hair with her fingers, went to meet him. He was shaking a fine spray of snow off his overcoat when she arrived, leaning over to kiss the top of her head lightly.

'I'll pour you a sherry, darling,' she said, just as the phone rang.

'Can't they leave me alone for one bloody second?' he said, going to answer it. She heard subdued voices, could not make out what was being said.

'Something wrong?' she asked when he came back in.

'No. Nothing.'

'You can tell me,' she said quietly. 'That's what I'm here for, darling.'

'Nothing is wrong,' he said with a smile. 'Stop worrying. Now . . . are we all organised?'

'Yes,' she told him. 'Every last thing. Oh, I love Christmas, Joe. My very favourite time of year.'

She sat beside him on the sofa. She daren't tell him, of course, that the only fly in the ointment, as it were, was Tess. He adored Tess so she had to be very, very careful.

'It will be wonderful,' she repeated softly. 'It's already beginning to snow. I feel it in my bones, Joe, that it will be the best Christmas ever.'

'You make the most of it, my love,' he said.

She felt a moment's unease. That seemed a very peculiar thing to say.

'We should have set out earlier,' Andrew said, peering through the windscreen. It was that awful half light of approaching dusk in this low-point of the year, short dark days. He hated driving on these narrow country roads. It was just starting to snow and it would be ten times worse up at Joe's.

'I couldn't leave the girls to do everything. It's my busy time,' Tess told him. 'One of my busy times. There's the mistletoe and the holly wreaths and everybody deciding at the last minute that they should take flowers along to their loved ones.' She stole a glance at the flowers in the back seat, the ones for Stephanie. Simple, nothing too elaborate. Appropriate. She had taken some flowers up for Constance Makepeace and again she had chosen to keep them simple. A simple posy often meant more to people and Constance had been delighted at the gesture. Tess was a little disappointed that nothing had been said yet about West House. The suspense, the not knowing for sure, was driving her mad.

Hearing Andrew sigh, she glanced at him. 'What's the problem? Worried about the weather?'

'I am. You know as well as I do what it can be like over the fell. Drifts and blocked roads before you know what's what. Look . . . it's just starting to snow.'

'God, I hope we don't get stuck there. Stephanie will have enough food to last us till spring but that's not the point, is it? I can't stick her for longer than a couple of days.' She sighed, put on a passable imitation of Stephanie's voice, 'Shall I do a goose, Tess, or would you really prefer turkey? Do say. I don't mind. It doesn't matter to me. I'm just a little housewife. I just aim to please.'

Andrew smiled a little even if there was an edge to Tess's playfulness.

'Behave yourself,' he said. 'The children will be building a snowman if we get many more flakes. And Yvonne has to get Mrs Whitworth from the home up to the house in her wheelchair. God knows how she'll manage if it gets thick.'

'Who's Mrs Whitworth?' Tess asked, against her better judgement. Did she really wish to know?

'An old lady who lives at Greenview Rest Home. She's going to Yvonne's for Christmas Day.'

'How very charitable of her. Have you noticed she's a bit into do-gooding,' Tess said with a short amused laugh. 'I didn't see Robin at all. Leaving it a bit late, isn't he?'

'Oh . . . I don't think he'll be there. He's working, apparently.'

'What a shame. I suppose somebody has to at Christmas.'

'Portia's said a few things. I'm not sure that all's well with Yvonne and Robin.'

'Aren't you, indeed?' She leaned forward and switched the heater on to full power. 'And just what has the little Miss been saying?'

'I hardly like to say. It wasn't meant to be for general consumption,' he said quietly. 'Out of the mouths of babes and all that.'

'I'm hardly general consumption, am I? I'm your wife. You might have told me.'

'What is there to tell? I didn't think you'd be interested.'

'Oh, come on . . .'

She sighed, fell silent. Maybe there was nothing to it but she didn't like him keeping secrets from her. It made little difference in fact whether or not Yvonne and that husband of hers officially separated. They'd been so in spirit for years. It had been perfectly obvious when they went for dinner that the man was an obsessive, a loner. He'd sat there, surrounded by his family, and been quite alone. Tess sensed it. She supposed she might be a bit that way herself.

She dismissed it. Why the hell should she worry about Yvonne?

The immediate problem was to get through another of Stephanie's jolly Christmases without losing her temper. Stephanie was like a little girl. She made her own Christmas crackers, her own this, her own that. They played games, sang carols and they went for a long long walk on Christmas Day afternoon, almost the only walk of the year for her father. And herself, come to that. Then it was tea, a fabulous affair, and yet more games. And this year, there was the added worry of her father's work problems. He had not mentioned them again so she hoped that all was now resolved. He had a knack of fearing the worst, before wriggling away intact.

'I can't understand why there's no interest in our house,' she said as it niggled at her.

'Have some patience. It's early days.'

She sniffed. 'Patience! If Constance offers us the house, what will we do if we haven't sold ours? I mean, she's not going to give it away, is she? She'll expect some sort of realistic price. What about the money you got when you left your last job? How much have we left?'

'It's rainy day money, Tess.'

'It *is* a rainy day. We are not going to miss getting West House on a technicality. We can use that money if necessary, and then pay ourselves back when we sell the house.'

'If she's going to practically give it away, as you keep on saying, then she's not going to be bothered about money, is she?' he said. 'Stop worrying. I think you might have this all wrong, Tess. Somebody happens to say a few indiscreet words and you jump to all sorts of conclusions.'

'She's weighing me up. And you. She likes you. I'd still like to be in a position to get things tied up, and being without ready cash is a bore.'

'There's always Joe. You can always ask Joe for yet another loan.'

She glanced at him sharply, hearing the sarcasm. 'You know I only do that if absolutely necessary. In any case, I don't want him to know about West House until it's all settled. I want to surprise him.'

'Hasn't he had enough surprises?'

'I don't understand you. You've been no help whatsoever to me recently. You refuse to help Joe with his little accounting problem and you're lukewarm about this. For God's sake, do you want West House or not? We've got to keep on at her in case she changes her mind or suddenly goes completely off her head. She must be half daft already to be even thinking of doing such a thing. She might die on us. Have you thought of that?'

'And you have no qualms about taking advantage of her?'

'No. Somebody else will if we don't. It's not for us to query her motives. She's in her eighties. People do peculiar things then. Look at the way she dresses. Tracksuits at her age? I ask you, darling. Tracksuits are so unflattering even to someone like me.'

Andrew managed a laugh at that and Tess smiled ruefully. She knew all was not well with his business. He was muttering about taking another job after Christmas. OK, if that's what he wanted to do, it didn't matter to her one way or the other although it had been rather useful to have him at home.

She frowned as the snow, gathering strength, dizzied towards them. Visibility was poor, getting poorer by the minute, and she knew the road surface was icy. One false move and they would end up in the stone wall at the side of the road. She stopped talking and let him concentrate on getting them to Caryn Lodge in one piece.

As they neared it at last, she saw the coloured fairy lights slung across a couple of trees on the drive.

'Just look at that. She'll be looking out for us,' she said with a short laugh as he swung into the drive. 'The mince pies will be warming through now and there's bound to be spicy punch. And then, we'll have a light supper and play charades. A little prize and a round of applause for the winner. Honestly, darling, is this woman a grown-up? Why did he marry her? My mother was so sophisticated. She would never have played charades. Steffi is so incredibly predictable. I bet she buys you a shirt and me a silk scarf. Frankly, Andrew, I sometimes wonder why I bother.'

He pulled the car to a halt beside Joe's.

'So do I,' he said.

# 27

Constance dressed with special care, for Penny's boys took particular notice of fine clothes. She wore a warm woollen dress under her camel cashmere coat and a rather fetching Robin Hood style hat with a feather. Her pearls, of course, and the diamond ring Archie had bought her, the one she wore on special occasions only. Smith was in a mood, well aware that she was going to be out for the whole day and that he would be alone. He sat haughtily, slit-eyed and silent, on the very best silk cushion on the antique chesterfield, knowing she disapproved of that.

She ignored him as best she could, looking out of the window impatiently, waiting for the taxi. The snow was several inches deep this morning, this Christmas morning. Unable to face a journey down to St Cuthbert's late at night, she had watched the midnight service on television instead, so she was feeling a little tired but no matter. She could relax when she was in the taxi, close her eyes, have a nap maybe.

It had stopped snowing but the sky was dirty white and low slung and looked as if it was ready to dislodge another skyfull. The garden was transformed into a theatrical snow-scene, bushes out of shape and weighed down. The near garden was looking particularly attractive with frozen catkins hanging like icicles, the grey and silver foliage stiff with frost. The very air was crisp. A trail of birdprints and some heavier unknown creature's marred the virgin snow, not Smith, for he disliked it and had not ventured out yet.

Ah . . . there was the taxi, or rather the splendid limousine that Mr Miller used for longer journeys, making its way slowly up the drive spoiling with its wheel tracks the picture-postcard perfection of the snow-scene. Constance gathered together the presents, her handbag and gloves, and prepared to leave, stroking Smith's furry head as she passed him by way of apology.

The taxi driver was known to her for she had specifically requested that Mr Miller himself transport her. It cost a lot to hire him for the whole day but he was alone like her and did not seem to mind, and indeed she always made sure he was properly recompensed with a generous tip for going so out of his way on Christmas Day.

He drove her there and was waiting for her when she was ready to leave. What he did in the meantime whilst he was waiting she had no idea. It was that awkward distance, a little too far for him to drive home in comfort and then return for her later. She thought he might visit some friends too in the neighbourhood but it was not her business to enquire, just as it was certainly not his to ask after hers. After all these years, she had not felt the need to enlighten him as to whom she was visiting and, to his credit, he did not seem to possess Mrs Bainbridge's conspicuous curiosity.

To her dismay, it was not Mr Miller. She realised that immediately for Mr Miller was a small, kindly man and this man was anything but. A ruffian, no less. A giant of a man with a flattened nose and a closely cropped head. He was wearing jeans and the kind of khaki jacket soldiers use when they are crawling through undergrowth to escape the enemy. He looked most disreputable.

'A happy Christmas, Mrs Makepeace, isn't it?' he called, smiling a crooked smile that managed to make him look slightly less menacing, reaching out his hand for the gifts she was carrying. 'Give us your parcels and I'll put them in the back for you.'

'Good morning. Whom am I addressing?' Constance asked coolly, handing over the parcels and offering him season's greetings with some reluctance. 'I was expecting Mr Miller. Mr Miller usually transports me.'

'That's right. I've stepped in at the last minute. Done you a favour, Mrs Makepeace. He had an eyeful last night. Conked out he is this morning. He's not used to booze, silly sod, and he can't risk losing his licence. He says to tell you he's very sorry. Right then, ready for off, pet?'

'I beg your pardon?' she said, tight with annoyance, her chill breath puffing out into the morning air.

He looked puzzled, smiled uncertainly at her, showing the uneven teeth once more.

'Ready for off then, pet?' he repeated, rather loudly as if she was hard of hearing.

As it was the season of goodwill, she let the quite appalling over-familiarity go for once. Mrs Bainbridge had only ever addressed her the once as 'pet'.

'Are you one of his employees?' she asked, still unsure. She was not usually anxious about her personal safety but he looked awfully huge and quite capable of dreadful atrocities even to sweet little old ladies such as she.

'Just started,' he said cheerfully, quite oblivious it seemed to her doubts. 'I'll get you there, pet, no sweat. I've rung up and the roads are passable with care, they say. That really means they're crap but have no fear with me. I'm a good driver. I'll have you there in an hour and a bit.'

It was a big comfortable car so Constance, having ascertained the driver's name was Colin Hawkins, left him to it. She would give him the benefit of the doubt as Mr Miller had done no less in employing him. Mr Miller, pleasantly taciturn as he was, was however always willing to engage in a little inconsequential chat on the journey but she did not feel she and this man would have very much to talk about.

How wrong she was!

All she could see from her comfortable seat in the back was the back of his neck, a bull of a neck below the very short haircut. He wore a thin gold necklace.

They were scarcely out of the gates before he was off.

'That *your* house back there, then?'

'Yes.'

'Do you live there on your own?' Disconcertingly, he half turned as he spoke. 'Bloody palace. You'd get my bedsit in the porch.'

'It is rather large,' she admitted, most irritated as it occurred that she was too late now to catch a glimpse of the house.

Another last glimpse.

The last time she would set off from West House at Christmas. Next year, she would be leaving from the cottage. Ah, well . . .

They were travelling swishily through an orangey slush brought about by the sand and grit that had been shovelled on the road last night.

'Do you mind if I smoke?' she asked for Mr Miller was such a nuisance. He had a bad chest and had once asked her, politely of course, if she might refrain. A No Smoking notice was prominently pinned to the back of the driver's seat but Constance was more than happy to ignore that if the driver was. She needed a cigarette to calm her ruffled nerves.

'Smoke? Only if that means I can,' he said cheerfully. 'I'll have one with you, pet, if you don't mind.'

'Can you smoke and drive?'

'Try me. Helps the concentration,' he said. 'Tell you what, it's hard currency where I've just been.'

A dreadful thought assailed her as she lit and passed a cigarette over.

'Her Majesty's Prison,' he said clearly, confirming her worst fears. 'Just out last week. For good. A miscarriage of justice, it was. Framed, you see. There's some nasty people in this world.'

'I see,' she said faintly, feeling in desperate need of the cigarette. There would be a formal complaint following this episode to Mr Miller. How dare he do this?

'Hope you don't mind me telling you but the way I look at it you might as well be straight with people,' he went on, cursing colourfully as the car slid to the right. 'Mr Miller is giving me a chance, you see, and I won't cock it up. I'm hoping you'll give him a good report, pet.'

Constance sighed. She was doomed to several hours of this! Dare she ask him to moderate his language, refrain from calling her 'pet', or would he take dreadful offence?

'Tell me, Mr Hawkins,' she enquired with just a tiny glimmer of curiosity. 'For what were you imprisoned?'

'What was I put away for do you mean? What was the *alleged* offence? Nicking. And I didn't do it. They have it in for you, you see, once you've done youth custody. And I couldn't come up with no alibi except my girl, but they didn't believe her. They said she was bound to say I was with her but you see the thing is, Mrs Makepeace, I was.'

'Nicking.' Leaving aside the validity of his alibi, she felt a relief. It could have been worse, much worse. 'And what were you accused of stealing?'

'There you are. You've made the same mistake they all make, pet. Nicking's not the same as stealing in my book. Stealing is taking something off somebody. Like . . . say I grabbed your purse, now. That would be stealing. Now nicking, on the other hand, is disposing of stuff that happens to come your way, stuff in transit, not really belonging to anybody proper. Get my drift? Car parts, anyhow.'

She puffed on her cigarette, feeling a little calmer. The snow was piled dirtily at the side of the road they were on and sprays splashed the windscreen whenever a car went by on the opposite side of the road. It was very quiet yet, most people probably still indoors unwrapping presents and having a late breakfast.

She would not argue with this young man for after all it was Christmas and one ought to be charitable to one's neighbours and certainly to one's driver. She would endeavour to ascertain what made the poor man do what he did.

'Bedsit, you said?' she said. 'Do you live alone too, Mr Hawkins?'

'Colin,' he said quickly. 'I'm Hawkins but I've told you to call me Colin. I've just got this place temporary until I get things sorted. My girlfriend's shacked up with somebody else. It happens when you're out of it. Can't blame her, can I? Don't you worry, I'll have her back in no time. This other bloke's a fairy.'

'How long were you in prison . . .' she hesitated and then realised he would not be content until she called him by his Christian name. 'Colin?'

'Eighteen months, pet. Got out early on account of good behaviour. Shit and sugar, did you see that bloody lorry?'

Constance gave a little warning cough. Really!

'So what do you intend to do now? You have a job and a bedsit, so that is a start, isn't it? The essentials for staying on the straight and narrow, I would have thought.'

'Were you a probation officer once?' The voice was suddenly suspicious.

'Good gracious, no. I wasn't anything. I've never had a job as such,' Constance said. 'One didn't necessarily need to have a job in my day. I was married, you see. My husband supported me.'

'But you have money. I don't.'

'Yes, but even if I did not have money, I would not steal it.'

'Nick, not steal,' he said sharply. The hand that rested on the steering wheel held the cigarette and he took a quick drag again. 'We never had no money, you see. And my girlfriend was always expecting. She only has to look at me and she falls pregnant. Four, we have.'

'Four children?' she said. 'You and your girlfriend have four children?'

'Yes. Jodie, Eugenie . . . that's after the princess . . . Chelsea and Ashleigh.'

'Four little girls. What charming names!' Constance said with a slight smile. So . . . she and Colin had something in common after all. They had both named their children after princesses.

'Shit! Accident up ahead. Do you want me to do a detour, Mrs Makepeace? We can take the back road.'

'Yes, if you're happy to do that, Colin. I must be there for lunch time. They expect me, you see.'

'No sweat,' he said, turning the car round in one deft manoeuvre and going down a side road that was worryingly narrow, made even narrower by the banked up snow.

'What will you do whilst you're waiting for me?' she asked. 'I'm sure it can be arranged that you wait indoors and I'm quite sure there will be enough food to spare an extra plate for you. Would you like me to ask?'

'I've got a flask and my snap,' he said. 'That'll do me, pet.'

'But you'll be very cold and bored,' she protested.

'I've been bored for eighteen months,' he said in a suddenly gentle voice. 'I can occupy myself. You go and visit your friends and don't worry about me.'

'Would you care for another cigarette, Colin?'

'You bet. Thanks. When I saw you this morning, I wouldn't have put you down for a smoker, not with a hat like that.'

She laughed, genuinely amused, passed him one.

She had another full packet in her handbag and she would make sure he got that at the end of the trip together with his tip.

'You'll have to give me directions when we get within spitting distance,' he said. 'I'm from Middlesbrough myself. Don't know this place at all.'

'I will certainly give you directions. It's quite straightforward, as I recall. Will you be seeing your children over Christmas?' Constance asked, immediately regretting the enquiry, for it was not a very delicate question under the circumstances.

'I'll drop in tomorrow,' he said, surprising her. 'I've managed to get some presents. Dolls. A mate of mine had a consignment. Not nicked, mind. Do you think they'll like dolls? Do they still like dolls?'

'Oh, yes . . . I'm sure so.'

After acquainting him with the last minute directions, she fell silent as they drew nearer. It always had this effect. A sobering effect.

She found herself worrying too about the gifts *she* had bought. The chocolates and sweets were easy, of course, and the socks, the brighter the better. For some reason, the boys adored socks and had a huge collection. The colouring books and those special sorts of pens, felt-tipped, and the jigsaws, were also fairly straightforward, but the music tapes had proved a major problem for she did not listen to the country and western music that Penny informed her they liked best. It had meant engaging the help of an assistant in the Woolworths store who had, despite her unfortunate multi-earringed appearance and slovenly accent, proved very helpful. The boys would play them, she knew with resignation, over and over today.

'We're here, Mrs Makepeace.'

He pulled up outside. Got out. Helped her out. Lifted the parcels out of the boot.

'Thank you Colin,' she said with a gracious nod.

He was on his way back to the taxi, turning to offer her an unexpected and rather pleasant smile.

'Have a nice day,' he said.

Ella walked up to the house in the afternoon.

Bernard did not fancy his chances of getting the car up Staine Bank and she quite liked walking in the snow anyway. She left Bernard to it, watching some old black and white film.

Why was it always such an anti-climax . . . Christmas!

You went mad just before. Sending Christmas cards, putting up the tree and the decorations. Queueing at the butcher's, buying in enough bread to last a week, the mince pies, the sherry, the last minute bits and pieces you always forgot. And even Christmas Eve was a bit special. She liked Christmas Eve when the shops had finally shut so it was too late if you'd forgotten anything.

Christmas Day itself was only exciting if you had children and she didn't. When she'd given Bernard his present – a new cardigan he'd better not use for gardening – and he'd given her hers – a nice butterfly brooch from the jeweller's in a little blue box – that was it. They had a nice meal but then they always did. They ate well.

So, when the Queen had finished her lovely talk, what else was there? A walk up the hill to West House would do her good and give her an appetite for tea and stop her stuffing herself with dates and chocolates.

She trudged on past One-Mile Bridge, stepping into the soft snow and leaving behind a trail of size five wellington prints. It was funny to think that this would be the last time she did this and no mistake. Next year they'd be at Primrose Cottage, Mrs Makepeace and the cat, if it survived the move. She'd heard cats were funny about things like that. She'd heard they thought more about places than people.

She'd asked Mr Miller once where he took Mrs Makepeace on Christmas Day in the taxi but he wouldn't say. Client confidentiality, he said, coming over all pompous. Come off it, Jack man, you'd think you were a doctor, she'd said, you can tell me, it won't go any further. But he didn't and she supposed, all in all, she respected him for that. If ever she had a secret liaison with another man planned, she'd know who she'd get to take her there. Secret liaison? She smiled at the very idea. As if. Even if Bernard snuffed it tomorrow, there would be nobody else for her. He was all right, was Bernard. You knew where you were with him and, although he never said as much, she knew he thought a lot about her. One decent man in a lifetime was enough.

Whilst she was feeding his lordship that cat, she might as well have another look in the cellar, see what she could find. It was a nuisance doing it when Mrs Makepeace was around because she got a sweat on when she thought she might be found out any minute. Mrs Makepeace took it upon herself to look at her bottles of wine sometimes. Check the labels, she said. So today, with no danger of being interrupted, she could search around in peace. She had told Bernard she might have a walk after so he wouldn't be worried. He'd drop off anyway after that big dinner so she could take her time.

She'd have to be careful, do the boxes up properly afterwards.

She let herself in the kitchen door and Smith was instantly at her feet. Miaowing.

A parcel, Christmas wrapped, was on the kitchen table and she went over to it, pushing him aside, ignoring the plaintive miaows. He could wait. She knew what it was of course for it had always been the same ever since the cat arrived. A present for her from him.

The card said, 'Thank you, Mrs Bainbridge, for looking after me today. Smith'

Crackers, it was, but you had to make allowances for the fact that old Mrs Makepeace was ever so slightly daft when it came to the cat, treating him like he was human. But the box of chocolates was lovely and it was nice to know she was appreciated. She and Bernard had already received a little Christmas bonus as well as a bottle of best whisky. It lasted them the whole year.

'Right, man.' She looked down into the bright green eyes. 'I can see I'll get no peace so I'll get you your dinner first and then I'll see what's what down there in that cellar.'

The best cat food, salmon and trout mixed, and today, because it was Christmas Day, he was to have real cream from a carton in the fridge.

Ella waited until he was happily lapping it up before she went down to the cellar. Whatever it was that Constance was keeping to herself, she intended to find out.

# 28

Stephanie flopped down on the sofa in the drawing room, smiled at Andrew.

'Lovely meal,' he said, patting his stomach. 'That last mince pie did it. I couldn't eat another thing.'

Stephanie sighed her relief.

'Do you want to listen to the Queen's Speech?'

'No disrespect intended, but I can live without it,' he said with a grin. 'Do you?'

She shook her head. 'We'll catch it later.'

Rather to Stephanie's relief, Tess had a headache and had retired to bed for a rest. Tess was frankly a wet blanket, distinctly half-hearted about playing the games she had devised for them. Joe, after consuming three glasses of red wine with his meal, was slumped half asleep in the sitting room so she and Andrew must make the best of things.

Another hour and she would have to start preparing the tea. A buffet with a boiled ham, a superb selection of savouries and a variety of salads. And of course the Christmas cake, home-made and iced, the chocolate Yule log and her speciality orange and lemon trifle. Nobody would eat a thing but that was beside the point. It still had to be there in great quantity and they could take the whole evening to nibble at it.

In the corner of the room, the tree sparkled, the whole room glowed with Christmas shades of red and gold and silver and she reflected happily that this was what it was all about. Joe teased her a little about all this and the fact that last night she had been quite unable to sleep with excitement. Finally dropping off into a deep dreamless sleep, she was awoken early with a kiss and a murmured. 'I love you' as usual. It was wonderful to be so adored by Joe.

This was the family Christmas she had often dreamed about and now it was happening. It was a shame that there were no children in the family for that would have really been the icing on the cake, but for her and Joe that idea had been discounted for purely practical reasons and for Tess and Andrew – well, she hardly liked to ask what the current thinking was in that camp. It was certainly not a question she could ask of Andrew. Nor for that matter of Tess. They did not share confidences. She had tried, after it happened, to be there for Tess but Tess had shunned sympathy in a very robust fashion and if that was her way of dealing with the situation, so be it. Joe had told her to let it be. Nowadays the subject was never referred to.

Tomorrow, they would eat less. A simpler meal and a walk, whatever the weather. Nobody felt like venturing out today and she was too overwhelmed with excitement herself to bother.

She had bought her husband a pure wool sweater from Marks & Spencer but Joe, prone to extravagance as he was, had bought her a beautiful diamond pendant. Tess had been quite jealous; she had seen it in her eyes. Poor Tess. Stephanie knew she could not compete with Joe's first wife and had given up trying. She was just glad that Tess was not a child, for then it would be much worse. On the other hand, Tess sometimes acted like a child in a quite ridiculous way and Stephanie felt awkward on occasions about showing Joe affection because of the effect on Tess.

She fingered the new pendant a little worriedly. Expensive jewellery that had to spend most of its time hidden away in the safe was not her thing at all but it was a waste of time trying to explain to Joe, and a bit ungrateful too. It was the thought that counted and he had wanted to buy it for her when, at the moment, he could ill afford it. He was saying nothing about his problems at work and she would not dream of asking.

Instead of the Queen's Speech, she switched on the stereo, very low so it would not be too intrusive, a beautiful collection of Debussy piano works. Mellow and perfectly in keeping with their relaxed mood.

She reached languidly for a chocolate, searching for something to say to Andrew. He seemed slightly preoccupied and, although she had said nothing to Joe for she did not want to worry him with other matters, she would swear there was a problem between Andrew and Tess. She had never thought them particularly suited but then it was hard to think of the sort of man who would happily take on Tess with her up and down moods and fierce ambition. Ambition was fine, in its place, but not when it was at the exclusion of everything else.

'How's your business doing, Andrew?' she asked. Just a polite question, not really intended to be anything other than that but Andrew looked quite startled and momentarily guilty.

'OK, thanks.' His shrug was explicit and she was reminded of her students, forlornly fibbing. Andrew had a very honest face.

'Only OK?' she asked gently.

'If you must know, Stephanie, not very well. I went for an interview for a job but didn't get it. I have applications in for a couple more.'

'I see. I'm sorry. So . . . working for yourself isn't a success?'

'It could be, I think, but I haven't managed to get it together yet. Tess is right. I'm too easygoing. Working from home seems great but you can be easily distracted by domestic problems, or I can. Added to that, I have a continuous cashflow problem. I seem to have got the worst payers imaginable as my clients. I don't chase people enough. It's a pity, because in many ways I like being at home.'

'So do I,' Stephanie said earnestly. 'I love it. As you know, Andrew, I worked twenty years in academia and thoroughly enjoyed it but now I'm perfectly happy to be at home and look after Joe. I see it as my new role in life and I'm not ashamed of it. I don't miss the lecture circuit one little bit. Well, not much.'

She looked round the room. She had changed it a good deal since she married Joe and moved in, and she was well aware that Tess did not approve which was understandable. However, she had felt it very important to make her own mark on it and that had to include masses of bookshelves for her masses of books. Joe's first wife had not been a reader. It also included quiet corners for her to sit and read and listen to the classical music she loved, and comfortable, if not necessarily fashionable, furniture.

Nothing matched. There were too many patterns, Tess had once told her, unable to hide her irritation, too many colours, and had she never heard of colour coordination? Next time she must ask for help. Tess would be delighted to offer assistance.

Stephanie knew better than to argue with Joe's daughter and had managed to look suitably crest-fallen at the criticism and certainly agreed that next time she would seek advice. However, she had not changed a thing. She always found that the low-key softly-softly approach worked best with Tess. Tess thought her so very dull but that was Tess's problem. Tess had no idea that she and Joe enjoyed a thoroughly satisfactory marriage, their roles clearly and happily defined, and had a buoyant sex life. She had a feeling that Tess might very well be appalled.

'Joe's lucky to have you,' Andrew's voice broke into her thoughts.

'Thank you.' She smiled her appreciation. What a generous thing for him to say. He was such a nice man, Andrew. Tess had no idea how to treat him. She treated him, in Stephanie's opinion, far too casually, sometimes she was downright hostile. She would lose him if she wasn't careful. A man needed a little cosseting, to be made to feel he was special. 'Can I ask you something, Andrew?'

'Fire away.'

He reached for the little glass dish of nuts, picked up a few, cupped them in his hands.

'It's about Joe. Do you remember the surprise party?' She laughed a little. 'Of course you do. Well . . . did you detect an atmosphere at the party among his colleagues?'

'Difficult to say,' Andrew said. 'I was too busy trying to be sociable to notice that sort of thing. They're not my kind of people anyway. I don't go in for corporate jollity and multiple back-stabbing.'

'Neither do I. But . . . I think there's a problem at work that he's not talking about. Do you know anything about it at all?'

She was watching him carefully. She had had enough dealings with people over the years to know how to interpret body language and of course she knew instantly that he did know something.

'He probably doesn't want to upset you yet,' Andrew said after a moment's hesitation. 'But yes, there is a bit of a problem. It's to do with the takeover. For a start, they're investigating his expenses. He's been on the fiddle, you know, with his company card as well as various other tricks.'

'Oh, dear . . . don't tell me. I wondered about that. He's always very cagey and I don't ask. He once said it was just something that everybody did and I wasn't to worry about it.' She pushed the box of chocolates towards him, unwrapped a coconut cream for herself. 'It's not serious, is it? I mean, the job is everything to him. He couldn't lose it, could he, Andrew?'

'I don't know. If there's enough evidence against him, then, yes, I suppose he might. But I doubt it. I think it will be settled in another way as it usually is at his level. It'll all be hushed up. Somebody lower down the pecking order would be sacked on the spot.' He looked pained at the idea. 'It's not the first time it's happened, Stephanie. He'll be asked to leave politely but they'll give him money to go. It will all be dealt with very cautiously and delicately.'

'But he's only been with them five years,' she said quietly.

She knew enough about pensions to be worried herself at the thought. She had her own modest pension, earned a very little from her paintings, but despite her own efforts to make him cut back a little, they lived life to the full. Joe spent a lot. Goodness me, why on earth had he bought her a *diamond* pendant? Costume jewellery would have sufficed. If he did get the push then very likely the house would have to go. It wasn't the end of the world, of course, but a pity. She liked this house and she loved the view. She had a few paintings of this very view.

'Hey, don't look like that. I shouldn't have told you,' Andrew said, smiling at her. 'Or I should have lied.'

She shook her head. 'I appreciate you being straight with me,' she said. 'I did ask. It's just like him, you know, to keep it secret.'

'I wouldn't worry,' Andrew said, and his calm and relaxed manner was a bit of a comfort even though he had just confirmed all she had feared. 'He won't go down without a fight. Leave him to it. He'll tell you when he's ready.'

'Will he?'

She knew Tess was his daughter and therefore special to him

but she sometimes felt just a twinge of jealousy. Like now. Tess knew an awful lot about Joe's work. Tess knew people *he* knew. And Tess took advantage. Tess could wind Joe round her little finger and frequently did. It was unforgivable that she should keep expecting him to give her huge loans that she never repaid. Stephanie had, however, only once made an adverse comment about it and got short shrift in return. Joe's relationship with his daughter was non-negotiable.

'I suppose he's spoken to Tess?' she asked, trying unsuccessfully to keep the dismay out of her voice.

Andrew nodded, grimaced, trying to be kind.

She stood up, smoothed down her new long skirt. It was scarlet for she had quite taken a liking to brighter colours but it had failed the Tess test miserably. Tess had already looked her up and down in that way of hers, commented to the effect that you couldn't get away from red in the shops this year. Simply everyone was wearing red. She herself was in pale silver grey.

'Can I leave you to yourself a moment?'

'Of course. This music's nice and relaxing.'

She left him to the delightful Clair de Lune and went into the kitchen where her buffet preparations were already in hand.

She was determined their little problem would not spoil the rest of the day.

Bad news or not, it could jolly well wait.

# 29

Agnes was sitting in an armchair in Yvonne's sitting room, propped up with extra cushions. She was wearing a black and yellow shiny print dress and a heavy cardigan. She had a new very tight perm, a fine white net covering it. Portia, fascinated for some reason by Agnes's varicosed legs, sat at her feet. Getting her here through the soft snow in the wheelchair had been a nightmare although Agnes had been surprisingly good humoured throughout, even when the children wanted a 'go' pushing her all at the same time, a minor scuffle following as a result.

'How very old are you, Mrs Whitworth?' Portia asked Agnes in that fearfully direct way of hers and Yvonne, hearing the question, intervened.

'You mustn't ask that, Portia,' she said. 'It's rude to ask ladies their age.'

'Why?'

'Because it is. Ladies don't always like to admit their age.'

'Why don't they?'

'I'm ninety-six in March,' Agnes said suddenly. 'And if you've any more questions, young lady, ask them now because I'm going to have a nap in a minute.'

'*Ninety*-six! That's nearly a hundred, isn't it, Mummy? I've never met anybody as really old as that before.'

Yvonne smiled. Shoes kicked off, she was relaxing now after the hectic preparations for their meal. Presents were scattered all around and she had filled a binsack with torn up wrapping paper. Samantha, wearing a nurse's outfit over her new dress, was playing with her dressing-up doll and Harry with a little multi-storey garage. She just left them to it but it occurred that her children were remarkably politically incorrect.

They had all watched 'White Christmas' as promised, although the children had grown bored with it and retired quietly into the playroom half way through. Strangely, for Christmas Day, they were managing to behave in a relatively sober fashion. Tired, of course, from lack of sleep last night. Samantha had tried to stay awake to see Santa arrive. Yvonne had crept into their rooms in the early hours, leaving their stockings at the foot of their beds. In a way that had been the worst time, evoking suddenly fond memories of Robin, and slipping alone into her big bed had been the final bitter reminder that she had better get used to this for this was how it was going to be.

Awake at half five, some sort of excited breakfast, a trudge up to Greenview, collect Agnes, a sherry for the two of them, dinner and then 'White Christmas.'

Yvonne, keeping Agnes company, had dreamed her way through it, thinking not of a white Christmas but of Christmases past and the break-up with Robin. Agnes, sipping another sweet sherry, had been entranced by the film and had tears in her eyes when it was finished. Yvonne, suspecting there were happy memories attached to it, did not enquire further. Robin had rung earlier, thank God, and spoken to the children. And, almost as an afterthought, to her. Strange, but it felt so final now and she felt she was speaking to a stranger who just happened to be the father of her children. That's what it felt like then, when love finally died. There would be no resurrection. She knew that with certainty.

'Why have you got bumpy bits on your legs?'

Damn. She had known the question was coming for Portia would not be put off.

'When you're nearly ninety-six, lovie, you'll have bumpy bits on *your* legs,' Agnes said, quite unconcerned. 'Won't she, Mummy?'

'That's right. Portia, why don't you go and play? Mrs Whitworth wants to rest,' Yvonne said helplessly. 'Or perhaps we'll have a walk. Who wants a walk?'

Nobody wanted a walk. Silly idea anyway because of the wheelchair. She had no idea how she would get Agnes back. If it froze over, she would *not* get her back tonight and that would cause a few problems. Nothing that could not be surmounted, however.

'Relax, Mrs Lonsdale, you're all on edge,' Agnes said as Portia disappeared. 'I don't worry about what children say. They're lovely children. Count your blessings.'

Yvonne smiled a little.

'Is he away then? The man next door?'

'What?'

She looked at Agnes in surprise.

'Away for Christmas? Is he away? I see there are no lights on.'

'Oh, yes. They've gone to Tess's father's, I believe. He lives up the dale. Tess's mother died and he married again.'

'What's this Tess like?'

'Well . . .' Yvonne considered the question. 'She's very smart. Very professional. Runs three or four shops, I think. Does amazing things with flowers. I don't like her.'

'I know you don't,' Agnes said with a short laugh. 'What's to be done about it then? Is he happy?'

'I don't know,' she said, uncomfortable with this. 'I'm sure he is. They both have good jobs. They have a lovely home.'

'That's nothing to do with it, Mrs Lonsdale. Is it? You're not telling me everything, are you?' She adjusted her spectacles which frequently slipped. 'You can tell me anything at all. I could be dead tomorrow. It's a wonder I'm not already, the food they serve at that prison of mine.' The glance was shrewd. 'It won't go any further, believe me.'

'Mummy . . .' Portia, indignation on full power, appeared at the door. 'Harry said "bloody". Twice.'

'No more sweeties for him then,' Yvonne said absently, still looking at Agnes.

Portia came further into the room, carrying a game. She showed it carefully to Agnes. 'It's called Connect 4,' she said, her voice gentle now when she talked to the old lady. 'Mr O'Grady bought it for me.'

'And *Mrs* O'Grady,' Yvonne corrected quickly.

'Oh, yes. Her as well,' Portia said, unconvinced. 'Do you want me to show you how to play it, Mrs Whitworth? You'll have to get down on the floor.'

They laughed.

Portia, persuaded that Mummy would play later, disappeared again.

'Well . . . ?' Agnes said, 'You're not getting away with no answer, girl.'

'All right,' Yvonne said miserably. 'All right, you old bat,' she went on, lowering her voice and glancing guiltily over her shoulder in case Portia was there. 'I've got a bit of a thing for him, if you must know.'

'Thought so,' Agnes said. 'And he must be half way there himself, otherwise why would he make such an effort with the children?'

'He likes them,' Yvonne said at once. 'He's not doing it for any devious reason.'

'I didn't mean that. I meant he probably doesn't even realise why he's doing it. But it's partly to do with you. He loves you but he'll still be at the guilty stage, seeing if there isn't something he can do to save his marriage. People do try. God knows why. I did. How I tried. Waste of time with my first two.'

'*Agnes*! . . .' Yvonne nearly exploded. 'Will you stop it? How can you say this about Andrew? You've never met him. And you forget he's married to Tess.'

'But not happily. You've said so yourself. No family, eh?'

'No . . . she doesn't want any.'

'Well then, that's one less complication, girl. It's up to you how you go about it. You've both of you done what I did twice. Married the wrong person. Easily done. Now you've got to sort yourselves out. Simple.'

Yvonne shook her head as she looked at the old lady.

If only it were.

'Thank you so much, Colin. You drove very well,' Constance said, stepping out of the car into a soft fluff of fresh snow. She passed him the fare plus a handsome tip and the packet of cigarettes, hesitated a moment. 'Would you like to come in a moment for a cup of tea or coffee? I believe there are some mince pies in the larder, if you would like one?'

'It's not that I wouldn't like to, Mrs Makepeace,' he said,

looking very embarrassed, 'But it's a bit much for me. Your place. Best not. I'll see you inside safe, though.'

'Thank you.'

She allowed him to escort her to the door, and once the key was inserted and the door opened, he barged in ahead of her full pelt as if there was somebody lying in wait to knock her on the head. He fumbled a minute and then the light flooded on.

'I do hope you'll let me know how things progress,' she said, cold now as the benefits of the warm car faded, 'Between you and Lisa Marie.'

'Right, pet. I will let you know. If you want me, you know where to find me. I'm living over the butcher's.'

'Good evening then,' she said, dismissing him. 'Thank you for transporting me. And a merry Christmas.'

'Cheers then. And thanks for the tip and the fags. Good on you, Mrs Makepeace.'

She watched as the limousine disappeared down the drive, its lights glowing in the dark. When it was gone, she stared out a moment at the whiteness of the garden, at that strange light that snow brings.

'Smith . . . I'm home, darling,' she called into the silence. He would no doubt still be in a mood and might not appear for some considerable time. He quite disliked the dark if she was not around.

There was no sound, so she switched on lights as she went through the house, made herself a cup of hot milk and carried it up to bed. It was later than she had anticipated for there had been fresh snowfalls and the roads had been treacherous. Colin's language was extraordinary but he was a good driver and she had felt perfectly safe. She had revised her initial opinion and would not now be making a complaint about him, although she was severely displeased with Mr Miller and his lack of control in being unable to limit his drinking.

All in all the day had been a success. She thought happily of how it had been and hoped she had not made a mistake in asking Penny to bring the boys over to West House when the weather improved. It had been an impulsive request that she had been unable to retract once offered. Penny liked to take them on little excursions up the Northumberland coast or to the North York moors, to broaden their horizons, she said, which was most commendable. It was when she was telling Constance about their outings that Constance had the idea of inviting them here. Bishopsmeade was most picturesque and they would certainly approve of it. They could walk a little on the hill or in the grounds of West House and have tea afterwards. They would so enjoy that. They had, of course, very hearty appetites and she would ask Mrs Bainbridge to prepare something special. They would eat in the dining room and have the best china. Like Smith, the boys were infinitely careful with precious items.

She left the bedroom curtains undrawn, wanting to look out onto the night. Taking her drink, relaxed in a royal blue housecoat over her nightgown, she sat awhile on the chair by the window. Dark and creamy, the whole gardens were spread with icing, the trees dusted with sugar. The sky dark and sparkling with pulsing silver stars. The moon a sliver of white. No more snow tonight.

Penny had made a magnificent traditional meal. Turkey and cranberry sauce, roast potatoes, a selection of vegetables. Plum pudding and custard. Constance had eaten sparingly but enjoyably, and after their meal, they had presented her with their little gifts. Lavender essence, a book on roses and some chocolates which she had shared with them later. They pulled crackers and laughed, sometimes incomprehensibly, at the so-called jokes. They all wore party hats as they ate their meal. It was all most convivial.

The boys had then built a snowman, a splendid creature that had afforded them much amusement even though they were soaked through as a result and Penny had to help them get changed into dry clothes afterwards. A brightly striped scarf was placed round the snowman's chilly neck, a rather beautiful scarf belonging to Penny that had given the iced creature a couture look. Penny was the sort of woman who cared not a fig that they draped her expensive scarf round a snowman. They wanted it to look good so she made sure it did. Constance had not participated in the actual building of the snowman, content to watch the whole proceedings from the window, pleasantly full and enjoying another glass of dry sherry. They sang carols later round the tree and played a few simple games.

Constance was in bed, her hair brushed out, by the time Smith put in an appearance.

She greeted him as he stole into the bedroom and came over to the bed, leaping up and picking his dainty way towards her across the oyster satin eiderdown. 'Did Mrs Bainbridge feed you, darling?' She propped herself against the pillows, knowing that tonight sleep would not be easy. 'I had a splendid day today although I was rather worried when it began because the driver of my taxi was not Mr Miller. He was called Colin. Mr Hawkins. Once I got to know him a little, he was tolerable. Poor man. He's lived a difficult life and it is not in my nature to be vindictive, as you know.'

She left that to Grace. Grace had more than enough venom in her for two.

Smith, she could tell, was quite delighted to see her back, relaxed, his furry body moving up and down as he breathed, his purr deeply content.

The clock at St Cuthbert's chimed midnight. She listened. Counted each chime. It was Boxing Day and she would spend the day, from choice, alone.

Boxing Day, 1955. Would she ever forget that?

# 30

It was already late January, cold, foggy and damp, and Christmas had slipped into the dim and distant past.

Tess was in a helluva mood. Up to her eyes in overseeing the complete and, in Andrew's opinion, totally unnecessary refurbishment of one of her shops, annoyed, more than annoyed, that he still refused to help Joe. With a bit of luck, that business might have sorted itself out. Joe hadn't said anything further anyway, which had to be a good sign. Knowing Joe, he would come up smelling of roses as usual, with a bigger better job and a nice lump sum in the piggy bank.

Since Christmas, it seemed to Andrew that Yvonne was going out of her way to avoid him and he hadn't seen much of the children over the school holidays. There had been not a sign of Robin and he was beginning to think that his suspicions were true. The guy had done a bunk.

Tess was in a world of her own, worrying about losing West House, which was a bit rich, because the way Andrew saw it they'd never had it in the first place. It was hearsay, all this. If he saw a whopping For Sale board by the front gates *then* he would believe it. She was also very busy at work and had decided to stay a whole week up at the flat Joe kept in Newcastle because she was in a regional floral competition. Highly competitive as she was, she was going at it hell for leather and didn't want the hassle of a daily drive. So he was alone and feeling it. He had a job interview the day after tomorrow and couldn't raise much enthusiasm for it, which was a sure track to not getting it.

Bugger . . . he'd go out for a walk. He needed a blast of cold air in his lungs.

He never planned to step outside just as Yvonne was going past his gate but that's the way it happened. Of course, polite neighbour that she was, she stopped, smiled, waited for him.

'I'm just having a breath of fresh air,' he said, awkward and a bit embarrassed. 'Thought I might take a walk round to the hill.'

'That's what I was going to do,' she said. 'Do you mind if I walk with you?'

He shook his head. God no, he didn't mind. He could handle this. He had had a serious talk with himself about this whole set-up, the reason for the cooling-off between him and Tess. The baby business was too important to be simply dismissed. It had to be resolved and sooner or later they had to talk. He would have to put aside all thoughts of Tess's sensibilities and get her to talk about it once and for all. Once she had a perfectly healthy baby everything would be fine. They would work it out, the two of them. She would come round, he felt sure. He was not giving up yet. And that's why he could handle Yvonne and any amount of teasing and sexy glances. Yvonne was off limits.

'Haven't seen you for ages. Not properly,' Yvonne said as they set off. She was wearing her long black coat and her hair was tucked into a big furry hat, Cossack style. Her lipstick was a bright pink and her eyes sparkling. She looked very well. 'Portia was asking after you only the other day. She misses you, I think. Will it be OK if they start coming to you again on Tuesdays only? Just half an hour or so. If you wouldn't mind picking them up from school and hanging onto them until I get back?'

He shook his head. 'It's fine,' he said, strangely relieved that she had asked. He had worried lately that she'd had terrible second thoughts about him and his ability to look after the children. Tess would not like it but that was just too bad, and he was getting just a tiny bit fed up of always doing what she wanted. It was *him* doing the child minding and he didn't mind in the least. He enjoyed it.

There was still a trace of snow around, dirty and slushy now where the traffic had churned it up, as they turned off Front Street and walked along the path beside the church. There were snowdrops pushing up in the churchyard, the tall trees silhouetted, branches contorted against the ash grey sky. Up on the hilltop itself, the snow was white and undisturbed.

'How did your Christmas go?' she asked. 'I never had time to ask. You were up at Middleton-in-Teesdale, weren't you? Tess was telling me once about her father's house. It sounds lovely.'

'It is,' he said. 'And his wife is a wonderful cook so we stuffed ourselves silly, as you can imagine. It was all very relaxing. Tess needs to relax. She can get pretty stressed. How about you? Did you have a nice Christmas?'

'Oh . . . all right really, considering Robin wasn't here. Once I explained to the children that Daddy wouldn't be home they were very good about it. It amazes me how they just accept things, the younger ones anyway. Portia sometimes asks questions. I worry myself sick, wonder how on earth I'm going to tell them and then they just accept it. We had Mrs Whitworth to stay on Christmas Day, so looking after her and trying to make sure Portia didn't say anything too dreadful kept me fully occupied.'

'I can imagine. Portia doesn't beat about the bush,' he said with a smile. 'Comes straight out with it.'

She glanced at him. 'They do at that age. She's very bright, you know. She hasn't been saying anything to you, has she?'

'About what?'

'Nothing.' She tugged at her hat, struggled a bit on a steep bit of path so that he held out his hand to her.

'Thanks.' She held onto his hand, did not let go as the path levelled out. They paused to look down at the church now below and the village beyond, still mainly white and grey with a few wintery touches of blue as the snow dallied. 'Is Tess away?' she asked after a moment, slipping her hand free of his in quite a delicate manoeuvre and setting off again. 'It's just that I haven't seen her for a few days.'

He explained.

'I hope she does well in the competition. She's very talented, isn't she? I'd love to spend time on arranging flowers but it's a matter of priorities when you have a family.' She blushed, rapidly changed the subject. 'Why don't you come over for tea tomorrow? Tess won't mind, will she? The children would love you to have tea with us.'

He hesitated, suddenly wary. So much for the bravado about being able to handle this. Tess would never know, but he wasn't sure about it himself. He had to avoid too cosy scenarios with Yvonne and the children. It made him think of happy families and he and Yvonne had better not start playing at mummies and daddies. He fished around for an excuse, a plausible one, but couldn't think of one off-hand. He did not say anything, therefore, neither a yes or no, but tried a distraction, pointing out the view of West House as they approached. Portia was always fooled with distractions.

'Have you been there? West House?' she asked as it loomed nearer. 'Inside, I mean. I know we were there for the bonfire night party.'

Andrew realised he had not told her about the tea invitation, decided not to bring it up anyway as it was something he preferred to forget.

'It's lovely inside. I take books to Mrs Makepeace every two weeks. It's a little service we operate. Bishopsmeade Volunteers.' She laughed suddenly. 'I didn't mean to confess that. Awful, isn't it? Don't tell anyone. It's coming to something when you're almost ashamed of being a volunteer. Joan who runs it is very persuasive, you see.'

'You should be about twenty years older,' he said, seeing what she meant. 'But why not? It's very public spirited of you.'

'You're not taking the mickey, Andrew, are you?' she asked, clicking her tongue at the 'public spirited'.

'No.' They exchanged a smile though and below them, West House retreated a little amongst the trees. The path was steeper now and a bit iced up here and there and he asked if she wanted to carry on any further.

'I know we haven't got our mountaineering gear with us,' she said mischievously, looking for a second as she tilted her head just like Samantha. 'But I think we can cope. We're neither of us in our dotage exactly. Come on, we've got this far. Race you to the top.'

'OK. You've asked for it,' he said, setting off up the steeper path at the fork, overtaking her quickly. Laughing, she followed, puffing a bit, but managing to keep up fairly well. The effort warmed them a little and by the time they reached the top, a surprisingly large level area, their cheeks were tingling and they were both breathing hard with the exhilaration.

'Wow! Just look at that,' Yvonne said, spinning round slowly and taking in the whole vista. 'Isn't it just beautiful? It would make a wonderful watercolour. It's quite perfect.'

They were alone.

Nobody to see.

The snow was just a feathery sprinkling here on the sheltered side, the green of the hill showing through. Above them, the sky was determinedly grey, heftily clouded. Yvonne was smiling and beautiful, her cheeks a little flushed, and very fair blonde wisps escaping from the hat.

To hell with the view.

He couldn't take his eyes off her. She was all a-sparkle and he found himself catching his breath.

'Yvonne . . .' he said, whispering her name as if for the first time, and there must have been something in his voice because she stopped spinning round, stopped with her back to him so that he could not see her face.

'Yvonne . . .' he repeated urgently, not knowing quite what to say. There was so much to say. He was, and the thought surprised and shocked him, tempted to tell her that he loved her.

'No, Andrew.' She wasn't letting him say it. 'We'd better get back. I've got all sorts of things I should be doing at home.' She spoke briskly, the no-nonsense tone she sometimes used with the children when they were up to no good.

And she was off, marching down the path.

'Careful. Take it slowly,' he warned, following her.

They said very little on the way down.

# 31

Constance had trouble walking in slush. She slipped and slid, and so she decided it would be wise to telephone for a taxi to take her down to the teashop. Mr Miller answered the telephone and she was distinctly cool with him, upset him, she thought, by specifically requesting that Colin be the driver.

'And how are you, Colin?' she asked when he had settled her most solicitously in the back of the car.

'Fabulously fantastic, Mrs Makepeace, pet,' he said and winked at her.

'Really? You seem to be in excellent humour.' She lit a cigarette, passed him one, as he started the engine.

'We're back together. Me and Lisa Marie,' he said proudly. 'And the girls. They loved the dolls. She's packed in that other bloke. Dead loss, he was. What did I tell you? Me and her, we're a team.'

'Good. I'm so pleased for you. But surely you have to find somewhere else to live? You can't all of you live in a bedsit?'

'We're a bit squashed but we manage. The girls double up and we have three beds.'

'Oh, dear. Then you are *all* in the bedsit? Does Mr Simpson mind?'

'He's easy as long as the rent's paid. I'm looking for another job, something that pays a bit more. This is only temporary. We're getting married, you see. Lisa Marie wants all the trimmings, she says. She reckons she's waited long enough. The girls will be bridesmaids.'

'Oh . . . may I be the first to offer my congratulations!' she said, smiling slightly. Ella would be affronted at such an idea but she liked to think she was more modern in her outlook. One simply had to move with the times. Her own father would have suffered apoplexy if she and Archie had lived together before they were married. Frankly, so would she. It was not done then.

They were at the teashop. Colin pulled the car to a careful halt outside and helped her out.

'Here. Before you go in . . .' He dug in his pockets, pulled out a photograph. 'Thought you might like to see my kids,' he said shyly. 'There they are . . . the whole bloody lot. That's Jodie and Eugenie . . .' he pointed with a grubby finger. 'And there's the little ones, Chelsea and Ashleigh. And that's my Lisa Marie. Bloody looker, isn't she?'

'Charming. What beautiful children,' Constance told him, meaning it, for they were indeed beautiful as was his Lisa Marie. She paid him the fare and asked him to call back in half an hour. She might visit the cottage first, before she returned to West House. Her tenants had moved out promptly and, as she had not visited it since their initial occupancy about a year ago, she needed to see it. She did so hope they had left it as they would wish to find it.

'Only moderate weather, Mrs Makepeace,' Florence Green said as she brought her coffee and toasted tea-cake. 'What did I say about the winter? I knew we were in for a bad one.'

'What's a bit of snow?' Constance said, dismissing it. Miss Green was a natural complainer. Too hot. Too cold. Too windy. Too this, too that.

She was sitting at a corner table by the window so that she could see what was going on. Across the road, she saw Mr O'Grady strolling along accompanied by – good gracious! – Mrs Lonsdale, surely. There was something about the two of them together that quite disturbed her. They looked comfortable together, much more so than mere neighbours ought. It disturbed Tess O'Grady also; Constance had noted that, particularly at the bonfire supper when Andrew had appeared with Mrs Lonsdale and her children at his side. Tess had been very annoyed although she had tried her best to hide it. It was probably completely innocent, but Mr O'Grady ought to realise how it might look to others and behave accordingly. In Constance's opinion, he was being a mite indiscreet.

She might have to rethink her strategy. She had almost, so very nearly, decided that the O'Gradys would be admirable that she had thought of asking them to dinner and breaking the news then. She was prepared to let them have West House for a figure to be negotiated, a figure, however, that would be well within their grasp, perfectly happy to wait until their own house was sold for the final settlement.

But . . . if their marriage was shaky then she would be making a big mistake.

One thing was sure; although she liked Andrew O'Grady very much, she found Mrs Lonsdale altogether too . . . too blonde . . . for her taste.

And yet West House needed a family to live in it again. These last few years she felt sure it had not enjoyed its solitary existence. Rooms were meant to be used, not dust-sheeted. Views were there to be looked at. The house needed a purpose once more.

'There's your taxi driver back, Mrs Makepeace,' Florence said. 'I can't think what Mr Miller's thinking of, employing characters like that? Is he all right? He looks a bit rough to me.'

Constance took money from her purse, deposited the correct amount on the table.

On Colin's behalf, she felt most offended.

Miss Green was far too keen to judge on appearances.

'No, not West House,' she told him as she climbed back in. 'Would you take me to my cottage, please? It's by the river in Pedlar's Lane. It's the end one and it's called Primrose Cottage.'

Pedlar's Lane faced the river, dark and deep and slow moving at this point, so the little terraced row of cottages was one side only. The road was rough, unmade up with a grassy verge, a shallow crumbling stone wall, the ground shelving away to reeds and weeds beside the water. Across the river, rolling fields with grazing sheep and trees in the distance. It was very quiet as they stepped out of the taxi but Constance could smell the river, felt the tingle of apprehension that being close to water always provoked. It was over a year since she had last been here and she had not missed it. A tiny doubt nudged at her even as she listened to the plop of water sounds nearby.

There was a small garden beyond the wooden gate, not terribly well cared for, as Constance saw to her regret as she led the way up the little path. The windows were grimy too and even before she stepped inside, she had a most dreadful foreboding.

She was right.

Primrose Cottage was in a disgusting state. Constance, two steps in, felt shaky with the sudden shock. The smell was quite dreadful. The windows must have remained shut fast for a year at least. The air was stale and nauseating.

'Bloody hell!' Colin said, coming in behind her although she had not specifically invited him to do so. 'Are you sure this is it? Who's been living here, Mrs Makepeace? Pigs?'

It was furnished with some old solid stuff of hers that she had not needed at West House. She had imagined that the people would look after it as if it were their own. She recalled she had interviewed them and they had seemed a charming couple, well dressed, nicely spoken, and the rent was always paid a month in advance on time into her bank account. She had never seen the need to check up on them. It would look as though one did not trust them. They had never requested any repairs or maintenance and she had merely assumed – naively, she now realised – that they were more than happy to do such things themselves.

Nervous now, Constance quickly looked in on the remaining rooms. A small kitchen thick with grease and grime, the smeary windows looking out onto a paved yard which was piled high with dustbins and uncollected rubbish. Two bedrooms upstairs and a bathroom. Hastily, she stepped in and out of that. She could not believe it of them. How could they? How could they be so dirty? This sweet old cottage needed rescuing quickly. It needed a good wash and brush up followed by a gentle airing.

'Scarpered did they, the lot who were here?' Colin said, when she came back down. He loomed large in the little living room, looking most comically indignant at the squalor. 'Tip, this is. Tell you what, Mrs Makepeace, my Lisa Marie would have this sorted in no time. If it was a toss up between Domestos and a square meal, she'd go for the bleach. Can't stand a mucky kitchen or bathroom, my Lisa Marie. Come on now, don't take on, pet,' he said gently as she let out a little shudder. 'Let's have you out of here. This is no place for a lady like you.'

Constance pulled herself together.

She had not anticipated this, but no matter. Things could be cleaned. Furniture brought from the house. However, she did not wish Mrs Bainbridge to have anything to do with this. For a start, she did not wish Mrs Bainbridge to know that these people had taken advantage. She felt terribly let down.

'Would Lisa Marie be willing to come in and clean the cottage for me?' she asked once they were on their way. 'And would you be willing to help, Colin? There are repairs to be done, that sort of thing, the furniture to dispose of.'

'Dispose of it?'

She smiled, hearing the delight in his voice.

'Dispose of it,' she repeated. 'And I don't care how you do that. You have carte blanche.' She smiled kindly at him. 'Complete authority, Colin, to do as you wish and you may keep any money you may acquire as a result. And will you be able to decorate it for me? Paint and wallpaper. Magnolia throughout I think. Can you do that? I will give you some money for that purpose. I need the cottage for myself in spring, you see. I will be spending some of my time there. When the decoration is complete, I will of course reimburse you both generously for your time and effort. I really don't wish to set foot in it again until it is worthy of a second look. Once it is finished, you can come up to the house and I will decide what items of furniture can be taken down.'

'You're on,' he said. 'By the time we've finished with it, you won't recognise it.'

Constance sighed.

'I sincerely hope not,' she said.

'Bernard said as he'd give you a hand with the cottage when you're ready, Mrs Makepeace,' Ella Bainbridge said. 'It might need a lick of paint.'

'Thank you, Ella. It will not be necessary,' Constance told her firmly. 'Everything's being taken care of.'

'Right.' Ella put their cups down on the kitchen table, opened the tin of biscuits, passed it over to Constance.

Constance declined, lit a cigarette instead.

There was a short reflective silence. Ella had a furtive look on her face and Constance glanced at her thoughtfully. Out with it, Ella!

'Of course me and Bernard were never able to have children,' Ella said at last, startling her with the out-of-the-blue statement. 'We never bothered to find out why. It's best not to know why, if you ask me, then you don't start blaming one another. At first we were very upset about it because I'd always thought we'd have four or five bairns. But afterwards we got to thinking that it didn't matter that much. After all, some people never have any happiness in marriage, do they, children or not? And we've been very happy together. We've always been friends.'

'Good. I'm so pleased for you.' Constance smiled.

Now what had brought this on? And where was it leading?

'And we looked on it this way as well. We thought . . . people who have children . . . all they do for ever and a day afterwards is worry about them. You spend your whole life worrying about them, so they say. Grown up or not. Isn't that true, Mrs Makepeace?'

'It is indeed, Ella.'

She drew on the cigarette, saw exactly where this was leading. Poor Ella would never give up.

'I mean to say, I know you had a son, Mrs Makepeace. You talked about him to Bernard.'

Oh yes. She remembered that. Bernard, for some reason, had been going on and on about the fat stream and how dangerous it was where it tumbled to the river and she finally had to tell him in order to put a stop to it.

'It must have been terrible for you,' Ella went on, nibbling on a chocolate digestive. 'And I'm here if you want to talk about it. Talk through your troubles, they say. Get it off your chest. I'm not pushing you, Mrs Makepeace, but I'm here and I'm listening.' She allowed the minutest pause to develop before she ploughed on with the delicacy of a tractor. 'They do say that to lose a child tragically is the worst thing.'

'The very worst.'

Ella waited.

The silence hung about the room.

Constance caved in.

'You blame yourself, Ella,' she said after a moment, feeling the need to say it. 'Especially when it's an unfortunate accident that could have quite easily been averted. You think afterwards . . . if only. But, you see, I usually relied on nanny and nanny didn't come on holiday with us because I wanted to have Thomas to myself. I think I was becoming a little jealous of nanny and the influence she was beginning to exert on him.' She stopped, amazed she had said that, especially to Mrs Bainbridge.

'I've heard they can be like that. Those nannies,' Ella said with a knowing shake of her head. 'They're usually women who've never had children. Have you noticed that? My mam wouldn't have had truck with anybody like that. She looked after us herself, did my mam. If you've not wiped a bottom or a snotty nose then you've not been a proper mam, she said. Oh, I'm sorry, Mrs Makepeace, I didn't mean that to sound as if . . .'

Constance waved her stumbling apology aside.

'Nanny was very strict with him, you see. My husband insisted on that so that when Thomas went away to school when he was eight, he would be able to cope with it. She would never have allowed him to go anywhere near the loch on his own. But I was trying my best to be something that nanny was not. Do you see? I was Mummy and I was much more lenient. My husband was recovering from an illness and was out shooting and fishing most days, so we ladies and the children were alone. I allowed Thomas to stay up later than usual. I allowed him to leave his greens. I even allowed him to get down from the table when he had not excused himself in the proper manner. And I allowed him to drown,' she added in a whisper. 'Nanny, I believe, never forgave me. And nor did my husband.'

'Oh no. I'm sure that wasn't so. You mustn't blame yourself, Mrs Makepeace,' Ella said, the biscuit forgotten in her hand, her expression one of shock and surprise. 'What a notion! Have you never heard of fate? What's meant to be is meant to be. Destined. I had an auntie who used to read teacups. Did I ever tell you about her?'

'I believe you did, Ella,' Constance said, rousing herself with some difficulty, turning to look as the cat fluffed and squeezed his way through his flap, a most welcome distraction. 'Hello, Smith. Oh dear, you are quite wet.'

'No wonder. It's torrential out there,' Ella said, stuffing the last of the biscuit in her mouth, obviously anxious now to leave the confessional when the moment was gone. 'I hope that's helped a bit, anyway. As they say, talking helps. Now if you'll excuse me, I have to get on. I have my floors to do.' She went to get the bucket and mop. 'So I'm to tell Bernard you don't want his help, then? At the cottage?'

'No, thank you.' Constance stubbed out her cigarette, rose to her feet, left Mrs Bainbridge to it.

She had no idea why she had told Ella all that about Thomas. Perhaps the woman was wearing her down, or perhaps after all it was a good idea to talk about it. Oddly, she felt a little better. Nanny had loved Thomas, of course, for she had looked after him since he was a baby but that was no excuse for being downright vicious. She could see her face even now, tear-stained and pale, as she spat angry words at her. The first time I let him out of my sight, she said, you let him drown, you incompetent bitch. Constance remembered she was speechless at the words. Hugh overheard and dismissed nanny angrily at once, although that was an empty gesture for quite obviously she was not needed any more, but it was too late for the words were said.

She had indeed been an incompetent bitch.

Ella was quite right, though, and there was no point in shouldering all the blame.

If a thing was meant to be it would be, and nothing could change it.

# 32

The cream and white narcissi edged with orange picked up the yellow of the daffodils in the pot that sat on the wide window-ledge of Joe's flat, his base when he had to stay over in town. He'd had the flat for years and Stephanie seemed happy enough for him to keep it on. It, much more than Caryn Lodge, still retained much of Tess's mother's influence as Joe had kept the duotone creamy scheme and the simple furniture. Often, Tess popped in with flowers, something bright, to add that splash of colour.

Tess glanced at the flowers briefly, satisfied with their condition, threw down her coat and keys, and went immediately into the ultra-smart little kitchen to make a cup of tea. She was completely fed up. Not only was this contest a fix – she was convinced of that – but she had made a shambles this morning of her own confection which was supposed to be a charming ensemble in dusky pastels. It had ended up looking sad and wilted even to her eyes. She wouldn't care but she had only entered the damned thing for the publicity it would attract in the local press, and by publicity she meant good publicity, of course.

She had assumed she would come first. Most of the others were palely provincial florists with very little expertise and absolutely no new ideas, but she had neglected to check who the judges were. They were, unfortunately, the old fashioned variety. They were just too old hat to take on board any innovations in floral design. More fool them, but it meant on this occasion she was destined to be an also-ran so, as a consequence, she had backed out as soon as that became obvious rather than face the final music of a group photograph with her in the back row.

She made her cup of tea, carried it through to the living room, wondering if she should ring Andrew again. She had rung him first thing this morning, waking him up in fact, for she had heard the sleep in his voice. She needed to hear his voice. Andrew was – for want of a better expression – her rock and just now, with things as they were, she needed him. The trouble was, it was all slipping away a little. Step by step, it seemed, he was retreating from her. And it was all to do with the baby and her decision to abort. If it had been up to him, they would have been lumbered with it. It sometimes seemed he was incapable of taking a rational decision. He was too swayed by his emotions.

Damn Joe also for adding to her worries. He was saying nothing. Had said nothing since that fiasco of a birthday party of his. Had said nothing over Christmas when she had given him every opportunity to speak to her about it in private.

And that infuriating woman Constance Makepeace had not uttered a word either. She had been up to the house twice more to take her flowers but to do it again might invite suspicion. The only encouraging thing was that there was nobody else in Bishopsmeade who could take on West House with any degree of competence and decorum as she could. Constance, she knew, would not give it to just anybody.

She turned the fire up a notch, looked out at the lit-up skyline of the city before drawing the curtains, and settled on the sofa. A quick meal later, and a look through some fashion and home design magazines, and then early bed. At least, having no firm date for taking over West House meant she could indulge in daydreams about the decoration. She was going over it in her mind, taking a few notes, in fact, room by enormous room. She had done the downstairs and was now contemplating what to do with the hall and the upper landings. She could not decide whether to go for a truly bold scarlet and gold or subdue everything in peach. Halls made such an impact, set the tone for the whole house, and she had to get it right. But she had to remember that she would be using floral decoration in the hall so a more neutral background might be preferable.

The telephone rang and she raced across the room to snatch at it.

'Oh . . . Hello, Joe,' she said as his voice came on the line. 'I thought it was Andrew.'

'Sorry to disappoint you, sweetheart. I was just checking you were at the flat. OK if I come by? I might stay over tonight.'

'It's your flat,' she said with a smile. 'You still at the office, then?'

'Working late. I'll be with you in fifteen minutes or so.'

'Do you want feeding?' she asked with a frown. There was next to nothing in the fridge and she hadn't bothered with shopping. She had been planning something simple with cheese and eggs for herself but it would not satisfy her father.

'I'll bring something,' he said wryly. 'Knowing your cooking, I'd better. See you later. I'll just let Stephanie know I won't be home tonight.'

It irritated a bit, the way everybody was bemused by her cooking failures. Steffi was such a wonderful cook, so was Andrew, and she was such a hopeless one. If she took the time, tried, she could do it but she did not have the inclination, and in a marriage it didn't matter so much so long as one of you could do it. Two cooks elbowing each other out of the way could only be trouble.

He arrived armed with a pizza and they ate it in the kitchen, washing it down with a glass of wine, following it with a dish of ice-cream.

'Your mother should have taught you how to cook,' he said thoughtfully when they had finished and were cosily entrenched in the living room. 'Funny, isn't it, how some people are reluctant to pass on their knowledge? Your mother had a good few failings but she could turn her hand to cooking as you well know. As far as I'm concerned, sweetheart, I'll do my bit to pass my expertise to you. I want you to know all there is to know about the big bad world out there. The whole sorry business.'

'Won't you tell me what's the matter?' Tess asked quietly, watching him. He had loosened his tie, opened the top button of his shirt, and as he sighed, she suddenly saw that he looked old and tired. 'Look, Joe, I'm sorry I couldn't get Andrew to help with . . .'

'The expense fiddles?' he asked with a crooked grin. 'I never thought he would. You married an honest man, Tess. More fool you.'

'Yes, but it wouldn't have hurt him to bend his own ridiculous rules for once,' she said, reluctant to own that she was angry with him but unable to stop it. 'It's family.'

'May I . . . ?' He pulled a cigarette packet out of his pocket, grimacing as he did. 'I know, I know . . . don't tell her or she'll have me pickled in aspic. It's the stress, it's got me started again. Now . . . about the job. Can you keep a secret, Tess? I don't want to worry Stephanie, so she mustn't know yet.'

Tess felt suddenly quite cold looking at him, at the familiar way he snatched at the cigarette. She took no pleasure in the fact that he was choosing to tell her the secret in preference to his wife. It was so obviously bad news. The worst. And she had somehow to keep him buoyed up. There had to be a way out of this. Good God, they weren't going to shop him to the police, were they? His fiddles were only minor, no more no less than anyone else. Surely they wouldn't be so vindictive? Although, remembering Ivan's cold eyes, she wasn't so sure.

'The thing is, I'm in the middle of my notice more or less,' he said, looking at her as he caught her sharp intake of breath. 'It's flexible either way, six months, but they imagine they're doing the decent thing and giving me the chance to pick up on something else. They'll supply a glowing reference, the bastards.'

'Oh no. I don't understand, Joe . . .' She struggled to find words of consolation. It was not a surprise, the revelation, just what she'd expected more or less. 'You're brilliant at the job. Are they so short-sighted? Just think of all the business you bring in for them, Daddy, all those overseas orders. Surely that outweighs the little . . . discrepancies? What can they be thinking of?'

'I'm no longer the man of the moment,' he said with a shrug. 'Bound to happen sooner or later. There's no room for two sales directors and the other bloke – from the outfit we've taken over – has got the vote. Ivan cast the deciding vote, wouldn't you know? I wouldn't mind, Tess, but he's the same age as me, this new man. That makes it worse, because they preferred him to me for some other reason. He's got no personality. Reminds me a bit of that husband of yours.'

He glanced at her with a wry smile.

Joking?

She chose not to rise to the bait.

'Anyway, that's the way it goes,' he went on, after another drag on the cigarette. 'Here today, gone tomorrow. The story of my life, sweetheart. Do unto others and expect the same bloody thing to be done unto you. The fact is, it's gutted me this time. I feel like packing it in.'

'What are you talking about?' Tess pounced at that. 'Packing it in? You have to do something, Joe. You're too young to retire. You can't afford to retire, can you?'

'I'll screw them for what I can get. Substantial sum that we can invest. But I've never stayed long enough with any one firm, as you well know, to get a decent pension organised. I never liked to plan long term strategy. Man of the present, me, and to hell with the future. I have nothing to fall back on at all.' His attempt at a smile backfired and he looked . . . well . . . frightened. 'I can buy the car, the company car, at face value but that's going to make a hole in the money, and then there's Caryn Lodge. You know your mother and I had just moved in when she died . . . the mortgage payments are bloody horrendous, rates sky high, heating bills out of this world. There's the gallery expense, and Stephanie spent over two grand at Christmas. Her only extravagance, she said. Two grand on turkey, tinsel and trimmings. Can you credit that?'

'Do you want a drink?' Tess was over by the drinks cabinet, rifling through it. 'Whisky and soda?'

'Thanks, sweetheart. A double.'

She poured herself a large gin and tonic, handed him his drink. Tried to keep calm. Tried not to think about the money she owed him for he had not mentioned that, not included that in his disaster list.

'You've got to get another job then,' she said at last. 'No other choice. Have you tried any of your contacts? Spread the word that you'll be available soon?'

'A couple,' he said quietly. 'No joy. The trouble is, it's bound to get around that I've been dumped and when people know that they won't lift a finger.'

'You must think in a positive way,' she said, somewhat desperately. 'It's not as if it's the first time this sort of thing has happened, is it?'

'No. But it feels more serious this time. The fact is, as you get older, it gets harder to shrug it off. It hurts, being dumped. Stephanie is a very practical woman, you know.' He looked across at her, smiled a bit. 'She thinks a lot about you, Tess. She likes you.'

'And I like her,' Tess said staunchly, for what the hell else could she say?

He nodded. 'Good. We've made our wills. I wasn't going to tell you this – bloody depressing, isn't it, talking about wills – but she made it clear to me that she didn't want you to think she'd married me for my money. She has a particular thing about that.'

'Really? As if I'd think that?'

'Quite. However, the point is she's happy to be left with just the house if I go. The house and my pension from work which is due to her, plus her own small pension, of course, and she says if she's left on her own, she'll probably move to a little flat somewhere, go back to work part-time. As I say, she's practical. So . . . the rest of the estate's coming to you with her blessing.'

'Is it?' Tess looked at him in genuine astonishment. She had just assumed that Steffi would take him for everything he had. 'The shares you got from Mummy and everything?'

'The shares and the lump sum that's due. That's if I cop it, of course. If I die in service. It's if I don't die that all hell will break loose. Then I'll have to sell the shares and use up the lump sum just to keep me going for a while. No option. Then you'll get bugger all, sweetheart.'

'Daddy . . .' She smiled. 'Don't talk like that. I hate it. We'll think of some way round this.'

Despite the unexpected and quite thrilling news about his will, she was worried, though. He was taking this extraordinarily badly. His career had always been volatile, jobs lost, but he had always bounced back straightaway, usually landing something bigger and better so that he was able to cock a finger at his erstwhile employers.

Was there more to it this time or was he just older and tired of it?

She was not going to allow him to lie down and let them walk all over him.

Time for action.

Although, at the moment, what kind of action escaped her.

Tess was damned near hysterical on the phone.

'Calm down,' Andrew told her. 'And tell me again. Slowly.'

'He's on his notice. Six months. Well, three now. He knew at Christmas but didn't want to spoil things, and he still doesn't want Steffi told. She's not to be worried, he says.'

'He'll soon get fixed up,' Andrew said with more conviction than he felt. Joe might have done this sort of thing once too often. 'What about all these contacts of his? Of yours?'

'I know. The trouble is he's so down about it, and you know as well as I do, Andrew, that if you don't exude confidence you're sunk. Who's going to give you a job if you don't think you can do it? Oh, by the way, how did your interview go?'

He thought she would never ask.

'Not bad,' he said, thinking back to it. 'They'll let me know soon.'

'Nobody been to see the house?'

'No. Not a soul.'

'Honestly!' she clicked her tongue. 'Nothing's going right at the moment. What is Joe going to do, Andrew? You know the sort of spending level he runs at? He's got overdrafts. Colossal debts on the cards. And the mortgage is huge. Something will have to go if he can't get a job.'

'Stephanie will be all right about it. He ought to tell her,' Andrew said thoughtfully, remembering the conversation at Christmas. 'She's not the sort to worry about status. Downgrading won't bother her.'

'But it will bother Joe,' Tess snapped. 'And it bothers me, for God's sake. It's just a matter of time before he asks me for some money back, isn't it? And I can't afford it. You know how finely balanced everything is.'

Ah! At last. The crux of the problem. Tess was worried for her own skin.

'Don't let's panic,' he said, trying to quieten her down. 'Why don't you have a word with one or two people? You have a delicate touch.'

'Yes, I do,' she said, and he knew she was smiling, pleased at the compliment. 'And maybe that's what it needs, Andrew. A woman's touch. A quiet word with Ivan, I think, to begin with.'

'Oh . . . I'm not so sure. Leave Ivan out of it. He's not going to give Joe his job back, is he? I'd concentrate on other people. Casually mention that . . .'

'All right,' she said, jumping in crossly. 'Don't tell me what to do. I'll handle it my way. As you say, darling, it's early days. And if I can fix him up with something else, then everything will be fine. He'll be quids in once more. A massive pay off and a new job.'

'When will you be back?' he asked. He was feeling lonely on his own and, on his own, his culinary efforts were sliding into frozen food oblivion. It was easier.

'Why? Missing me?' she asked in delight.

'Of course.'

'A few more days, I think. I need to chat a few people up. See who I can spot at lunch.'

He looked up as there was a tapping at the window, said a hasty goodbye to Tess, and went to open the door. Yvonne and Portia stood there. Yvonne holding aloft a foil-wrapped container.

'We made one extra,' she said. 'It was no trouble and we knew Tess was away.'

'Thanks. Come in a minute,' he said leading them into the kitchen. 'I can cook, you know,' he said, slightly irritated by her gesture. 'Portia knows that. You helped me cook, didn't you?'

She nodded, smiling. 'We made crispy cakes,' she said, looking up at her mother, 'and fudge and chocolate muffins.'

'My goodness! No wonder you've had to go to the dentist for a filling, Portia Lonsdale,' Yvonne said with a reproving smile. 'Robin and I do try to limit the sugar in their diet,' she told Andrew and he nodded, feeling well and truly put in his place. 'I hope you don't mind me doing this,' she went on and he smiled, for what else could he do?

He was glad she was chaperoned. The fluffy sweater left

nothing to the imagination and the longish skirt hugged her body below a wide leather belt with a big buckle. Black hosed legs were slipped into the high heels she liked. Since the walk on the hill, he had taken to dreaming about her sometimes.

'Off you go then, darling,' she said now to her daughter. 'I want a word with Mr O'Grady.'

Oh God.

He watched Portia skipping down the path, blonde curls bobbing, smiling as she turned to wave.

'Shan't be a moment,' Yvonne said, 'but they know where I am if they need me.' Her glance round the kitchen said it all.

'I'd be hopeless living on my own,' he said, seeing it through her fastidious eyes. 'I can't be bothered with cooking just for me.'

'Quite. It's hardly a nutritious diet, is it, though?' she said, pointing to the frozen food packets.

'Is that what you've come round for? To lecture me on my diet?'

'Sorry.' She flushed her dismay and he was instantly sorry for the sharpness of his tone. 'How did your interview go?'

'Fine,' he said. 'I have to wait and see.'

'I hope you get it,' she said, beginning to fiddle with cups and saucers, carrying them over to the sink. 'At least – oh, this is terrible, Andrew – but I shall miss you if you start going out to work again. There'll be not a soul left.'

'How's Robin?'

She looked at him, flushed. 'He's fine. He might be back in a few weeks for a weekend. You'll see him then probably.'

He couldn't care less.

He couldn't care if he never saw Robin again.

'It's about Tess really . . .' Yvonne said, turning away from the sink and giving up on the dishes. 'Have I upset her? She's been very peculiar lately.'

'She's got a lot on her mind,' he said hastily. 'Family problems. Concerning her father.'

'I see. Then it's nothing to do with me,' she said, looking quite relieved. 'Good. I thought perhaps . . .'

'No, no. Nothing to do with you,' he said.

'Right then.' She brightened, pointed to the container. 'Pop that in the oven at two hundred degrees for about forty minutes. Oh . . . you are OK about having the children, aren't you? Do say if you're not.'

'They can come round until I get a job,' he said. 'But then you will have to make other arrangements, I'm afraid.'

'That's very honest of you. Thank you.'

He was relieved to see her go.

He had to get away from Yvonne if he was to save his own marriage.

Putting a stop to his involvement with the children was an obvious first step.

The trouble was, he would miss them like hell.

# 33

The wheels were in motion for the divorce and Yvonne felt Robin was happier communicating via solicitors. A mutual feeling. He did ring though to speak to the children and it seemed as if it was no different from before for them. He might just as well be up in Aberdeen than somewhere on the Med.

Since all this had happened, she allowed Portia to stay up half an hour longer than the others, a small concession much appreciated. Although she tried to make it a special time for just the two of them, sometimes they did very little of shattering importance. It was just the being together, just the two of them, that mattered.

Tonight, Portia sat close beside her on the sofa as a wildlife programme flickered on screen. She was ready for bed, her hair freshly shampooed, smelling of her sweet pink bubble bath, wearing her 101 Dalmatians nightshirt under the lilac towelling gown. Clean little feet. Strangely babyish feet.

Yvonne found her attention wandering.

She had to plan for the future now, but she wasn't sure how.

Financially, Robin was being brilliant but then he always had been so there would be no unseemly arguments about maintenance. In fact, and it was funny to face up to it, Robin was essentially a good man but he should never have got married and had children. He was a loner. Happier on his own. She had known it from the beginning but had hoped she could change him. It helped, she supposed, that there was no other woman. The other woman was the sea. When he was too old for diving, he would go into business with Jean-Louis and open a diving school tied in with leisure breaks.

Oh, yes, it was all mapped out for him. The children could go to visit, perhaps when they were a little older, and he would come to see them in the summer. All in all, now that it was going ahead, it *was* going to be an amicable divorce, God help them.

It was not all mapped out for her, though.

She knew what she would like to happen but a future that included Andrew did not seem possible. For it to happen, he had to split with Tess and she did not want to feel she was responsible for that.

She heard his voice saying her name and it said everything. He might just as well have embraced her at that moment when they stood at the top of Staine Hill, for it could not have been made any clearer. It was the voice of a lover. She treasured that moment, held onto it, brought it back with a delicious frequency.

She had been frightened of the consequences.

She had not dared to look at him at that moment, for she might have given her own feelings away. What on earth were they thinking of?

'Mummy . . . ?'

'Yes, darling?'

'It's not very nice of the lion to eat the deer thing, is it?' Portia asked and Yvonne realised the programme had moved on and they were watching a family of lions tucking into a recent kill. 'To run after it and chase it because it had a poorly leg and it couldn't run very fast.' Her eyes were filling with tears at the thought. 'It was very old, the man said, like Mrs Whitworth. It didn't want to be eaten by the lion. I hate that lion.'

Yvonne smiled, pulled her close.

'It's all to do with nature,' she said, as Portia's bottom lip wobbled and her tears began in earnest. 'Don't cry, darling. That's what happens with animals. Other animals kill them. It's sad but that's what happens. You mustn't get upset about it.'

Something Portia said reminded her of Agnes.

She was due to visit tomorrow and lately, she tried her best to avoid all mention of Andrew. Agnes would not let the matter drop, however, and always managed to turn the conversation round to him. It was so irritating, particularly as the very mention of him made her feel warm and tingly and happy.

She was in love and Agnes Whitworth had guessed. Stupid, stupid, stupid.

'All right now?' she asked Portia, gently pushing her away and planting a little kiss on top of her head.

Portia nodded, sniffing, disconcertingly enquiring in that jumbled-thoughts way of hers if Mrs Whitworth could come to her birthday party in June. And Mr O'Grady?

'It's ages away,' Yvonne said, thankful that it was. 'And I don't think grown-ups like to come to birthday parties.'

'Why not? They're my friends,' Portia said stoutly. 'I can ask who I like. It's my party.'

'Portia . . .' Yvonne gave a warning at the petulant sound.

Andrew was not setting foot in this house. In fact, she resolved to take great care that they were not alone again. What on earth had possessed her to take a meal round to him? She had to stop trying to look after him. She had to stop worrying about him. It was Tess's place to do that.

She had rebuffed him once. But she did not trust herself to be able to do it a second time.

'Oh, Mrs Lonsdale . . . can I have a word before you go through?'

Yvonne slipped off her coat, turned, smiled at Joan. She felt in a slightly happier mood today for, as she set off, she had noticed clumps of snowdrops in the garden and the other bulbs were just beginning to push through. A faint hope then that winter was on the turn although they had a long way to go yet. Up here, it had been known to snow in April.

She followed Joan into the little office at Greenview Rest Home.

'Sit down, Yvonne, would you? I'm sorry to have to break some bad news this morning . . .' Joan smiled a little, fiddled with a pencil. 'Agnes Whitworth passed away peacefully during the night. One of the nurses found her this morning, just lying calmly on the pillows, when she took in her tea, looking as if she was asleep. I know you were close to her. You seemed to get on very well together.'

Yvonne nodded, managed a little smile too. It could not be a surprise, not at nearly ninety-six, but it was a shock.

'Peacefully?' she repeated. 'In her sleep?'

'Yes. Wonderful way to go, isn't it? Just what she would have wanted. Last night, apparently, she was complaining about the bingo. She was campaigning for them to start up a bridge club, so they were going to do just that. Nobody else could play but Agnes said that didn't matter. She would teach them. It was about time they exercised their minds, she said.'

'That's Agnes . . .' Yvonne took a deep breath. 'The children will be sad. I'll tell them when they get back from school. Portia was fearfully impressed that she was so old. She wrote about it in her news. She wanted Agnes to come to her birthday party.'

She and Joan exchanged a smile at the ways of children.

'Maybe it's not the time to say it but matron says she believes you're mentioned in the will,' Joan went on.

'Oh, no, I'm not, am I? I don't want anything,' Yvonne said and for some reason that did it. She felt the tears starting up. She hoped to goodness that Agnes realised that she had never ever done it for any possible gain. The silly old bat. She didn't have to leave her *anything*.

'Cup of tea, I think. You look a bit shaken up,' Joan said, standing up and filling the kettle, organising cups and saucers. 'Shall we go to the funeral together? The two of us? I feel we ought to represent the volunteers.'

Yvonne nodded. 'Oh, yes. The children won't come. They're too young.'

She left after her cup of tea, not feeling quite up to visiting anyone else. She had, she realised now, homed in rather on Agnes, become too involved as usual. The secret of coping in a professional capacity was that, although you were always sympathetic, you never allowed it to get to you personally. You kept your distance if you had any sense.

At least that was the theory, but it did not always work in practice. Losing one of the children as they sometimes had at the school she had worked at had been very hard to take. Often it was a blessed release if the handicap was profound. Yes, that was the official line, the official religious line. Blessed or not, it was still a deeply felt bereavement for the staff as well as the family.

Quickly now, she did the shopping she had meant to do in a leisurely, argumentative fashion with Agnes, and returned home. Tess was just climbing out of her car, wearing a gorgeous navy and white suit, and paused to say hello.

Yvonne smiled with an effort, not wanting to be drawn into a conversation. At the drop of a hat, she knew she could cry. Coming on top of her impending divorce, this was just too much. She had liked Agnes. She would miss her.

'We've got somebody coming to look at the house,' Tess called to her. 'The agent says that there'll probably be a flurry now. According to him, it does this. Comes in waves of interest.'

'Good. I hope it goes well.'

'We mustn't get our hopes up too much, but . . .'

Yvonne walked on, cut her short, knowing she wanted to talk some more.

Not caring too much if she appeared terse, she clattered up her path, opening the door and going inside with some relief. At last she could have a little weep in private.

# 34

'I've just been cold-shouldered by Yvonne,' Tess said, carrying parcels in and shutting the door behind her with difficulty. 'You must be right, Andrew. Robin must have left her. He's not been home since before Christmas as far as I can remember. Anyway, she looked extremely miserable.'

'Did she? Poor Yvonne.'

'Yes. Poor Yvonne. What time are these people due?'

She carefully put the flowers on the kitchen table, hunted for a favourite vase. She had taken the afternoon off, deciding that this time she would be on hand to do the showing round. She was sure Andrew somehow managed to put people off. This time, there would be no putting off.

'An hour,' he said, glancing at the clock. 'Are all those for us?'

She nodded. 'I want to make a good show in the hall. First impressions, darling. If I have some over . . .' She eyed the vast bunch, decided she need not use them all. 'I might have a run up to West House later. Take Constance a few flowers. She loves them.'

'You could take Yvonne a few too,' he suggested. 'Peace offering. It sounds as if she might appreciate them more.'

'I am not into "Relate",' Tess said with a quick grin. 'Let her sort out her own marital problems. *We* have to, don't we?'

She busied with the flowers.

She and Andrew were not sorted out, not in any way. By the total avoidance of certain subjects, life was just about tolerable. She tried not to mention her father. Or his expenses.

Or Stephanie. Or the baby that he was beginning to be a bore about. Or West House.

The list was getting longer.

And some things on it were very important to him. Frankly, she was amazed that he was holding out about the expenses. Not that it mattered now for the die was cast. Joe was leaving the company in a little under two months and, although she did not like to admit it, time was running out.

She had run round in circles up in Newcastle. She had spent time and money lunching various people who might conceivably come up with the offer of a job for Joe. Time well and truly wasted by the look of it, for not one of them had got back to her. Difficult fraught lunches, because she had to think of some discreet way of throwing in the fact that her father would be available shortly, that he had grown bored with packaging and was looking for something more challenging. All bullshit, of course, but how else could she play it? Sometimes people responded, asked a few pertinent questions, and sometimes they did not which made her begrudge the cost of the lunch.

'Have you nearly finished?'

Andrew was standing watching her. She turned away from him, busy with the final fussing. It was a fairly informal mixed bunch and its abundance pleased Andrew as she had known it would. She carried it through to the hall and then checked on the other rooms. Andrew had gone through the house with a fine-tooth comb and it was looking very good, considering they had no help with the cleaning.

When they moved to West House, serious attention would have to be given to the matter of staff. A house that size needed more than just one part-time cleaner and Tess had no intention of running herself into the ground coping with it. She was not entirely sure how they would pay all these extra people, but she would do a bit of shuffling around, perhaps dispense with a couple of staff at the shops. It would be worked out. She would work it out herself, for Andrew could not be relied on.

'Do you mind, Andrew, if I go up to Caryn Lodge in a couple of weeks for the weekend?' she asked, as they waited with some anxiety for the people to arrive. 'I'd go this weekend but Stephanie has some sort of stupid exhibition at the gallery. She's providing wine and nibbles. Admittance – would you believe? – by invitation only, as if she was famous. She actually asked if we wanted to go.'

'I wouldn't have minded,' Andrew said. 'We've got to give her some support.'

'Why?' Tess raised her eyebrows. 'Anyway, you haven't answered my question. Do you mind being on your own again? I feel rather bad about it.'

'I don't mind, but why the mystery? I'll come with you if you want.'

'I want to speak to Joe, and . . .' she smiled and moved closer to him. 'Please, darling, let me do this my way. I want to find out what's going on and – don't take this personally – I need to be alone with him. We need to talk. I know he's up to all sorts of tricks with his contacts and I want to know, once and for all, what's happening. I can't stand the suspense of not knowing . . . and I don't think he'll tell me if you're there.'

'If it was good news, he'd soon let you know,' Andrew pointed out, reasonably enough. 'So I would take it that nothing's doing yet. I still don't see why you have to go to the trouble of going to see him. What about Stephanie? Won't it be awkward? We both know she suspects something's up but has he still not told her officially?'

'I don't know. He's being so annoying. That's one of the things I'll find out.' She glanced up as the clock chimed. 'You sure you got the time right? These people should be here by now.'

'Absolutely. I'll put the coffee on, shall I?'

Tess nodded, taking another glance round the room. Fine. As fine as it could ever be, a house like this. What had ever possessed her to think that something brand new could ever have any style? After this, she was never going to live in a new house again.

Ten minutes later the telephone rang. It was the estate agent ringing to apologise but the people had decided not to bother after all. It wasn't exactly what they were looking for.

Fuming, Tess had snatched her car keys and was out of the house within minutes, a bunch of flowers on the seat beside her, heading for West House.

* * *

She was a little calmer by the time she rang the bell. The door was opened by the grumbly housekeeper who showed her into the drawing room where Constance was enjoying a cup of tea.

'Do join me. I'll get Mrs Bainbridge to bring another cup,' Constance said, smiling her delight at the flowers, an old-fashioned bouquet that she liked. 'Those are lovely. Thank you so very much. I'll get Mrs Bainbridge to find a vase.'

Mrs Bainbridge reappeared, muttering something about 'only one pair of hands,' and Tess, managing to keep her irritation at the afternoon's events under control, smiled.

'We're having some trouble selling the house,' she confessed, deciding it might be better to be honest, for Constance knew they were trying to sell. 'Although I am perfectly sure we *will* sell. I suppose we have to be patient.'

'Do you have another house in mind?' Constance asked, pouring her a cup of tea and handing it over. 'It seems rather a risky business to sell your own if you have nowhere to go.'

'Oh no, it's the right way to go about it. I think,' Tess said hastily. 'It's what we've always done. We sold the house in Jesmond before we bought this one. Sellers are always happier that way. Bargains can be had. It gives you a bit of negotiating power.'

'Where will you go? And what sort of house are you looking for?'

Tess glanced rather irritably at her. She had told her before. Did the woman never listen?

'We want to stay in Bishopsmeade,' she said. 'But we want something bigger so that we can think about starting a family. I made a mistake with the new house. It's not what I really wanted.'

'Would you like something like this?' Constance gazed around the room, making it quite obvious she meant West House itself.

'Something like this?' Tess pretended great surprise. 'Oh, well . . . that would be dreaming, Constance. I might dream about a house like this but I know, in all honesty, it's out of the question. Some day, maybe.'

She sipped her tea. Wondered when the old woman would get round to saying it. Come on, come on, you know you want us to have the house. What's stopping you?

'Are you aware, Tess, that I'm thinking of moving in spring? I have a cottage down in the village that I'm having done up at this very moment.'

'Oh . . . really! I had no idea.' Tess smiled brightly, clattered her cup onto the saucer. 'That will be a dreadful wrench for you, surely? You've been so happy here, haven't you?'

Constance laughed. A short sharp laugh that signified pain rather than mirth.

'In some ways, yes,' she said. 'The time has come for me to leave. I shall be cosier in the cottage.'

'So you will be putting this house on the market?' Tess said, choosing her words with care. 'I wish we could afford it, Constance, but as I've already said, it's quite out of the question. What will the asking price be, if that's not too impertinent of me?' She spread her hands wide. 'Sorry . . . don't answer that . . . I'm just curious, that's all. It's absolutely nothing to do with me.'

'I know I have what might seem a ridiculously romantic attitude to this house,' Constance went on, rather infuriatingly refusing to be drawn on price. 'Mrs Bainbridge, for instance, obviously thinks me partially unhinged.' Her smile was unexpected, a little wicked. 'Suffice to say, Tess, that I do feel dearly for the house for various reasons, mainly because it has always been a family home belonging originally to my great-grandfather. I spent time here when I was a little girl. The views are much the same, some of the trees a little larger, of course. It's comforting.'

'Yes, I can see it must be. How wonderful!'

'Hugh and I were delighted to move here, take it on, as it were, keep it in the family. But now . . . there is nobody left, no Parkinson blood anyway.'

Tess was silent. She knew when to keep quiet.

'So . . .' Constance perked up. 'I am therefore determined that I shall have some say as to who takes it on when I'm gone. I particularly want to ensure that nothing is changed. I mean the basic structure. I abhor the thought of the new people demolishing interior walls, that sort of thing.'

Tess shuddered theatrically.

'What an idea!' she said, although that's precisely what she had in mind. All the bitty bits to the kitchen – a wash-house, pantry and under-pantry, for God's sake! – would be amalgamated into one fantastic kitchen. 'It's perfect as it is,' she added. 'I wouldn't change a thing.'

'I'm glad you think that. If I were to put it in an estate agent's hands then I suspect I would lose all influence. He would wish to get the best price, as it were, and that does not concern me in the least.'

'I would love it. If we had it, we could start a family straightaway,' Tess said, deciding it was time to go for it, wondering though if she had gone a bit far, for Constance had this ever-changing expression that was sometimes difficult to judge. She could mask her feelings very successfully. 'If only . . .'

'Ah, if only . . .' Constance smiled and then to Tess's extreme irritation, signalled in that awfully aristocratic way of hers that the conversation was at an end.

Thoroughly miffed and feeling as if she was being toyed with like a kitten with a ball of string, Tess had no option but to leave as graciously as she could manage. The housekeeper had stuck the flowers in a vase anyhow, and Tess shot an annoyed glance at them as she passed.

Damn the bloody woman. Damn both of them.

She stormed off to her car, climbed in, drove off at speed.

She was half inclined to tell her to stuff the house.

The trouble was she wanted it so very much that she had no alternative but to keep dancing around in this humiliatingly ingratiating manner for just so long as it took. Once they'd signed things, Constance Makepeace, frankly, could take a running jump. She wouldn't care if Constance never set foot in West House again. She certainly would not be inviting her.

# 35

Andrew stood at the school gates, off to one side, alone.

Whatever had happened to this new man they were always on about? He'd just this very morning read an article about the changing face of the workplace. In this very region, working women outnumbered the men and the role of househusband was growing. Or so it said. New Man did not live in Bishopsmeade, that was for sure, for the entire contingent at the gates consisted of mums, grannies, aunts, big sisters, assorted pushchairs, dogs, an array of badly parked cars, and him.

He had been coming here to collect Portia, Samantha and Harry for weeks past, and he was still invisible. To hell with them. They looked at him, some of them, as if he was some sort of pervert. Oh yes, he had heard the suspicious mutterings, seen the sly glances, the way they held tighter onto the hands of the snotty-nosed siblings.

It upset him more than he cared to admit, to such an extent that, even if he didn't get a job, he might have to tell Yvonne that it was off, all this. He smelled a witch-hunt, wondered how long it would be before the accusations began. Even if they let him off being a pervert, a child abuser, they had probably decided long ago that he and Yvonne were at it.

Bloody annoying, that, being accused of something he was only dreaming about. He was being extra sensitive these days. Tess was leading him a dance, flitting about here, there and everywhere, off tomorrow to Caryn Lodge for the weekend, supposedly to have it out with Joe, find out what was happening on the packaging front. West House, she assured him, was theirs for the taking but they would have to be patient a while longer until Constance got her act together and got her solicitor on the job. In the meantime, they had to push that useless estate agent of theirs, she said, get him to do something. She was giving him two more weeks and then that was it. She was switching to somebody else.

Andrew had been for a second interview for the job he was currently after, which had to count for something. Actually he thought he might have it and they had promised to let him know on Monday. A weekend of nail-biting, he supposed, for he really wanted this one.

It was cold standing in a small huddle of people waiting. He felt very alone. Maybe if he made more of an effort, people around might unbend a little. He tried as he caught the eye of the nearest woman, wearing one of those puddingy all-in-ones under a peculiar looking cape. She had an alarming frizz of orange hair and looked as if she was expecting quads. A toddler with a red nose leaned languidly against the bump.

'Nice day,' Andrew said, plucking up courage and giving her what he hoped was a nice ordinary sort of smile. 'For the time of year, that is.'

She looked at him with supreme disinterest and he felt himself flushing. As a chat-up line, if it had been a chat-up line, it was an explosive non-starter.

She turned very deliberately so that all he could see was a puddingy rear view, the child leaning round to peep at him.

Sod it, then. That was it. That was the last time he made any effort.

The doors opened and the children filed out in that excited three-thirty exodus. Anxiously scanning them, he picked up on Portia and Harry, took a second or two longer to spot Samantha. There followed the usual few minutes of zipping up anoraks, pulling up socks, sorting Harry out with his laces. Portia, immaculately clad herself, helped. One day, as well as being a supremely efficient career woman, she would also be an irritatingly perfect mother.

Right.

'Ready then?'

'Where's the car?' they asked in unison.

He had been a bit lazy these last few times, driven here, but today they were on foot.

They groaned as if he was asking them to do a marathon instead of walk down the length of School Lane and Front Street and thence home. Firmly holding Harry and Samantha's hands, with Portia walking briskly beside, he set off on foot as everyone else piled into cars. The lollipop lady smiled at him, thank God, told the kids to stay there with Daddy whilst she leapt, pole extended, into the road with a bold disregard for her personal safety.

They crossed quickly, Portia causing a small problem by trying to stop to explain to the lollipop lady that it was Mr O'Grady, not Daddy.

'Daddy's on the ship now,' she said when they were safely across. 'He sends us letters.'

'Wonderful,' Andrew said, glad she was too young to understand sarcasm. This walking lark wasn't such a good idea, for he had forgotten about the stuff they carried with them in assorted cheerful bags. A couple of sherpas in tow wouldn't come amiss.

It occurred to him, as they struggled along, picking up things dropped, proceeding at snail's pace, that this might be one of the last times he did this. They would want him to start promptly, so he might well be working next week. He had enjoyed the time with the children, though, and he thought he was pretty good at it.

One step forward, two steps back.

Children slowed you down. They stopped dead to look at things. Things you never even noticed. A window cleaner up a ladder caused them to stare in wonder. A cat sitting on a wall watching them and darting off at the very last made them stop to peer over the wall to see where the creature had fled.

'Mrs Whitworth is dead,' Portia said, as they were passing Greenview Rest Home. She spoke in that matter of fact way of hers, grabbing his attention with the words. 'Like the rabbit we had. She was really Harry's and she was called Snowdrop because she was all white. She was very, very old. Going to be ninety-six. She had bumpy legs and funny hair but she was nice. She did not like carrots, so Mummy said it was all right she could leave them. Mummy bought her some perfume in a little bottle. It cost a lot of money. She's dead,' she repeated, tugging at his arm as he made no reply.

It took a few minutes to decipher the slight mix-up between the recently-deceased Mrs Whitworth and the white rabbit. Not able frankly to drum up a terrific emotional response, as he had never known the aforesaid Mrs Whitworth or the rabbit, he nevertheless put on a suitably sober expression.

'Mummy cried,' Samantha said, looking up at him with Yvonne's eyes.

'That's a secret,' Portia said crossly. 'We weren't supposed to tell.'

Andrew tried another of his distractions before the girls started on one of their fortunately infrequent but very wearing arguments.

'When we get back there's kitten cakes,' he said, knowing that would stop them in their tracks.

It did.

They would have to wait until they got back, he told them, to see what they were.

In fact, they were ordinary little cakes with Smarties pressed into the icing for eyes, jelly diamonds for ears and angelica pieces for the nose and whiskers. Fiddly but effective. The kids' cookbook he had bought was full of natty ideas.

When he went out to work again, it was goodbye to things like that.

He was under no damned illusions.

When he went out to work again, it was curtains for decent meals.

Tess had gone off for the weekend, laden with suitcases. Would he be OK? Was he sure he would be OK?

She didn't usually show such concern but, at last, assured that he would indeed be absolutely fine, she went.

He felt a bit guilty at the relief he felt at her departure, even guiltier when on Saturday morning he felt such an intense pleasure when he caught up with Yvonne who was pottering about in her garden. Of the children, there was surprisingly no sign.

'Where are they?' he asked, for Samantha in particular was a bit of a dab hand with the gardening, a Tess in the making as far as the love of flowers went.

Yvonne rubbed a hand over her forehead, unknowingly leaving an earthy trail.

'Portia and Samantha are staying over at a friend's,' she said, pulling a worried face. 'The first time ever. And Harry's at a birthday party. They're going swimming and then having a fish and chip supper. Jonathan's mummy is bringing him back about seven o'clock. So . . .' she looked up brightly, 'I can hardly believe I am on my own for the entire day. On Saturday too. I did think of going shopping but it's best I stay here in case there's a phone call.'

'I'd ask you to come over for lunch,' he said after a moment, 'but it might be misconstrued because Tess is away for the weekend.'

There were people about this morning. Car washing. In the garden. Looking up the road at them even now as they conversed.

'Indeed it might,' she said crisply and with a certain delectable primness that quite astonished him. The blush that accompanied the words told him what he wanted to know though. He had a sudden wicked idea that she might very well include him in her dreams.

'Oh . . . I meant to say how sorry I was to hear about your friend Mrs Whitworth,' he said quietly. 'Portia told me. I had no idea. Ninety-six, though? A good enough innings, that.'

'Yes. Dear Agnes. We mustn't be too sad. It was peaceful. In her sleep.' Yvonne pulled secateurs out of the little flowery bag she used for gardening, 'The funeral was exactly as she wanted it. We sang "White Christmas". We were not supposed to be sad although that wasn't easy. She had three husbands, you know, and yet no living relatives. She had no children.'

He shared a little wistful smile with her. 'At least she had a nice last Christmas,' he said, for something to say. 'With you.'

Yvonne nodded. 'The awful thing is she left me her fur coat. Portia is horrified. She told Samantha it was made of real live rabbits dead. Samantha adores it. I keep catching her stroking it in the wardrobe.'

'Oh. I see.'

'It's not rabbit, it's mink. I shan't wear it, I don't suppose, but I shall treasure it. I owe it to Agnes.'

'Is Robin coming back? Or is he in the Med for ever?'

There was a short silence.

'I beg your pardon?' She looked up at him. 'I'm sorry, is that your business?'

'No. No, it isn't,' he said, surprised at what was quite obviously a change of mood. 'And I'm sorry I asked.'

'Children, particularly Portia, pick up things sometimes and get them wrong,' she said stiffly. 'Robin and I are working things out, that's all you need know. Now . . . if you'll excuse me, Andrew, I must get on and I expect you have work to do. Oh . . . and by the way, I have arranged for the children to go to a friend of mine on Tuesdays. She'll pick them up from next week.' Her smile was brief. 'Thank you very much for helping out. You've been very kind and I'm most grateful.'

'Not at all. It's been a pleasure,' he said, reflecting that they were ending this conversation very comically correct.

He did not look back as he went up his own path but he damned well knew she was looking after him.

# 36

Stephanie wanted to be at the gallery on Saturday but, because Tess was visiting, she had changed her plans, decided she ought to be the attentive hostess, and it took a considerable effort on Tess's part and an awful lot of apologising on Stephanie's before she changed her mind a second time and went.

'You still haven't told her,' Tess said accusingly to her father as they watched the little car disappear. 'You'll have to sooner or later. You can't just suddenly not go to work one morning. She might just query that.'

'I will tell her,' he said, his irritation showing. 'But not just yet. Not when things might happen. I have one or two things pending. A few more contacts, people who've been out of the country.'

Tess sighed. She did not bother to tell him about the efforts *she* had made, for she was not sure he would appreciate it, and it looked increasingly as if it had all been a waste of time.

'Let's have it, Joe,' she said, sitting opposite him in his study. It was a bold bright room, the only room in Caryn Lodge that Stephanie had made little impact on. Some of his more personal possessions, including a map of old Durham that her mother had bought him, emphasised that this room was his. His desk was tidy, a couple of expensive pens and executive leatherwork on it beside the telephone. A second smaller desk held the computer and printer. 'How bad is it? The truth, please.'

'I've told you,' he said and for a moment the old aggressive light was in his eyes but it was quickly gone. 'All right, sweetheart. If you must. The truth is, it's all over,' he went on, digging into the drawer and bringing out cigarettes, pulling one out of the packet before pushing it roughly back and shutting the drawer almost in disgust. 'I'm finished, Tess. Nobody wants to know. My contacts, as if you haven't guessed, are pretty near exhausted. I've spoken to everybody. Spent a fortune – personally, this time – on lunches. I've had it up to here with grovelling. The word's got round, if you ask me, and I have no chance of landing anything else. I have enormous debts, overdraft, cards. The lump sum won't stretch far, not for long anyhow. God knows what we're going to do, me and Stephanie.'

She was not too concerned about the effect all this might have on her dearest stepmother but the lump sum was a different matter. The lump sum that was, under the terms of his will, due to come to her. Tess hoped she had got all the financial facts straight because she hadn't talked to Andrew about the will, managing to stop herself in time. Wills were hypothetical things anyway, depending as they did on somebody's unfortunate demise before they were realised and, short of killing someone, you as a beneficiary had no say in the whys and wherefores of the outcome. How could she talk to Andrew about it without giving away her own thoughts? Andrew would be utterly appalled. Andrew would not even fight for his own skin. He had no instinct for self-preservation. But she had. By God, she had. She was not giving up the good life without a struggle.

'As a family, we've had it,' Joe continued, going suddenly pompous on her. 'We're bloody disgraced. It's bound to get round that I was on the fiddle. It'll probably find its way into the local paper if I know that editor. He's always hated my guts. As for bloody Ivan . . . he's letting me off the little discrepancies. Blackmail, of course. He'll be back to me someday for a favour. Thank God your mother never knew. You know what your mother was like. Why spend a tenner when you can spend a hundred? Your mother had class, sweetheart. Just like you.'

For a brief moment, despite all this, she felt a glow at the praise, on her mother's behalf as much as her own. 'I would pay you back, Daddy, what I owe you . . .' she said quietly, 'but at the moment I don't have it. I could lose one of the shops, I suppose.'

'Hell, no. No need to panic. What you owe is nothing,' he said roughly. 'Neither here nor there with my debts. We'll have to move to something smaller. Downgrade. And that's assuming we can sell this place. I'm going to have to try to get a job by applying for one. I might even have to sign on. Christ . . . it's going to be a nightmare, Tess. I know what Stephanie will want to do. She'll want to go back to work, support *me*. Well, I'm not bloody having that. I didn't marry her for that. I married her to look after her.'

Tess sighed, looking at him a little despairingly.

'Let's go for a walk, Joe.'

'A walk? What, now?' He looked at her. Astonished.

'We can think better in the fresh air,' she said. 'And we need to think. There has to be a way out of this.'

They went down to the road, walked a little way along it, facing the sparse traffic, before climbing a stile and taking a path that skirted the house and led up to the gentle hills behind the property. In some ways, this location reminded Tess of West House although West House had the advantage in her eyes with its softening effect of woodland close by but it did not have the forward view of the Tees as Caryn Lodge did. After a week of heavy rain, it was full, the level well up.

They walked beside the beck, a tributary of the river, a stream that tumbled fast, pouring coolly and cleanly over rocks and ledges. The grass was springy and moist, still drying off from the winter snow and the rain, but spring flowers were a little prematurely in abundance in what must be a peculiarly sheltered spot. Delicate blue gentians and pink primroses and the sheer stark hill-beauty of it all suddenly and unexpectedly caught at Tess, made her all too aware of her father's dark mood. He strode on, head bent, concentrating on each and every step, the views passing him by. She hated him like this. She'd only seen him like this once before and that was understandably after mother died.

She wanted him to be brisk and energetic and confident. He was a good actor and she had no doubt that he did not present this mood in public, particularly to the contacts he had been trying to impress, but it was getting harder for him as time passed. He was getting desperate and he was developing a corresponding look. If he was running out of ideas then it was up to her to come up with something. Fast.

'Things are never as bad as they seem,' she said at last as they paused to look back at the house. It was a ridiculous statement and she realised that as soon as she uttered the words.

He laughed.

'Aren't they? You could fool me. Things are every bit as bad, worse if anything. How about you and Andrew? Things aren't right between you, are they? Stephanie's worried. What's wrong? You can tell me, sweetheart. I'll help all I can. Do you want me to have a word with him?'

She looked sharply at him. What the hell did this have to do with him and Stephanie?

'No, I do not want you to have a word,' she said hastily. 'Nothing's wrong. At least . . . all right, if you must know, he wants a family, and I'm not going to go through that again. You know how I went to hell and back. I haven't actually told him as much.'

'Oh . . . that'll take some sorting out then,' he said with a slight smile. 'It won't happen again, you know. Chance in a million. Next time it will be fine.'

'One chance in nine hundred and fifty at my age,' she corrected him quietly. 'I've swotted up on the subject. And, no . . . I don't want to talk about that. I have no regrets, Joe. I did the right thing. I ask you, am I the sort of woman to cope with an idiot child?'

'They're not idiots,' he said and for a minute she saw in his face the same expression as Andrew sometimes had. 'They're not called that.'

'Just as they don't call them mongols any more,' she said. 'What's in a name? Anyway . . .' she frowned her irritation, 'stop changing the subject. We're talking about you and what we're going to do about you.'

Joe looked up at the clouds. Way in the distance, one of the hill tops was softly swathed by them, looking as if it was wearing a silky sombrero. A solitary spit of rain fell but it seemed isolated. He shivered nonetheless.

'Of course, as I've said before, if I pegged out within the next couple of months before my contract expires then everything would be OK,' he said. 'A quick heart attack would do it. Stephanie would be all right. I'm still employed by the company, you see; it doesn't matter that I'm working my notice, and she would get all the benefits from me dying in service. You'd be OK as well. I hope I've got another thirty years ahead of me and by then your business will be fantastically successful, but you would have been pleased to get a bit from me, wouldn't you? Parents always want to leave their children something.'

'Don't talk about it, daddy,' she said. 'It upsets me. You'll live to be ninety at least. You're fit. Aren't you?'

'Oh, yes. I had a medical a while back. Got the all clear. I've got the heart of a thirty year old. So . . . that's not going to happen, is it? And the bloody annoying thing is there might be nothing to leave you if everything goes sour. It'll all have been frittered away.'

'You don't have to leave me anything,' she said. 'Do you really think I'm so shallow that all I'm worried about is what I'm going to get?'

She looked at him. Held his gaze.

They walked on. In silence.

And then he said the unthinkable.

He said the thing she had once suspected but put out of her head as quite ridiculous.

They had reached the top of the walk, a small bumpy plateau of tough rough fell grass, where they would pause a while before starting down. Joe was puffing a bit but for once he seemed to be taking an interest in the surroundings, in the high green beauty of the hillside. For a moment, his worries seemed forgotten, as he pointed out hills all around, to Tess's surprise putting names to some of them.

'Stephanie loves it here,' he said. 'She has a great sense of place, does Stephanie. She'd miss it a helluva lot if we have to move. I can see us having to move up to Newcastle. Cut down costs, etc. She'll want to sell her little car, of course, and the gallery – that goes without saying, and Caryn Lodge. She'd do all that for me. I know she would.'

They were then silent, Tess burrowing into her mind for some fresh ideas. There must be someone amongst his contacts, amongst her own. Someone who would jump at the chance of employing him, a man of his expertise.

And it was then he said it.

'I can't let her down.' His voice was soft yet sure. 'Not Stephanie. You see, Tess . . . can I tell you this? I love her very much. I know people thought I married her just because I was lonely after your mother died. You thought that too, didn't you?'

She made little demurring sounds but he seemed not to hear, intent on his thoughts.

'People thought I did it just because of that. Don't think I didn't hear the comments. After all, I'm hardly the greatest catch in the world, am I? People are cruel. They can't always see that love, just that, can be the reason, however old you happen to be. I wish we'd met when we were young. Oh, don't get me wrong – of course I loved your mother – but this thing with Stephanie . . . it's different. She is my special lady.' He laughed shortly. 'God knows why I'm telling you this, but I want you to know the truth. I can't let her down,' he repeated. 'So I'm going to sort this out if I can without telling her.'

Tess managed a smile, somehow hiding her deep shock.

Oh Joe, you have just made a dreadful mistake.

You have just admitted to me – your daughter – that you love Stephanie more than Mother. You love that plain, clever woman more than Mother. Mother, who lit up the room when she walked into it. Mother, who made up for her lack of academic intelligence by a sharp wit. Mother . . . who was beautiful.

Oh no, Joe.

This cannot be allowed.

It made it easier, though. It made what she was now going to do easier. The idea that she had dismissed as most definitely not on could now be brought out into the open. It was a long shot but it was worth a try.

'And how are you going to manage that?' she asked, keeping her voice even, even though she was still seething at his words. He didn't realise how much he had hurt her. He did not realise. 'How are you going to sort it out without . . . your wife . . . knowing?'

'I don't know yet,' he said. 'I'm working on it. I'm starting to cover all possibilities.'

She stole a quick glance at him. Her heart gave a single thump. If she didn't do it now, this minute, she would never do it.

'The Romans were good at this sort of thing,' she said as they began the gentle curving descent. 'Stephanie . . .' She had some difficulty uttering the name. 'Steffi lent me this book about them. It was a good read.'

'Didn't know you had time to read,' he said, looking a little bemused. 'You're like your mother sometimes. She was always going off at a tangent. Tell me, what the hell has this to do with my predicament?'

She shrugged.

'Let me explain. Family honour was everything to them.'

'And so it should be,' he said, drawing himself up even as he said it. 'It is bloody important. We don't think half enough of the family these days. Disintegration of the family, Tess, is the ruin of civilisation as we know it.'

'Quite.' She nodded her agreement. 'I was reading about this Roman . . . I think his name was Piso . . . he was the governor of Syria, anyway. I couldn't make head or tail of the politics and he seemed pretty ruthless himself but for various reasons there was this plan to discredit him and his family. They were forever plotting and scheming in those days.'

'Nothing changes. Just like my business colleagues, particularly Ivan,' he said bitterly. 'I did think of suing them but I could come a cropper on that. That's the trouble when there's an element of truth in what they claim. It puts you in an impossible position.'

'Exactly . . .' She drew him back to the tricky subject of Piso. 'He had the option. He could fight it out, challenge the Senate, but with even the emperor turned against him, the verdict was a foregone conclusion. Guilty, of course, which meant death by sword. In other words, complete disgrace for the family, for his wife, sons and daughters. Forever and ever. However, the emperor very kindly offered him another way out. It was left to his wife to explain what it was.'

'And?' He glanced up again at a fresh gathering of cloud, at a few more spits of rain, took her hand as the path sloped. 'Come on, you've got me curious now.'

'He could kill himself,' she said, the words spinning into the cold hill air. Her father's grip on her hand tightened even as she said it and she knew she had hit the nerve. Bull's eye. 'That way the family honour would be restored, and his wife and children would still inherit.'

There was a short disbelieving silence broken only by the gurgling of the stream source nearby as it splashed hidden. The moorland stretched, walled into neat variously-shaded green fields, sheep on the lower slopes, the outline of the hills blurring as the cloud thickened. The spits of rain intensified into a more persistent drizzle, cold on their faces.

'Neither of you would get a thing if I topped myself in company service,' Joe said. 'So that's no use. If I die of natural causes, of course, then that's a different matter. What are you suggesting? That I make my suicide look like natural causes?'

'Daddy! For heaven's sake. I wasn't suggesting anything of the sort,' she said hastily, mustering great indignation at the very idea. 'I wish I hadn't told you the story now. I can't think why I did except I was just reminded of it when you were talking about love.' She glanced at him, at the wry smile on his face, gentled her voice. 'Thank you for sharing that thought with me. Forgive me, I'm an old romantic. I was thinking of Andrew and wondering if he would do it for *me*. I think it's just wonderful that a man can love his wife enough to do that. Kill himself for love.'

And hadn't he just told her that he loved Stephanie more than anything in the world? They hadn't sounded like empty words. He damned well meant them.

They did not say another word until they got back to Caryn Lodge.

Tess immediately excused herself and locked herself in the bathroom, feeling suddenly nauseous, holding her hand over her mouth until the moment passed.

Was she so very wicked?

She was not wicked, she told herself. She had to do this for her mother's sake, for her mother's beautiful, perfect memory. How dare he love that woman, that grey plain woman, more than her mother?

She looked at herself in the mirror, at her flushed face, her bright terribly excited eyes. She was also trying to save her own skin and unfortunately desperate situations called for desperate measures.

She could not get cold feet now.

She was well aware that, in his present extremely depressed state, she had managed to sow the seed of a way out for her father. An honourable way out, moreover, and Joe was a surprising pushover for the honourable solution. She did not bother to tell him the rest of the story. That Piso had refused to take his life, a coward at the end, and so Plancina his wife had taken the knife and plunged it into his heart for him.

Somehow that seemed inappropriate.

# 37

'Close your eyes then, Mrs Makepeace,' Colin told her as he helped her out of the taxi. 'And I'll tell you when you can open them.'

Constance heard the gate latch, allowed him to lead her up the garden path, heard the key being inserted into the lock, stepped inside. It smelled so different. Now new paint mingled not unpleasantly with a clean pine disinfectanty smell.

'Right then . . . open your eyes!'

The first thing she saw was Colin and the delight in his big brash face. Then she saw the room, the little living room at Primrose Cottage. It was unrecognisable. The wallpaper was pink with big silvery pink flowers and there was a border and a pale pink ceiling.

'She picked the wallpaper. We got it at a special price from B & Q. End of roll. She likes flowers,' Colin said, his smile fading a little as he saw her face. 'You do like it, don't you? I know you said magnolia, but Lisa Marie said you'd love this. Flowers, she said, for Mrs Makepeace. Look . . .' He dashed across the room to where some blue and white hyacinths sat in a little vase on the window ledge. 'She likes the smell. Got you these, she did, so it wouldn't look so bare. Bloody awful without furniture, isn't it, pet?'

'They're lovely. Thank you,' Constance said, stuck momentarily for words. She was touched by the gift. By the thought. Much less spectacular than Tess's flowers, the huge mixed bunches she was fond of giving.

'And upstairs, we put in coving, a ceiling rose and a bloody great chandelier from BHS in that front room. That was her idea.

She's always liked them and she knew you would. It'll remind you of the big house, she said. And she's run up all the curtains herself. She didn't skimp on material. I've got the receipts, like you said. Every last one.' He fumbled in his pocket and pulled out a heap of small bits of paper. 'Here you are, pet . . . they're all here. And after we'd scrubbed the bathroom, we got some tufted carpet, two toned, and it all looks a treat. Lisa Marie said you'd like carpet, better than tiles anyday. And she got a new toilet seat. Wooden.' He flushed. 'It's only right, she said.'

'Really!'

His excitement showed in his face as he showed the upper rooms off. The chandelier was his pride and joy and Constance assured him she loved it, unwilling to say anything that would deflate his enthusiasm.

'Come and have a look at what we've done to the kitchen. Now I've got you a new cooker off a bloke I know – the latest, timer and all. Cheap at half the price. The other was knackered, Mrs Makepeace, otherwise we'd have made do. Lisa Marie said we couldn't expect a lady like you to cook on that. And the fridge – they'd buggered that up good and proper. So – off this same bloke . . . mind you, pet, there's no receipts for these. But nothing's nicked. I wouldn't have you with hot stuff, not the Colonel's lady, eh? More than my life's worth.'

'It's all very nice, Colin,' she said, peeping into the kitchen and withdrawing. It was clean and very bright. Yellow. 'I do hope you disposed of the furniture to your satisfaction.'

He flushed deep. 'Kept a bit for ourselves,' he said. 'That's all right, is it? Lisa Marie says as you wouldn't mind. Scrubbed it up a bit. It's all old but it'll do until we get some modern stuff. We can't use it proper until we get out of the bedsit. Not room to swing a cat. It's getting on her nerves, it is. It's a bugger being so bloody squashed. And now that we've got the furniture stored, it's worse.'

Constance picked up the vase, smelled the strong scent of the hyacinths, touched the pale blue and pink petals, smiled a little.

'And what about a job, Colin? Are you any nearer finding something else?' She eyed the room carefully, noting that the wallpaper matched perfectly. 'You're very good at decorating.'

'Partially served my time,' he said. 'I should be good at it. Should have stuck at it but you know how it is. Lisa Marie fell pregnant and that was that. Thrilled to bits, she was. She always is. Thrilled now.'

'Oh . . .' Constance looked at him. 'Oh dear, not another baby?'

'She thinks so and she's never wrong. She's over the moon. A boy, this time, she says. Would you credit it, Mrs Makepeace. Once at Christmas, a quickie . . . and that's it. I told you, she only has to look at me.' Pride surfaced, coupled with sudden embarrassment and a muttered red-faced apology.

'Yes, well . . .' Embarrassed herself, not knowing what to say, Constance went to look outside.

The little paved yard was swept clean. There was a high stone wall and a back gate. She might ask Mr Bainbridge if he would organise a little border, remove a few of the stone flags, perhaps plant some rambling roses and clematis to cover the plain wall. Gracious me, it was so small. This tiny yard was about the same size as her herb patch in the kitchen garden. She had forgotten quite how small Primrose Cottage was. She really did wonder how she would cope with its sheer lack of size. West House might be too large but this was just too small. Smith would be most sniffy about all this. And she had forgotten what effect the river had on her. She dared not look at it too long, and living here, she would not be able to get away from it for it was opposite the front door. A quite dreadful place for children.

'Great yard, isn't it?' Colin said, looming up behind her. 'Room for a slide there and a washing line. What Lisa Marie would give for a washing line!'

'It would be very difficult living here with children,' Constance said quietly. 'Because of the river. Some children are fascinated with water. You would have to watch your little girls very carefully.'

At her side, Colin was suddenly silent. She could hear him breathing.

She stole a glance at him. At the hope in his eyes.

'Very well. You may have it rent free for six months, Mr Hawkins, and then we will review the situation,' she told him.

'I will draw up the necessary papers. There is, however, one condition.'

She smiled as she saw the hope die fractionally.

'What's that then?' he asked. 'What condition?'

'That you marry Lisa Marie,' she said. 'And quickly.'

Tess was back up in Newcastle for a few days, beavering about with contacts again, staying at her father's flat.

Andrew knew why she was taking all this on herself, but frankly he was getting fed up with it. Why didn't Joe do what any other man would do? Get off his backside and go job hunting instead of fawning around with these so-called contacts? He could always take something lowlier for a bit for a stop-gap, although when he had mentioned that to Tess, she had vetoed that idea in no uncertain manner. Joe had done the same. If he couldn't get a directorship or a senior executive position, then nothing else would do. It was equivalent, didn't Andrew see, to a cabinet minister taking a part-time post in a local constituency office. Not bloody on. He was not going to be a laughing stock amongst the people he had known and worked with for years.

Sod him, then. Andrew had offered advice and had been rounded on, so that was that. Joe would never forgive him for not helping to cook his books.

In the meantime, he was on his own for another couple of days and, now that he had a job, coming home to an empty house was pretty grim. He let himself in and shook off his wet overcoat. What a day! It had rained solidly from the moment he stepped out of the house this morning at half past seven. Torrential stuff, so that he was wet before he even got himself into the car. He'd sat in dampish trousers all the way up to the audit he was doing for his new company at some god-forsaken spot way up the coast.

He thought it was pretty bleak where Joe and Stephanie lived in Upper Teesdale but parts of the Northumberland coast made bleakness an art form. Sharp rain, sleet even, slanting in from the North Sea, a bitterly cold sea not yet warmed up, not that it ever did warm up much. The accounting staff at the factory that stood inches from the beach informed him proudly that the views on a clear day were out of this world. Rugged and raw and breathtaking.

He had to take their word for it for the weather closed in, steamily grey, switching the view off. Halfway through the afternoon, the figures had started to swim on the page and the screen but he'd stuck it out manfully until finishing time. He was not going before they did. The journey home, skirting Newcastle and then coping with the hazards of a spray-filled A1, had been hell on wheels.

He felt chilled to the bone and his limbs were aching, throbbing. He was, he just knew it, catching the cold that the senior accountant at the factory had been wafting everyone's way all week. Sneezes. Red nose. Temperature. The man had infected everybody. The cold was on the rampage. The trouble was, he could not afford to be ill, not when he'd just started the job and was trying to make a good impression. He had no option but to nip this in the bud. Hastily, he stripped off his clothes, stepped into a hot steamy shower, sneezing through it. He put on some old pyjamas because he liked them best, wrapped himself in a towelling robe, hurried back downstairs.

Tess should be here. Her kind of low-key sympathy was better than none. He shouldn't have to cope with this alone. With the fire full on, a lemon aspirin drink in a mug, he huddled into the chair drawn close to the fire, feeling miserable. Tess might have made the drink for him, tucked him in the chair, a blanket round his legs – stroked his fevered brow, dammit! – rubbed his chest and back with Vick and told him to sit there and not move a muscle. She might have, but then again she might not.

His head ached. Thumped like Big Ben. And his eyes were watering so that he had to keep wiping them. God, he felt rotten. Worriedly, he felt his forehead. Hot. It was one step up from a mere cold, flu probably, or something worse . . . malaria, for instance . . . Could it lie dormant for four years? That was the last time he'd been anywhere where he might catch it. He sipped the hot liquid, feeling as he did so the beginnings of a sore throat. Bugger it . . . he'd be lucky if he got to work tomorrow. He would have to *crawl* in, no matter how bad he was, show willing and then be sent home.

Andrew shivered, listening to the silence. In a few minutes, he told himself, when he felt a bit less like death, he'd heat up some soup and open a can of rice pudding with sultanas. Funny, the things you fancied when you were out of sorts. It was a bit like being pregnant, he supposed. Tess had adored peaches when she was oh-so-briefly pregnant. She had looked very well and had indeed bloomed with health, and that was another reason it came as such a shock.

Don't start on that again. Any further attempts to discuss that little matter had met with a resounding display of petulance on her part. She was getting worse. After she'd been up to Caryn Lodge, she'd been very peculiar, withdrawn and uncommunicative.

She had also done something she had never done before. She had let the flowers in the hall die. He'd watched them wither himself, determined not to do anything about it until she did, and at last she seemed to notice them, had them whipped away and some leaves and bits from the garden in their place in no time. She'd made no effort with them unless just poking up stiffly in the vase was some sort of new-fangled design. He didn't say a bloody word. There was no joy, no vitality, for them any more. Joy had gone out of the window recently. He was beginning to dread waking up, wondering what heights of tight uncommunication they might achieve today.

Awkwardly, he rose to his feet, feeling distinctly dizzy, steadying himself as he headed for the door. Malaria could kill, but this was just a cold. He knew that but he needed someone, a sympathetic woman, to tell him that, to laugh at his stupid irrational fears. He wished Yvonne would suddenly appear, flowery-scented and gorgeous, with one of her food parcels. He would have no strength to argue and it went without saying she would treat him like one of the children, have him tucked up in bed in no time. He knew there would be a lot of sympathy from Yvonne. She could even, if she so desired, have her wicked way with him. On second thoughts – he glanced at himself in the hall mirror – he was at a low ebb in the fanciability stakes just now, nose reddening nicely, eyes bloated and bleary, energy zero-rated.

Late out this morning, he had left his breakfast dishes, and they still sat there, of course, accusingly, on the sink over the dishwasher which was full of yesterday's dishes. He left them there and rummaged in a cupboard for a pan and a tin of soup. He did not even look at what kind of soup it was. It didn't matter as long as it was hot and wet. Another pan for the rice pudding, and that was it. Dinner preparations complete.

The soup was fawn coloured with bits. Chicken, he thought. He felt a minuscule amount better by the time he had consumed it and the whole can of pudding. Still groggy, though, and he ought to go to bed and sweat it out. For God knows what sane reason, he felt compelled to tidy up the kitchen a bit. Suppose he died in the night and Tess found him when she got back. She would never forgive the state of the kitchen.

He had a picture on the wall, a picture Samantha had drawn as a thank-you-for-having-me present. An out of doors picture with green grass, a bright blue Caribbean sky with a golden sun. His hair was not so curly as before and he had a very big smile and enormous feet sticking out of short legs. She'd run out of paper but it had to be said that there was still that indefinable essence.

Andrew sat down with a bump and stared at the picture. Portia had wanted to know all about his new job when he had last seen her.

He explained it in simple terms she would understand

'I wish you were *my* daddy and not Mrs O'Grady's,' she said after a moment studying him alarmingly closely when he thought she had been weighing up the intricacies of his job description.

It took him a moment to fathom that one.

'You have your own daddy,' he said quietly, wanting to close this conversation before it became too difficult. He was not trying to wheedle family secrets out of her.

She was a smashing little girl.

He picked up the letter that she had written him. A formal thank you letter for looking after them for so long. Harry had added his signature and there were kisses at the bottom of the page. Samantha had cried and said she wished they could still come to his house and not have to go to Ellie's mummy's house on Tuesdays.

He was sorry too, but he couldn't let them see that. He'd see less and less of them now and that's how it should be, he thought. Things had been getting too bloody cosy.

You pathetic bastard, he said aloud, as he practically crawled upstairs. If he got any worse, he'd ring the doctor or Tess or somebody. The way he felt, he wasn't entirely sure he would make it through to morning. He would expire sometime during the small hours.

Alone and unloved.

The way he felt, he didn't even care.

# 38

Constance had broken the news to Mrs Bainbridge about her decision not to move to Primrose Cottage and, as expected, Ella had taken it badly.

'Mrs Makepeace . . .' she said accusingly. 'What a thing to have done! Why didn't you have a word with Bernard first? He'd have put you right.'

'I do not need "putting right",' Constance said, giving her a sharp glance. 'It was my decision and I stand by it. I was less than enthralled by the cottage anyway. It's too near the river.'

'Ah . . . right you are then,' Ella said after a moment. 'That is a bit of a facer for you, but where are you going to go, Mrs Makepeace? Or are you staying here now?'

'No. I shall find alternative accommodation. Another cottage. There are several available, I notice, and I shall choose one of them. There is one in the little lane beside St Cuthbert's, and I think I might be very happy there. Smith would have a garden too, and that was another thing that was worrying me about Primrose Cottage, the absence of a garden of substance.'

'But he's a layabout, he is, that Colin Hawkins and they're not married, him and that woman of his. All those children. They say he's been inside.'

'I am aware of that, and it does not matter, Mrs Bainbridge,' Constance said wearily. 'They are getting married a week on Saturday. I have been invited to attend the ceremony.'

'You're not going!' Ella asked, quite horrified at the idea. 'Are you?'

'I have not decided,' Constance told her, dismissing her with an irritated wave of her hand. She had had quite enough of Ella this afternoon.

The day had started well. Springlike. Daffodils were sprouting in the beds and the sky was developing that high bright look of spring. It was still capable of feeling quite cool first thing though, and Smith was still staying indoors at night. She had taken her usual stroll down to the teashop and enquired of Miss Green whether or not she had seen anything lately of Mr O'Grady.

'Got a job,' she told her. 'So he told me the last time I saw him. Up over Newcastle way somewhere. Anyway, he said he wouldn't be able to get in much any more. Nice man. Do you know his wife at all?'

Yes.

Tess had been up several times bringing her flowers. It was kind of her, of course it was, and Constance almost hated herself for thinking there might be an ulterior motive. She so hoped she could trust Tess. Tess of the bright eyes, the friendly manner.

Trust was everything.

Hugh, for example, had to be trusted. He had to be trusted to stay loyal to her, despite everything. And he had. He stayed loyal because she supposed he had loved her truly and it was hardly his fault that she had been unable to return that love because hers belonged to Archie. She hoped Hugh never regretted marrying her instead of Grace. It was, of course, never spoken of. After Hugh's 'accident', there had been a letter from Grace. One of those vicious letters of hers.

*My dearest Constance* (she always started them like that), *Please accept my sincere condolences at the untimely accident that has occurred. Poor Hugh! I heard the news from Walter's wife with whom, as you may know, I retain some small contact. I am sure you would have wished to have Hugh with you, beside you, for longer than this and you must try to be brave as he would have wished you to be. We shall never know, shall we, what prompted such an action. Deep despair, obviously, that you were unable to assuage. As before, my invitation to you to visit me stands, although I do appreciate the difficulties of our discoursing in a civilised manner. I will be unable to attend the funeral, detained as I shall be elsewhere, as I was on the occasion of both your marriages. In deep sorrow. Your ever-loving sister, Grace*

Ever-loving!

Constance sighed, annoyed to have remembered the letter. She had read it recently again, her fury at Walter spilling over once more. How dare he tell Grace the circumstances of Hugh's death, as he so obviously had? She had read the letter word by incriminating word, or was it just her own tremendous guilt that read so much more into the words? They leapt off the page at her, accusingly, reminding her of just what she had done. For a few months back in 1945, Grace had glowed with her love, only to have it extinguished by the announcement she and Hugh had made. Seeing the colour drain from her sister's face, hearing her sharp intake of breath at the shock, had marred her own joy just a little.

There was no address at the top of Grace's letter so she could not have replied even if she wished to do so, but she did observe on the envelope a Devon postmark, so it was more than likely she was ending her days in Smallcoombe Manor. So far as she knew, she herself had no claim to Smallcoombe Manor. It had gone first to Eleanor and then to Grace. Nobody had thought fit to tell her and she was most certainly not going to enquire.

Constance made no effort to trace Grace at the time of the last letter or since. Why should she? After fifty years, the unpalatable truth was that Grace was still as livid as ever. Wouldn't you think she could accept the fact that not only Archie, but also Hugh, had preferred *her*, Constance. They had wanted to go to bed with her, not Grace, and she still took comfort in the fact that she had been the desired one, not her sister. Grace only had herself to blame for being so appallingly ill-presented. One had to make some sort of effort, and Grace never had.

Serve Grace right, therefore, and how fortunate she was that Hugh had been loyal to the end to her. For all his many faults, she had trusted him.

Trust.

She was having serious doubts about Mrs O'Grady and yet all this shilly-shallying about was getting her nowhere. She had not yet found the people who would move into the house when she left.

She was not going back on her word to West House.

She was leaving in spring.

And spring would soon be here.

# 39

'Hello there.'

Yvonne heard his voice, turned. Saw him standing there, looking pretty good in a smart suit. She managed a smile. She had avoided him for weeks, easy now because he was working and off at the crack of dawn. She had avoided him precisely because of this . . . this stupid, warm, loving feeling . . . this ability the damned man had to make her feel teenagerly weak-at-the-knees. It was, frankly, not far short of pathetic and she would have to pull herself together, snap out of it. She couldn't stop thinking about how short she had been with him that day he had enquired after Robin. She wasn't ready to admit to other people that it was over, although she knew it was daft. Sooner or later the secret would be out.

'Oh, hello, Andrew. Feeling better?'

'Thanks, yes. Did Tess tell you I'd been under the weather?'

Yvonne nodded as the children, unbidden, dashed over to see him. Portia wanted to tell him about something she had done at school that had been highly praised, and Samantha was not to be outdone, pulling at his jacket, trying unsuccessfully to get a word in.

'Come on, you lot, we'll be late if we don't get on,' she called, trying to keep her voice light and level. Until just now, she'd almost forgotten what Andrew was capable of doing to her. She wished Agnes was here to talk to. Agnes could see things for what they were. Agnes talked a deal of common sense. In the meantime, with no Agnes, she was trying her best to be adult about it and that had meant stepping back, trying to cool things down before she well and truly landed herself in it. It would take nothing to set them off. She knew it and so did Andrew. It sizzled between them, and Agnes would have spotted it right away if she were here now at this very moment. Agnes would have very likely given her a nudge of encouragement.

'Do you want a lift to school? I don't need to be at my audit until ten this morning,' Andrew said by way of explanation, for he was later than usual.

'We're walking,' she said as the children clamoured to get into his car. 'No . . . we're walking,' she told them sharply. 'Come on, let Mr O'Grady go. No, Portia . . . we are *walking*.'

She found she was glaring at him rather, irritated because he'd managed to get the children in a bad mood when a few moments earlier they had all been quite happy. Her car was sitting in the drive, for heaven's sake, and if she'd needed to drive them to school, she would have done so.

'Do what your mummy says,' he said, gently pushing them aside as he stepped into his car. He looked at her, over their little heads, and the look was hard to fathom.

Then he was gone.

Ignoring the children's grumbles and the way they dragged along, she walked them to school, which involved passing Greenview Rest Home, looking up and seeing the window through which Agnes had seen their comings and goings. Her prison cell! The silly old bat, she had no right to come into her life like that and make an impact, Yvonne thought, feeling herself fill up with tears. Emotional over-reaction, that was what it was. The result of the pending divorce and the fact that she would have to have a rethink about what she was going to do with the rest of her life. If Andrew and Tess sold up and moved, fair enough, but she did not think she could damned well cope with him being stuck there for much longer.

She kissed and waved the children into school, wandering back into Front Street. Shopping first and then she had to do her volunteer book-round. She wondered if Mrs Makepeace would deign to see her this morning. The housekeeper usually acted as go-between, looking at Yvonne with a distinctly supercilious expression.

Yvonne found it faintly amusing, the way people judged so very much by appearances. It was hardly fair, was it?

She couldn't help the Portia-type thought as she struggled home with the bags. She supposed she could tone herself down a little so that Samantha's pictures of her were not quite so flamboyant, multi-crayoned as they were with her hair a shining mass of yellow, but why should she? She was how she was and trying to be different just would not work. People had to accept her.

Some wouldn't, of course, especially people like Mrs Makepeace.

'When Mrs Lonsdale comes at eleven o'clock with my books, you may ask her if she wishes to come through and have a cup of tea, Mrs Bainbridge.'

Ella looked up. She was on her knees in the kitchen, sloshing sudsy water over the floor. 'You want her to come in?' she asked in surprise, pausing in mid-wring of the cloth. 'That Mrs Lonsdale?'

Constance nodded.

'I do, indeed. Thank you, Ella. Have you seen Smith this morning?'

She shook her head. 'Not seen hide nor hair of him, but he's been on that blue chair again. Orange bits all over. One of these days I'll catch him at it.'

'And then what?' Constance said, in that nasty voice of hers that she could sometimes use.

Ella muttered something as the door closed behind her. Had the old dear taken leave of her senses? What was she thinking, of letting that Colin Hawkins have the cottage . . . rent free! . . . him and that woman of his? He must have seen her coming and no mistake, wormed his way in.

It left her and Bernard in a bit of a pickle, because they needed to know how they stood. They were all jollied up to leaving in spring, taking it easy, and she might even persuade him to take a holiday this year. Cornwall, she thought, where Mrs Makepeace was born. It sounded nice. They'd take the car and self-cater.

She stood up, rubbed at her knees which had gone to sleep nearly, and surveyed the floor with great satisfaction.

That blonde woman would be here soon, and she was to take a cup of tea, was she?

She set the tea things out on the tray. She didn't know why Mrs Makepeace was bothering to make an effort with a woman like her. Now that nice Mrs O'Grady was a different matter. Beautifully spoken and always so elegantly dressed. The flowers she brought! And last time, she'd given her a few tips on how to arrange them.

Not that she'd ever be able to do it as well as her.

She had a special touch, did Mrs O'Grady.

A lovely light touch.

'These are a bit bloodthirsty, Mrs Makepeace,' Yvonne said, handing the books to her with a smile. 'They'll make your hair stand on end.'

Constance gave her a look that put her firmly in her place for being over familiar. Yvonne blushed, sitting down quickly when invited with a regal wave of the old lady's hand to do so.

She sank into the soft cushions of the big winged chair that sat in a cosy area by the window. There was a low polished walnut table between the two chairs and a silver tea-tray was laid on it. She smiled, a little awkward, fiddling first with the bracelets on her arm and then with her rings. Opposite her, Constance Makepeace was so still. A very calm figure in a royal blue tracksuit today. The training shoes she wore, clumpy and hugely laced, were an interesting contrast to her own skimpy high heels. Yvonne wore a dark skirt that was shorter than usual which she now tugged down as she saw Constance glance with some disapproval at the display of barely-black tighted knees.

'I have not seen you to speak to since Christmas,' Constance began, inclining her head graciously. 'Did you and your family enjoy the festivities?'

'Yes, thank you,' Yvonne said, feeling like a child speaking to some sort of formidable great-aunt. 'The children enjoyed it especially. Did you?'

'Indeed. I spent the day – Christmas Day – with some dear friends. On Boxing Day Smith and I were alone, but we spent the time most pleasantly.'

'Smith . . . ? Oh, the cat,' Yvonne said with a smile, remembering. 'How is he?'

'He's disappeared. Oh – he's done it before. He's been missing since yesterday morning, but I don't worry, Mrs Lonsdale. He needs time to himself sometimes. Cats are contemplative creatures.'

Yvonne nodded. The view from the window was distracting, mellow this morning, and one of the trees in her sight was tight already with buds. Spring was like this. Full of anticipation. Holding its breath.

She made no comment as Constance lit a cigarette when they had finished their cup of tea. She was not yet comfortable in the old lady's presence as she had been with Agnes, and she struggled for something to say, preferably something non-controversial. If only Portia were here, Portia would have struck up a conversation at once, probably would have asked her why she wore a tracksuit at her very old age. On second thoughts, it was just as well Portia was not here for Constance might not be as understanding as Agnes of the ways of children.

'How old is your little son?'

'Sorry.' Yvonne struggled to the surface, smiled. 'Oh . . . Harry's four. He started proper school young because his birthday's in August. He's quite a sensitive child, Mrs Makepeace, and I would have liked to keep him at home with me a bit longer but you can't hold them back, can you? My husband thinks I treat him too much like a baby and I suppose he's right. He is my youngest, you see, and I think . . .' she paused and then, seeing that Constance seemed genuinely interested, continued, 'I think I know he will be my last child. So perhaps I do cling onto that. Do you see?'

'I see very well,' Constance said. 'I had a little son who died when he was just a little older than yours.'

'Oh . . . I had no idea . . .'

'I don't discuss it very often. However . . .' the smile was very slight, 'you have quite an understanding face, Mrs Lonsdale, if I may say so.'

'If you want to talk about it,' Yvonne said gently, 'feel free.'

Constance shook her head. 'Feel free? What an odd expression! But thank you for saying that. However . . .' She stubbed out her cigarette and Yvonne, sensing the slightest rebuff, pushed her chair back.

'Goodness, is that the time? I must go,' she said. 'It's been really lovely talking to you, Mrs Makepeace.'

'Would you like to see round the house before you go?'

Having made an excuse about the time, Yvonne consulted her watch. 'I've just a few minutes,' she said. 'Yes, thank you. I would like that.'

Yvonne followed her upstairs where they paused at a half-landing. The view towards the woods and Staine Hill quite took Yvonne's breath away and she was reminded of the walk she and Andrew had taken up there. The mood had caught at both of them at the same time which was highly dangerous. For two pins, she knew they might have ended up in an embrace and then the great pretence that they both aspired to would have been blown apart forever.

It only needed one kiss.

'Mrs Lonsdale . . .' Constance's voice was quiet at her side. 'I gather from your silence that you rather admire the view?'

Yvonne turned from the window, looked around. 'I don't know what to say. It's just so lovely. Compared with my house, it's huge. The children would love it. Especially Portia. Oh, yes . . .' She peeped into a bedroom, her heels clicking on the wooden floor. Dust sheets covered furniture but the views of the side garden this time were unobscured, sweeping into the distance. 'Samantha would think it was a palace and she was a princess.'

Yvonne sighed her pleasure, her delight undiminished as they toured room after room, moving up a floor and doing the same.

She wondered why Constance was doing this, making a gallant effort to be friendly, showing her round when previously she scarcely managed to pass the time of day with her.

She wondered also what was the interest in Tess O'Grady. Constance Makepeace had enquired on a couple of occasions how Tess was, and did the two of them get on? Yvonne had bluffed it out, explaining that she didn't see much of her because Tess was at work but that they got on very well. It was certainly not her intention to cast any doubts the old lady's way. Let her find out for herself, as she would in time. Certainly Tess seemed to take a curious interest too in Constance, for on several occasions she had mentioned that she'd dropped off some flowers for her. It seemed uncharitable to wonder why.

Tess was brittle and, if there was a soft centre, Yvonne had yet to find it. She hoped she was not being unkind because of her feelings towards Andrew but she prided herself on her judgement of people. She was aware of the danger of a snap decision, but she was normally proved right.

She remembered the first time she met Tess.

She did not like her then.

And she did not like her now.

# 40

'Tess is out,' Andrew said, smiling into the receiver. 'Did you want to speak to her, Stephanie?'

'No. I wanted to speak to you. Have you time for a little chat?'

'Sure.' He sat down, tugged at his tie, unbuttoned the top button of his shirt. 'I've not been in long but I've got myself a coffee and I needed to unwind a bit before eating. Tess will be late, I think. Business.'

'I see. How's the new job?'

'OK, thanks. Better than I thought,' he said. 'How about you? What the hell is going on with Joe? Tess has been very quiet about it.'

'Ah . . . Joe is still pretending that all is well,' Stephanie said, her voice light. 'I know differently, but I'm going along with it because I know he's only doing it so that I'm not worried. He thinks I'm a little girl. No matter that I was a senior lecturer holding down a most stressful job for years; Joe still thinks I have to be protected at all costs against unpleasantness.'

'That's rather nice,' Andrew said, meaning it. 'Time's getting on, though, and presumably he's not got anything else fixed up?'

'I think not. I'm thinking of selling the gallery, in fact. It's a little frustrating having to admit, even to yourself, that you're just not good enough. A middle-age dream, that's all it was, Andrew.'

He knew better than to contradict. Her paintings, even to his inexperienced eyes, would not set the world alight. Even so, it seemed a bit drastic, and would it help the situation that much?

'And I've been making enquiries about part-time lecturing. It pays reasonably well but . . .' she paused, 'I can hear a question. Come on, Andrew, out with it.'

'You and Joe have got to talk,' he said. 'Can't you see that? Get it out into the open, all this. Then perhaps you can help him get through it.'

'Do you and Tess talk?' she asked sharply. 'I get the impression you don't.'

'You're right,' he said. 'She won't talk about important things. Just like her father, I suppose.'

'I know she's Joe's daughter,' Stephanie said. 'And I know therefore that it's very foolish of me to criticise her but . . .'

'Careful, Stephanie' he warned, managing a little smile. 'This is my wife we're talking about.'

'I know, and of course you're bound to defend her. I'm sorry,' she said and he heard the sigh. 'I shouldn't have started this. But she manages to get Joe terrifically depressed. They went for a walk recently when she was here and when I got back he was in an awful state. If I didn't know him better, Andrew, I'd say he was very nearly suicidal.'

'Never,' Andrew said, the response instant. 'Never in a million years. This only reinforces what I'm saying; you two have got to talk.'

'You don't understand our relationship,' she said softly. 'Joe needs to protect and I am the protected. That's the way he wants it, and that's why I work very hard to keep it that way. Maybe you're right about the gallery . . .'

Andrew was startled. As far as he could remember, had he said anything at all about the gallery?

'I won't do anything rash,' she said. 'I'll hang on a bit. This situation requires nerve.'

'Do what you think best,' he said, feeling it was the only advice he could offer. 'If you want to talk about it, give me another ring. Sorry, I don't feel I've been very helpful.'

'Andrew . . . can I ask something of you?'

'Sure.' He smiled. At last, the point of all this.

'Keep Tess away from him for the time being, would you? I'm worried about the influence she has on him.'

'I'll try,' he said, trying to keep his irritation hidden. 'But I'm not her keeper, Steffi. I don't control her movements. She meets him for lunch sometime and I can't do anything about that.'

'Do your best,' she said and he was surprised at the earnest note in her voice.

What did she think was going to happen?

He put the phone down thoughtfully.

Tess certainly could twist Joe round her finger. No problems.

Stephanie, though, seemed to be over-reacting.

Whatever else, Tess loved her father.

Whatever she did, beavering around with contacts on his behalf, she was only doing for him.

Wasn't she?

'They recorded a verdict of accidental death,' Ella Bainbridge said to Bernard as they trudged this morning up to West House, the car being in for a service. 'She kept the newspaper cutting. There it was, as large as life, a picture of the both of them. Former Member of Parliament, they called him, lately a business man. Apparently, he'd gone out shooting, like they do, and tripped, and the gun had gone off.'

'Careless,' Bernard said with a click of his tongue. 'Very careless.'

'And she wasn't there at the time, so she couldn't have done it,' Ella said. 'Could she?'

'What? Killed him, you mean? Why would she do that? Her own husband?'

'People do.' Ella glanced at him affectionately, slipped her arm through his. 'Not everybody's as happy as we are, Bernard. And I don't think she was happy with him. My late husband, she calls him, and there's no love in her voice.'

'Soppy, you are, my flower,' Bernard said, cheerfully enough. 'You always want a happy ending and most times there isn't. I wish you'd leave her be.'

'I have to keep my eye on her. If she's losing her marbles then I have to make sure she doesn't do anything too daft. That cottage, for instance . . .'

'That was nice of her,' Bernard said. 'She went up in my estimation for doing that. They got married, you know, and I've heard she keeps that cottage as neat as a pin.'

'I know. But that's not the point. The point is, where is she going to live when she leaves the house?'

'Is it your problem?'

'Of course it is. I worry about her. And that cat of hers. Where is he? He's been gone for over a week. I think he's dead but she won't have it. She says he's just in retreat, whatever that might mean.'

She glanced at him, at his gentle face, wondered if she should mention all the letters she'd read. Perhaps not. Bernard didn't take kindly to reading other people's letters.

The ones from that Archie of hers, the first husband, were lovely. Sentimental stuff. He must have thought a lot about her. Tied together, showing their age, with a blue ribbon. She'd been frightened of tearing them but she had been very careful. Retied the ribbon afterwards. It made her wish that Bernard had written to her. She'd never in her whole life had a love letter. Just scruffy notes scrawled on scraps. 'Dear Ella, Gone to the shop. Back in half an hour. Love Bernard. XX.' That was the extent of her love letters. But Constance had all these letters, pages of how much he loved her, how he longed to be with her, bits of poems as well that she didn't quite understand but they sounded lovely.

That was as far as she'd got with the letters. She'd got a bit carried away with them and by the time she'd finished reading every last one on Christmas Day, it was getting late and dark and she'd had to ring Bernard to ask him to come and get her. He'd turned up, not asked what she'd been doing, and that had been that.

Those letters, those lovely words, remained in her heart for a long time though.

She found herself looking at Mrs Makepeace, the beautiful Mrs Lennox as was, in a different light.

Tess was profoundly irritated. Andrew had tried to put her off visiting her father. No other explanation. Well, he could take a running jump. She would visit Joe whenever she chose, and she chose to do so today. She had seen him up in Newcastle a couple of times and there was no joy, absolutely no joy, on the job front. The depression was really settling in and time was running out and still . . . still . . . he refused to worry Steffi.

The love of his life!

It was reaching the point of no return. He just needed a little push now. He needed her to reiterate what it would mean if he were to disappear off the scene. She and Stephanie would be all right and the family honour would be restored. She would leave the details to him. She had no wish at all to hear details. One thing, though . . . it had to be recorded as an accident and not suicide. Joe was crafty and she knew, however the end came, there would be no doubts that it was an accident. In fact, only she would ever know otherwise.

Sometimes, she could not believe it of herself.

Sometimes, she talked to her mother about it. In her mind. Telling no one.

She and her mother were so very much alike.

All this nonsense about material things not being important. Steffi said stupid things, like it didn't matter where she and Joe lived so long as they were together. Looking adoringly up at him as she said it.

Tess knew for certain that she and Andrew would not survive five minutes if they were suddenly down and out. She would not waste any more time on him. She would find herself somebody else with money.

You *could* buy happiness. It was a very difficult thing for most people to stomach, that particular thought, selfish as it was, but she prided herself on her honesty, especially to herself. Unfortunately, Andrew had never seen eye to eye with her on this. Frankly, Andrew was a constant irritation these days and she was no longer sure that he fitted into her future scheme of things. She needed a man who would happily throw his weight behind all her ideas for the business, not somebody who constantly fretted and fussed that she was 'over-stretching' herself.

She stopped off on the way up to Caryn Lodge to buy flowers, of all things, for Stephanie. For once, she had quite forgotten. The florist she chose was barely adequate but she managed to select some passable blooms herself, discarding the first few attempts of the young assistant. Trying to palm *her* off indeed with past their sell-by date offerings!

Back at her car, the mobile was ringing and she answered it.

'Hi! Glad I got you, Tess. How are you?'

'Fine.' She smiled into the receiver, recognising the voice at once. One of her erstwhile contacts, someone she had lunched recently. 'How are you?'

'Very well. Just thought I'd let you know that we're going to offer your father that job I was on about. We like the look of his experience. Just what we're looking for. I thought I'd check with you first. As far as you know, is he still available?'

'Well . . .' She hid her delight, counted to three slowly before replying. 'I think there might have been another offer, but, yes . . . I do believe he didn't accept it. So, yes, he is available.' She grimaced as she said it, keeping her fingers firmly crossed.

'Good. Thank God. I'll get in touch with him then. We can match his salary and there'll be the usual perks on offer. Lucky I lunched with you, Tess, or I'd never have known. We don't want to let him slip through our fingers, a man of his experience. He's just what we need.'

She sat a moment, stilled, when the line was dead.

Bingo!

Talk about cutting it fine!

She tried Joe's number but there was no reply. Better anyway to surprise him with the news, the wonderful news. Toying with the idea of buying a bottle of champagne to celebrate, she decided against it. The important thing was to get up to Caryn Lodge and break the news herself.

# 41

'Andrew, how lucky that you're at home,' Yvonne smiled. 'I wouldn't ask, but . . .'

He sighed. Looked down at the children, smiling.

'Problem?' he asked, finally looking at Yvonne.

'Dentist's appointment for Samantha and Harry,' she said. 'I would take Portia but she's been a bit off. A mild stomach ache. She just needs to sit quietly. Would you mind? Were you going somewhere? I saw Tess leaving earlier.'

'I'm on my own. Got some time off,' he said. 'It's OK. You can leave her with me. I'll make sure she sits quietly.'

Yvonne nodded. She looked lovely in lilac, a floaty ribbony thing anchoring her hair, the flowery distinctive scent drifting his way. She issued instructions quickly to Portia, kissing her and telling her to be good for Mr O'Grady before she was off.

He and Portia were left in the hall. A somewhat subdued little girl.

'Right . . .' he said cheerfully. 'Sitting down quietly, eh?'

'I'm writing a letter,' she told him, producing it from the little childish briefcase she was holding. 'To Daddy.'

'Good. You can sit at the table if you like while I have my coffee.'

'Where has Mrs O'Grady gone?' she asked, perking up suddenly now that Yvonne had disappeared. Andrew wondered about the reality of the stomach ache. Useful things, stomach aches, to get out of things you didn't want to do. Tess used that excuse more and more these days. In fact, their sex life was at an all-time low. He couldn't help thinking about the way she used sex to get her way, which made him think it didn't matter to her. It was a big turn off. In fact – and this was the single most depressing thing – it didn't seem to matter much to either of them any more.

'Mrs O'Grady's gone to visit her daddy,' he said. 'He lives in a big house near Middleton.'

She nodded. 'Do you have a daddy?'

The writing paper, pale yellow with a picture at the top of the page, was on the table and she was scrabbling about for a pen.

'He's dead,' he said, deciding beating about the bush was useless with somebody like Portia.

'Like the rabbit and Mrs Whitworth?'

'Yes. Like them.'

'Daddy and Mummy are getting a divorce. I can spell it. Mummy showed me.' She started writing. 'But we'll see Daddy sometimes like we used to. Sometimes . . .' she looked up at him, her eyes big and blue and bright. 'When people are grown up, they still want to be best friends but they don't want to be married. They don't want to live in the very same house.'

'Right.' Andrew smiled, sipped his coffee, not entirely surprised but determined not to quiz her. Yvonne would go daft if she knew her little girl was betraying the family's innermost secrets like this.

'But he still loves us and that's why I'm writing a letter to him. He writes to me. I might be a diver when I'm big if I can't be a flower lady like Mrs O'Grady. I've seen her shop. Mummy took me once. It's all pink and very pretty. I like daisies best.'

'Want some orange juice?' he asked. 'Or blackcurrant?'

'Orange, please.' She wrote several more words. 'We might get another daddy sometime, Mummy says, but if we do he won't be our real daddy but he will be our . . .' she struggled a moment for the word, '. . . our friend daddy. Like you.'

'Right.'

Good God! Andrew poured her the orange juice, passed it over. Her hands were so tiny, he thought suddenly, as he watched her put her pen down carefully and cup the beaker in them. Poor little sweet. Here she was, not fully understanding, trying to come to terms with it, and Yvonne was doing her best with a desperate situation. He liked the way Yvonne was trying not to set them against their father. It must be bloody tempting when things had fallen apart, when you'd fallen out of love, to plump the blame on the absent partner. If it was them, he knew with a terrible certainty that Tess would have him down for some sort of unfeeling monster.

He looked again at Portia as she busied herself with her letter, her blonde hair falling over her face. He felt a fondness for her, for all Yvonne's children, and knew without a doubt that, if ever he got the chance, he would take them on without a second's thought. To hell with Robin. He would make a better dad than him. He would be their 'friend daddy' OK.

'Harry doesn't like going to the dentist,' she said, turning the page over and beginning a new one. 'Do you know what he said this morning? It was really naughty.'

'No.' Andrew looked suitably crestfallen at her indignation.

'It begins with an f.'

Oh God!

Whatever it was, she was just about to tell him.

Tess couldn't wait to see her father's face. There would be a big celebration after this. And she would have been instrumental in fixing it up, so that meant she would retain that special place in his affections. What the hell had Stephanie done to help him get a new position? Sweet nothing.

'Why, Tess, this is a surprise,' Stephanie said, as she ushered her inside. 'I wasn't expecting you.'

'I told Joe,' Tess said with irritation. 'Don't tell me he's not in.'

She shook her head. 'No. Sorry. He must have forgotten. It might be tea-timeish before he's back.' She led Tess into the kitchen where baking preparations were in hand. 'Do you mind if I carry on? I'm making pies for the freezer.'

'Not at all.' Tess sat at the kitchen table, tempted to tell Stephanie the good news but refraining. She wanted to be the one to break the news. You always remembered the messenger. 'Where's he gone?'

'You'll never believe this,' Stephanie said, rolling out pastry with Delia Smith panache. The smell of stewed apple and cinnamon gently filled the air. 'He's gone out for a walk, of all things. Can you imagine? Up to High Force.'

'A walk?'

Stephanie nodded. 'What a fuss! You'd think nobody had ever been walking before. He insisted on buying some proper walking boots. He quite looked the part this morning, in fact. I would have gone with him but he wanted to go alone. A bit of thinking time, probably. Fresh air, that sort of thing. It gives me time to get on with this anyway.'

'High Force?' Tess stared at her, a most awful thought occurring to her.

'Yes. Should be pretty spectacular, shouldn't it, after the rain this last week, and Joe said the snows are only just melting up on the top of the hills so it will be brim-full, I expect.'

'Who wants to see a waterfall just trickling?' Tess said quietly.

'Exactly. I told him to be careful. Now . . .' she popped the pastry lid on the last of the pies, wiped her hands. 'Cup of coffee and a chat?'

'Sorry, no.' Tess whipped her car keys out. 'What time did he set off?'

'Oh . . . half an hour. Not long. Why?'

'Nothing . . .' Tess, quite cold, managed a smile for her stepmother. 'I've just remembered I've got to go somewhere. Terrible mix-up with my appointments. Do you mind, Steffi, if I dash off?'

'No.' Obviously puzzled but not worried, Stephanie kissed her goodbye, waving from the window as Tess hurried back to the car.

She had to restrain the car, hold back from doing seventy and above as she drove towards Middleton, slowing down painfully as she drove through the main street and over the bridge. Trust her father to do it in style. If he slipped off High Force, he would not survive. A seventy-foot drop via jagged rocks into the pool beneath should just about guarantee it. The water in that pool churning, eddying and with his heavy walking clothes . . . looked just the part, Stephanie had said . . . he would be dragged instantly down into the depths. He couldn't swim either, just for good measure.

It was a good choice. It would be quick, surely, and there would be no mess. No mistake. The verdict would be that he had been out walking, inexperienced at that, gone a bit close to the edge up on top and slipped. A pure accident, yet another accident at the spot where there'd been more than enough in the past. There'd been a death only last year. They would pay up without a quibble.

There were only a handful of cars, including Joe's, in the car park beside the High Force Hotel as Tess drove in, shuddering the car to a halt. She ran over to his car, but it was locked and empty, as she had known it would be. He was gone already. For a moment, as she set off across the road towards the falls, she was tempted to enlist the help of a man nearby. But what on earth could she say? *Come and help, I think my father's in the process of throwing himself off the waterfall?* What sort of idiot would he think she was?

She'd forgotten you had to pay to see the falls. It meant precious moments lost as she rummaged in her bag for change. Sensible shoes recommended also, which let hers out absolutely. Hers were infinitely unsensible, highish-heeled two-toned black and cream to match the black suit with its cream piping. It was brand new, hugely expensive, and she'd wanted to show it off to Stephanie today otherwise she might have been more casually and appropriately clad.

Quickly she paid her money, not offering any conversation to the woman in the little wooden kiosk. She could not trust herself to speak. She had no memory whatsoever of driving up from Caryn Lodge. For all she knew, she might have left a heap of dead rabbits or worse at the side of the road. She had driven quickly, she knew that much.

She started off briskly along the path that led to the waterfall. She and Andrew had been here years before and it looked different now because they'd cut a lot of trees down. Mystified that such an unimportant thing should occur to her now, she hurried on. The river to her left looked quite calm and surprisingly shallow at this point, recovering as it was from its tremendous drop upstream. God, how this path meandered, heading momentarily away from the waterfall via a little picturesque bridge. Cursing the path and the effect of its roughness on the brand new heels of the Italian leather shoes, keeping her feet with difficulty, Tess walked quickly on.

Heart pounding both with anxiety and the rate she was

pushing herself, she rounded the bend, vaguely taking in the beauty of the stacked smooth rocks, the greened-up trees and now . . . the sound of the gushing water itself. There was a moist feel to the air, that pleasant spring feel of sweetness and new leaf, the recent rains emphasising it. A moment later, through branches and budding leaves, she could glimpse the very top of the waterfall, the creamy froth spilling deliciously over the rocks, tumbling into the as-yet-unseen pool far beneath.

There was not a soul around.

She stopped, panting, heels sinking into the mud of the middle of the path, scanning the river just in case she spotted something. She didn't know what she expected to see. Joe's body floating delicately downstream, mercifully in one piece? Please God, don't let it be too smashed up.

The rain was starting.

The suit was a suede material and would not tolerate being wet. Angry, she looked up at the sky, at the dark heavy clouds. Oh, no. A sob escaped her. What the hell had she done? Even her mother, who was not known for her squeamishness, would have drawn the line at this. If she had wanted him dead before, she did not want him dead now, now that she could have him alive with a new fantastic job and money. She hoped he understood her motives. All she wanted was for things to be the same so that when she needed a loan, she knew she need look no further than Joe. Banks were such a bore.

She searched the river with a frantic gaze for a sign, any sign. Turning, she failed to see a tree root in her way, tripped over it and landed with a bang that knocked the breath out of her, full length on the path. Hastily struggling to her feet, embarrassed that some unseen eyes might have seen her, she retrieved a shoe, stuffed her foot back into it, ridiculously smoothed her skirt down before ploughing on, all dignity lost, arms aching from the sudden jolt.

Her skirt and tights were muddied and one hand was grazed, bloody with bits of grit embedded in the wound. More slowly, for she was a bit shocked by the fall, she carried on, at last reaching the foot of the waterfall itself. Now what?

Steps carved out of the hillside led up towards the top but first she chose the others that led down towards the dark pool and the flat smooth rocks at the edge. Standing close as she dared, she peered into it, searching every inch of the brown gurgling water. The frothy cream tumbled into what looked like brown ale. Swirled with a very big finger.

Oh God!

Her panic complete, she started up the uneven steps, holding onto the handrail, dragging herself up and up. Ignoring the warning notice about the dangers of unsuitable footwear up here, she stepped through the stile onto the glistening worn rocks. The river looked so innocent, little more than a wide running stream not unlike the fat stream in Bishopsmeade. The very top edge of the waterfall was out of her sight, hidden by bigger rocks, and it was only the spray and the roar that hinted at its presence. Sure enough, she slipped into the cold shallows, her shoe and foot wet through in an instant as she regained her balance.

Someone on the opposite bank waved at her and she waved back, not hearing the words he shouted at her, carried away as they were by the roar of the falls. As he looked at her, a young man in walking gear, she was reminded – for God knows what reason at a time like this – of her appearance. A mess. Her designer suit ruined. Her shoes an absolute disgrace. Her hair wild. It was a relief, frankly, to see him disappear along the trail and, after a moment, making sure he was out of earshot, she called Joe's name. A few helpless hopeless calls.

A bigger sob, childlike, catching at her, she set off down, mercifully not meeting a soul. She took a final despairing look at the dark whirling water, but it was holding onto him if he was deep in there. She ran nearly all the way back, quickly crossing the road to the car park. His car was still there, of course, and she passed it, returning to her own car and leaning against it, trying to get her breath back. She felt awful. Wretched. But after a few moments, she calmed a little.

Think, Tess, think.

If he had already done it, then it was too damned late and the important thing was that nobody must ever connect her in any way with it. Therefore, it was unwise, wasn't it, for her to be here in the first place. When they found him, when they told

Stephanie, she did not want her to know that she had chased after him.

She had to concoct some tale.

Suppose . . . suppose after all he had talked of suicide to her; when Stephanie mentioned High Force then of course she would have been instantly worried. He'd been having a few dizzy spells lately – nobody could dispute that if it was privately told – and a dizzy spell on top of the waterfall could be fatal.

So . . . her being here was perfectly understandable, even commendable, for she hadn't wanted to worry his wife at this stage. What would she do now? Ring the police?

Yes, she thought, she would. Incoherent, but that wouldn't be too difficult for she felt unable just now to string two words together. She would ring from the hotel. Brushing off the worst of the mud from her skirt, using an old car cloth to rub at her shoes, she found a packet of moist tissues and dabbed at her hand. She combed her hair, put on a shaky layer of lipstick. On closer examination, she found her tights were miraculously intact. Thank God for that.

She walked across to the pub beside the car park and opened the door. She needed a drink first before she did anything else, just one drink to calm herself down. And for some inexplicable reason, she was also ravenous. She ordered a gin and tonic and a sandwich and was just on the point of taking her drink to a quiet corner when a voice hailed her – a very familiar voice.

'Tess! What the hell are you doing here? Come on, join us. Squeeze in.'

Her father was sitting at a table with another man. He was very much alive tucking into a mountain of a meal.

He introduced her, making no comment about her appearance, but the raising of his eyebrows told her he had noted it nonetheless.

'I thought you were at the waterfall,' she said, trying to regain her composure. 'Steffi said you'd gone for a walk, and I thought I'd catch you there.'

'I did go for a walk. Tom here is into walking. Aren't you?'

'That's right. I can tell you're not, Tess. Not with those shoes,' Tom said with a cheeky smile. 'Your father and I thought we might discuss business out here rather than at the office.'

'Business?' she asked carefully, as the sandwich she had ordered arrived.

'Tom's made me a proposition,' Joe said, wiping his mouth and grinning. 'I've told him I've had several offers, so it's a question of deciding between them.'

'You're a wily devil, Joe,' Tom said. 'He only told me last week that he might – just might – be available when I've been scratching around at the bottom of the bloody barrel for months trying to get a replacement for my last sales director.'

'Mild heart attack,' Joe said to her, deadpan. 'But he decided to take early retirement because of it. Wise man. What's the use of killing yourself?'

'Excuse me a moment.' Tom rose, headed for the gents.

'Saved by the bloody bell, eh?' her father said when they were alone. 'Bluffing about the other offers, of course. Great sounding job. Bigger salary. New car. I've even wangled a two-month stint in the States. I'm taking Stephanie with me. I didn't tell her I was meeting Tom, by the way, in case things didn't work out. There was always the other option, you see.'

Tess forced herself to say something. 'What wonderful news. I always knew something would turn up. Didn't I say so? Congratulations.'

He smiled the same old smile but his eyes were quite chill. 'Stuck with me a bit longer, sweetheart.'

'What?' She tucked into her sandwich although she might have been eating cotton wool. It was something to do to avoid looking at him. No point in mentioning the other job now. He'd find out about that soon enough. 'What do you mean?'

'I mean, I can read you like a book, Tess. Did you really think I'd do it?' he asked, his voice a mere whisper. 'Did you really think I'd take your advice? You did a good job of planting the thought but I'm a survivor, sweetheart.'

'I don't know what you're talking about, Daddy,' she said, laying her sandwich down. 'As I said, I just thought I might catch you here. Take a walk with you.'

He smiled but it was a very strange smile.

'Know something?' he said. 'You're just like your mother. She was sweet on the surface, too, but under the skin . . .'

If he expected her to rise to the bait, she did not give him the satisfaction. She would have to be very careful after this. She put out her hand towards his that lay very still on the table. OK, she might as well admit it because he knew.

'Daddy . . . I'm so glad you didn't do it,' she said.

He nodded.

But she knew then, as Tom cheerfully returned, that it was over between them.

Dammit to hell, she had finally blown it.

Love, trust, it was all out of the window.

As Joe might very well put it, she could whistle for any more loans.

# 42

After almost two weeks, Smith returned. Constance and Ella were having their afternoon coffee, sitting at the kitchen table, when the cat flap gave a warning rattle that signified he was on his way in, just testing.

Constance, who was beginning to worry about him, spun round and there he was. A little bedraggled heap of orange unkempt fur, his good ear torn and bleeding, a huge lump on the side of his face.

'My God!' Ella said, cringing at the sight. 'Look at that cat! Ugh! Look at him, Mrs Makepeace. What has he been up to, I'd like to know? And look at my floor. Blood all over. Mrs Makepeace . . . look at it.'

Constance was busy attending to Smith.

'We must take him to the vet, Mrs Bainbridge,' she said. 'At once. Would you telephone for a taxi, or perhaps Bernard could take me?'

'He would, of course he would, but the car's waiting for a new something or other. I did tell you, Mrs Makepeace, that we'd had to walk up again. Gets on your nerves, it does, when things keep going wrong.'

'A taxi then. Quickly, Ella.'

Whilst she waited for the taxi, she gave Smith some milk and biscuits. He lapped the milk but left the food, which worried her. He looked quite dreadful. She wrapped him in his blanket and put him in his cat carrier.

'What's he been up to then?' Colin said as he carried him out to the car. 'Right bruiser, he is, isn't he?'

'Quite,' Constance said, wishing that for once Smith was not quite so pugnacious.

They smoked as he drove her out of Bishopsmeade to the vet up the dale.

Constance barely listened to his chat about his wife and the girls. They loved Primrose Cottage, that was the general gist. And he had a bar job now, weekends at a public house, and all in all, they were managing.

She was worried sick about Smith.

Please God, let Smith be all right.

She told herself that, if he recovered, she would stand by the decision she had finally reached last evening. She was going to offer West House to the O'Gradys. There! No going back. She would invite them over for dinner and open one of her good bottles and over the meal, something special, she would give them the good news. She would have the necessary documents drawn up but she was happy to let them have the house for . . . let's see . . . half its true value.

But if Smith passed over, then she would take a day or two to recover sufficiently to give a congenial dinner party, so she would postpone it.

'My wife . . .' Colin began proudly. 'That's Lisa Marie, Mrs Makepeace,' he went on, as if she didn't know. 'Well, they think it might be twins. Amazing they can tell that so soon. We have the photo thing. I'll bring it to show you. Twins, eh? What do you think of that, then?'

Constance sighed. 'What do *you* think of that?' she asked.

'We think it's fantastic, pet. Lisa Marie's thrilled to bits,' he said. 'We'll have to get another cot but we've plenty of baby stuff. Gets passed on, it does. It's all girl stuff, pink and that, but it doesn't matter.'

Constance had a thought. She had baby clothes in the cellar at West House. She would get them out, have a look to see if they were still in good condition. She remembered packing them away, wrapping each item carefully in tissue, pressing them softly down, doing the whole thing in secret, for Hugh would have been displeased if he had seen her. He had not been one for sentimental gestures.

'There . . . you're all right, darling,' she said to the cat as he miaowed most pitifully. 'Can you . . .' She hesitated, looking at Colin's broad neck. 'Can you put your foot down?' she asked.

'I rather think this may be an emergency.'

He did as requested and they sped on their way thereafter in rather a thrilling manner.

'Here she is now,' Ella Bainbridge said, coming away from the window. 'Now, Bernard man, off you go. I'll put the kettle on, because if he's had to be put to sleep, that cat of hers, she'll want a cup of tea for the shock. I half hope he is dead,' she added as her husband struggled to his feet, frowning at what she'd just said. 'All right, I don't really hope that, but I've got used to not having to pick his hairs off that cushion. And that peach silk chair – ruining it, he is.'

She shooed Bernard out, and adjusted her expression to one of suitable grief and, by the time Constance came back in, carrying the little wicker basket, the kettle was boiling and the plate of biscuits was out. Ginger creams, because Mrs Makepeace was partial to them.

'Good news,' Constance said as she came in. 'He's poorly but he will recover.' She lifted him out of the basket, laid him gently on the chair by the window. 'He's had a scrap, been bitten by another cat on the side of the face but it's burst now, the abscess, and he'll be fine. He's on antibiotics.'

'Is he now?' Ella eyed the recumbent cat with dismay. 'Well, then . . . that is good news, Mrs Makepeace,' she said after a moment. 'I'm very pleased. I said to Bernard, I hope that cat's not had to be put down. Break Mrs Makepeace's heart, it will, I said.'

'I have decided to give a dinner party next week,' Constance said, sitting down with a sigh at the table. 'Will you be able to manage, Mrs Bainbridge, or shall I get some outside help with the catering?'

Ella sniffed her displeasure. 'I will manage,' she said tightly. She was having no caterer in the kitchen, coming in with her own pans and what have you, creating a mess. She could do a very nice dinner, and Mrs Makepeace was always very generous with a little extra money for the effort she would put in.

'Good. I hoped you would say that. Mr and Mrs O'Grady will be coming to dinner.'

'Right. That's nice,' Ella said, looking at her closely. Sometimes she found it hard to equate this Mrs Makepeace with the young beautiful girl referred to in those love letters. He sounded lovely, did that Archie. What a waste. 'Any particular reason, Mrs Makepeace? I mean, do we want champagne or anything? Is it a celebration?'

Constance said nothing, rising instead and going to check on the comatose heap of ginger fur.

'We'll leave him to sleep it off,' she said quietly. 'Poor darling, he's had a most difficult time.'

'He's only himself to blame,' Ella said, regretting the remark instantly as Constance gave her one of those looks that only she could give. 'He's like all men,' she went on, powerless to stop herself now. 'Do first, think after.'

'I will discuss the menu with you later,' Constance said. 'Thank you, Mrs Bainbridge, that will be all today. You and Bernard may depart early as Smith and I wish to spend the remainder of the day quietly.'

In a huff, Ella washed up the dishes. She eyed her floor with irritation but it would have to wait until tomorrow now as milady wanted rid of them.

# 43

Coming home later than usual, Andrew found to his surprise Tess already in, cooking a meal. Inexpert, she was however trying on this occasion and wisely he left her to it, pouring himself a coffee and carrying it through to the garden room.

'Nearly ready,' she said, following him through a few moments later. 'Had a good day, darling?'

He smiled. 'To what do I owe this sudden housewifely concern?'

'Does there have to be a reason?'

'Yes. With you, there usually is.'

If the warped nature of the comment irritated her, she made no response, sitting opposite him, casually clad in tight blue jeans and white top. She looked pretty good too but it no longer registered in quite the same way with him and he found himself thinking why she was doing it and what she was after. In other words, there had to be a reason.

'I need financial advice, darling. I'm going to start up floral design workshops in the summer. I need a venue, of course,' she said in that well-known throwaway manner of hers as if it was the easiest thing in the world to organise. 'I thought evening sessions to attract beginners, spanning a week, but I'm also planning a four-day intensive course for the more advanced. They'll pay roughly £800 for the course which will include all materials and lunch, an absolute bargain. What do you think? A friend of mine put me onto it and he's willing to come into partnership with me on it. He's a chef looking for a special niche, so it can't fail, can it?'

'Oh, Tess, you've only just got the other shop up and running.

It might be best to wait a while before you blast off with something else. Who's the friend, anyway?'

'He's called Mark and he's more a business acquaintance,' she said. 'He and I go back a long way. Since before you, darling.'

'Really?' If she was trying to make him jealous, it was not working.

'He's looking for something different and he likes the sound of this. Wants to know if I'll come in with him on it. He's a useful person to have around, Andrew. He also has a pilot's licence and we might think about using . . .'

'Hold on,' Andrew put down his cup, tried to calm himself down. 'It's no go, Tess. It's too soon. You have to give things time to settle. You can't just go leaping about from one mad scheme to another. What is it with you?'

'I want to expand,' she said, face flushed. 'And I resent that implication, Andrew. I do think things through. God, you're so tame. If it was up to you, we'd still be living in our first flat and I'd have one measly shop. Have you *no* ambition?'

'Ambition yes, but stupidity no,' he said, quiet in his anger. 'You have no available capital to put into this unless your father's going to lend you yet more money.'

'No. No, he is not. We've had a slight disagreement. Sort of,' she said. 'I don't wish to discuss it.'

'You don't wish to discuss too many bloody things, Tess.' He stood up, picked up his cup. 'Let's eat.'

In silence and with extreme ill grace, she dished up the meal.

They ate in silence too, and only when it was over did they resume their conversation.

'I don't know why I'm bothering to tell you this because you'll only bite my head off,' she said at last. 'But, guess what – Constance Makepeace rang me this afternoon. She wants us to go for dinner. She told me she'd made up her mind about West House. And I was right, darling. She wants us to have it. She couldn't wait to tell me. She was going to tell us apparently over dinner.'

'Oh God.' Andrew groaned at the implication. 'Does she know we haven't sold this?'

'We might have. We've had an offer,' Tess reminded him

tartly of the offer that had come out of the blue following a lukewarm visit the previous week by a couple who'd seemed singularly unimpressed. 'OK, so it's a pretty miserly one but it's an offer and we're going to get West House really on the cheap. Half price, more or less. I knew my persistence would pay off in the end.'

'I don't want it,' he said, as it dawned. 'It's a wonderful house but not for us. I don't care whether or not we get it on the cheap. I don't even care if she gives it us for nothing. It'll be too costly to run. The upkeep – have you considered that?'

'Oh, for God's sake, you can't back out,' she said. 'You can't. I need that house, Andrew. So what if I might have been having second thoughts about it; I still need it short term. We can sell it at a huge profit, don't you see, and I need capital.'

'Sell it?' he yelled, feeling like tearing his hair out. 'Bloody hell, Tess, we haven't even bought it yet and you're talking of selling. Constance thinks she's selling it you so that the house will be lived in by a *family*, the family that you told her we were having! She wouldn't sell it to you if she thought you were going to sell it straight off. How will you look her in the face if you do that?'

'I don't care much frankly what she thinks,' Tess said calmly, her callousness making him do a double take. Yes, she meant it. 'It's too late afterwards for any come-uppance, once we've signed papers. I've decided I want something up in Northumberland on the coast. In fact, I've been making a few casual enquiries of estate agents. I can't stand it round here and I want to be as far away from dearest Stephanie as possible, Daddy's darling little wife.'

Andrew glanced sharply at her. He didn't know quite what had happened, but sure as God something had.

'I won't do it,' he said. 'I won't go to dinner and lie.'

'Then I'll go myself,' she hissed at him, pale with fury. 'And I'll lie and scheme all I can until we've got something in writing. Something concrete. She won't go back on her word. She's got dignity.'

'Which is more than you bloody have.' He sighed deeply, 'Oh, Tess . . . what are we doing?'

'Having a row,' she said with a short laugh. 'And it's all because you've got such a damned straitlaced attitude to life, Andrew. I can't believe now that it actually used to turn me on.'

'It's not too late,' he said, but even he could hear the desperation in his voice.

'West House is mine,' she said. 'And I hope you love me enough not to do anything to prevent me getting it. Whether or not you stay with me afterwards is beside the point. I am moving to Northumberland, Andrew, and you can come along if you wish. I hope you do,' she went on, 'but I'm not going to lose too much sleep if you do not.'

The cat was recovering, although he still did not look his best with half the fur on his face missing. He was lying on Constance's bed and she was stroking him carefully so that she did not touch his poor hurt face. He had started to purr again.

Smith's illness, self-inflicted or not, had upset her very much and Constance realised that she had not felt like this for a long time. She had considered the possibility that he might have to be put down and that had been difficult. It was a long time since she had felt the pain of loss.

She felt a little sob beginning as she stroked the little body nestling beneath her hand, murmuring soothing words.

'Why did you do it? Run off like that?' she whispered. 'You had no need. You have a good home, Smith.'

*A good home.*

She remembered Hugh saying that on the evening of Boxing Day, 1955.

Billy went to a good home too.

In November, she and Hugh had travelled to their London flat to spend a few days there and, whilst she was there, Constance, heavily pregnant, was taken ill. It was just a minor chest infection but it meant they decided to remain there rather than risk the journey home as the weather was quite appalling. It was in hospital in London, therefore, that Billy was born three weeks early. He was a good weight, though, and the labour was relatively easy. Hugh was not present at the birth, but fathers seldom were then and she would not have wished it. Pleased – that was an understatement – pleased that the ordeal was over and they had another son, Constance was lying in bed in some small discomfort only.

Memories of Thomas intruded, of course, but she pushed them aside. One had to look forward to the future with their new son. He would be William but they would call him Billy.

The knock at the door was gentle and the almoner, a most pleasant lady, appeared a moment later, smiling.

'Mrs Makepeace . . .' she came across and pulled up a chair. 'How are you feeling now?'

'I'm feeling well, thank you.' Constance smiled too, seconds before she looked at the woman and knew that something was wrong. The woman's smile was tipsy, off-centre. 'What is it?' she whispered as a chill settled on her head, tingling on her scalp before travelling slowly down the length of her body. Her toes were suddenly very cold and she felt quite nauseous.

'I'm sorry, Mrs Makepeace, but I've always found it's best if I come straight to the point. Have you heard of babies being called mongols?'

'Yes . . .' The word came from afar, from somewhere deep where she could hear her heart thudding. There was no need for the gentle explanation that followed. No need, and she did not listen anyway, hearing only isolated phrases although she did not interrupt either, letting the woman finish.

'There are places we can send him. We have foster parents, very kind people, experienced with these sort of children, who will look after him.'

'But I don't want that,' Constance protested, raising herself up a little, feeling a little sore as she did so but persisting. 'I want to look after him myself,' she said, and no smile would come, not even to make the woman in the chair feel less awkward about all this. 'Is my husband outside? Has he seen him?'

The almoner nodded.

'And what did he say?'

She looked to the woman for some sign of hope but she knew it was hopeless as the woman struggled for a kind reply.

The decision had been made.

By the time Hugh came in, her desolation was complete. His eyes, she noticed, were cold but then they'd always had a steely glint. She'd once found it very attractive. She knew as she looked at him that he blamed her for this. He blamed her for Thomas's accident, and he blamed her for this too.

'It's out of the question, Constance,' he said when, just for a few painful seconds, she pleaded with him. 'I cannot contemplate having a child like that around the house, not a man in my position. It's just as well it happened as it did. Here in London. We'd never have got away with it at home.'

He paced the room as he spoke, saying words that she knew Archie would never have uttered.

'I shall issue a statement to the staff and to your family when we return. Unfortunately the child was born prematurely and died. That's all they need know. I'll proceed with the necessary arrangements now.' He looked at her with irritation barely concealed as she struggled for control. 'You must keep your chin up,' he said. 'It's most unseemly for the nursing staff to see you in a state. Pull yourself together, Constance.'

She wiped away a tear.

Then and now.

'You'll like Billy,' she told Smith. 'And he will like you. He may be a little rough at first, wanting to pick you up, but once I explain that you don't like that, he will be gentle with you. He's a very gentle man, you see.'

Billy was such a happy person, and quite delighted her with his achievements. He was in his forties now and most content in the group home where Penny was the chief carer. He did not know who *she* was, of course, and she did not confuse him by telling him. As far as he was concerned, his parents were the people who had lovingly cared for him for so long. Hugh had dealt most efficiently with the arrangements and it was coincidence indeed that Billy had spent most of his life up here, so close, and at first she had been quite unaware of it.

From choice, she had never met his foster parents who were now deceased, but she knew them to be exceptional people. Billy's move into the Centre had been kindly and carefully arranged, a gradual process when he grew up, short day visits at first and then longer ones until he adjusted. He worked in the training centre most days and enjoyed his free time. He was a country and western fan and had gained a medal for ballroom dancing. He loved painting, although, left to his own devices, his colour choice was most garish.

He had his own room and was so proud of it.

She was so proud of him too.

'I'm a man now, Constance,' he told her when she had made the mistake of referring to him as a boy. 'A man.'

His speech was only a little slurred and it was perfectly easy to comprehend what he was saying. As he only saw her at Christmas, he had to be reminded when they first used to meet who she was – Constance, a friend of Penny's – but she liked to think he did remember her from the previous visit. He was certainly keen enough to hug her, as were all Penny's boys, his face breaking into that lovely smile.

She could not keep her eyes off him, greedy to look at him. Despite his disability he was one of the brighter boys with an IQ of nearly 60 which Penny told her classed him as having only mild intellectual disability. True, he needed supervision but he could live fairly normally. He was healthy and mercifully free of most of the medical problems he might have been afflicted with.

When she died, half of her money was going to the cats' home and the other half to the wonderful Centre that had cared for Billy and others like him for so long.

Constance, her spirits lifting, felt a tremble of excitement.

Very soon, she told the cat, Billy was coming to West House for the very first time.

Billy was coming home. It was right that he should come home, just the once.

Later in the week, she would speak to her solicitor and arrange for the necessary documents to be drawn up so that the O'Gradys could have the house.

# 44

Andrew was having nothing more to do with West House. He was sick of it. If Tess was fool enough to try to deceive Constance, then so be it. It would never go through. He knew that with certainty. She would fall at one of several hurdles and come a cropper.

And he would not be picking up the pieces.

Never again.

It was drifting towards separation, their relationship, in a very steady hold-as-you-go fashion. Like a boat being tossed towards rocks. Inevitable. And he had known it for a long time but had ignored it, tried stupidly to resurrect it, take it back to what it once had been.

That decision three years ago had done it.

Wrecked things.

For better or worse, he had wanted that baby, that little slightly misshapen baby. He remembered that morning when she went into hospital. All he could think about was that they were killing it. Call it what you like, but that's what it was.

He had a day off today.

He had been asked to take it because the audit had finished early and the office had said he might as well take time off as come in to do nothing. It was knocked off his leave quota anyway, so he didn't feel in the least guilty.

It was like the old days, seeing Tess off and pottering round.

The phone rang as he was standing at the window watching Yvonne and the children set off for school. Portia had seen him, turned to wave, and then they all stopped and waved. Yvonne had ushered them on their way, glaring at him rather for the interruption to the procession.

'Oh hello, Stephanie,' he said, smiling into the receiver. 'Haven't heard from you for ages.'

'Hello, Andrew. I rang your office but they said you were off today so I hoped I might catch you. Joe's got another job,' she went on. 'Did Tess tell you?'

'She mentioned something but wouldn't discuss it. What did I tell you? I knew something would turn up.' He smiled his satisfaction, for if nothing else he was glad for Stephanie's sake. She was a nice woman. 'What is it, exactly?'

Stephanie told him about the job which sounded frantically important. 'We're off to the States in a couple of weeks for six weeks,' she went on. 'Joe's taking me, although I'll have to make my own amusements whilst he's at business meetings.'

'That sounds great. Whereabouts?'

'The East coast and Washington, DC. Yes, it will be fun, won't it? I'm looking forward to it. All those museums for me to browse in.' After a slight hesitation, she asked after him and Tess.

'Fine,' he said, trotting out the usual. 'Tess is busy. Would you believe that she's after organising floral design workshops now? OK, so it's a good idea, but for the future when she's got a bit more behind her. It's not on, Steffi, and I've told her as much. I'm surprised she hasn't asked Joe for a loan.'

'No . . . she won't be doing that, Andrew,' Stephanie said and there was something in her voice, sadness coupled with anger almost, that he couldn't quite fathom.

'Have they had a row?' he asked, scarcely able to believe it. Tess knew better than to force a wedge in that particular set-up. She needed Joe.

'Andrew . . .' Stephanie sighed. 'I need to see you. I don't want to tell you this over the phone. It's not fair.'

'God, this sounds serious,' he said, trying to lighten the mood with a short laugh but, to his dismay, it provoked no response.

'Would it be too much trouble for you to come over? I can fix us a light lunch.'

'No trouble,' Andrew assured her, giving her an approximate time.

He was just relaxing with a coffee when the doorbell rang and Yvonne stood there.

'Are you all right?' she asked. 'Only I couldn't help noticing you weren't at work, and I remembered that you'd suffered in silence once before. Why on earth didn't you give me a ring when you were ill? I'd have come over.'

Quite.

'Come in a minute,' he said, rather rudely glancing at his watch as he offered. 'I have a lunch date with my stepmother-in-law.'

She smiled. 'What a funny sounding relationship! Stepmother-in-law. Mind you, with all the marriage break-ups these days that sort of thing is going to become all too common, isn't it?'

He poured her a coffee from the pot and they went to sit in the garden room.

'Andrew . . .' she shook her head as he passed a plate of biscuits. 'I think you ought to know that Robin and I are getting a divorce. There's nobody else,' she added quickly. 'It's just incompatibility. We've spent so much time apart and it's been a terrible strain.'

He nodded, not letting on he already knew, not wanting to drop little Portia in it.

'I'm so sorry,' he said, knowing how inadequate that was. 'I don't know what to say.'

'There's nothing to say. At least you haven't said that we seemed such a well-suited couple,' she said a shade bitterly. 'That's what one of my friends said. We were not well-suited, Andrew. We never were. I thought I could change him, that it would be all right once we were married, and that was my mistake.'

'We all make mistakes,' he said quietly, wincing in his mind at the idiocy of that statement. Why was it you always said the wrong things, stupid things, at moments like this? He had to think of something positive, something that might help. 'Are you all right financially?' he asked. 'Not that it's any of my business,' he added quickly, remembering she could be a mite touchy on this subject.

She smiled a little. 'Oh, yes. Financially everything's fine. And I will think about going back to work sometime. Yes, Robin's been very good about that. He always was. It was the emotional support that was lacking.'

And suddenly, quite without warning, her eyes filled, Samantha-style, with tears and she gave a little sob as they spilled over.

'Hey . . .' He was over to the chair where she was sitting in a few seconds, taking her cup from her before the coffee spilled too. 'Don't *you* cry . . .' he said, laying his hand on her arm. 'I have enough with Portia and Samantha turning on the tap.'

'Do they try it on with you?' she said, sniffing and regaining some hold on herself. 'They do that to me too. It's a useful weapon.'

'OK now?' he whispered and she nodded, reaching once more for her cup.

He returned to his chair, letting out a sigh himself.

'Sorry,' she said. 'Silly thing to do. I've got myself into a bit of a state. I usually save that sort of thing for when I'm on my own.'

'He's not worth it,' he said. 'Not worth you crying for. Do . . . do you still love him?' he asked, not daring to look at her as he said it, willing her not to say yes. He looked instead at the garden outside the window at the spring flowers as they flooded the beds, while nearer at hand the feathery fronds of one of Tess's plants almost brushed his face.

He heard no answer but when he dared look, she was shaking her head and looking at him but, even as he drew breath, sought to decipher that look, she blushed and rose to her feet, muttering that she had to go and she was glad he was all right because she'd only popped by to ask that.

Like a pale blue whirlwind in a fluttery loose dress, she was through the house and out of it before he had time to say anything else. Hurrying down the path without a backward glance. Hurrying up her own. Shutting the door.

Her perfume remained, though.

Stephanie was wearing a new dark skirt and a rather military style cream jacket. Joe, delighted with the new job and all it meant, had insisted she treat herself to some new clothes for their American trip and he had come shopping with her helping her to choose. Car brochures littered his study as he searched for something even bigger and better than before. He would make bloody sure Ivan saw him in it. He wanted to rub Ivan's face in it.

She was out of the house even before Andrew had stilled the engine, smiling as he stepped out, kissing him a little self-consciously on the cheek. He looked his usual self.

'This is nice,' she said, tucking her arm in his. 'Joe doesn't know about this.'

'A liaison?' Andrew said, a twinkle in his eye. 'Careful, Steffi; people will start to talk.'

'I thought we might take lunch in the sitting room,' she said. 'Cosier there. It's very simple, Andrew. I've made some soup and there's sandwiches and a cake.'

He murmured his approval. He felt a little underdressed in jeans and sweatshirt as he followed her through. A small table was set in the window alcove but she motioned him to sit first on the sofa and brought him a drink.

'I knew everything would work out for you,' Andrew said. 'About the job and everything. He's a survivor, is Joe. He always lands on his feet.'

She nodded, tucking her legs under her, reaching for her glass of mineral water. 'Promise that you won't go huffy on me, Andrew, if I tell you something?' She waited for his bemused agreement. 'It feels a bit sneaky and behind her back, but I know I have to tell you. It's about Tess.'

'I thought it might be. If you must know, things aren't too good, Steffi. You'll never guess what she wants now.'

'Nothing will surprise me,' she said. 'Is it the house?'

'We've sold ours – yes, it's all going through – and she's got herself excited because she believes she might have the chance of getting West House. You know it?'

'In Bishopsmeade? The house on the hill?'

'That's the one. It belongs to this old lady, Constance Makepeace, and she's moving out shortly – according to Tess, that is. She never put the house on the market but . . .'

'Don't tell me,' Stephanie said, seeing what he was getting at. 'Tess is being devious again?'

'But that's not all,' Andrew went on. 'Now she tells me that, even before the signatures are dry on the page, she intends to sell it, at a vastly inflated price of course, so that she can fund this new thing she's set her sights on. And she's informed me she's moving to Northumberland with or without me.'

'Is she? You don't sound unduly upset,' she said, seeing the set of his face, knowing this made it easier. Their marriage was crumbling fast and she knew now that what she had to tell him would clinch it. Snap it completely. But she had to tell him. 'I know this sounds melodramatic but I worry about Tess's sanity sometimes. She's not far short of . . .' she searched for the word but the only one that sprang to mind was 'wicked' and she couldn't say that, not to Tess's husband. 'Is she under some terrible strain?'

'No more so than usual,' Andrew said. 'She can't use that as an excuse. She thrives on stress.'

'So does Joe,' Stephanie said with a small smile. 'Shall we eat?'

They moved to the table and she served up the soup, carrot and tomato, with crusty bread. For a while they ate in virtual silence. Stephanie watched him, however, and wondered what he would do, how he would take it.

'Tess tried to persuade Joe to commit suicide,' she said at last, saying the words, the most awful words, even as she politely passed him the butter dish.

He almost dropped it.

'It had to look like an accident, though, so that everyone would pay up without a quibble,' Stephanie went on, knowing she had his full amazed attention.

'Suicide?' His laugh was uncertain. 'Oh, come on, Steffi . . . she's done some awful things over the years, but I don't believe that. Is this a joke?'

'I wish it were. She came here in rather a state the day Joe went up to High Force for a business meeting . . .'

'Business meeting at High Force?'

Stephanie smiled. 'I know. It does sound odd, doesn't it? He was meeting this man who's a keen fell-walker and Joe thought it might be better if they had an outdoor meeting. He thought it might put him in a more receptive frame of mind and, as it turned out, he was absolutely right. That's when he was offered the job.'

'I see. At least, I think I do.'

'She planted the idea in his head. Something about family honour, but she would have come out of it very well . . . financially. He only told me about it the other day. He needed to tell someone. He wanted to know if he had interpreted it correctly and as I see it . . .' She shrugged. 'I remember now the look on her face when she shot off after him to High Force. She thought he was going to do it, you see, Andrew. And she'd just had good news herself. You'll not believe this, but after all the worry, Joe was offered not one but two positions. One of them as a direct result of Tess's efforts.' She frowned as Andrew continued to stare. 'Sorry . . . this is so complicated. Am I making myself at all clear?'

'I don't believe it,' he said at last but his voice, his whole being, contradicted that.

'I hated her at first,' she said. 'I could not believe it either. But I can now. Everything fits. And to think that it was I who insisted that she was well provided for under the terms of Joe's will. The last thing I wanted was for her to think I'd married him for what I could get. So, as the will stood then, I just got the house and his pension and she got the rest. The lump sum and his shares, etcetera.'

'Did she know?'

She nodded. 'Oh, yes. She knew. We've changed the wills now. Now I get everything. Oh, Andrew . . . why did she do it? It's shaken Joe. He believes, you see, that, short of pushing him off the edge, she did everything else. I almost feel sorry for her. Almost. What can have possessed her to contemplate that? Her own father?'

He sighed. Said nothing.

'I'm sorry, Andrew.'

'What have you to be sorry about? It's been on the cards for a long time . . . a separation,' he said at last. 'The rot set in when she lost the baby. I wanted that baby, you know.'

'I know,' Stephanie said, reaching across and lightly touching his arm. 'You don't have to explain, Andrew.'

'There's Yvonne next door. She has three children and she's getting divorced,' Andrew said as they sat quiet and still looking onto the gently awakening spring garden. 'We both know, sort of, but we haven't got round to admitting it. It's a helluva thing to admit to. That you've, both of you, messed up your marriages. You'll like her,' he added. 'We get on fine, me and the kids.'

'That's it with you, isn't it?' Stephanie asked gently. 'Children?'

'Yes and no,' he said. 'If Tess were more . . . if she were less . . . bloody hell, Steffi, I don't know what I'm trying to say.'

'Me and Joe won't have children either, but it doesn't matter for us,' Stephanie said, explaining it for him. 'If you're right for each other, it doesn't. But you and Tess are not right for each other. I've known that for ages.'

'The thing is, I don't think Tess will mind too much. I think she almost expects it. She's been working towards it for a while. Independence. She doesn't need me any more. She doesn't need anyone any more.'

'I won't say a thing to Joe until you want me to,' Stephanie told him. 'But you have my support, Andrew. I hope things work out for you.'

# 45

'Post, Mrs Makepeace,' Ella said, bringing the letters through. 'Two circulars, another of those things from Reader's Digest, your milk bill, a leaflet on double glazing, something from the Inland Revenue and a nice letter in a white envelope marked "Private and Confidential" with a Darlington postmark.'

'Thank you, Ella,' Constance said with a slight smile, wishing Ella would not take it upon herself to feel the need to discuss the contents of her mail. She did it every day. But then, Ella Bainbridge had a thing about letters, didn't she? Hadn't she read every single one of Constance's letters that were down in the cellar? Constance was not too concerned. The ones from Archie were quite as beautiful as she had been herself. And there was nothing incriminating in Hugh's letters. Nothing at all in Hugh's letters. The ones from Grace would appear on the surface to be nothing more than letters of condolence, although Constance was surprised that Ella had not yet got around to quizzing her about Margaret and Billy.

Time enough for that.

'That will be all, thank you,' Constance said, fingering the stiff white envelope with some interest. From whom could this be? It certainly looked official and in that case it may not necessarily be a 'nice' letter as Ella had judged it.

She waited until Ella was gone before she slit it open with the paper knife she kept in her desk, her walnut lady's desk, that graced the gap between the chesterfield and the window. Smith was on the chesterfield, on the best silk cushion. Since his illness, he had taken a few liberties and because she did not wish to scold him in his delicate state, he had regrettably taken up an almost permanent residence on the chesterfield.

The letter which she removed from the envelope was from her solicitor.

*Dear Mrs Makepeace,* it read, *Re Your Deceased Sister Mrs Grace Curtis*

Grace was dead.

Constance looked up from the letter a moment, reflecting on the news. She was not surprised by it; in fact, she had assumed Grace had died long since, and she could not drum up much sorrow, which was despicable of her and she felt most ashamed of that, but Grace had never made the slightest effort to forgive. Hate was a destructive emotion and Grace ought to have put it aside, all the happenings of the past, and forgiven her. They might have enjoyed each other's company in their declining years.

She sighed and read on.

*I would be obliged if you would come in to see me to discuss aspects of your late sister's estate.*

*Please contact my secretary on the above number to arrange a suitable time.*

*Yours sincerely,*
*J. K. Nicholls.*
*For Partners and Self.*

Most interesting.

Constance put the letter aside. When had Grace died? The family – and she knew only of a son – had not thought it necessary to inform her so that she might have attended the funeral. And then again, she might not, for Grace had not thought fit to attend Hugh's.

'Bad news, then, Mrs Makepeace?' Ella asked, directly she went into the kitchen. She was doing her cupboards under the sink, every last item taken out and sitting beside her whilst she scrubbed and disinfected the shelves. 'That letter?'

Constance chose not to answer. Mrs Bainbridge really took too much on herself and it was time she was put firmly in her place.

'The daffodils are up a treat,' Ella went on, undeterred by the silence. 'And the harebells just coming through. Bernard reckons it's going to be a good year for the fruit. And the roses. Any news of that cottage you're after?'

'Thank you, yes. It is proceeding,' Constance said, reaching for her jacket. 'I am going down to the village,' she said. 'The letter is in my desk, Ella,' she added mischievously, zipping up the waterproof. 'I will telephone my solicitor when I return.'

'Solicitor?' Ella perked up, sprinkling lemon cleaner liberally on her cloth. 'Have you come into some money, then, Mrs Makepeace?' she laughed to show no disrespect was intended. 'Wish we would, me and Bernard.'

Constance took pity on her.

'My sister has died,' she said quietly. 'And there are matters to clarify.'

'Oh . . . well, that is sad,' Ella said, flushing, awkward on her knees at such a moment. 'I am sorry, Mrs Makepeace. You should have said. Here's me twittering on and not knowing. Why didn't you say? Do you want me to make you a cup of tea?'

The sympathy was not entirely welcome. It made Constance feel suddenly and totally unexpectedly upset. Grace, after all, had been her sister and as such she ought to feel something. She had shed a tear for Eleanor.

Mrs Grace Curtis. She had never met Alistair Curtis but that hadn't stopped her feeling sorry for the man, for he must have been not only second but third best as far as Grace was concerned. What a trial, to be a woman's third choice! There had been a son but she had never met him either.

Walking down the drive of West House was curious these days because it was beginning to feel as if it didn't belong to her any more. She was looking after it now for Mr and Mrs O'Grady. She felt like a trustee.

How very convenient that Mr Nicholls should ask to see her, for hadn't she just been about to see him? The meeting would kill two birds with one stone, as it were. When she telephoned to request the appointment, she would mention that she wished him to have to hand the relevant documents pertaining to the sale of West House.

There was a tiny hint of warmth in the air this morning, a

spring feel. The meadows were aglow with yellow and blue and the sun, timid still, was strengthening nonetheless in a pale sky.

She paused only briefly at One-Mile Bridge, daring to look at the cool splashing water.

It was true.

Time healed.

# 46

Tess was outside her shop in an alley off Northumberland Street, examining the window display.

A gorgeous blue arrangement dominated, intended to illustrate that blue need not be cold. It could be warm as a summer sky, as a sun-kissed sea, and there was a wonderful variety of shades of blue flowers. Forget-me-nots, cornflowers, grape hyacinths, delphiniums and early spring bluebells. A blue bouquet could move within the colour spectrum from deepest cobalt to palest azure. This particular shop veered very much to blue. The assistants wore pale blue jumpsuits and the interior decor closely matched. Tess found it worked very well as a marketing ploy. People remembered the blue florists.

Satisfied, she went inside, but merely to pick up her car keys for she was off. Finishing early for once, and she intended to drop in on Constance Makepeace. No harm now that it was all more or less settled, and she had asked one of the girls to put together a mixed bouquet. She found that if you picked a compatible assortment of blooms they would almost arrange themselves and that housekeeper woman needed that as she was totally useless at producing any sort of imaginative display.

She was in a remarkably upbeat mood as she drove home. To hell with Andrew and his doom-laden predictions about the business. The man had no style whatsoever, and it had taken some considerable time to discover that. Why in God's name had she married an accountant? She might have known. One thing was sure, though. He would huff and puff in outrageous fashion about the iffiness of all this but he would do damn-all about it.

He had lost his fire.

He had lost all interest.

She wanted out.

She had had a good think recently about their relationship and where it was heading, and the truth was it was going nowhere. It never would and she was hanged if she was going to spend the rest of her life apologising and making excuses for the decision that she had taken that weekend three years ago. He would never forgive her. Do what *you* want, he had said, and so she had taken him at his word.

Just imagine it.

Someone like Yvonne Lonsdale would have coped most stoically with the tragic situation. Dear God, yes. She would have coped. Andrew would have been better off with a woman like her. If Andrew wanted to be lumbered with her and those chattery children of hers then God help him. He'd soon find out it was no bed of roses. He had a rosy pink view of family life, did Andrew. She bet Yvonne didn't look half so good when she woke up in the morning before she'd got herself tarted up.

Tess hummed a tune as she neared West House.

Andrew would do this last thing for her. She knew that. He would sign on the dotted line. Pity she might have to sell almost before the ink on the paperwork was dry, but that was the way of the world and there were other equally grand properties up in Northumberland. She and Mark the chef might think of opening a hotel.

She wondered fractionally about Mark and if there would be any point in making the relationship a little more intimate. Yes, they did go back a long way, and they had been lovers once until their paths parted and she married Andrew and he went off with a woman whose name she quite forgot. That was over, he had been at pains to tell her. And she knew he still hankered after her, for she saw it in his eyes. It might be worth considering, but not yet. She needed his undivided attention and an unspoken promise was worth a lot.

She turned into West House and saw she was not the only visitor. Oh well, this was just an impromptu call and she would leave the flowers anyway.

'Mrs Makepeace is taking tea,' Mrs Bainbridge said, eyes

brightening at the flowers. 'Oh, those are lovely, Mrs O'Grady. What a nice big bunch. I'll put them in water straightaway.'

Tess passed them over. 'Don't forget to snip the bottoms,' she said with a smile, stepping just inside the hall and looking longingly towards the drawing room and the sound of voices. Constance might as well be aware that she had called even if she only stayed a moment as there were other guests.

'Go on through, hinny . . .' Mrs Bainbridge said. 'She'd like you to meet them, I'm sure. I'll bring in an extra cup.'

'Thank you.'

Mrs Bainbridge tapped on the door, opened it, announced that Mrs O'Grady was here, and Tess followed.

She stopped dead.

Mrs Makepeace was entertaining a whole group of people. Five anyway. A bulky woman with dark hair and a quite appalling flowery print suit and four . . . boys, young men, whatever . . . all gazing at her now with that stupid look, one of them protruding his tongue, one of them pointing even now at her, a silly grin on his face, standing up . . . good God, coming towards her . . .

'Now, Billy, let Tess come in first . . .'

She heard Constance's voice from a distance, looked across at her in horror as the young man reached her and stopped. For an awful, awful moment she thought he was going to embrace her but instead he held out his hand stiffly and said something in a slur that she did not comprehend.

Shocked, speechless, Tess stood still. She couldn't take her eyes off him. Good God, she might have had to put up with this for years . . .

Constance, she noticed vaguely, was at her side too.

'I'd like you to meet Billy,' she said. 'And then come and meet the others. You must take tea with us. Mrs Bainbridge has made a chocolate cream cake for the boys.'

Tess looked at the hand still outstretched, at the chubby smallish hand, and then into the face of the child-man.

He smiled.

She recoiled.

She could not bring herself to touch him.

She glanced helplessly at Constance but nothing would have induced her to touch him, not even the certain knowledge that she was burning all her boats in this very minute. She saw that in the other woman's eyes.

Constance gently turned the boy round and he trotted back to the other lady.

She then looked at Tess. Her eyes were bright, her head held high, her look could have cut through stone at that moment.

'I just brought some flowers,' Tess stumbled over the words, difficult for she could still see them all sitting there, staring at her. God . . . why did they stare so?

Constance inclined her head, gracious to the last.

'Mrs Bainbridge will see you out,' she said.

# 47

'I'm sorry to trouble you, Andrew . . .'

Yvonne stood at the door, a dream in cream linen, a little different in a smart suit and a big-brimmed hat with a cream rose centred on it.

'We're off to the christening,' she said with a smile. 'And you're never going to believe this, but the car won't start. I can't think what's wrong and we're going to be late if we don't go in a few minutes. If only I'd found out earlier, we could have gone on the bus or something. Isn't it such a nuisance?'

She drew breath, smiled up at him in that way of hers.

'Your car won't start?' He hid his own smile. 'Off to a christening, did you say?'

'Lyn's baby. Do you remember when he was born?'

Ah yes. The very first time he looked after them. The start of everything, you could say.

'Mummy's going to be fairy godmother,' Samantha said, looking rather natty herself in a navy dress with a big white collar, carrying a little red handbag and wearing red shoes.

'Not *fairy* godmother,' Portia corrected her promptly. 'That's the pantomime, isn't it, Mummy?' She was in pale blue with a matching ribbon holding her hair in a ponytail. 'And Mrs Forbes says I can hold baby Alexander if I'm very good. She won't let Samantha hold him in case she drops him. Samantha's always dropping her doll right on the head.'

'Stop it, girls.' Yvonne looked up at him anxiously realising he had said precious little. 'I know I'm a nuisance, but could you possibly run us over to church? I wouldn't ask but . . .'

'Which church?' he asked, wondering how on earth he was

going to cope forever with this wonderful, wonderful dotty woman.

'Over towards Middlesbrough, I'm afraid. I've got directions. I suppose I could get a taxi,' she said anxiously as Andrew reached for his car keys. 'I feel terrible, imposing on you. But I mean, you don't expect the car not to start, do you, in this day and age. Not a new one, anyway. I shall play hell at the garage. They think just because you're a woman, you know nothing about cars.'

She spoke with great indignation, as if she was a mechanic.

'Come in a minute. I just need to do something.'

They followed him into the hall, the entire gang, and, as he hunted for some paper and a pen, he realised that Yvonne had trailed behind him into the kitchen.

'What are you looking for? Can I help? Oh, no . . . you were just about to eat,' she said, seeing the preparations for his meal. 'Now I feel even worse.'

'Yvonne . . . for God's sake.' He swiftly closed the kitchen door, almost pinned her against it so that her hat shifted on her head. 'I am sick of this. All this bloody tiptoeing round on broken glass. Tess and I are finished. It's all over and I love you, dammit, *and* you know it. Don't you?'

He stopped, reflecting that as a first 'I love you' it was considerably less than romantic.

She nodded, said nothing, but a slow smile lit her face.

'I wondered just when you'd get round to it,' she said.

He kissed her then.

A most wonderful first kiss.

Just enough to show her what was in store.

She kissed him back as the doorknob rattled, adjusted her hat and pushed him gently away, reaching for her bag so that she could make repairs to her appearance.

'Mummy, what are you doing? We're going to be late and Mrs Forbes will be very cross.'

'We're just talking, darling,' she said, as Portia came through. 'Mr O'Grady was just explaining something.'

She shooed Portia out, turning to give him a lovely smile as he followed her.

More out of habit than anything, he scribbled a note for Tess should she deign to come home. She had rung the other evening saying that something dreadful had happened and she needed to be on her own for a while so she was staying at the little flat she used as a store quarters over one of the shops for a few days. She would be in touch later. They needed to discuss the sale of their house, she said. And they would need the services of a solicitor, wouldn't they? She had not mentioned separation or divorce, but she didn't need to. They were implied in letters six feet high in her voice. He hadn't realised until he put the phone down that it had been a conversation between ex-lovers. No matter how gradual it had all been, what Stephanie had told him had finally snapped it clean. He had not confronted her with it. He could not do that but neither could he make excuses any longer. It was over. Tess knew it too. Her tone had been freezer-cold. It was all over bar the legalities. They would sell this house, sort things out, and that would be that. He was on his own to do what he wanted. A few months ago, the future might have been bleak but not now, because now he had Yvonne. His beautiful Yvonne.

'Where is Tess?' Yvonne asked, as soon as they were all installed in the car. He had made a brief attempt to start hers but she was not fooling. It needed an urgent garage appointment. 'Only I haven't seen her for ages.'

He shook his head, frowned towards her. 'Not just now,' he said quietly, anxious not to say too much in front of the children.

'We've got to learn to talk, Andrew. It's important,' she said, keeping her voice low. 'We've got to be honest with each other.'

'Honest is not telling lies,' Portia said loudly from the back seat. 'And not stealing things. Isn't it?'

Yvonne leaned a little towards him. 'You're right. We'll talk later . . .'

'My button's just pinged off my new dress,' Portia continued. 'All on its own. I wasn't twisting it at all. It just pinged. It's on the floor under the seat.'

'I *can* hold the baby if I sit still and I'm very very careful,' Samantha said, tightly cross. 'Mrs Forbes promised.'

'Oh, Mummy . . . did you hear what Harry said? It begins with a b and it's a very naughty word.'

'I don't want to hear. Stop telling tales, Portia. And, Harry . . . that's no pocket money for you again this week. What will Mr O'Grady think of you all?' Yvonne sighed, caught his amused expression and managed a furtive smile in return.

And so it went on. And on.

Portia was unstoppable. Samantha was peeved about holding or not holding the baby as the case may be. And Harry was muttering. Indistinctly.

They played I-Spy to pass the time but it quickly disintegrated into a shambles and then they played a game Andrew originated which proved to be mildly distracting but a bit too complicated. He reflected he would have to give this matter some serious thought. How to survive a car journey with kids . . . wasn't there a book on the very subject? At least nobody was sick.

Yvonne gave a sudden shriek in the midst of all this.

'I've left the camera at home. I knew I'd forget something. It's pandemonium, Andrew, when you're trying to get yourself ready *and* the children. Portia, I did ask you to remind me. You don't carry a spare one in the car with you, do you?'

'No.' He laughed at the idea. 'Actually, no. Sorry.'

'Oh well, never mind, it can't be helped. I'll have to get copies of photographs from other people,' she said. 'Nearly there,' she went on, addressing her remarks to the children. 'And let me go through the rules again before we get out of the car. Quiet in church. Not a word. You will all do a wee and blow your noses before you go in. Is that quite clear? And afterwards, if you are all very good, then I expect Mrs Forbes will let you all have a go at holding the baby. Isn't that right, Andrew?' She gave him no time to comment before ploughing on rather desperately as they arrived at the church. 'And Mr O'Grady will want to know if you've been good when we get back, won't you, Mr O'Grady? Now, here we are.'

Andrew helped them all out. Yvonne's hat was at a curious angle again and she adjusted it and the suit, asking that immortal feminine question of him with her eyes. Do I look all right?

'You look beautiful, my sweet,' he murmured, for her ears only, passing her her handbag. 'I'll let you know just how beautiful later.'

She bit her lip. Stood alone a moment, looking at him.

The smile that followed a moment later was for him.

'Will you wait for us?' she asked. 'I wouldn't ask but . . .'

'Yvonne, will you stop it!' he said. 'Of course I bloody will. It's what I'm for, isn't it? Fetching and carrying you lot. Isn't that my role in life?'

'Hardly,' she said, looking pained. 'I can do my share, thank you very much.'

'OK.' He held up his hands in mock surrender. He wanted to take her in his arms there and then, and sod the fact that there were all these people about. She wanted it too, he knew that, but she was being terribly discreet, bending down as Portia tugged at her skirt, holding aloft the lost button, asking if it could be stitched on right away.

'How? Portia, do be reasonable. I don't carry a needle and thread with me,' Yvonne said with some exasperation. 'Later, sweetheart. Look, pop it in my bag for now, so we don't lose it.'

'But Mummy, everyone will see . . .' The muttering started.

'Portia . . . don't start,' Yvonne said, looking at Andrew for support.

'Nobody will notice. Your dress is very pretty,' Andrew said, smiling her into a reluctant smile. 'All you ladies look very pretty. I'll see you later. Take you home.'

'Bye, Andrew,' Portia said, the button forgotten, setting off briskly, blue skirt flaring round her little legs, very clean white frilled socks above the polished shoes. He thought she looked smashing. They all did. He was bloody proud of them.

'Bye, Andrew,' the others said, trotting off with Yvonne.

Andrew? He noticed Yvonne did not bother to correct them.

He watched as they disappeared in the direction of the church hall where people were assembling, heaving a sigh of relief as he returned to the blissfully quiet car.

Their presence was all around.

Yvonne's perfume lingered and there were signs of a few sweetie wrappers in the back, a hairslide and some scrunched-up tissues. Amazing what they were capable of.

It was by no means its usual pristine state.

This was what it was like.

This was what it would be like from now on.

And he loved it.

# 48

A lucky escape, Constance realised.

Tess O'Grady would most certainly not be moving into West House, which left her in a dilemma for, having decided to leave the house and move into an adorable little cottage near the church, she did not wish to put it off. However, she might have little choice. She would not leave West House empty and alone.

She was offered a cup of coffee as she waited for Mr Nicholls but declined, because she saw it would be in a paper cup and she could not tolerate that. She glanced pointedly at her watch, not able to actually see what time it was, but knowing he was keeping her waiting, which in her view was unforgivable.

'I do apologise,' he said, suddenly rushing in and smiling so fulsomely that she forgave him his lapse. 'Unavoidably detained, Mrs Makepeace. And how are we this morning?' he asked as he showed her into his inner sanctum.

'I am very well, thank you,' she said, graciously nodding her appreciation as he fussed a moment with her chair. 'The weather is pleasant, isn't it?'

'Indeed.' He nodded towards a sad-looking thirsty plant on his desk. 'My secretary likes to liven the place up a little,' he said, almost apologetically.

She did not succeed, Constance reflected, for the room was dark and dismal even on a bright day, the blinds at the window half shut. Whereas she had noticed an array of modern-looking equipment in the outer office, this room looked very much as it always had. She had been here last after Hugh died.

'Now . . .' Mr Nicholls opened a file. 'May I first of all offer you our sincere condolences on your sad loss?'

'Thank you.' She was wearing black because it seemed appropriate to do so, for no other reason. She was sorry but she had been totally unable to feel anything for Grace.

'Your late sister Grace left instructions with me, to be followed in the event of her death. She requests that you receive her son, your nephew, Mr Peter Curtis, at West House, time to be arranged.'

'Of course,' Constance said. She was somehow pleased that he was still alive. It didn't necessarily follow that he would be, not with the bad luck her branch of the Parkinsons had been dealt. 'I will be happy to receive him.'

'Thank you.' Mr Nicholls closed the file. 'I will inform him duly.'

'Is that all?' Constance asked. 'Is that what you needed to see me about?'

'Thank you, Mrs Makepeace. Now, I understand you wish to sell West House. We will be pleased to act for you in that respect as and when you find a buyer.'

'Thank you. I thought I had a buyer, Mr Nicholls, however unfortunately it has not worked out. I will be in touch later.'

When she got back, Ella was hovering in the hall in a spasm of anxiety.

'This gentleman's just been on the phone,' she said. 'Lovely voice. I took a message.' She pulled a scrap of paper from her pocket. 'A Mr Peter Curtis, Mrs Makepeace. He said he was your long-lost nephew – his very words – and would it be all right if he came over tomorrow, only he's had a change of plan with his flights or something and if he doesn't get over tomorrow he's going . . .' she struggled to recall the words, 'he's going to be hard pressed he said to fit it in at all and he has something to give you. So I said – oh dear, Mrs Makepeace, I hope I did right, and I won't get wronged by you – but I said he could. I said he was to come for tea.'

'Thank you, Ella. That's perfectly all right.'

She knew what Grace was up to. She was almost sure of it but, in bed that night, unable to sleep, Constance decided the only thing she could do was to be gracious to Peter. A family disagreement was most distasteful but, if Grace had instilled in her son her own hatred, then a disagreement might be unavoidable.

Grace wanted her to see that she, Grace, had got what she did not have. A fine healthy son. She knew nothing of Billy being alive, of course, which was just as well for that would have been another thing for her to gloat over.

Billy . . . Constance smiled. He had so loved the house and the afternoon was not marred too much by the unfortunate arrival and subsequent abrupt departure of Tess O'Grady. Penny had seen that sort of reaction before and just breezed it away. Those sort of people, she told Constance, were just not worth thinking about.

Constance agreed.

She strolled in the garden after lunch the following day whilst she waited for Grace's son to arrive. She had to confess to feeling a little curious about him. She hoped he would not have inherited his mother's irritating inability to forgive. It would be impossible if the friction were to continue through him.

Walking along the western perimeter of the estate beside the rough meadow, Constance enjoyed the spring warmth. It was a glorious day, the meadows full of early bluebells and primroses, the cherry trees in the orchard in blushing pink bloom and, nearer the house, the canary yellow of the forsythia shot droplets of colour against the paler golden walls.

She sighed her delight.

If she dropped dead now, this very moment, it would never be a better time.

But she could not, because she still had to sort out what was to happen to the house when she was gone. What a bore that the O'Gradys, or rather Mrs O'Grady, had turned out to be unsuitable. She had been right. The marriage was doomed. She had seen it first at the bonfire evening and then when they came for tea. They did not realise it, perhaps, but she saw that they were at the tolerance level in their relationship which did not usually last long before the final plunge into separation. She and Hugh had spent most of their married life at the tolerance level, so she knew the signs. She also recognised the signs of love between Mr O'Grady and the blonde lady who brought her books. Mrs Lonsdale was nicer on acquaintance than she had thought, and she obviously adored her small children.

Beside the orchard, there was a small secret garden which one entered via a high wrought-iron gate. Mr Bainbridge kept it in a very formal fashion with neat beds surrounding a central ornamental fountain. It trickled and tinkled, a joyous summery sound, as Constance sat on one of the benches. A lot of yellow and white at this time of year and it was pleasant on the eye, not too demanding. She wondered about the wisdom of trying to go another year without spectacles. One could buy extremely handsome ones these days and she had to own to a slight fuzziness in the middle distance. For instance, just as she entered this garden, she could have sworn she saw Hugh coming her way across the lawns from the house. A trick of the light or a failing in her eyesight. One or the other. She was far too practical to believe in ghosts.

No rush. She lit a cigarette and relaxed. She was not nervous, she assured herself, not in the least. It would be a courtesy visit, she hoped, for what else could it be? There was no money to come to her or her solicitor would have informed her of that. She would not accept money in any case from Grace. What an idea!

She closed her eyes, feeling the warmth of the spring sunshine on her old face. She could smell her cigarette and the open air. Wonderful combination.

'Aunt Constance?'

She opened her eyes.

Hugh stood before her.

'Hugh . . .' Befuddled, she sat up, knocking the cigarette from her hand and retrieving it quickly before she set herself on fire. 'Oh . . .' She regained control as the man leaned over her.

'I'm sorry, did I startle you? How do you do? Your housekeeper said I'd find you here,' he said with a smile. A nice man, with a kinder face than Hugh, but a man so like him that she could not quite believe her eyes. 'I'm so pleased to meet you at last. You're a complete mystery to our side of the family. I always wanted to search you out but Mother wouldn't have it. Wait until I'm gone, she used to say, and then go to see her.'

'Do sit down.' She took a deep breath, offered him a cigarette which, rather to her surprise, he accepted. 'So you are Peter?'

'I am. I wanted to see you before I go back home. I live in France with my wife,' he said. 'Our children are grown up.'

'Of course.' She realised he was no longer young. In his fifties, she guessed.

'I feel badly about not visiting you before now,' he said at last, stiff in his discomfort. 'I wanted to, but as I've explained, Mother . . .'

'We were estranged,' Constance said carefully, wondering how much he knew. 'What did your mother tell you?'

'Only that you married and went away. She said you were . . . let's see . . . flighty, I believe. Sorry, but Mother was a little staid in outlook.'

Constance smiled. 'And did she tell you that I lost two husbands?'

'No. I'm sorry. As I said, you are a mystery to us. Mother did not wish us to come up here to see you, so we never did.'

'When did she die?'

'Two months ago. A mercifully short illness. I'm sorry – I keep saying that – but her instructions were quite clear and I made her a promise. You were not to be invited to the funeral but I was to come to see you afterwards. We've just sold the house down there. None of the family wanted it, you see.'

Constance looked at the man who looked like Hugh.

'Tell me about yourself,' she said. 'I never met your father.'

'He was all right, Father,' he said, and his face lit up as he said it. 'He always regretted he wasn't very energetic because he suffered from arthritis, but he was a wonderful man. I'm rather like him. He was an art historian too.'

'That's what you do. How interesting,' Constance said politely. 'I hope you don't think me rude, but how old are you, Peter?'

It confirmed what she already knew. Hugh and Grace had resumed their affair after her marriage to him. Those weekends in London at the club or the apartment had been in truth assignations with her sister.

It hurt. It hurt that Hugh had turned away from her beauty. No matter that she may have been cool with the physical side of marriage, for Hugh was not Archie and never would be. He ought not to have done that, though, with Grace. Shame on the pair of them. How dare Grace do that to her?

'Our older son Simon is a consultant gynaecologist at a hospital quite near here,' Peter went on. 'He only took up the post six months ago and he and his wife are looking for a house. Mary has stayed with the family down in Lincolnshire until they find something suitable. Something with a bit of space and a good garden where the children can play. He has four children under seven,' he added with a smile. 'If you like, I'm sure he would visit you. We should try to make amends, Aunt Constance, now that Mother's gone. I hate family feuds.'

'Yes . . .'

The idea was not only brewing, it was well and truly fermented. Her great-nephew Simon, his wife and four children would love West House. She could feel it in her bones. A doctor and his family . . . how admirable! And what made it even more admirable was the sure knowledge that Grace would disapprove of such an arrangement. Grace would be appalled.

'Shall we take tea?' she asked, tucking her arm in his as he escorted her indoors. By the time they finished tea, not only had she told him about his cousin Billy but he had also acceded to her request that he would take personal responsibility for making sure Billy was cared for for the rest of his life. It was a weight lifted from her mind. A great weight.

He gave her a letter when he left. His mother, he said, had specially requested that he hand over the letter personally. He took his leave with Hugh's smile and a little bow. Walked away to his car with Hugh's walk.

A letter from Grace.

A letter from the grave.

'I'm glad I lit the fire, Mrs Makepeace. A bit chilly, don't you think, this morning? What a nice man he was. That Mr Curtis who came yesterday,' Ella Bainbridge said, as she brought Constance a cup of tea. 'Lovely looking man.'

'My sister Grace's son,' Constance said.

'Oh, yes, she would be the one who . . .' Ella's voice tailed off and she busied about with the silver teapot and the sugar bowl.

'She is the one who wrote me letters of condolence,' Constance said with a smile. 'And here's another, Ella. Peter gave it to me. Her last letter.'

'How sad!' Ella sighed. 'I don't think I could bring myself to read it, Mrs Makepeace, if it was mine. Not when she's passed over. It was bad enough when my sister Sylvia died – all the stuff we had to sort through. It broke your heart, it did. It was a blessing, though. Did I ever tell you how she suffered at the last, Mrs Makepeace?'

'I believe you did, Mrs Bainbridge.' Constance nodded graciously. 'Thank you, Ella.'

Smith leapt onto her lap when Ella was gone.

He was much recovered, quite his old self, his coat smooth and silky, his eyes bright and clear, the bare patch of skin on his cheek beginning to fur over with new gingery growth.

'So . . .' she murmured, stroking him. 'What *are* we to do with this letter, Smith?'

The envelope was addressed in Grace's rather elegant handwriting.

Simply.

*To Constance.*

Constance fingered it. Stiff and white. One of those letters Mrs Bainbridge would think of as 'nice' because of the quality of the notepaper. It was very bulky, in fact, and, oddly, it felt as if there might be an additional envelope within. A letter within a letter.

She slit it open and – yes, she was right.

She pulled out another envelope, an opened one, addressed in Hugh's handwriting this time. Addressed to *My dearest Grace.*

It came to her even as she was about to pull the second letter from the envelope.

After the 'accident' she recalled Walter saying there was no note, or rather that he had disposed of it in the confusion.

There had been a note.

But it was for Grace, not her, for, after all, hadn't Grace presented him with the son he craved whilst she, Constance, failed miserably?

Not quite. She thought of Thomas and dearest Billy. She ought to have – what was the expression? – fought her corner over Billy. She ought to have insisted on keeping him. It had taken a long time for her to realise the truth, that beauty, perfection, is indeed under the skin.

Grace was welcome to Hugh.

She would not read his final words.

She would not give Grace the satisfaction of being heart-broken.

Deliberately, she tore the letters, both of them, into pieces before throwing them onto the fire. She watched the paper brown at the edges and curl, twist into strange shapes, and then, just as the heat seemed to lose its power, it suddenly blazed afresh in flames of orange and yellow with streaks of blue until just the grey ashes of it were left.

A fireball.

'Archie . . .' She stirred as the cat leapt startled from her lap and drew her eyes away from the flames. For a moment then, she had had the most extraordinary feeling.

She had things to do first before she joined Archie.

She must issue an invitation to her great-nephew and his lovely wife to come for the weekend, and of course they must bring the children. They would adore the house. There was no question but that they would adore the house and best of all, they were family. Grace's family, true, but one had to show compassion at the last. If Grace could not be gracious, that was no reason why she should not be.

There was so much to do.

She rang the little bell for Mrs Bainbridge. There were the rooms to prepare, and flowers to arrange, and meals to organise . . .

'What is it, Mrs Makepeace? I'm ever so busy in the kitchen . . .' Mrs Bainbridge appeared, flustered, at the door.

Constance sighed.

Staff nowadays . . .

'I wish to inform you that I am expecting guests, Mrs Bainbridge,' she told her. 'They will be joining us for the weekend shortly, the date to be confirmed. My great-nephew Simon, who is a hospital consultant, and his wife Mary and their four children. All under seven.'

'All under seven? That'll be a to-do,' Ella said with a sniff. 'We're not used to bairns here.'

Constance left her to her grumbles and took a stroll in the grounds. She loved the feel of spring approaching, a time of promise, and as always a close inspection of the gardens did not disappoint. Mr Bainbridge loved them too, and it showed in the way the flowers and plants responded. The Japanese garden cherries were heavily laden with blossom as she walked past and the waxy blooms of the magnolia were opening out, the branches still bare of leaves.

She waited until she was at the end of the blossom walk before she turned to look back at West House. A last glimpse of it before she passed it on.

The morning chill had quite vanished and the spring air was sweet. The sun, though gentle, was shining and the golden house bathed in its glow.

It was so beautiful.

Rosy and happy.

Constance sighed, and she imagined the house did too.

With relief and contentment.

As well it might.